THE NOTORIOUS BAD BOY

K.M. SCOTT

THE NOTORIOUS BAD BOY

Cade March loves his life. Free to do as he likes and wealthy enough to afford whatever his heart desires, he's all about having fun.

As the only son of Stefan March, he's the spitting image of his father in every way.

And that's the problem. At least for everyone else.

Hailey Canton lives a very different life. Still recovering from a betrayal that's left her shaken and no longer believing in love, she only has the desserts she makes for her parents' small restaurant to make her feel like she can do anything.

The cakes and cookies she lovingly creates are works of art, but to her, they're simply a lifeline so she doesn't give up.

For the first time in his life, he loves a woman enough to make things right. Whatever it takes, Hailey's worth it.

And for the first time in too long, she's willing to take a chance because what she feels when she's with Cade makes her truly happy.

But what happens if his past never goes away?

Published in the United States

ISBN: 978-1-955335-28-7

The two full-length books included in this one-volume book are Notorious and Infamous (NeXt #1 and #2). The extras included are new to this edition.

CHAPTER ONE

ade

"THIS IS THE LIFE. YOU KNOW THAT?" I SAY AS I weave in between cars on my way to nowhere in particular.

It's a gorgeous spring day that would be a crime to waste inside, so Alex and I are riding around listening to music and enjoying the freedom that comes from being single guys beholden to not a damn soul.

When I glance to my right, I see him nod his head and lean back in the passenger seat of my Jag. Closing his eyes, he says, "It's days like this that make going to work hard as fuck sometimes. Thank God I don't have to go in today. The last thing I want to do is spend an eight hour stretch slaving in that kitchen."

"I don't know how you do it. Really, I don't. If I had to work with my father and uncle day in and day out, I'd kill someone. I'd turn into one of those guys who goes on a rampage and then when the cops and the news talk to the neighbors, they always say things like, 'He was a quiet guy. Never bothered anyone. I can't believe he took a meat cleaver and hacked up an entire kitchen staff and both the owners of such a fine restaurant. I just can't.'"

Alex laughs at my imitation of every next-door neighbor ever seen on the news talking about some homicidal maniac who lived next to them. "Yeah, and they always have that look on their faces like they really can't believe that was the guy who lived in the blue house across the street. 'He looked so nice. I swear I never knew.'"

I take the corner hard onto a side street and chuckle. "They just can't believe their dumb luck that the crazy guy who snapped didn't come over and kill them that time they let him borrow the weed whacker."

"My favorite is when they say things like, 'It's such a shame. He comes from such a good family. I know his mother. She's a very nice lady.' As if that's why he's a mass murderer. Like it's in the genes."

That thought rolls around my head for a minute. Is there some DNA marker for mass murderer? I don't think so. Not that I've ever heard of, but maybe. Anything's possible.

If that's the base, though, the whole lot of us in my family would be screwed. My mind wanders to the idea of seven mass murderers. That would be something. A whole family of killers.

Although I can't imagine Ava even killing a fly, and Annalea doesn't seem to have the killer instinct in her either. Wilder's definitely got it. That's for sure. But he's not blood, even if he is part of the family.

"Hey! Pull over into that restaurant," Alex says, ripping me from my thoughts about the March and Jackson family's potential as killers.

"What?"

I look around and don't see anywhere we'd want to go. Just some diner that makes me think I can taste the grease by just looking at the place. He can't want to go there. Alex is a chef, for God's sake. There's no way he wants to eat at this greasy spoon.

Pointing at the very building I'm sure he can't want to go to, he repeats himself. "Pull over! Let's stop in that restaurant."

He looks like he's going to practically jump out of the car while it's still moving he's so eager to get to this diner. What the hell did I miss?

"Relax. It's not like the place is going to disappear before I get the car parked. Jesus. You'd swear this is some five-star restaurant. It's a diner. I would have thought you hated these kinds of places."

I look up at the sign as I pull into the parking lot. Comfort Food. Catchy name for a dive. They probably have things like meatloaf and grilled cheese sandwiches on the menu. Not exactly what I ever pegged Alex being into.

When I stop the car and kill the engine, I look over to see him flinging the door open. "Wait! Why are we here? You have a craving for some fried food or something?"

He shrugs like I'm making a big deal out of nothing. "Not really, but don't worry. It'll be fine. This place has great desserts."

Before I can ask when he became such a big dessert fan, he jumps out of the car and slams the door. Great desserts, huh? By the looks of the building, I'd be surprised. Gunmetal grey block walls with silver trim around the windows makes me wonder if he's gotten this place mistaken with somewhere else.

I walk toward the entrance and mumble, "You'd think at somewhere called Comfort Food the outside wouldn't look like I was walking into some dive bar off a dusty highway. Doesn't feel very comforting to me."

By the time I find him, he's all settled into a booth complete with silver seats that have a distinct pleather vibe to them. It's not pleather, though. By the way the seat squeaks as I slide into the booth, I know it's vinyl.

"Is this place going for some retro vibe or something? I feel like there should be a jukebox somewhere around here. You know the kind with actual little records in them. Forty-fives I think is what they were called."

Alex taps his knuckles on the table. "Check it out. Real, honest to goodness Formica! Definitely retro. I love it."

I arch one eyebrow and study him suspiciously, sure someone has stolen my best friend and replaced him with this hipster sitting across from me admiring the white Formica table with silver and gold designs that look like the nuclear symbol. He actually traces the design with his fingertip, like he's enchanted by it.

"Remember in fifth grade when the teacher told us all about fallout shelters. That's what that looks like. Not a good omen for a food place. Radiation poisoning on the menu?" I joke.

He looks up at me and scowls. "It's not a nuclear symbol. I think it's got more of a Star Trek vibe with the two swooshes, one silver and one gold."

Sitting back against the silver vinyl behind me, I shake my head. "You're sort of freaking me out here, Alex. I was worried that maybe being a serial killer runs in our family, but now I'm more worried about whatever you're exhibiting at this moment."

Alex rolls his eyes and goes back to studying the oh-so-interesting ancient table. "Do you remember that server I was seeing a while back? She was into all that fifties stuff big time, so I got to know a little about it. That's all."

My mind wanders back to which girlfriend of his he could be talking about, but there have been a lot, so I can't be blamed for not recalling this particular one. "Which one? The girl who had the Minnie Mouse obsession and loved to wear those big bows in her hair? That, by the way, was bizarre. If you hadn't told me she was a freak in bed, I would have thought you lost your mind going out with her in public."

His dark eyebrows come in toward his nose as he makes that pissed off look he gives me any time he's really angry at something I've said. "No, I don't mean Misty, asshole. And she wasn't that bad with those bows. She just liked dressing up sometimes. You didn't like her because of her friend."

Ugh. That I do remember.

Shaking my head, I try to get rid of the image of her best friend Sandi and her ruby red lips plastered with lipstick. "Damn. How did I let you talk me into going out with her that time? You still owe me for that, and since you made me remember her, you owe me twice. Dude, that was a nightmare."

"Well, you brought up Misty. That's on you, not me. But I wasn't talking about her. I was talking about Tori. You remember. She had black hair, and she wore it in that way that pin-up models from the fifties did."

I vaguely have a sense of who he's talking about, but because I can't get Sandi and that horrible lipstick that tasted like plastic when I kissed her out of my mind, I don't think I can focus on anything now. Alex's taste in women runs the gamut from wild to utterly bizarre. It's so odd too because he doesn't look like he'd go for anyone other than hot women, but he's got a thing for the strange ones.

"She's not really registering with me at the moment, but it's fine. I'm glad she expanded your horizons regarding the fifties diner style."

"Just open your mind, okay? The pastry chef here makes the most phenomenal desserts. My father and Kane tried to woo her to come work at CK a few months ago, but she wouldn't even take their calls."

Looking around at the diner and wondering why we don't even have menus yet since there are no more than two other booths filled with customers, I doubt this place even has a pastry chef. That's probably just Alex throwing around his chef lingo again. Nobody's just a cook with him. Everybody's some kind of chef. Pastry chef. Sous chef. Executive chef. The person making desserts here is probably just some schlub who knows how to slap on some frosting on a cake.

A server finally makes her way over to our table a minute later. All smiles and very pretty, she looks about seventeen, if that. When she opens her mouth and I see braces, I think I might have given her too many years with my first guess.

"Hi, welcome to Comfort Food! I'm Hannah," she says with such enthusiasm that I question if she's going to leap over the table and sit down with us.

"It's great to have you here. Here are menus, and let's get you started on some drinks."

My cousin looks up at her like he can't open his

eyes wide enough and says, "I'll have a Coke, Hannah."

"Make that two," I mumble as I let my gaze slide over the plastic-coated menu.

"Got it! Two Cokes. I'll be right back, but I wanted to mention that our sandwich of the day is a grilled cheese with tomato and herb mayonnaise. Be right back!"

I lift my eyes from the menu to watch her ass in her too-tight shorts as she walks away. Interesting place. Diner décor with a touch of Hooters.

"That grilled cheese sounds good," Alex says, sounding a little too peppy for my taste.

"Is that girl rubbing off on you? She was only here for a minute, at most, and now you sound as up as her. Or is it the shorts and white T-shirt that's got you all excited?" I ask, still reading the menu of more fried and greasy foods than I've ever seen in my life.

He doesn't answer, but I know him well enough after all these years, so I lift my head and see him glaring across the table at me. "You know what your problem is? You're a snob, Cade. Comes from going to that school up north."

His insult misses its mark entirely, especially coming from him. "You're the guy who calls everyone who owns a goddamned spatula a chef, and you work in a five-star restaurant, for God's sake. You went to school for culinary arts, and I'm a snob?"

That little bit of truth stops him cold, so he twists

his face into a sneer and says, "Just give this place a chance. You never know. It could be great."

As much as busting my best friend's balls is something I enjoy, I don't say anything back to him. After another quick glance at the menu, I look around for any sign of our server and those drinks she promised to bring right back. She's nowhere to be found, but in the window of one of doors leading to the kitchen, I spy a woman staring out at our table. I only see her for a split second before she disappears.

Too bad. I was hoping to get her attention so maybe she could send over Hannah.

CHAPTER TWO

ade

BY THE TIME HANNAH FINALLY BRINGS OUT MY hamburger and fries and Alex's turkey club sandwich with fries, I've caught the person in the kitchen staring out at us three times. She disappears every time she realizes I see her, and as much as I doubt anything as exciting as a mystery is occurring at Comfort Food, I can't help but wonder why she keeps looking out at us.

Then it dawns on me. She knows Alex. She probably worked with him at the restaurant at some point, and now she's working here. Maybe she's embarrassed since this place is nothing compared to CK, or maybe she thinks it might be him, but she isn't sure.

So much for the latest episode of Diner Mystery Theater.

Alex points at the last bite of my hamburger left on my plate and nods. "See? I told you this would be good. Tell me you didn't love that burger."

As much as I hate to admit it, I loved the burger. In fact, I loved the fries too. I don't want to give him a reason to gloat, though, so I merely shrug. "It's a decent burger. Jeez, Alex. You sound like you're trying to sell this place. I'm not in the market for a diner, thank you."

He finishes his club sandwich and sits back, shaking his head. "I'm not trying to sell anything. I did hear the desserts are the best in the area, though, so we have to try them."

"Quite the hard on for cupcakes, huh? You need to go out more, man. You're starting to turn into some deranged version of that celebrity chef dude I watched the other night."

"Whatever. Don't try the desserts. Be a grumpy guy who refuses to enjoy anything," he grumbles under his breath.

Times like this show how different the two of us are. Alex is all about the senses. He gets off on how good things taste or feel. The chef in him talks about how things are presented, like that's a big deal.

I, on the other hand, am not as much a hedonist as he is. Oh sure, I indulge in almost anything that makes me feel good, but he takes it to places I never would.

Like desserts.

I can't remember the last time I had a dessert. Maybe my grandmother's birthday party last year? She had a cake, which Alex talked about like it was the goddamned Taj Mahal of food, so maybe then?

But he's my best friend and practically my brother, so I accept how he is. Born three months after me, we basically grew up together. For the past twenty-three years, other than my time in college, we hung out every day. I'm closer to him than anyone else in the world.

"I guess I could try something. Maybe they have some kind of doughnut I'd like."

Alex shakes his head and laughs. "You give me a hard time about stopping here because it's a diner, but you want a doughnut?"

"Don't bash the doughnut. It's the breakfast of champions."

"The person who makes the desserts is an artist. I don't think she makes doughnuts."

Now it's my time to do an eye roll. "An arteest?" I say, making sure he understands how utterly ridiculous I think he sounds about all of this.

Before he can give me a hard time about not taking this whole pastry chef and their desserts seriously enough, a man stops at our table. I look up to see him smiling as he notices our empty plates.

He points at them and says, "I hope this means you enjoyed your meals."

Quickly, Alex shoots me a nasty glance and smiles back at the man. "They were great. Best club sandwich I've had in a while."

As they talk about the turkey and something about the lettuce tasting some particular way, I glance past the man and see the woman in the window again. For the first time, I smile. She doesn't smile back, and after looking panicked that I noticed her, she disappears once more.

Strange.

"I'm dying to see what desserts you have today, Robert. I've heard great things about them," Alex says, practically gushing about these fucking desserts again.

What the hell has he heard about these cakes? Now he's on a first-name basis with this guy too?

Robert walks away to check what they have, but he returns a few seconds later looking all long-faced. "I don't see any. Let me check in the back to see if there'll be any ready soon."

"I'd love the chance to meet your pastry chef. I work as a chef at CK," Alex says with a smile.

"Oh, I wish I could, but I can't let anyone back there because she's very particular about her work."

Alex nods. "I completely understand. Trust me. I do. I wouldn't want strangers loping through my kitchen either."

"Let me go check to see what she has. I'll be right back."

After he walks away, I nudge Alex's forearm. "So the pastry chef is particular? Here? Sounds like bullshit to me."

"She's an artist, Cade. You don't fuck around with an artist's area. I get it."

"Well, I don't. This sounds utterly pretentious. Dare I say, snobbish?"

Alex shakes his head. "You don't get it. I do. She has a space where she creates things. Having people she doesn't know in that space affects her."

"Can we leave yet, or are we sticking around for some cake or pie we could get anywhere else on the damn planet? I have things to do."

"You have nothing to do that can't be pushed off for an hour more. Whoever she is, she can wait."

That he assumes it's a woman that's making me want to leave here is a logical guess but an incorrect one. Since I don't want to start a discussion about my love life, I sit back and let out a huff of disgust.

All of this for something that isn't even a doughnut.

Out of the corner of my eye, I see one of the kitchen doors open, and there in full view for me is the woman who's been peering out the window at us for the last half hour. In her arms, she carries a tray of what look like cookies, but I barely waste a second studying them since she's stunning.

Is this the famous pastry chef my cousin can't talk enough about?

I barely get enough time to see she has light blond hair that goes to just below her shoulders and blue eyes. She looks like one of those stunning girls that hang out at the beach, not someone who spends her days in a kitchen.

When she sees I'm looking at her, she hurries back behind those doors, but now she doesn't sneak any peeks out at me. Disappointed, I look across the table at Alex and see by the look on his face he noticed her too.

"Is that her? The person who makes the desserts?" I ask, suddenly curious about these tasty treats he can't talk enough about.

"I don't know, but damn, whoever she is, she's gorgeous. I got the feeling she liked what you looked like," he says with a chuckle.

"She's been looking out at us the whole time we've been here. I figured she knew you from the restaurant. You know, since you both work in the same business."

Shaking his head, he laughs again. "Trust me, if anyone who looked like that worked at CK, I'd know. Kane's been doing the hiring for the past few months, and I swear to God the guy won't even consider someone to work in the kitchen who doesn't have ten years' experience under their belt. That pretty much ensures everyone, male and female, is in their forties, at least."

"Thank God for nepotism, right?" I say, taking this one opportunity to bust his balls.

He shrugs off my jab at how he got his job. "I guess, but that means I don't get to work with anyone even close to my age."

I look around for the mystery woman and don't see her. "So what do you know about this pastry chef?"

"Suddenly interested?" he asks with a chuckle.

"I'm not dead, man. I'm just jaded and a snob, remember? But even someone like that can appreciate a woman that gorgeous."

Robert returns a few moments later and blocks my view of the kitchen doors. "These are the creations for today. Hailey calls them lace cookies."

He sets a plate with a cookie down in front of each of us. "I hope you enjoy them."

I want to ask him more about this Hailey, but he hurries away before I can get a word out. Alex stares down in awe at the rectangle cookie that looks like white lace over a dark chocolate dough.

"Look at these scalloped edges and what she's done with the icing. It looks like actual lace. What did I tell you? Artist. That's the only word for the person who can create something like this. I need to get a picture of these."

As much as I don't usually go all crazy for cookies, I can't disagree with what he's saying. I've never seen anything that looks like this cookie in front of me. The icing truly does look like real lace, and not just some basic design. What look like delicate flowers and leaves made out of icing sit on top of this dark cookie, and I'm not even sure I should eat something so beautiful.

Alex doesn't have that issue, though, and once he gets finished taking half a dozen pictures of his cookie, his hedonistic ways take over. With one bite, he looks like he's in heaven. His eyes roll back in his head, making him look like he's about to get off right here in the booth.

"It tastes even better than it looks, Cade. Holy fuck, you have to try this cookie. It's chocolate but not like anything I've ever tasted before."

Lifting it to my mouth to take a bite, I joke, "You going to be okay over there? We need to leave this place sometime soon, so try to tamp down the hard on you've got going on."

One taste of that cookie when it hits my tongue and I know why he's acting like he is. It's delicious. Actually, that isn't a good enough word for it, but I don't know what would be good enough to explain how sweet and light it tastes at the same time.

When Robert returns wearing a hopeful look, I don't give Alex a chance to talk and say, "I'd love to meet the person who made this. It's incredible."

Alex immediately joins in on the praise. "They are fantastic. From one chef to another, I'd be honored if we could tell her how wonderful we think they are."

Robert seems to hesitate for a moment but then nods, giving us a smile like he's proud of his pastry chef. "Okay. I'll get her."

The two of us wait, and Alex says in a low voice, "Try not to be your usual dick self. She might actually like you if you aren't."

Nice. My best friend thinks I'm a dick. And a snob.

I consider asking him what the hell that comment means, but before I can, Robert returns with the person I'm silently calling the woman of my dreams. A couple yards away before, she looked stunning. Up close, she's even better.

Twice in the span of a few minutes, I don't have the right word to describe something regarding her.

"Gentlemen, this is Hailey, my daughter. She's the one who makes the wonderful desserts for our restaurant," Robert says, beaming pride.

Hailey. At least now I officially know the name of the woman of my dreams. The problem is my dream woman isn't even looking up at me. Not that she's looking at Alex either. In fact, her gaze seems plastered to the floor.

"I'm Cade, and this is Alex. We loved what you made. It's delicious."

Finally, she lifts her head and gives me a tiny smile before glancing over at Alex. "My father told me you're a chef and you loved the cookie? That's so nice of you to say."

Alex's face lights up at her mention of his job. "I am, and I can say for certain I've never tasted anything as incredible from any of our pastry chefs at

CK. Just don't tell them I said that because they'll never let me live that down."

Unlike with me, Hailey gives him a big smile that shows off a beautiful mouth and white teeth. "Thank you so much. I really appreciate it."

She gives me a quick glance and then quietly says, "It was nice meeting you two. I have to get back to work now."

And with that, she hurries into the kitchen and the last thing I see is the back of her right before the doors swing closed and she disappears. Robert and Alex continue to talk about desserts and how talented Hailey is, but I can't take my eyes off those kitchen doors, hoping for one more glimpse of her.

She doesn't appear, though, and when her father walks away and Alex starts talking about how much the check is compared to how great the food was, I simply nod my agreement. I can't think of anything but Hailey.

Is she cool like that with everyone? No, it's obvious she isn't. She didn't act all chilly with Alex.

Is she just shy? Maybe. I can work with shy. Shy girls are some of the sexiest girls going.

Or is she just not interested? Or worse, interested in my best friend?

"Did you hear me? I said I'm going to pay the bill."

Alex's voice pulls me from my thoughts, and I give him a fake smile and nod again. "Yeah. I'll be right there."

Left alone, I look over at the kitchen doors one last time and see her face in the window. This time, she doesn't immediately run and hide. I notice she doesn't look over toward where Alex was sitting either.

When she gives me a tiny smile like she gave me before, I give her one in return. So she's a shy girl. I can definitely work with that.

CHAPTER THREE

$\mathcal{H}$ailey

I HEAR MY MOTHER WALK IN THROUGH THE BACK door of the restaurant and know she's going to come right over to see what I'm making. She means well. Really, she does. It's just that at this very moment the last thing on my mind are cookies.

Shaking my head, I try to push out the image of that guy. Cade. A guy that gorgeous has no business being in our restaurant. Either does his friend, especially since he works as a chef at the best restaurant in town, but I could tell by the way he was talking about the cookie he had that he really liked it.

"Hello, honey," my mother says as she leans over

my back to kiss my right cheek. "What do you have cooking today?"

It's her way of being sweet and asking me how I'm doing. When I was little and Comfort Food was new, she would always say, "Hey, good looking! What you got cooking?" every time she came home from working here.

Back then, I loved when she said that to me. Now when she asks what I'm making, all I feel is anxious. I want these cookies to be as wonderful as they can be so my parents' restaurant does better business, but so far, all they've attracted are over-the-top food bloggers who write long-winded posts that don't get to the point until ten paragraphs in. I can't imagine most people are that patient to wade through all that chatter to find out about my cookies, even if they do include pictures that make them appear even better than they do in person.

I look back at her and give a smile I know she needs to see. "Just a little lace cookie thing I wanted to try. Chocolate shortbread cookies with lace designs on top. Daddy already took them out to the case if you want to see them."

Her blue eyes get big, lighting up at my description. "Oooooh, that sounds incredible! I'm going to go take a look right now. Do you need anything, honey?"

"No, I'm good, Mom. Thanks."

Hearing I'm fine, she runs off to see my latest

creations. I hope she doesn't notice how empty the restaurant looks today and focuses only on the cookies.

No sooner does she leave to go out front, she returns with one of the cookies in her hand. "You could be working somewhere incredible, honey. That's how good this is. I wish you'd consider it. Your talents are going to waste here at the diner."

"I'm not interested, Mom. I do this because it makes me happy. I like working here with you and Daddy."

She takes another bite and gives me a sigh like she's in heaven with how good it tastes. "I know, but you're young. You could be out working at somewhere great and meeting people instead of staying in this kitchen every day."

I glance over at the cook at the grill and give him a smile. "I'm sure Hector loves to hear you say that."

A hint of regret fills my mother's eyes. "He knows what I mean." Turning toward him, she yells across the kitchen, "You know I meant no harm, right, Hector?"

My mother couldn't willingly hurt a soul, so he just nods and smiles. He has no interest in getting involved in this conversation. I don't really want to have it either. It seems like lately, that's all my mother wants to talk about with me.

Working somewhere great and meeting new

people. I know what she means, even if she doesn't say it.

She means meeting men.

My mother is nothing if not old-fashioned. The time period the diner is meant to simulate would have fit her perfectly. That she was born long after the fifties always amazes me, especially when she gets talking about how I should find a nice young man and settle down.

Settle down? I'm twenty-four, for God's sake.

"Did you hear anything I said, Hailey?" she asks, pulling me from the thought of my life ending before it actually gets started.

I sheepishly shake my head. "No, sorry. I was off in my own head thinking about this macaroon I might want to make," I lie.

"Oh, that sounds delightful. Now as to what I was saying."

Damn. I hoped the macaroon idea would have changed the subject. No such luck.

"What do you think about the young men your father told me he introduced you to today?" she asks, hope filling her eyes like it always does when she mentions me meeting that elusive fine young man she wishes for me.

"You sure did get a lot of talking done in the few seconds you were out front, Mom," I say as I begin to set up my area to make some more desserts, already so done with this conversation about those guys from earlier.

Should it be cookies or something else? I saw a lemon tartelette that could be great for a beautiful spring day. Do I have what I need? If not, I'll happily run out so I don't have to stay here in this kitchen and talk about this subject that seems so top of mind for my mother.

"He called me on the phone and told me. Now what did you think of them? He said they raved about today's cookie. He also said they both seemed to be very nice men. What did he say their names were? I can't remember the one, but I think he said the one who's also a chef is named Alex. You two would have a lot in common, Hailey. Did you like him?"

I struggle against my nature to tell her Cade's name because I know if I do, she's going to read something into the fact that I remember it when that means nothing. I remember everything. She knows that. She used to joke that I had a mind like a steel trap, but I know if I even mutter his name, she's going to make it something it isn't.

So I just shrug like none of what happened earlier made any impression on me whatsoever. "They were like any other two guys, Mom. How do you and Dad know they aren't gay? They came in together and I saw them talking and it looked like they were bickering. I'm sorry to tell you, but that might mean they're both taken."

The mere thought that those two handsome young men who would be perfect for me could be gay stops my mother for a long moment, and she stands in front of my dough table with her mouth hanging open. It's like her mind is processing the likelihood that those two fine specimens she'd already had me choosing between could possibly not be available, and with every second that passes, she hates the idea more and more. Her expression morphs from one of shock to one of utter unhappiness.

"Well, your father thought they might be brothers since they resembled one another," she says, practically snapping at me for ruining her fantasy.

They did look alike. Both had dark brown hair and brown eyes, and they did both have tattoos up and down their arms. It never occurred to me they could be brothers, though, but in all honesty, I only paid attention to the one named Cade, especially once I found out Alex is a chef at a five-star restaurant.

I'm not a chef, by any stretch of the imagination, so being around someone who actually is instantly makes me feel self-conscious. A chef at the best restaurant in town? I couldn't have focused on him if I wanted to.

"Well, I have no idea, Mom. It's not like we had a deep conversation or anything. They liked the cookie and told me so. I thanked them and came back here to do work. That was it. If Daddy made it out to be anything else, then he was seeing something I wasn't."

My mother's five-foot five body seems to deflate

right in front of me at my disinterest in Cade and Alex. "Oh. I just thought since they came in and they were young like you that you might have wanted to get to know them. It's not every day young men come into the diner here, Hailey."

"Sorry. I didn't have my man-hunting thing going on today. Maybe if they come in again."

She grimaces, twisting her face into a disapproving scowl. "You know, honey, it's no crime to like people. You're a beautiful young woman who shouldn't think she should spend all her time hiding away in a kitchen. When opportunity knocks, you want to make sure to answer that door."

I grab the rolling pin from the rack next to me and drop it onto my table. It makes a loud thud that startles my mother.

"Oh, my God, Mom! Opportunity did not knock just because two good looking men came into this restaurant. I don't care if one is a chef or not, and just because he works around food doesn't make us have anything in common. I'm not a chef! There is no comparison to what he does and what I do here. As for the other one, I didn't even catch his name, so I'm sorry to disappoint you, but this episode of Set Up Your Daughter With Hot Strangers has come to an end."

Instantly, I see in her eyes that I've hurt her feelings. Frowning, she gives me a nod and silently turns to leave the kitchen as regret fills me.

"I'm sorry. I didn't mean that. Well, I did, but not that way, Mom."

Without turning around, she nods again. "It's fine, honey. I'm just going to go out front and see how things were this afternoon."

Every word sounds sadder than the last, so by the time she gets to the end of her sentence, I think I hear a tiny sob. Nice going. First, I'm my usual backward self with those two guys, and then I'm my other usual self, the defensive one, with my mother.

Grabbing the dough from the mixing bowl behind me, I slam it onto the table and begin working it. I better get used to working alone here because at the rate I'm going, even Hector is not going to want to be around me.

So much for thinking I'd made so much progress this past year. That was obviously as wrong as wrong can be.

I look up toward the kitchen door, hoping to see my mother come back so I can tell her I didn't mean to hurt her feelings. I understand what she's trying to do. I do. She has that whole mentality of getting back up on the horse after it's thrown you off. It's how she and my father continue to fight to keep this business open year after year long after other people would have given up.

That attitude is to be admired, but love isn't like running a struggling business. Sometimes, a person can't find the will to get back up and dust themselves off after being thrown. Sometimes, it just feels better to stay down where you are on the safe ground.

It's been almost a year since I've been down here, and as much as I thought I was getting back to who I was before it all happened, that was just wishful thinking. I'm still that brokenhearted soul Malcolm threw away that beautiful June night eleven months ago. All the hours spent talking to the therapist have added up to one sad truth.

I'm not ready to get back up on that horse again. I'm still hurting from the last fall.

CHAPTER FOUR

ade

BRIGHT AND EARLY THE NEXT DAY, I HEAD DOWN TO CK to see what I can find out from my uncles about this Hailey person. Unlike Alex, they should know something since they supposedly tried to lure her to CK as a pastry chef.

I find Cassian and Kane both in the office, which is a surprise. I'd have been happy simply trolling for information with one of them. Maybe this is a good sign.

"Hi! It's your favorite nephew come to visit," I say to announce my arrival as I walk into the office the two of them share.

Kane looks up and gives me a big smile. "Hey,

what are you doing here? Decide you want to put that business degree to good use finally?"

Cassian just shakes his head. "What's up, Cade?"

I grab a chair on the other side of the room and take a seat. "You sound like my father, Kane. Have you two been meeting to compare notes on how to shanghai me into the club or restaurant business?"

My question makes him laugh. "The last time your father came here to talk to me, we almost got into a fist fight. Trust me, we are not comparing notes on anything."

"Good, because one of him is enough. I don't need two of you trying to convince me what to do with my life."

Kane holds his hands up in front of him like he's surrendering. "No convincing here. But whoever thought it would be Stefan who turned into the dad who wanted his son to figure out life so young?"

Cassian laughs, and I'm tempted to ask exactly what Kane means by that, but I'm not really interested in taking a trip down memory lane with my uncles today. I already know a little about how my father was when he was my age. I can hear more another day.

Right now, I have other topics I want to discuss with them. Other more beautiful and interesting topics.

Might as well jump right in. "So, what do you guys know about the pastry chef over at that restaurant, Comfort Food?"

"We were definitely interested in having her work for us, but she denied us cold. No way. Wouldn't even return our calls, no matter if it was me or Kane."

Interesting. Then again, Comfort Food is her family's restaurant. She probably feels allegiance to them. But to give up the chance to work at the best restaurant in town to stay at the family diner seems foolish.

"Okay, but what do you know about her?" I ask, hoping to get more than this scratching the surface bullshit.

"For the longest time nobody knew it was even a her," Kane says. "A few local food bloggers got a hold of her treats and asked the owners of the restaurant, but they didn't tell them it was their daughter who made them. Only when the bloggers went snooping around did they find out it was a young woman named Hailey Canton, the daughter of the owners of the restaurant."

"Do you know anything else?"

Kane looks at me like he can't understand why I'd be asking about this woman at all. Clearly, he hasn't seen her.

"Like what? What else is there to know? Have you tasted any of her desserts? It's not an exaggeration to say they're the best most people around here have ever had. That's why we wanted her to come work for us, but she said no. Or more correctly, her father told us she wasn't even interested in talking about it."

"Alex says she's some kind of artist. He was raving about her like she was the Michelangelo of cookies yesterday."

Cassian laughs at his son's over-the-top response to that dessert. "I saw the pics of the cookies she made. The lace ones. I don't think he was wrong to rave. He told me they were delicious."

"They were," I admit with a shrug. "I mean, as far as cookies go, I guess. So she makes nice cookies. Why does she act like some kind of diva? She wouldn't even talk to either of us yesterday when Alex asked to meet her to compliment her on the cookie. It was weird. Then when she came out, it felt like she didn't even want to bother talking with us."

"Artists are like that, Cade. We've had some chefs who act like her. They're passionate about what they create. You have to give them that," Kane says as he stands from behind his desk.

"Artists. The way you guys talk like these people are DaVinci or something...I don't get it. Does that give people license to act like dicks?"

Both my uncles look at one another and laugh. "Sounds like she got under your skin a little bit. Not used to having women not interested in you?" Cassian asks with a chuckle.

Well, at least I got a little information out of them before they started busting my balls. Leave it to my family. Too bad Olivia and Abbi weren't the ones I could ask about Hailey. They'd give me chapter and verse, every detail from what she does in her spare time to how long she's been single.

Or maybe she's not single. Is that why she was so cool yesterday?

No, that doesn't work because she was fine with Alex.

I stand from my chair and push it back against the wall where I got it from. "Well, thanks guys. I better get going."

As I turn to walk toward the door, Cassian asks, "Why do you want to know about this pastry chef?"

His tone says he knows exactly why I want to know about her. Alex probably told him everything that happened yesterday.

When I don't answer his question, Kane chuckles. "Alex told us what she looks like, Cade. Guess the whole diva thing isn't that much of a turn off."

I look back over my shoulder and throw him a cocky smile. "I'm not against a challenge."

"Oh yeah? Turn over a new leaf or something?"

He's not wrong mocking me on that. I do have a history that indicates the exact opposite of liking a challenge when it comes to women. I'll admit that.

But something about Hailey makes me think I might be interested in one with her.

"I actually like the idea of having to work through whatever she has going on. Personally, I'm not sure it's not a shy thing instead of a diva thing, and if that's the case, I'm all in."

My uncles look at one another in disbelief. So maybe my history more than indicates challenging women haven't been my thing. Fine. A guy can change, can't he?

"You know what they say about shy girls, don't you?" I ask them.

Kane stares at me blankly, and Cassian shrugs. "No idea."

I shake my head at the state of the two men I thought were the coolest guys in the world growing up. "You two need to get out of this office more. Seriously."

"Well, I'm wondering if you aren't aiming above your level, Cade. Alex couldn't say enough about how gorgeous she is. Good looking and talented? Maybe she was cool because she's just not into you," Kane says with a laugh.

"Yeah. I mean, she might have told you everything you need to know yesterday. You just don't want to see it," Cassian adds.

Before they have a chance to bust my balls about trying to date out of my sphere, I head toward the back door of CK. Leave it to family to act like I'm the one who can't get her and not vice versa.

So she's beautiful and talented? So what? I'm not exactly some loser walking around without any skills here. True, I don't have my entire life planned out like nearly everyone else in my family. It's not because I can't do that.

It's because I won't.

Anyway, what woman wants a guy who's all settled down at the age of twenty-three? Women want excitement and fun, and that's what I offer in spades.

Leave that life all planned out shit for guys as old as my uncles. I'm way too young to be dealing with that yet.

And I'm betting that Hailey is a woman who could use some excitement in her life.

CHAPTER FIVE

*H*ailey

POKING MY HEAD INTO THE KITCHEN, I GIVE MY father a smile. "Hey, what's new?"

He shakes his head and sighs. "What's new is it's your day off. You don't have to be here every day, honey. You made more than enough desserts yesterday, so why don't you go out and enjoy yourself on such a beautiful day?"

"Coming through!" Ginger announces as she practically barrels through the kitchen doors, nearly taking me with her.

I quickly step out of the way so the doors don't come back and slam into my face. After a few seconds,

I walk back to where my father is working near my area and answer his question.

"Don't worry. I'm not here for long. I just wanted to see how the lemon tartelettes did, and it seems they went over pretty big. There are only a few left, and it's only two o'clock in the afternoon. Did one of those food bloggers post about them and that's why people came in to grab them?"

He gives me his usual confused look that he always wears when I start talking about the food bloggers. My father simply doesn't understand why anyone would write about my desserts like they do. When they first started featuring my creations, he read a few of their posts and complained the entire time that they said almost nothing about the restaurant or how good my desserts are but instead talked about their childhoods the whole time.

I tried to explain that's how they do it, but he wouldn't listen. Since then, whenever I mention them, he looks at me like I've switched from English to Greek and he doesn't comprehend a word I'm saying.

It's the same look he used to get when I was a teenager and had a crush on a boy. He didn't want to understand I was growing up then, and he doesn't want to understand those food bloggers and their posts now.

So instead of discussing them, he switches to business mode. "We had a bit of a lunch rush pretty early for midweek. It started even before eleven, and it just ended a few minutes ago. I mentioned the dessert of the day, which is what I'm calling them now, to a few people, and from there they took off."

"I'm so happy to hear that! Anyone new seem to come in?" I ask, more curious about if what I'm making is bringing new customers in than if the tartelettes were a hit with the regulars.

In his stoic way, he nods and thinks about the question for a moment. "Maybe. I thought I saw a couple new people today. But you don't need to shoulder the responsibility for bringing new people into the restaurant, Hailey. We're fine with the customers we have right now."

The two of us know that's a lie, but I don't let him see I know the truth. My father is a proud man, and I would never want to hurt him like that.

It doesn't change the fact that I hope my desserts help people find this place and make it a go-to restaurant for them in the future. He doesn't have to know that, though.

"Well, I'm going to get out of here then. It's a beautiful day, so I thought I'd get a little Vitamin D and then catch up with Meadow after her big job interview. She's meeting with the owners of the biggest design firm in town right now."

My father's face brightens at the mention of my best friend. "Tell her we said hi and that we hope she gets the big job. If she does, you have to go out and celebrate."

I know what he's doing. My mother has rubbed off on him and now he's slyly trying to get me to go out more. He's just not as obvious about it.

"We will. Don't worry. You know Meadow. If there's a chance to celebrate, she's there. She'd celebrate days ending in y if she had the time," I joke before waving goodbye to him. "See you tomorrow, Dad."

"Have fun getting your vitamins!" he calls after me, thinking he's funny.

I do have to admit it, though. He is cute when he tries to be amusing.

On my way out the front door of the restaurant, I give Ginger a smile, which she doesn't return. She saves the niceties for the customers. That's good, I guess, but it would be nice if she sometimes didn't act like everyone else who works here is a sworn enemy of her family who she must growl or bark at every chance she gets.

Even my parents and I don't get a break from her rudeness, and my family owns this place. But she's good with customers, so she stays, snappy attitude and all.

As I head toward my car, I see a red Jaguar with tinted windows pull into the parking lot. Maybe those food bloggers are helping. It's pretty rare we get that kind of clientele here. Maybe they'll like the lemon tartelettes and tell some of their wealthy friends. That would help my parents.

I watch as the driver's side door opens and see Cade, the guy from the day I made the lace chocolate cookies. My attention switches to the passenger side door while I wait to see if his friend came back with him, but it doesn't open.

He's alone. But why is he here at all? He didn't strike me as the kind of guy who's a big fan of cookies. His friend maybe, but not him.

Unsure what to do, I hurry to my car. I fumble with my keys to get my door open, and while I'm silently wishing I hadn't locked the damn doors in the first place since it's the middle of the day and I'm at my family's restaurant, I hear footsteps behind me.

When I turn to look, there he is coming toward my car. What does he want to talk to me about? We don't know one another. I barely spoke to him the other day.

God, he's good looking. Like the kind of good looking that makes you wonder if he's real. Men like that don't tend to come looking for women like me. So what is he doing walking this way?

Maybe he is a guy who loves cookies. Too bad I have to tell him all we have are tartelettes today.

"Hey, Hailey? How are you?"

I stop dead and slowly turn my entire body around to face him. Jesus, up close he's even better. I didn't think he was this good looking the other day. Then again, I spent most of my time looking at him through the dingy kitchen door window and barely made eye contact with him when I went to his table.

He's wearing a light blue T-shirt and a pair of jeans, but I swear I've never seen anyone look this good in clothes like that before. It's got to be the muscles. He looks like he works out.

That's what he is. A gym rat. But a gym rat who cheats by eating sugary desserts? That doesn't sound right. Or maybe it is. I don't exactly have a wealth of knowledge about that kind of man.

All of this runs through my head as I stand there staring at him and then realize I haven't answered him. How am I? Not good, Cade. A nervous wreck would be the appropriate description, I think.

"Hi. What are you doing here?" I ask, knowing how rude that must sound, like I've been taking nasty lessons from Ginger. But I can't help but be curious at what's brought him back for the second time in a week to a restaurant he's never been to before the other day.

"I came to see you."

The way he says that, as if it's the only answer and I should know that, makes me even more nervous. He's way too confident. That I can tell already.

He smiles, and I think my insides begin to melt. I'm like chocolate morsels in the sun looking at that sexy grin. Oh, yeah. Way too confident. I bet women really like that smile.

Then again, why wouldn't they? Nice teeth. White. Straight. What's not to like?

Out of nowhere, my brain switches into idiot

mode, and I ask, "Do you mean you came to see me because of the cookies?"

Cade looks confused for a moment but shakes his head. "Not really."

"Because I didn't make any today. It's my day off. I made a different dessert yesterday, though, and if you love lemon, you should definitely go in and check it out."

"I didn't come here for food."

Now I feel foolish and uncomfortable, so I blurt out something I know is a lie. "Oh, because I thought you and your friend might be food bloggers. Some of the local ones have been doing write-ups about what I make."

He smiles and shakes his head again. "No. My friend is actually my cousin. Alex is a chef like you. I do nothing with food other than eat it. That I'm very talented at."

I can't help but let my gaze roam down his muscular, toned body as I decide he's a liar like I am. Or maybe he just eats really healthy stuff to get to look like that.

When I don't say anything to what I'm sure can't be the truth, he says, "So it's your day off? Want to go do something?"

"You mean you and me? Us do something?"

"Yeah," he says and then chuckles. "I thought maybe we could hang out and get to know one another. I saw you looking through the window at me the other day. It's fine that you're shy. I have enough confidence for both of us."

"It seems like you do."

"That's not a bad thing, though. I mean, the shyness. I like that. I bet once you get to know someone you aren't so quiet anyway, so I thought we could start on getting to know one another today."

"Are you always like this with women?" I ask, unsure if I'm put off by how forward he is or intrigued that he truly is this confident.

"I don't hesitate when I see someone I like. I think you like me too. I mean, unless you were checking out Alex the other day, but I didn't get the feeling you were. You seemed more interested in me," he says in that smooth way that seems so natural to him.

Hearing he likes me makes every ounce of anxiety that lives inside me rear its ugly head. I should have never looked out that kitchen window at him. That's what I get for listening to Dr. Thorpe and Meadow.

Put yourself out there, Hailey. Let people know you like them. Try it.

This is what happens when I take their advice. I end up in a parking lot talking to some gorgeous guy and feeling like the only thing I want to do is run away before I say or do something so utterly ridiculous that I humiliate myself.

Looking down at my keys I'm gripping tightly in my hand, I mumble, "I have to go. You should go inside and have one of the lemon desserts I made. You might like them."

And then before he can say another word, possibly that it was a mistake to come here today because I'm just a basket case, I run inside the restaurant and hide in the kitchen back near my station.

Ten minutes later, after pretending like I was looking for something just in case someone saw me tear back here, I look out that same kitchen door window where he saw me checking him out the other day and see there's no red Jaguar in the parking lot. For a moment, relief washes over me, but then that's replaced by regret, like always when I push people away like I just did with Cade.

I sneak out the back door of the restaurant this time and walk out to my car, silently berating myself for being exactly who I swore I wouldn't be anymore. But if you're not ready, you're not ready. It doesn't matter what the horse looks like or that he likes you.

By the time I reach my car, I can't remember what I wanted to do today because all I want to do now is go home and crawl underneath the covers. As I slide into the driver's seat, a white piece of paper stuck under one of my windshield wipers flaps in the breeze. When I grab it and open it up, I see it's from Cade.

Hey, give me a call sometime. I think we could have fun. I promise I don't bite. Unless you want me to. 555-2466

Cade March

Quickly, I stuff the note into my pocket and decide right there and then there's no way I'm ever going to call him. I may be afraid to get back on the dating horse, but some people you should be afraid of.

Men like Cade March.

CHAPTER SIX

ade

AFTER CHECKING MY PHONE FOR THE FIFTH TIME, I toss it onto the other side of the bed in disgust. She got my note. I'm sure of it. So why hasn't she called? It's been almost twenty-four hours.

Maybe this arteest isn't for me.

Bullshit. She and I could be having a good time if only she'd call. I should have stuck around to get her number, but after watching her run away into the restaurant, I can't be blamed for calling an audible. It's not every day a woman flees from me like she's running from a house fire.

She'll call. They always do. And why not? Who doesn't want to have a good time?

I close my eyes and ease my palm over my cock. Just thinking about her gets me hard. I can only imagine how incredible it's going to feel to actually kiss her. After that, it's all good from there.

And then in the middle of my daydream about how fucking fantastic it's going to be with Hailey, I hear a voice I know all too well call out my name. Thanks for crashing my fantasy, Dad.

"Cade? Where are you? It's the middle of the day."

I know damn well what time it is. Why does he have to do his Big Ben impression for me this afternoon?

Quickly, I get into a pair of shorts and scrub the remnants of last night's sleep from my face before heading out into my living room. There, standing in the middle next to the coffee table, my father swivels his head left and right examining the room like he's never seen the place before.

"Hey, Dad. How did you get in?"

It's a valid question, if not a polite one. I'm all for family togetherness, but just walking up into my condo and interrupting what was going to be a fine jerk off session is a bridge too far.

"You left the door open. Pretty trusting, don't you think?" he says with all the disapproval he can fit into those few words.

"Not trusting. Forgetful. I thought I locked it when I went to bed," I say before turning to walk toward the kitchen. "Can I get you anything, Dad?"

"No, not unless it's juice. Your mother has me on this juice cleanse for the next two days. I think she might be trying to kill me."

I look back at him and see in his expression he's serious. "She's not trying to kill you. She's just trying to make you healthier. I might have orange juice, but I can't promise it's still good. Someone left it after the party a couple weekends ago."

He follows behind, begging off the possibly rancid juice that's sitting in the back of my refrigerator. "I'm good. I'm thinking I might just stick with water until this whole cleanse thing is up. Water has to be better for you than juice."

I grab a bottle of spring water and hand it over the refrigerator door to him. "It might be, but it doesn't have the vitamins and nutrients juice has."

My father thinks about that for a moment and smiles. "Don't tell your mother then. I just know I can't drink another glass of carrot juice or I'm going to turn into a rabbit. Does my skin look orange to you? Someone at the club said I was looking a little orange and asked if I went heavy on the self-tanner. As if I'd use that shit. If I didn't need all the bartenders I could find, I'd fire that little shit Antonio. Asshole."

My father's stream of consciousness makes me laugh. One second he's talking about turning into a rabbit, and the next he's threatening one of his bartenders.

"So what can I do for you, Dad? I'm guessing it's

important since you didn't bother to even knock before you came in."

"It's not like I broke in, Cade. The door was unlocked, so I walked in."

Why this sounds right to him I have no idea. It's not like I'm still a kid living in his house and he found my bedroom door unlocked.

"Yeah, you said. Do you routinely check to see if people's front doors are unlocked when you go to someone's house?" I ask as I take my place across the kitchen from him and lean back against the countertop.

His expression hardens into a grimace. "You aren't someone. You're my son."

Somewhere in there I sense there's a sentiment I should be unhappy with, but there's no point in getting into it with my father today. He's just being his usual dad self.

"Got it. So what's up?"

He looks around my kitchen that could use some cleaning and sighs. Okay, maybe it could use a sandblasting to dislodge the crusty food stuck on the stove. And the countertops.

"So, is this what you're planning to do today? Just hang around?" he asks before wincing, like my condo is causing him some terrible pain.

I can't help but get defensive when he does this. It's not like it's rare that this happens either. Lately, it seems like at least once a month, he drops in and examines my place like some kind of disgruntled housekeeper come to heap shame on someone for not keeping it tidy enough.

"Well, I wasn't even up when you barged in, Dad, so I'd say I've accomplished a few things already today," I snap back, all the while smiling because I really don't need to get into an argument with my father not a half hour after waking up.

More wincing is followed by him silently taking a drink of water while I wait for the inevitable discussion that's going to occur. I know my father too well to believe he's going to be able to leave here without giving me the lecture about how it's time for me to grow up and settle down.

At twenty-three.

It's the height of hypocrisy too, if you ask me. I've heard the stories of how legendary his twenties were working at Club X and living a life others could only dream about. Money, women, and all the alcohol he could want was his everyday life.

Yet I'm expected to be settled down into a responsible life at my age.

"Do you have any job prospects, Cade? It's been a year since you graduated from college. You have a degree, you're a smart guy, and I have to think there are hundreds of companies that would love to have you work for them."

As he speaks, I anticipate every word that will come out of his mouth next. I've heard this speech so many times, I could give it to myself. That would actually be better. It would cut out the middleman and make having to do this with him a thing of the past.

That wouldn't work for the great Stefan March, though. No, he enjoys coming over here on his monthly tour of my house, sighing disapprovingly as he scans the rooms and mentally ticks off all my household failures, and then giving me his same old dissertation on how I should be working at a job he would have never considered at my age and likely wouldn't even now.

"Dad, you know the answer, so why do you ask the question? I haven't found what I want to do yet. I have time. It's not like being twenty-three and unsure of my future makes me a lost cause. I have money, so I'm not going to be homeless anytime soon. Don't worry. I got this."

My father narrows his eyes like he can't believe what I'm saying. "You got what, Cade?"

I spread my arms out and smile. "This. Life."

"You've got a condo because of your trust fund your mother and I set up. You've got that car of yours because of that same trust fund. Don't you think it's time to make your own way in life?"

"I am. I'm just not doing it the way you would prescribe for me."

He acts like that trust fund isn't exactly like the money he got from his father all those years ago that allowed him and his brothers to start up Club X. Fuck, he's such a hypocrite!

Taking a step forward, he lets out another frustrated sigh and sets his water bottle on the island that separates us. "Cade, you have the very skills necessary to take over the club. You'd be perfect. I'm not going to be running it forever, and it's turnkey. Literally, you'd walk in, and it would set you up for life. Then you could do whatever you want with it. Change it to be exactly what you want it to be. It's there for the taking."

And there's the pitch that comes right near the end of every one of these monthly discussions. Now it's my turn to say that's not what I want to do and his turn to get angry, throw his hands up in the air, and storm out.

At least all of this is predictable. I have to give him that.

"Dad, I don't want to manage a club or own a club or do anything with your club. It's not who I am."

Right on cue, disappointment fills his dark eyes and he lowers his head to look at the floor. "Your mother and I always thought we were doing right by you when we set up that trust fund to begin paying out when you were twenty-one. We wanted to make sure we took care of the future because we love you, son."

He stops for a moment and looks up at me with anguish written all over his face. This isn't how our usual talks go. Why isn't he raging like always? This is when he's supposed to list all the ways I should be acting like an adult and how I should have some job that he approves of by now.

But that doesn't seem to be happening this time. Interesting. My father has changed things up on me.

"We see now we made a mistake, and we intend on rectifying that. From this year on, the payments won't occur unless you have a job. We don't care if it's flipping burgers or delivering pizzas. A job is a job, and as long as you're doing an honest day's work and you're happy doing it, we'll be happy for you."

I stand there in my kitchen staring at him, stunned at what he's just said. "You're taking my trust fund away from me?"

"No, Cade. You will, if you don't get a job. Again, your mother and I don't care what you choose to do, as long as it's legal and you earn money doing it. We put no restrictions whatsoever on you. Now, if you want, you can work at the club, and this will be solved. I always need bartenders, and since you have no interest in managing the club, maybe you'd like to do a job that's less work and more fun. It's entirely up to you."

Barely able to contain my anger at this blackmail he's decided to use on me, I snap, "So as long as I work behind the bar serving those goddamned drunks you call customers, you won't cut me off? Nice, Dad. Hell of a way to treat your only son."

He takes a sip of water and smiles. He's won, so why not? "The choice is up to you. You can start whenever you want. Or not. If you want to do something else, do it. If you want to start up a business and make things, do it. If you want to deliver those pizzas or flip those burgers I mentioned before, do it. Just do something, for Christ's sake, Cade!"

And there's the anger I'm used to in our lovely talks. At least he didn't disappoint me with that.

As he's leaving, I quietly give him what he wants. "I'll do some bartending at the club starting this week."

My father doesn't say a word before walking out of the kitchen. From the other room, I hear him say, "Afternoon, Alex. Your cousin is in there. How are things going?"

Sounding as happy as a clam, Alex answers, "Great, Stefan! Nice seeing you. Have a good one!"

By the time he pokes his head around the wall, it's all I can do to force myself to say hi. "You just missed a delightful conversation with my father, the wonderful and hypocritical Stefan March."

A look of pain comes over my cousin's face. "Was it that day already this month? I thought those talks came later in the month and not so early. So did it go the same as always?"

I shake my head, still amazed at what he pulled on me. "No. Daddy's got a brand-new routine, and it's utter bullshit."

ade

ALEX WAITS TO HEAR WHAT I MEAN BY THAT AND finally says, "A brand new routine? What does that mean?"

"Seems I'm not going to get any money this year from my trust if I don't get a job."

As much as I wish Alex would be supportive on this, I can see by the look on his face and the shrug he gives to my announcement that he either isn't surprised or may even think what my father's doing is cool.

"Thanks for being there for me, man."

"Cade, I'm your best friend, but even I can say it's time you stopped playing around. You've been back from school for almost a year. You can't be surprised he and your mother pulled this card on you."

Huffing my disgust at that little nugget of truth coming from Alex, of all people, I head over to the refrigerator and grab the two of us beers. I hand him his and push past him on my way to the living room.

At least I can enjoy a couple more days of freedom before I get chained to the workaday world. Leaning back, I close my eyes and take a sip of ice-cold beer while the realization that I haven't even had breakfast yet runs through my head.

Oh well. Forget doughnuts. Beer is now the breakfast of champions.

"Come on, Cade. It's not so bad. I work, and it hasn't made me some uptight pain in the ass who doesn't have fun. As my father likes to say, the world is your oyster. You can work at any number of jobs. Just find something you like and do it."

I look across the room to see he's serious about this. "The world is my oyster? Dude. And you've always been a pain in the ass. You working at your job has nothing to do with that."

"Fuck you too," he says with a chuckle, lifting his beer in the air. "To Cade finally joining the ranks of us working stiffs."

That toast sucks, but I take a drink of my beer anyway. "What kills me is he was even worse than me at this age. Remember hearing the stories your father and

Kane were telling a few summers ago at the Fourth of July party about my father? To hear them talk, Stefan March spent all his days sleeping and all his nights partying. So that was okay for him, but now he's older so he wants to make sure I don't have any fun? He acts like responsibility is some wonderful thing and having a job is the mark of a good person. What a fraud he is."

Alex nods, even though I have a feeling he agrees with my father at least a little. "By the way they were talking, all three of them were living the life. I guess time changes you, though. We'll probably be that way when we get to be their age."

I couldn't be more horrified at that prospect than if he had the power to show me the future himself. "No. Fucking. Way. I'm not going to turn into that. No, thanks."

"So what kind of job are you thinking you might want? You have a degree in business from a good school, so it's not like you're not qualified for a lot."

Just the thought of what job I might want to get makes my head hurt. If I knew what I wanted to do this past year, I would have done it. While I make it seem like I'm all about living the life of leisure and enjoying myself, even to my best friend, the truth is I don't want to do any job.

Not because I don't want to work. Work is work. If you hate what you're doing, it feels like a jail sentence. If you love what you're doing, time flies. I got through four years of school just fine, so it's not that I can't handle work.

I just have no idea what I want to do.

"No clue," I say shaking my head. "How did you know you wanted to be a chef?" I ask, wondering if hearing this story again might help me figure out what I should do.

Alex thinks about it for a few moments before taking a drink of his beer. "I just always did. I grew up hearing all about what was happening at the restaurant, and I thought it sounded great. I found out when I started working at CK when I was a teenager that it wasn't as fun as I'd made it out to be, but I knew I wanted to be a chef."

"I have no idea how you work with your father. I spent last summer working at the club with my father, and I don't know how I'm going to do it again now. I told him I'd do some shifts, but I swear to God I hate the idea more than I can put into words."

My misery makes Alex laugh. "It's not that bad for me, actually. My father and Kane don't really hang out in my kitchen, so I only see them when they pop in or when I go into the restaurant after my shift is over. And Kane is my uncle, and you know how he is. I swear there are some nights I don't hear him speak a word to those of us in the kitchen."

I blow the air out of my lungs in frustration. "Too bad I'm not the son of Cassian March or Kane Jackson."

"It's not bad for me, but Cash gets most of the grief from my dad like you do from your father. I'm guessing that's why my brother's going to be a lawyer and not a chef, like me. He never liked hearing about how the kitchen worked, and remember the first time he saw me making a meal? He laughed in my face."

"If only I loved something as much as you love doing what you do. I still don't get the whole loving cooking food, but at least it's something you're passionate about. I have nothing like that."

Alex smiles and gets that look of pure happiness on his face like whenever he talks about his job. "It's an art form. You take something that's a raw material and you create a masterpiece. Even better, people then eat it and gush about how delicious it tastes. I can't imagine doing anything else."

"An arteest, like that Hailey girl, huh? You should be interested in her. You have that whole food thing in common."

"I love how committed she is to making what she creates so beautiful, but she's not my type," he says like he's thought about getting together with her.

From out of nowhere, jealousy rears up in me. That's never happened before when it comes to him. We've dated sisters, friends, cousins—you name it, and never once have I thought he might be a rival for any woman.

But now with Hailey, he seems perfect for her compared to me. They both do that chef thing and they both love food for something other than putting it into their faces and eating. I doubt she'd run away from any conversation with him.

"What do you mean she isn't your type? She's gorgeous, talented, everything a guy could want. Why wouldn't she be your type?"

"I don't date women in the industry," he answers flatly.

What the hell is he talking about?

"Who are you? Some big movie star? You don't date in the industry? What kind of bullshit is that? I can't count the number of servers you've been with."

Still, he shakes his head with a definite no. "Servers are different. Fellow chefs? Never. You don't want to date someone just like you."

Now he sounds like a diva. I roll my eyes and shake my head at the nonsense coming out of his mouth. "That's ridiculous. I thought having things in common was what you need for a relationship."

He seizes on my use of the word relationship, practically leaping out of the chair when he asks, "So now we're talking about relationships? First you have to get a job, and now you're talking about settling down with someone? I'm guessing you've decided you want Hailey Canton. She's definitely got it all."

Under my breath, I mumble, "Which she ran away with while I tried to talk to her."

Alex leans forward and gives me a strange look. "What did you say?"

He's been my best friend from practically the minute we were born, so I guess I can confess the truth of what happened to him. "I stopped by to talk to her yesterday afternoon. You know, to chat her up and see if she wanted to go for a ride or something."

"No need to explain your methods, Cade. I've seen every move you have. So what happened?"

Blowing the air out between my lips, I sit back in frustration. "Nothing. Well, nothing good. We talked for about five seconds. She sort of looked like she was happy to see me. At least I think she did. Well, after she got over being surprised that I had stopped into that diner again. I asked her if she wanted to hang out, and she said no. She actually thought I had come back for more of those cookies. Wild, huh?"

He hums at the memory of that chocolate lace cookie. Typical Alex. "That cookie was pretty fucking good. She has a gift."

"Yeah, I guess, but I didn't go there to talk about desserts. So I'm trying to talk her up and feel the situation out, and she suddenly said she had to go and ran away. No kidding. She just ran back into the restaurant, even though she was on her way out when I caught up with her. I waited around for a few minutes, but she never came back out. What the hell was that about?"

My cousin's eyes grow wide for a second and then he throws his head back and laughs. "She ran away from you? Dude, you are totally losing your touch. I

67

can't remember a single time a woman has run away from me while I was talking to her. Too funny."

So much for having a best friend you can confide in.

I take a swig of my beer and then chug the rest of it. Slamming the empty bottle on the coffee table, I whip him off. "Fuck you, Alex."

Still laughing, he waves off my irritation. "Okay, my bad. I didn't mean to laugh at your humiliation. You have to remember she's someone who's creative, so maybe she saw your moves coming from a mile away and wasn't having them. Maybe you'll have to do more with this girl than just show up as you with that great car as your calling card."

"Dude, I wasn't standing there in the middle of the Comfort Food parking lot showing her all my moves. I was just trying to have a conversation to get to know her and she…"

I can't bring myself to say she ran away again. I've replayed the scene in my head a hundred times since yesterday, and then every time I checked my phone to see if she texted or called when I was asleep. I may not be the world champion in seducing women, but even I know when one runs away, it's not a good sign.

"She bolted," he says in a serious voice I know is taking every bit of strength he has because he probably wants to continue laughing in my face.

"So what are you going to do? Maybe she's not

your type?" Alex asks, giving voice to something I've wondered more than once.

No. I don't know if Hailey is my type, but I want to get to know her before I cross her off my list. Maybe she really is just a shy girl. Nothing wrong with that. I can work with shy.

As long as she doesn't keep running away when I try to talk to her.

"I don't know if she is or isn't, but I'm not ready to throw in the towel quite yet. She's a beautiful woman. I'm me. I don't see why we can't get together and have a good time, right?"

"You're one of a kind, Cade. I can't decide if you're funny or just way too fucking cocky. Either way, you're okay, man. So are we going to sit around talking about your failure with women all day or head out and get this day started? I have to be at work by six, so time's wasting."

He doesn't give me a chance to answer his questions before he grabs my bottle off the table and walks into the kitchen. Alex is one of those creative types. He and Hailey are a lot alike in that way, especially since they both like to create with food. Maybe she's a lot like him, which would be great since he's my best friend.

Sounds like the best of both worlds in one beautiful woman. How could I not take a chance on that?

CHAPTER EIGHT

$\mathcal{H}$ailey

MY PHONE VIBRATES AGAINST MY SIDE, TEARING ME from my thoughts about how I acted with Cade yesterday. I grab it and see it's Meadow calling me. She must want to talk about the interview again, but I'm probably not the best cheerleader at this moment.

"Hey, Meadow! What's up?" I say into the phone as I pretend not to be miserable.

"Hailey, I got it! I got the job! Oh, my God! I can't believe it. Can you believe it? Durkin and Chestnut offered me a position in their firm. I'm going to be designing for the best firm in Tampa!" she squeals into my ear.

I sit up in bed, finally excited about something

after the last twenty-four hours of regret and recriminations I've beat myself up with over running away from Cade like some scared rabbit. "That is so great! I knew you'd get it. They'd be crazy not to hire you with your experience. Ten to one they decided after your work on the Tamsin project."

She sighs into the phone at my mention of her favorite achievement since she started designing homes. "I loved working on that house. It will forever be the best time I ever had. Tamsin."

"The best until now."

"True. So we have to celebrate. Sabrina made reservations for us tomorrow night, so get out your best dress, girl, because we are celebrating."

"Okay. Sounds good!"

That part came out forced because while I love Meadow, her sister Sabrina can grate on my last nerve sometimes. She's like every Barbie doll, supermodel, and overachiever all rolled into one when she gets going after a few drinks.

Too perky, too perfect, and too much.

"She's going to send me all the particulars, so I'll text them to you when she gets them to me. Oh, Hailey, I'm so excited. The best design firm in the city wants me. I can't get over it. I keep pinching myself to see if it's really real."

"It's really real," I say with a chuckle at how adorable she is. "You deserve this. Twenty-five and on your way to the top. Will you remember us little people when you get there?" I tease.

"Of course," she answers, giggling. "How could I forget my friends who've always been there for me?"

"Make sure you mention us in your speech when you win designer of the year."

"I will. I have to go now. I feel like all my clothes for work look like rags, so I'm going to splurge on some new skirts and tops. Maybe even a suit to replace the one I've had all this time since I started. I can't wait to see you tomorrow night. As soon as Sabrina texts me the details, I'll send them along. Do you want to grab a ride with us, or are you flying solo?"

The thought of being trapped in a car with Sabrina to and from the restaurant, in addition to sitting at the table with her for dinner makes that answer easy. "I'll drive my car. Just let me know when and where and I'll be there with bells on."

Meadow is so delirious with happiness she's forgotten how her sister and I get along. That's okay, though. It's her night, so we can behave for a few hours and celebrate her success.

At least I can. As for Sabrina, I can't say.

"Great! It's going to be so much fun!" she squeals.

"Congratulations, Meadow. You deserve this. I'll see you tomorrow night."

I lay back on my bed and try not to let my jealousy get the better of me. I love Meadow like I love my sisters. She's been like a member of my family since we were kids in elementary school. I'm happy for her.

Really.

Meadow deserves everything she's getting. She's worked her ass off to make a name for herself in the design business around town. She's talented and disciplined.

Then why is it that all I feel as I lie here staring up at my bedroom ceiling is jealousy?

ALL DAY, I WAIT FOR HER TEXT AS I TRY MY HAND AT making rose cupcakes for the restaurant. They turn out better than I expected, and no sooner do I put the pink, white, and peach colored cupcakes out in the case, I finally get word from Meadow where we're going and what time.

Be at CK at six. Can't wait to see you!

CK. That's the restaurant Cade's cousin said he worked at. I stare down at my phone and wonder if I should text her back for the address or if she'll realize she forgot to send it. A second later, another text from Meadow makes my phone vibrate in my hand, and I see she did remember.

Money must be no object for Sabrina tonight since CK is one of the best restaurants in town. Definitely not in my usual price range, but for Meadow, I'll swing it.

Catching a glimpse of myself in the glass window

of the display case, I grimace. I might be able to afford CK for one dinner, but with the way I look, I'll stick out like a sore thumb at a place like that.

Unfortunately, I don't have enough time to go shopping for a new outfit, so I'll just have to muddle through with that dress I bought last summer before everything happened. I close my eyes and try to push away the negative thoughts that immediately pop up in my mind.

So things went horribly wrong, and your boyfriend cheated on you. It happens. At least you'll get to wear that dress you were supposed to wear to the rehearsal party.

I repeat those words over and over for a few moments, just like Dr. Thorpe always says to, and for the first time ever, it actually works. I take a deep breath in and let it out slowly—also a trick she swears by—and open my eyes to see my reflection staring back at me.

Still not great, but with some makeup and my trusty hair straightener, I'll look good enough for Meadow's celebration dinner. It doesn't really matter what I look like anyway. With her sister there looking like Miss Florida, who's going to notice?

"IS THIS PLACE NOT THE MOST GORGEOUS PLACE you've ever seen?" Sabrina gushes as Meadow and I scan the menu.

Normally, her exaggerating gets on my nerves, but tonight she isn't overstating how incredible CK is. Dimly lit by lights in the ceiling, sconces on the dark colored walls, and lamps on end tables scattered around the restaurant, the bank of windows that takes up the entire wall facing out toward the water provides not only enough light but a breathtaking view.

Gorgeous is the least CK is.

"I feel like I've died and gone to heaven," Meadow whispers as she leans over toward me. "This menu has so many things that look so good. What are you thinking of getting?"

My eyes roam over the large parchment menu in my hands for a moment before I turn to face her. "I have no idea. Maybe the shrimp risotto?"

"You have to get the steak, Meadow," Sabrina says, interrupting us. "I've heard people say it's the best they've ever had. Something about the way they treat it or where they get it from. That's what I'm getting."

Meadow stifles a laugh and points at the steak section on the menu. "Steak with rosemary chimichurri? I can do rosemary, but I'm not always a chimichurri fan, Sabrina."

Her sister waves away her concern about the

spiciness of the dish. "It'll be fine. Places like this never go full tilt on the spice anyway."

I roll my eyes behind my menu, and as Meadow leans away to sit back in her seat, she says, "I'll think about it, but I'm really feeling salmon tonight. The only thing is I like it well-done. Do you think that will be a problem?"

Before I can say she's the guest of honor so she can have her salmon any way she likes, her sister leans in toward the center of the table shaking her head. "That's like blasphemy to chefs at a restaurant like this. You can't ask for that, Meadow. What's wrong with salmon like it's usually done?"

Meadow gets a sheepish look and shrugs. "The texture is too soft. It makes eating it almost impossible."

"Then you have to get the steak. That's it. Steak it is."

We've been here fifteen minutes, and already I want to stick a fork through Sabrina's forehead. I promised I wouldn't say anything to make anyone uncomfortable tonight, but before I can stop myself, I mumble, "Why don't we let the woman who just scored the job of her dreams choose what she's going to eat and how she's going to eat it?"

Despite the fact that every table around us is filled with other people, I swear I can hear a pin drop when those words come out of my mouth. Meadow pulls her menu so close to her face that she can't possibly even see the words to read them, and I glare across the table at Sabrina with a death stare since I've already gone back on my promise to not get into it with her.

The entire scene feels like someone's put the world on slow-motion speed. Nobody seems to be moving around us, and all I can hear is the sound of my heartbeat pounding in my ears.

Sabrina glares back at me from across the table, her perfectly made-up eyes with her fake lashes ever so slightly narrowed to let me know she didn't appreciate my little comment. Well, too bad.

"Meadow, you do what you want. Tonight is your night, so you don't have to listen to anyone."

Typical Sabrina. She gets bossy and then makes it seem like everyone else is pressuring people to do things.

Lost in my disgust with how easy it is to predict Meadow's sister would act like this, I don't see the man approaching our table until he's right next to my elbow. I look up and see it's none other than Cade's cousin himself.

He smiles, showing off perfectly white teeth and lighting up his face so even his dark brown eyes seem to sparkle. I hadn't noticed how stunning he was that day, but now as he's standing over me looking down like he's happy to see me, I'm taken aback by how he looks, even in his chef uniform.

Oh, my God! I can't remember his name! What was it? Damnit, I can only remember Cade's name.

He's going to think I'm so rude. He said such wonderful things about my cookies, and I can't even remember his name.

"Hailey, isn't it? The woman who makes the incredible desserts at Comfort Food?"

I give him a smile I hope hides the terror racing through me as I try to recall what his name was. Cade and... Oh, God. How could I have forgotten?

Finally, after a pregnant pause that surely must be making him wonder if I'm suddenly a mute, I say, "Hi! Yes, that's me. Thank you so much for remembering..."

His smile grows broader, and he finishes my sentence, mercifully. "Alex. It's great to see you again, Hailey. I don't remember if I mentioned where I worked, but I happened to look out and saw you sitting here, so I thought it would be only right that I came out to say hello to return the professional courtesy."

I smile and open my mouth to introduce everyone at the table to Alex, but Sabrina chimes in with, "Professional courtesy? Did you get a promotion, Hailey? I thought you made desserts at your parents' restaurant."

Every cell in my body screams for me to lash out at her for that little swipe at what I do, but I don't get the chance to even give her a nasty look before Alex says, "What Hailey does at her job is very much the same as what I do. If you can't see that, you need to look again

79

at what she creates. She and I are equals when it comes to our professions."

Meadow squeezes my arm under the table, and I turn my head to see her gazing up at Alex like he's a fantasy come true. I can practically read her mind.

Gorgeous, great job, and so considerate.

Trying to beat Sabrina to the punch before she opens her mouth again, I quickly thank him and add, "Alex, this is my friend Meadow. Her sister Sabrina and I are here celebrating Meadow landing a job with the design firm of Durkin and Chestnut."

He graciously congratulates her and reaches out to shake her hand. I think Meadow might pass out she's smiling so much.

"Interior design? I should definitely call you because my place could use some real help. I'm ashamed to say it looks the same as it did the day I moved in, and that's not saying much. It's a combination of just graduated with bachelor, and it's not good."

Meadow presses her knee so hard against mine I'm afraid she's going to push me off my chair. She quickly rifles through her purse and hands him her business card. "I don't have any new ones made up yet since I just got the job, but this one has my number on it. Give me a call. I'd be happy to see what we could do to get that place of yours in much better shape."

"Will do," he says with a smile, and I notice he can't take his eyes off her.

"Well, I better get back to the kitchen or they're going to think I abandoned ship. Enjoy your meals ladies, and it was wonderful meeting you. Hailey, don't be surprised if Cade and I come back to Comfort Food to try more of your creations. I look forward to seeing what you make next time."

Alex gives us all one more smile and walks away. Sabrina lets out a disgruntled huff that I can't figure out, but Meadow and I let out a collective sigh before turning to look at one another.

"Okay, who is Cade and why didn't you tell me you met my future husband?" she asks with a giggle.

"Cade is his cousin. Yeah, I think that's it. He actually looks a lot like Alex. Maybe a few less tattoos. Or maybe more. I'm not sure. I only saw them together that one time. They stopped into the restaurant last week when I made chocolate lace cookies. I think that was Thursday."

Meadow scrunches her face up at me. "Stop getting lost in the minutiae. Tell me everything about them. Who are they? Why haven't I ever seen them before in my life? This city isn't that big."

"I don't know much more than you do. His name is Alex, and his cousin's name is Cade. He drives a red Jag. I do know that."

Her dark eyes get wide like saucers. "That man, the man who's the star of every fantasy of mine, drives a red Jag? I think I'm in love."

Shaking my head, I explain, "No, I don't know what he drives. Cade drives the Jag. Sorry."

Meadow lets out a sigh. "It's okay. I can live with Greek god who has a great job and is sweet and sexy no matter what he drives."

CHAPTER NINE

ade

ON MY WAY OUT THE DOOR TO DRIVE OVER TO THE
club and do my time behind the bar for my father, my
phone vibrates in my pocket. I consider not answering
since it's probably just boss man wondering why I'm
not in the building yet.

As if I need to be positioned behind the
goddamned bar at six o'clock at night. Did he fire
every other bartender he has in anticipation of having
me work day and night there?

When I lift the phone out of my pocket, I see it's
Alex calling and quickly answer. "Hey, I'm on my way
to prison. What's up?"

"Prison? What are you talking about?" Alex asks, obviously confused by my attempt at humor.

"Club X. I'm doing my bartending gig tonight and probably for the rest of fucking time. I'm guessing I have to wear all black and the white stripes come after a few months. Speaking of working, aren't you doing just that tonight?"

"Yes, and if you'd stop riffing about how much you hate your job, I'd be able to tell you what I called you about," he says, every word dripping with frustration.

I stop at my car and open the door to get in. "Nobody's stopping you, man. What's got you so upset tonight?"

"Not upset, and shut the hell up so I can tell you this. That Hailey girl is here with her two friends. They just ordered their meals, so get down here and coincidentally run into her."

"What is this? Eleventh grade and you found out where some girl's locker is so I can coincidentally run into her? Who the hell does that?" I ask as the thought of driving to this job makes me hate life.

"She looks really good, Cade. I just thought you might want to try your hand at getting to know her here. Maybe she won't run away this time."

Just what I need from my best friend—some ball busting about her running away from my last attempt. "Fuck you, man."

Alex laughs at my frustration. "Okay, don't then. I already made inroads with her friend, who is fucking hot, so you just stay at home alone or behind the bar dealing with drunk women and their slurring when they tell you how much they want to fuck you. Your choice. Either way, I have to get back to work."

The call ends, and I know I have a choice to make. I can go to the club and do what I promised my father I would and hate every minute of it, or I can rush down to CK and hope to catch Hailey and maybe make some progress with her.

I press my foot on the gas and scream out of the parking lot of my condo toward the restaurant. No fucking way am I ready to give up a good time with a beautiful woman.

Not yet.

AFTER I SCHMOOZE THE MAÎTRE D' AND HAVE TO throw my family's name around to finally get in since I'm not dressed for CK, I catch a glimpse of Hailey sitting at a table in the middle of the restaurant. Good. I'm not too late, even though I swear every last soul in this damn city is out tonight and clogging up the streets.

I duck into the kitchen to find Alex before I try to chat Hailey up again, but I hear someone follow right behind me. Turning around, I see my uncle standing there smiling like something's amusing.

"What's up, Cassian?"

His eyebrows slowly raise up into his forehead. "I

was going to ask you that very question. It's not every day you come waltzing into my kitchen."

I can't tell if he's angry or busting my ass, so I quickly give him a smile to smooth over whatever feathers I've possibly ruffled. "Just here to talk to Alex for a minute. I'll be out of here in no time."

Cassian nods, but I still don't know if he's pissed. "I thought maybe you'd decided to come work for us after all these years. Your father told me you're going to be starting a new job soon, so I wondered if maybe I missed something and Kane hired you."

Okay. He's busting my balls.

"No, thanks. It's bad enough I have to go bartend at the club so I don't starve. At least I know how to pour drinks. Cooking food I have no idea how to do."

"Okay. Alex is over there," Cassian says, pointing toward his younger son.

I flash him another smile, and when he walks out of the kitchen, I hurry over to the kitchen doors to see if I can get another glimpse of Hailey. A second later, two servers nearly bash me in the head on their way in.

Jesus, is this a racetrack? I'm trying to see out this damn window, people.

"Cade, why are you getting in my staff's way?" Cassian says from behind me. "I thought you were here to see Alex, who is in the room you're in."

I turn around to answer him and another server comes bounding through the door, nearly knocking me over. I quickly step out of the way and over toward my uncle, who's giving me a look that says he's about to throw me out of this kitchen in about two seconds.

"Alex is the person I'm here to see. I just wanted to look out at the dining room. That's all."

Truly the dumbest thing I've ever said, and considering my past, that's pretty bad.

This time, Cassian gives me that single raised eyebrow look that says he's not buying a word of this bullshit. I don't blame him. I wouldn't buy it either. It wasn't my best attempt at concealing what I'm really doing.

"What's going on? You never come here, Cade, and now you're standing in my kitchen, blocking my servers' way, and staring out the window at my dining room."

No point in trying to lie anymore. It seems that I'm incapable of conjuring up a good enough answer, so I admit the truth. "Alex called me to let me know someone I've been interested in is here having dinner tonight. I was hoping to get a look at her before I go out there."

For a few seconds, Cassian doesn't seem to know what to do with that answer. It's the truth, but he probably doesn't believe it. Again, I don't blame him.

Then he finally smiles and says, "Is this how you usually meet women? You definitely take after your father if it is."

Just what I need—another reminder I'm like my father, or I'm supposed to be.

As Alex joins us in the corner of the kitchen out of the way of the staff, I answer my uncle's question. "No, it isn't how I usually meet women, thank you."

"Why are you still in here?" Alex asks before turning to his father. "The girl he likes is here tonight. I told him he should come down and talk to her. I don't think she'll run away here."

Of course, my uncle seizes on that wonderful tidbit of information and throws his head back in laughter. "Run away? Oh, I have to see this. Just don't make my restaurant look like some kind of crime scene she needs to flee from, Cade."

Hanging my head, I mumble, "I fucking hate this family sometimes. I really do."

"Awww, Cade. We're just teasing you," Alex says, not helping.

"Like father, like son with you two?" I ask, truly believing it was a mistake to come down here tonight. "This whole thing is stupid. She liked you better than she liked me."

"I already went out there and talked to her. Trust me. She isn't into me, and I already told you she isn't my type. Her friend, on the other hand, I'm all in on. Stop talking to us and go out there."

"Fine. I'll do it just to shut you two up. I swear this family sucks," I say as I walk out the kitchen doors into the dining room.

I look over at her table and see it empty. Fuck! All that talking to those two made me miss her.

Well, I'm not ready to give up just yet. I've already blown off my job for this attempt to talk to Hailey, so I might as well see it through. Hurrying around guests and tables, I run outside to find her walking to her car.

"Hey! What's new?" I call out as I do my best casual fast walk toward her.

"Are you stalking me or something?"

Not exactly the response I was hoping for. In fact, she's even chillier than the last time.

"What? No."

"Then why are you in this parking lot when I know you weren't in the restaurant. You have no business being here."

Definitely not a good start to this attempt to get to know her. I try to be cool, but I have to explain I'm not some crazy stalker dude creeping up on her in a parking lot at night.

"I was in the restaurant and I have every reason to be here since my family owns this place. Well, not my immediate family but my uncles. My cousin Alex is a chef here."

She levels her gaze on me and hums as if she doesn't like what she's hearing. "I know. He came over to our table and was very gracious."

Great. Alex is gracious, and I'm a stalker who she might mace at any moment. I'm not thinking I could chalk that up to an improvement on our last meeting.

When she doesn't say anything more, I take a step toward her and ask, "So did you enjoy your meal? My uncles run a great place here."

"I have to go."

Not good. She doesn't even want to make small talk. Things are going from bad to worse. Well, not worse since she hasn't maced me yet.

"Would you like to go for a drink?"

She looks surprised at the question and doesn't answer for a long moment, so I hold out hope things are improving. Then with just a few words, she dashes my hopes.

"No. I have to go."

"Are you meeting your boyfriend now?"

"No," she says, shaking her head.

This is my in. I just have to finesse this right so she doesn't run away again. Or drive away, as the case may be this time.

"Then why not go for a drink with me? We can get to know one another. It could be fun."

Again, she shakes her head. "I don't really drink."

"Then let's go for a walk. You walk, don't you?"

That makes her smile, and I can't help but notice how beautiful she is when she smiles. It's like someone has lit her up from the inside.

"Of course I walk. Why are you so interested in me, Cade?"

A woman who gets right to the chase. I can

appreciate that. No beating around the bush is the way she wants it, so that's what I'll do.

"Because you're beautiful and I liked that you were watching out that window in that kitchen door at your parent's restaurant the other day. After tonight, I know how dangerous that actually is and I appreciate it even more."

She narrows her eyes like she doesn't understand what I'm talking about, but that doesn't matter. I just need to get her to say yes to the walk.

One yes and we can see what happens next.

"So you walk. I do too, so let's do it together. We're right here at the Riverwalk, so why not?"

"Because you might be a serial killer," she says with a tiny smile.

"I'm not, but if you want, we can go back into the restaurant and my uncle and cousin can vouch for me. You might get trapped listening to stories about when I was a kid, though, and to be honest, I'd rather not have that humiliation heaped on me tonight. I'm willing to go back in so you can hear I'm definitely not a serial killer, though. You decide."

Hailey rolls her eyes. "Don't try to make me laugh. I'm trying to be serious here."

"So am I. My uncle can't stop himself sometimes, and he loves to tell the story about when Alex and I were around seven and found his razor and shaved off our eyebrows. Or the one about when Alex's brother Cash heard about what happens when you stick someone's hand in warm water while they're sleeping. He got both of us that night."

The admission of two humiliating experiences from my childhood makes her giggle, and I watch her icy façade melt right in front of me. She really is so beautiful. I don't know why she pushes people away, or maybe it's just me she likes to push away, but I want to see more of this person standing here with me now.

"What happens when you put someone's hand in warm water while they're sleeping?" she shyly asks.

Good. I've got her curious.

"I'll tell you on our walk."

CHAPTER TEN

*H*ailey

A MINUTE INTO OUR WALK AND I'M ALREADY regretting agreeing to this. Cade is charming and sexy, but there are very few people on the path with us. I assumed there would be a lot of people like always, but then I always come here during the day, not at eight o'clock at night.

"So does walking make you get quiet? I thought we were doing so well back there, but now you're back to not talking to me," he says in a sweet voice that should calm me.

It doesn't.

"I'm just hoping you're not an ax murderer."

He laughs, which only makes him more charming

or more possibly a real ax murderer. "I've been accused of many things, but I think this is the first time anyone's ever wondered if I was an ax murderer. Personally, I don't see me as an ax guy. I'm more of a gun guy or even a knife guy."

I look at him and see him smiling. "That's not making me feel any better."

"Well, how about I tell you what happens with the warm water trick and then you'll know I'm not an ax murderer?"

That sounds like a non sequitur if I've ever heard one.

"How is that going to convince me you're not a serial killer or ax murderer? You're dressed in all black, so maybe I just got your crime wrong. Are you a burglar?" I ask, knowing I shouldn't be so worried.

People go for walks down here all the time. Maybe not tonight, but I'm sure they do other nights.

My questioning makes him chuckle. "Fair enough. Well, to prove I'm not an ax murderer, the fact that I can't fit an ax anywhere on me is all the proof I have."

He opens his arms to his sides and turns around for me, I guess so I can inspect him for that hidden ax. As much as I should be looking for some weapon stashed away somewhere, it's hard to concentrate on anything other than how great his body is.

Probably spends hours at the gym every day. Yep. That's what's wrong with him. He's an egotistical, self-involved guy whose sole focus is on his body.

With a smile that's entirely too sexy illuminated by the pathway lamp overhead, he says, "See? No ax. As for the black pants and black shirt, I was going to do a shift at my club, but I decided at the last minute to come down to CK because I heard you were there."

His explanation makes me more curious about him. "You have a club? What kind? Like a nightclub or a smaller bar?"

"First, I have to fulfill my promise to tell you about that gag Cash pulled on us that night. When you put someone's hand in warm water, they have to go to the bathroom. Like right then and there. So he did it to Alex first and then me since we were sleeping downstairs at Alex's house after playing video games for hours. Two ten-year-olds in sleeping bags full of piss."

He looks entirely too charming telling me what sounds like a horrible experience that at first I don't know how to react. I want to laugh since it's funny, but I don't want to be rude.

"Feel free to laugh. You should. Looking back, it was hysterical. My cousin Cash thought so that night when we both woke up drenched with him standing over us laughing until his sides hurt. My aunt and uncle didn't think it was so funny, though, and we got the last laugh watching him wash our smelly, wet clothes and the sleeping bags. And that's your introduction to the March family. Sorry to say this is a pretty common kind of story with us since there are five male cousins and only two females."

I finally let myself giggle at his description of that night, amused at how self-effacing he can be. "Are you and Alex around the same age? You said you were both ten, but you can't be born on the same day to brothers, can you? What are the odds of that?"

Cade shakes his head. "No. I'm three months older. Alex just seems older than me because he's more serious. Always has been. You should have seen him that night with his brother. I thought he was going to kill Cash he was so mad. Not that I wasn't mad, but Alex looked like he was going to rip him apart limb from limb."

As we walk, I try to imagine the man who was so nice and who came to my rescue when Sabrina hurled that not-so-veiled insult at me at the table that angry. "You know, I can't see him being like that. He was so sweet when he came over to introduce himself to my friend and her sister tonight. He didn't have to come out at all since we'd only met that once last week, and then he was kind enough to say he and I were peers professionally, which definitely isn't true."

"Alex meant that. He thinks you are colleagues," Cade says, but I sense in his voice he doesn't believe it either.

That's okay. I know my level when it comes to what I do. And everything else, for that matter.

"Well, that's very nice of him, but I think he was

just being chivalrous after my friend Meadow's sister made a dig about my dessert making compared to his being a chef. She's not my biggest fan."

"Screw her. She doesn't know what she's talking about. I trust Alex on this."

For a moment, I don't know what to say. Cade seems uncomfortable after that brief outburst too and puts his hand on my arm to stop me from walking. Facing me, he lowers his head like he's embarrassed.

"Sorry about that. She's your friend's sister, so saying that wasn't cool."

God, he's cute. I imagine this man could talk the birds out of the trees, and the ones who didn't want to leave, all he'd have to do is give them one of his sad looks with those dark brown eyes of his and they'd willingly do as he asked.

"You don't have to be sorry. I don't like Sabrina much at all. The feeling's mutual too. She doesn't think highly about any part of me, but I don't usually say much to her in my defense when she takes her swipes at my job or how I look because I would never want to hurt Meadow. So no need to be sorry. I appreciated how Alex set her straight in his very professional way, and I appreciate what you said. Truth be told, I silently thought the same thing when she made fun of my dessert making tonight."

Cade's face brightens at hearing I'm not offended by his attack on Sabrina. "Okay, then back to screw her then."

We begin walking again, and thankfully, more people start to fill the pathway around us. Not that I feel like he's an ax murderer. I don't know if I ever felt that way, but no matter how good looking he is or how nice it felt to hear him come to my defense about what I do, I don't really know much about Cade. Better to be safe than sorry with an almost perfect stranger.

Breaking the silence, he says, "You know, you shouldn't think what you do is any less than any other chef. I admit I didn't understand what you do at first, but Alex set me straight. He's serious about food, and he says you're an artist. That's pretty impressive considering what your canvas is."

Excited to tell someone about the rose cupcakes I made today, I begin to explain what they looked like and how I sculpted the frosting to look like real flower petals. Halfway through my description, though, I stop myself.

"God, you probably don't want to hear about peach colored roses being my inspiration for these silly cupcakes," I say quietly, embarrassed that I let myself get so wrapped up in telling him about those stupid petals.

"No way," he says with a smile. "I loved listening to you talk about them. I was trying to imagine them the whole time you were describing them, but I'm not really creative, so I'm probably thinking all the wrong things. I don't honestly even know what a peach rose looks like. Is that a color or how they smell? You probably think that's pretty stupid, huh?"

"The peach is the color. I took a picture with my phone. Would you like to see it?"

"Absolutely!"

I reach into my purse and grab my phone, happy I changed my wallpaper the other day from that hot guy Meadow and I saw in that movie last month to a sunset scene. A few taps on the screen and the image of my cupcake creations from this afternoon comes up.

Turning my phone so Cade can see, I point at the frosting petals. "That's the peach rose cupcakes. I saw them online a couple days ago and wanted to try my hand at making them. I love how they turned out, and from the way customers at the restaurant grabbed them up, I think they were a hit."

Cade stares at my phone for a long moment and then looks up at me and gives me a smile. "You really are talented, Hailey. I couldn't do that if I had someone standing beside me giving me step-by-step directions, much less from only seeing a picture online. I bet they tasted incredible too, just like that cookie I had the other day."

I sheepishly admit the truth of how many I sampled before putting the rest out for customers. "Although I shouldn't have, I ate two of them, and although I'm completely biased, they were delicious. I made them as vanilla cupcakes this time and used a special ingredient. Sour cream. People sometimes get turned off when they hear that's part of my vanilla cupcakes, but it makes them taste so good! I'm thinking next time I want to try to make different flavors for each rose color, so peach cupcakes for the peach roses and vanilla for the white ones."

God, I meant to just say I ate two damn cupcakes, and there I go again giving him every last tedious detail on cupcakes. Dr. Thorpe is right. Without practice around people my age, I've started to forget how to behave. I'm turning into a middle-aged woman before I reach twenty-five!

Looking away, I try to hide my embarrassment. "I'm sorry. This must be so boring for you walking around and talking about cupcakes."

"Not at all. I'm enjoying this a lot. You're passionate about what you do. There's nothing wrong with that," Cade says.

When I don't look over at him because I just feel so awkward still, he takes my hand in his and stops me from walking. Surprised and unsure what to say or do, I don't have a choice but to face him. I haven't been this close with a man since Malcolm, and my brain seems to shut off as I look at Cade now.

"Don't be ashamed for who you are. I'm having a great time listening to you talk about all of it—the cupcakes, the ingredients, even the color peach. Maybe it's because I've spent years listening to my best friend talk about food like it's something to be worshipped. I don't know. But if you're worried you're boring me, let me tell you, you're not."

"Maybe you could tell me something about you. I feel like I've been monopolizing the whole conversation, so you tell me about who you are for a while."

With a nod and one of his sexy smiles, he agrees to talk about himself, which will keep me from blabbering on about cupcakes and clue me into who Cade March really is. I know he's good-looking and very tolerant of my food obsession, but is there more to him?

As we begin down the pathway again, he keeps his gentle hold on my hand. At first, I wonder if I should pull away, but I push away that instinct that comes from fear.

"What do you want to know? I went to school up north and graduated with a degree in business. It's the last thing I want to do in life, though, so I haven't used it much since I came back to town."

"But you own a club, so that must be useful for you to know all you learned in college," I say, instantly wishing I could brag about going to school without having to explain what happened.

His hand tightens around mine slightly for a moment before he eases his hold. "I guess, but real life is never the same as what you learn in school. I went to school because I had to. I graduated because I had to. I work because I have to."

Turning to look over at me, he smiles. "See, that's why listening to you talk about what you do is so interesting. You want to do that. You love what you do, and it shows when you talk about it. I don't love what I do, and I know how I sound when I talk about it."

I want to hear more about his club, but since he clearly doesn't enjoy his work like I do, I quickly change the subject. "Well, what do you do when you're not working?"

With a chuckle, he answers, "I've just now decided I'm the most boring person in the world. I don't do much when I'm not working. Alex and I hang out on his days off, and sometimes our other cousins join us and we go jet skiing. Alex's father has a boat, so we go fishing too."

He looks at me and winces. "I think we should go back to talking about cupcakes or you're going to decide you never want to see me again because I have no life."

I give him a sympathetic smile and try to think he's a boring guy who does nothing. I can't, though. He's not boring at all, and if I'm not careful, I'm going to find myself letting him past all those walls I've so carefully constructed this past year.

CHAPTER ELEVEN

ade

THE TIME I SPEND WALKING ALONG THAT PATH WITH Hailey and talking like we've known each other forever is the best hour of my day. I knew my instincts weren't wrong about her, even if she ran away from me the other day.

She's every bit as incredible as I'd built her up to be in my mind. Passionate and committed to her work, she's also sweet and sexy and not that shy once she gets talking.

All I had to do was make the effort and it paid off. Now I want to see how far we can take this thing between us.

We get back to her car and I sense she's nervous

because she's gone quiet on me again. She lowers her head, fixing her gaze on the ground while I talk about anything that pops into my mind so our time together doesn't have to end. I'd much rather stand here talking gibberish than go to the club to serve drunks for the rest of the night.

"So what do you think about doing this again? How does tomorrow night sound?" I ask as I take a step closer to her.

But she doesn't look up at me when she answers, "Tomorrow night? I don't know."

"You had fun, didn't you? You got to hear about me pissing the bed and how my family is one step away from insane ninety percent of the time. And I got to find out about what makes peach roses peach, which I guess I should have known by this point in my life, but to be honest, I don't think most guys know exactly what the color peach is. We lump that in with salmon and colors like mauve, which I have no idea what it looks like but I'm guessing it's like peach."

Hailey finally lifts her head and looks at me, smiling at my color ignorance. "Mauve is not like peach," she says with an adorable giggle. "As for salmon, I guess I can see why you might get that confused with peach."

I take another step toward her, shrinking the space between us to only a couple inches. She really is so beautiful right now looking up at me with those crystal blue eyes that seem to sparkle under the streetlight above where her car is parked.

"Now I know the surefire way to get you to talk is to show you how stupid I am about something. Good to know."

She tilts her head like she isn't sure if I'm being serious or not and she wants to decide before saying anything else. "I don't think you're stupid about colors. You're just a guy. Guys think of things in basic colors. Black, white, blue, red, green, yellow and maybe orange is pretty much all men consider when it comes to colors, so you're no different than anyone else and definitely not more stupid."

The way she tries to make me feel better about being so utterly ignorant about something she understands so well charms me. I'm not even sure she realizes how sexy it is that she's sweet like that.

Still, I like the banter that's part of the chase with any woman, so I put on my fake sad face and tease her about saying I'm no different than anyone else. "So I'm just like every other guy you've ever met? Ouch. That hurts a guy's ego, and we're practically all ego, you know."

Instinctively, she waves her hands in front of her, brushing up against my chest since I'm so close now. "I didn't mean it that way. No, I don't think you're like everyone else. I don't. Really."

Leaning down, I stop her explanation with a kiss I've been dying to sneak since she started talking about those delicious sounding cupcakes nearly an hour ago. Her lips are soft, and although I've been nearly hard for the past few minutes, just the touch of her mouth on mine makes my cock stiffen so it's pressing against the front of my pants.

She returns my kiss with a soft kiss of her own and lets her palms graze my ribs as with each second that ticks by she relaxes more and more. I lift my hand to caress her cheek, but that startles her, and she quickly pulls away.

"I should go. It's getting late," she says, looking down at the ground again.

"Tomorrow night then."

My making a date for us without her agreeing makes her lift her head, but I don't see anger in her eyes when she looks at me. If anything, I see fear. Why? She can't still think I'm an ax murderer, can she?

"I don't know if I can, Cade," she says in a shaky voice.

"Why? You had fun. I know you did. You smiled. You laughed. You talked about things that make you happy. Sounds like the kind of time you'd tell people about and say I'm a fantastic guy. I know I'd tell people I had a great time tonight and you're definitely a fantastic woman. So what's the problem?"

Her eyebrows draw in and she frowns for the first time since she accused me of stalking her here in the parking lot tonight. I instantly hate that frown on her.

I hate that I had some part in putting it there even more.

"I'm not really good at things like this," she says shyly.

"Talking and walking? Don't sell yourself short. I think you've mastered those quite well," I say with a smile.

My attempt at a joke doesn't get me a smile in return, but at least her frown eases a little. "I have, yes, but everything that comes after that with someone I'm not good at."

"I can tell you you're great at kissing, so put that in the mastered column with walking and talking."

She lets out a heavy sigh and finally says what I suspect has been on her mind since the day we met. "Why are you interested in me? I don't drive an expensive car like you do. I work in a little restaurant that's nothing like the one your family owns, and I doubt it's as impressive as your club. I'm not the type of girl who a guy with a red Jag wants, so why do you keep coming around?"

Taking her hand, I bring it to my mouth to press a kiss against her knuckles. "I like you because you're you. I don't know why I was interested in you that day I saw you looking out the kitchen window at me. I just was from that day. I don't care what kind of place you work in. I think you're interesting and fun, and you're talented at what you do. You're also beautiful, and why wouldn't a guy with a red Jag want you?"

"Because I don't have legs that go on forever. Just regular legs on my five-foot five body. My hair isn't gorgeous and most of the time it stays up in a ponytail. Look at the way I'm dressed. Red Jag women wear little dresses that show off the goods. I'm in a navy-blue sundress that's nothing special. I just wonder if someone like me belongs talking to someone like you," she says before pressing her lips together, as if she needs to stop herself from saying anything more.

Hailey isn't wrong. I've spent most of my life chasing after women who look like they should be in a red Jag. I've had a lot of them too, but they want me for what I have, especially how much money I have. The fact that this is the first time she's even mentioned my car and still hasn't asked me to take her for a ride tells me what I have doesn't matter to her.

Maybe that's why I like her. Because she doesn't want anything anyone else has from me before.

"I like the way you look and the way you dress. To be honest, I don't care what you do with your hair or what you wear. From the first moment I saw you, I wanted to know more about you. Then I found out you were just like Alex, except way prettier."

Hailey smiles at my joke, so I continue. "I figure if he and I can get along famously for all these years as best friends, maybe you and I can be together and have a good time. You're both into your work in the same field, and while I don't do much with food other than stuff it into my mouth, I like being around someone who cares that much about what they create that they could talk about it for half a mile."

"You have a way of putting things that makes me want to say yes to you. Are you like this with everyone?"

I think about the talk with my father earlier and can't stop myself from grimacing. He's going to bust a blood vessel when I finally get to the club tonight, and I'd be willing to bet all my trust fund that he won't want to say yes to anything I say to him.

"Sadly, no. My charm and persuasive abilities do not work on everyone. I like that they work on you, though. Tomorrow night we can go for another walk again or do anything you want. You name it and we'll do it."

"Okay. I'll text you since I have your number," she says, giving away that she kept my note.

If she'd thrown it away, I might have to do a lot more persuading, but knowing she decided to keep it, even after running away from me that day, tells me things might be going better than I had thought.

"Text or call me anytime. Until tomorrow night, thanks, Hailey."

Confusion fills her expression. "For what? All we did was walk and talk a little while."

"For not thinking I'm like everyone else."

I can't tell if her eyes get wide out of fear that she might be wrong and I am like every other guy or fear that's she right. As long as I have another chance to get to know her even more, I'll show her just what I am.

And how much I want her.

"WAKEY, WAKEY," I HEAR A VOICE SAY ABOVE ME. "Are you going to spend all day in bed?" it taunts.

Am I dreaming, and if I am, why am I dreaming some asshole is waking me up? I need to reconsider what I eat right before I go to bed if this is the quality of dreams I'm having.

Slowly, I open my eyes to see Alex standing at the side of my bed. Covering my eyes with my arm, I groan.

"Go away."

"We're supposed to go jet skiing today, remember? Time's wasting. I've got until four to have fun, so get up out of that damn bed and let's get going."

I lower my arm and see he's still here. His hazy figure doesn't move from where he stands. He's planning on forcing this issue. I don't even remember making plans to do anything today. What day is it?

"Give me ten minutes and come back then. Thanks," I say before rolling over and covering my head with the pillow.

He rips the pillow from my grip and tosses it across the bed out of my reach. "Nope. Time to get up, sleeping beauty."

With a sigh, I try to not let all the aggression building up inside me out on my best friend, but it's hard. Very fucking hard.

"You sound like my father. Are you sure you're not his kid? Because you're both fucking slave drivers," I mumble into the bed.

"Come on, Cade. It's nearly noon, for Christ's sake. It's a beautiful day, although you'd never know since you keep this place like a fucking morgue. The sun's out, the water's waiting for us, so let's go."

I struggle to sit up, still half-asleep and exhausted from getting home after four. "You have no respect for the dead. None whatsoever."

"Did you work at Club X last night? Your father must have kept you there until he locked the doors," Alex says with a chuckle.

Like any part of that reality is even slightly amusing.

"Fuck off and go jet skiing by yourself, dick."

From across the bed, he hurls a pillow at me, hitting me in the head and knocking me over. "Get up, man! And you haven't told me anything that happened with Hailey yet. Did you get anywhere with her?"

"Things went great. I have a date with her tonight. Why are you interrogating me first thing in the morning? Did you at least bring me something to wake up with? Coffee? Energy drink?"

"I'm not your butler, man. Get your own caffeine. So you got a date with her tonight? Good."

Setting my feet on the floor, I slowly stand from the bed as I gradually come alive. "Yeah, good. She's going to pick the place and the time. I'm letting her do all the work."

"Why?" Alex asks, like he's horrified at the suggestion that I'm not dictating every minute of our time together.

I scrub the last remnants of a wonderful, albeit short night's sleep from my face and pad across the room toward the bathroom. "Because I thought I might not give her any reason to fucking run away again. Sometimes you don't come in like a goddamned wrecking ball. Sometimes you use the velvet hammer to get what you want. I think I know why you're single, dude. These are simple concepts."

By the time I get out of the bathroom, I'm wide awake. Well, as wide awake as I can be without some serious infusion of caffeine.

"You know, some people actually call or text before coming over to wake people up, dude," I say as I walk toward the kitchen. "Try it sometime."

"Sorry. I'm not used to you working, Cade. I just figured you'd be lounging around when I got here."

Alex sounds almost like he feels bad, so I give him a whatever shrug and grab a water from the refrigerator. Standing in the doorway, he watches me drink, but I have the sense he's got something on his mind.

"I feel like one of those animals in the zoo with you

staring at me like that. 'The wild Cade, newly awake, saunters down to the watering hole, noticing in the distance a far too alert Alex keeping a watchful eye on him.' What's up?"

For a moment, he hesitates to answer my question, piquing my interest even more. I know Alex as well as I know myself, so the fact that I have no idea what may be on his mind makes me think I'm not as awake as I thought I was.

"Are you going to tell me, or am I supposed to read your mind? I mean, we've known each other practically since birth, but I don't think we've developed that skill yet."

"Are things going to be different with this one?" he asks in a tone so full of what sounds like judgment that I'm stunned for a second.

"Things? Like what things? Are you asking if I'm going to buy different clothes to go out with Hailey or if I'm planning on trying out some new sexual positions? Because it would be a no to the clothes but maybe to something freaky, assuming she's into that."

My smart-ass answer doesn't satisfy him, if the scowl he gives me is any indication. I know what he's talking about. I just don't want to tackle that issue regarding Hailey yet. Things are going good between us so far. There's no reason to think they'll crash and burn.

Like they do with every woman I date.

"She's a nice girl, Cade. She's talented and sweet,

and from what I saw last night, she's not a bitch, even when it calls for her to be one."

I take another swig of cold water and try to keep my cool, even though I'm quickly losing it. "I know she is. And she told me how you stood up for her when that friend's sister tried to say she isn't a chef like you. What's this about, Alex?"

It's been a long time since we had a knock-down, drag-out fight, but I have a feeling that might be happening instead of the jet skiing today by the way he's looking at me right now. His eyes narrowed, he looks pretty fucking judgmental, and I'm not feeling that.

"Say what's on your mind."

He doesn't need any more than that to tell me what he's thinking about me with Hailey. "Well, how about we go over your recent history with women, shall we? There was Cassie, who you couldn't get enough of, but she found out you lied to her about who you were and she said adios. Before her was Emma. That crashed and burned pretty quickly, and why? You lied to her about who you were. How about before her? Amber, I think. And what happened there? Lied."

"Fuck off, Alex."

I push past him to go into the living room, but he follows me, continuing with his dissertation on my love life. "And the worst of it is you lie about bullshit stuff. Why lie about how you could afford the Jag? It's not like Cassie thought you were some Silicon

Valley whiz kid who had come up with the replacement for Facebook, Cade. And Emma? With her, you lied about this condo and said you shared it with me, which was ridiculous."

"You're here often enough that it was only technically a stretch of the truth."

"And what was it with Amber? Well, that was a huge whopper. You lied about being single since you were still with Sarah. So I guess you can include her in with Amber's lie."

I point the water bottle at him, intent on at least defending myself on that point. "We were technically not together anymore. She had ignored my calls for three days. That said to me we were done. So you can't count either of those as lies. And in my defense, I didn't lie to Sarah and that ended, so I think your entire thesis about my lying leading to the end of all of my relationships is total bullshit."

"Yes, you did. You told her you were going to be managing your father's club, which we both know you never planned to do. So you did lie."

That very lie I told Hailey last night flashes through my mind, and I turn my head so I don't have to face Alex. As I said, we've known each other for nearly our entire lives, and while we can't read each other's minds, I doubt he'll miss the look I know is on my face as I remember telling her I manage the club.

"Dude, you lied to her already, didn't you? What's wrong with you? This sounds pathological."

I wave away his concern, pretending it's nothing. "I just told her I was doing something I'm not exactly doing. That's all. We barely know each other, so it's not a problem."

"You lied about managing Club X, didn't you? Why do you do that? It's not like you're some poor guy mooching off his parents and living in their basement. Look at this place. You own it. Like your car. And the jet skis. And everything else you have because of your trust fund. Most guys in your place brag about that kind of shit, and yet you insist on lying. Why?"

I spin around, not worried about what expression I have on my fucking face now. "Stop busting my balls. I don't have to let any woman know about my finances. Do you go around sharing your bank account balance with every woman you get into bed with?"

"That's not the point and you know it."

"If all you're going to do is lecture me, then leave me alone. You sound like my father."

The insult hits just like I wanted it to, and Alex shakes his head. "I sound like me. She's sweet, and you're already lying. This isn't even about you hurting her because, fuck, I barely know Hailey. This is about you sabotaging every relationship you have. You love the chase. You're notorious for it, and I have no problem with that. But you've got a problem, Cade. This lying isn't okay."

On my way back into my room, I yell back to him, "You know the way out. Don't slam the door when you leave."

A minute later, I'm back in bed and I hear my best friend close the front door when he walks out. Nice start to the day.

CHAPTER TWELVE

*H*ailey

MY FATHER STOPS AT MY DOUGH TABLE AND RAPS his knuckles off the metal rack next to it. "You've got a visitor out front, honey."

I lift my head from the cupcake I've been frosting and look at him in shock. A visitor to see me? "Who?"

"One of the guys from the other day. I don't remember his name. They both look alike, so I'm not sure which one."

Quickly, I tear off my gloves and look at my reflection in the metal case next to me to see if I got any cupcake batter or frosting on my face or in my hair. I don't see any, but I want to make sure, so I turn toward my father.

"Do I look okay? Too much a mess?"

A slow smile lights up my father's face. "You look beautiful, like always, honey."

Pushing the hairs that have escaped my ponytail from my face, I roll my eyes. "You're not helpful, Dad. Okay, I'm going to go out there."

"Knock 'em dead, honey."

I throw him a look like I can't believe he said that and hurry out into the dining room before stopping dead just outside the doors. I'm still wearing my apron. Damn! I hurriedly pull it over my head and toss it onto the counter near the sink.

Now I look presentable enough to see Cade.

Looking around the restaurant, I don't see him, though. I don't see anyone who looks like a male in his mid-twenties. The only customers around are the usual old men who sit at the counter forever drinking cup after cup of coffee and a family in one of the booths near the windows.

"Hailey, hey," a male voice says behind me.

I turn around and see Alex, not Cade. Why is his cousin here? Oh, God. He's here to tell me Cade doesn't want to be bothered with me because I waited too long to text him. I was going to do it after I finished that batch of cupcakes.

"Hi, Alex. What are you doing here?" I ask, hating how rude that sounds considering how nice he was about what Sabrina said at dinner last night.

"I had some free time this afternoon since my plans

fell through, so I thought I'd stop in and see what you're making today. I looked in the case but didn't see anything. Did they sell out already?"

"No. Well, yes, but I was just working on some more cupcakes. I can show you them if you like."

Alex gives me a warm smile and nods. "Great. I'd love to see them."

"Okay. Come back into the kitchen," I say as I turn to head back to my station. Then I realize he's probably used to the best chef's kitchen, which is definitely not what we have here, so I stop and spin around to face him.

"I should warn you this probably isn't what you're used to a kitchen looking like."

"It's not the kitchen that makes great food. It's the chef, so don't worry."

Forcing a tortured smile I know isn't reaching my eyes, I move toward the kitchen silently praying to God Hector cleaned up and my father hasn't made another mess back there. It's bad enough my area looks like a cake factory exploded around it.

My hands are shaking by the time we walk through the doors. The moment I step foot inside, I frantically scan the kitchen for anything horrible, but it looks okay.

Well, okay for what I'm used to. What Alex works in probably looks like a million bucks compared to here.

I listen for any gasp of horror coming from him as

we make our way to my table, but I don't hear anything but the usual sounds of the kitchen. The afternoon cook, Sylvie, is humming some tune she said reminds her of when she was a girl back in Austin, the ice machine is making that ka-chonk-a-chonk noise that tells me someone needs to kick it again, and my father's radio way back in the corner plays some Beach Boys' song I recognize but can't for the life of me remember the title right now.

"My area is back here," I say, pointing to where I left the cupcakes I'd been working on in the corner nearest to the doors.

Before I can say anything else, Alex stops in front of my table and looks down at the last of the peach cupcakes I'd just started when my father said I had a guest. "That looks exactly like a rose, Hailey. It's uncanny. If I didn't know it was a cupcake beneath that frosting, I'd say you'd sculpted an actual flower. What flavor did you use for the cake?"

His compliment makes me beam with pride. "I decided to do a peach cupcake for this color icing. I'd offer you one, but our customers bought them all up this morning and I'm saving this one for something special. I have vanilla ones, though. Would you like one of them?"

With a smile that reminds me of his cousin, he nods eagerly. "I'd love to try one."

Reaching around, I grab a white rose cupcake and hand it to him. "It's just a cupcake, you know. Nothing terribly special. These are more of an artistic project for me. I saw a picture of some online and wanted to see if I could do it."

"Can we sit in a booth and talk for a few minutes?" he asks. "I won't take up too much of your time."

I hope he can't see how surprised I am that he wants to sit with me when I smile and start moving back out to the restaurant. "Sure. That would be great."

When we're settled in a booth in the corner away from everyone else in the dining room, Alex takes his first bite of the cupcake. "This is delicious. You have to put something special in these because they don't taste like ordinary vanilla cupcakes."

"I do. Sour cream. It makes them taste so good, doesn't it?"

"Mmmm…that's it. I thought maybe I tasted a hint of almond, but sour cream makes sense. This is fantastic, Hailey. I hope the next time you make the peach ones I'm around and can grab one before everyone else buys you out. I bet they're out of this world."

As much as I want to talk shop with him and explain how I use pieces of fresh peaches in the batter, I'm too curious about why he's here and why Cade isn't with him to let myself gush about my recipe ingredients. Maybe he came alone because Cade's busy, or is it that he's not interested in me or my cupcakes?

"So what would you like to talk about?" I ask quietly, bracing myself for his response being that he's here to be the one to break it to me that his cousin doesn't want to see me again after all.

He reaches across the table to grab a napkin from the dispenser and wipes his mouth. "So good. Well, let me get right to the point. I showed my father and uncle the picture of the chocolate lace cookie I had here last time, and they want to know what they'd have to do to be able to get your desserts on a regular basis for CK. Our customers would love them. We'd be willing to pay you well, of course."

Relief washes over me as he makes his offer, every word making me smile even as I know I have to decline. "I wish I didn't have to say no, but I can't do it, Alex."

He frowns, but I don't think he's unhappy as much as disappointed. "Is this because you don't think your desserts are good enough? They are, Hailey. Trust me."

Hearing him say that makes me want to burst into tears I'm so happy, but he's wrong. While I may not be the most confident baker in the world, that's not the reason why I have to say no to him and his family.

"Thank you, but no that's not why. I just don't have the time or facilities to make more than I do for my parents here. I'm trying to help them bring in more business."

I look around the restaurant at the mostly empty

tables and booths and sigh. "I thought if people had something to come in for, they'd come back again and again. So far, it hasn't turned out like that, but I'm still hoping. I have to keep making my desserts for them, so after that, I don't have enough time or the right equipment to say I'll be able to contract with you to make enough for CK. I'm sorry, Alex. Please tell your father and uncle I'm so flattered. Last night was my first time at your restaurant, and to think that a place like that would want to sell my desserts is almost too incredible to believe."

"I understand. What you're doing for your parents is a good thing, Hailey. Just keep us in mind if you ever get the chance to branch out, okay?" he asks with a smile that's like a cherry on top of this beautiful cake his visit's been.

"Absolutely."

When he doesn't continue the conversation, I can't stop myself from mentioning Cade for the first time. "You know, I saw your cousin last night after my friends and I left the restaurant. We're supposed to get together again tonight."

"I think I heard something about that," he says with a sparkle in his dark brown eyes.

"He told me about his club, so maybe he'll show me that tonight."

Something in Alex's expression changes so imperceptibly it's almost not visible, but I sense the difference in him immediately. "Maybe. I have to get going, but keep my offer in mind, okay?"

And with that, he stands from the table and gives me one last smile. "Take care, Hailey."

"Thank you, Alex."

As I watch him walk toward the front door, I can't help but wonder what made his mood change so suddenly. Was it the mention of Cade's club? Is there something he doesn't approve of in that, or is it that he doesn't think I'm the type of person who belongs at a place like that?

I press the piece of paper with Cade's phone number on it against the table, smoothing the wrinkles and creases from it being in my pocket all day. My hands tremble as I hold my phone, ready to text him.

Am I ready for this? Dr. Thorpe says I am. Meadow thinks I'd be crazy if I didn't at least give myself a chance with Cade.

Then why do I feel like a nervous wreck when I even think about seeing him tonight?

My mind whirls with what could happen, what might go wrong, what it would be like to kiss him again. Pushing all that out of my head, I smooth the paper one final time and press the numbers into my phone before beginning my text.

Hi, this is Hailey. Hope you're having a great day. If you still want to get together tonight, I'm free.

I stare at the words, reading them over and over

and wishing they sounded sexy or even fun, instead of such boring words. Of course I'm free. I'm always free. He probably knows that.

Maybe I should mention our kiss last night. But what am I going to say? Hey, thanks for kissing me? Your lips are soft? You have nice breath?

Definitely not. I'll just leave the text as it is. He's already met me. He must know by now I'm not exciting or sexy.

Or the type of woman who belongs in a red Jag.

I send it off, surprised that my anxiety doesn't abate but only gets worse. He might not reply. He might have decided after last night that he's not interested. I mean, if he was really into me, he could have come over with Alex this afternoon. Then again, maybe that's why Alex got so uncomfortable and left so quickly right after I mentioned Cade.

God, I wish I was a red Jag kind of woman.

While I mentally spiral out of control, my phone vibrates against the tabletop. I look down to see his response to my text and smile.

Meet me at CK at eight. See you then.

CHAPTER THIRTEEN

$\mathcal{H}$ailey

ABSOLUTELY SURE I LOOK LIKE AN OVEREAGER teenage girl, I get to CK ten minutes early. I'd expected traffic to be heavier, but the drive took much less time than I thought it would. I could drive around, but then I might get stuck somewhere and be late.

It's fine. I can check my makeup in the rearview mirror since I have a few minutes.

I pull into a parking space and turn the car off before turning it back on. Looking down my body, I frown at my pink sundress. It looks so silly. I should have chosen something sexier.

That's a ridiculous idea. I don't own anything sexy. That's sort of the problem, isn't it?

"You're going to have to get out of the car for us to have any fun."

Spinning my head to look out my window, I see Cade standing outside smiling at me. "What? I didn't think you'd be here so early."

He looks incredible in jeans and a grey dress shirt. How does he do that? He's casual but sexy at the same time.

And I'm whatever the opposite of that is.

"Are you ready to go?" he asks before opening my car door.

"I guess," I say tentatively as I put up the window and turn off the engine. "Where are we going?"

"Are you hungry? We can get something to eat," he suggests when I step out of the car.

"Not really, but if you are, we can."

"I'm not, so cross eating off the list."

I want to ask if he would want to show me his club, but I keep that idea to myself. Something about the way Alex reacted earlier hints at that being an issue of some kind.

"We could go for a ride. Then you'd be able to definitely say you're a red Jag kind of girl. You already are, but that would make it official."

He slams my car door shut and guides me to his car on the other side of the parking lot. So now I become a red Jag girl. Not sure how that's going to look.

"So, other than sitting in a red Jag, what does a

red Jag kind of girl have to do? I feel like I should have studied or something. Is there a handbook? Maybe that would be good for me to look at first," I say, hoping my jokes sound as funny as they do in my head.

But Cade isn't smiling. In fact, he looks like he's sizing me up like animals do with their prey. Oh, God. He is an ax murderer!

Just as we reach his car, he stops and leans in to kiss me. "You don't have to do anything but be you. Whatever that is, that's what a red Jag girl does as long as you're in the car. Easy, right?"

When his lips touch mine, I can't think of anything but how good he kisses. Gorgeous, has a hot car, and an incredible kisser. God, is there anything wrong with this guy?

If so, I don't want to know. Not right now, at least. Let whatever his flaws are come out later after I've enjoyed this night.

AN HOUR LATER, HE PULLS INTO A PARKING LOT AND points at the white building in front of us. "What do you think of doing something other than riding around for a while?"

"Is this where you live?"

"Yeah. I figured we could hang out for a while, but if you want to go somewhere, just tell me and we're there."

Again, I consider mentioning his club, but since it's only nine o'clock at night, it's highly unlikely the place is busy yet. I may not be a club kind of girl, but I do know things don't start happening until much later in the night.

"No, we can hang out. That's okay. This place looks nice. Do you live on your own?"

Cade turns the car off and nods. "Yeah. Sometimes I tell people I live with Alex, but you get the truth. It's just me."

I want to ask why he lies about a thing like that, but he jumps out of the car before I can and then a few seconds later, he's at my door opening it for me. Maybe he was kidding? Does he really tell other people that?

Instead, I ask what seems like a more obvious question at this moment as I crane my neck to look up at the enormous building looming in front of me. "What floor do you live on?"

Maybe that's why he's in such good shape. Walking up twenty flights of stairs each day would make anyone look good.

"One of the upper floors. Wait until you see the view from the balcony. It's what makes living here all worth it," he says like the beautiful surroundings, professional landscaping, and gorgeous building aren't enough.

"Oh. I bet you have a lot of very successful neighbors."

Cade shakes his head and grimaces. "Actually, I have a lot of old neighbors who complain and make up ridiculous rules at the HOA meetings. The last one I went to some lady raged on and on about someone's Christmas wreath being a choking hazard for like a half hour. I haven't been back since then."

I can't tell if he's serious, so as we walk into the main lobby, I look at him and smile. "Really?"

He nods but returns my smile. "I wish I was joking. This building wasn't like this when I bought the place. I figure I'm young enough to wait them out, though, so maybe in a few years it won't be bad. Or maybe I'll move. For now, the view from the balcony makes it all worth it."

I look around for a stairwell, but Cade guides me toward a bank of elevators that I silently thank God for. As the doors close, I watch him press the button for the fifteenth floor, and then the elevator starts moving up.

"This is a very smooth elevator," I say, suddenly nervous and needing to make small talk.

For a moment, Cade doesn't say anything, but then he laughs. "Yeah, I guess it is. I never noticed that. I think I'm usually so preoccupied about just getting to my place that I don't pay much attention at all to the ride."

He likely thinks I'm the most boring person in the world to pay attention to the smoothness of the elevator ride in his building. I couldn't argue with him if he did. So much for the ride in the Jag making me a red Jag girl. I bet the other women he brings to his home don't comment on the smooth elevator ride up.

I feel something against my pinky and look down to see him taking my hand in his. When I look up at him, he gives me one of his all-too-sexy smiles that make me feel like my insides are melting.

"You don't have to worry, Hailey. I'm not an ax murderer, and this is just us going to hang out. Honest."

His touch calms me, but I still have to make a joke. "You know, I think only real ax murderers say they aren't ax murderers. Non-ax murderers don't say anything about not being one."

His smile broadens, and he leans down to kiss me, taking my breath away this time as the elevator stops at the fifteenth floor. "Point taken. Now if you see any wreaths, don't eat them, okay? I hear they're dangerous."

We walk down the hallway to his apartment as one thought fills my head. How is it possible this man is single?

God, I really hope he's not an ax murderer.

He opens his front door and says, "Welcome to my world. Excuse the mess. The maid hasn't been here this week."

No sooner do those words leave his mouth, Cade stops and turns around to face me wearing a look so earnest I'm not sure what he's going to say. "I don't have a maid. That was more of a joke than anything else."

"Oh, okay. I don't either, so it's not like I'm going to look down on you for having to straighten up your own mess."

"Good. Well, come in and relax. I'll get us something to drink. Alcohol or no?" he asks as he walks into another room.

"No alcohol, thanks."

I quickly scan the living room he's left me in. Open to the dining room with an actual table and chairs set that doesn't look like it's ever been used as anything other than a place for Cade to drop his mail, this room contains a sectional that takes up most of the space. The walls are painted a tan color that doesn't clash with the black couch or the dark wood tables. It looks like a normal room a person would expect from a grown man.

Nothing in this room says he's a murderer or that he has a wife stashed away and this is his place where he cheats on her.

Cade hands me a glass of sparkling water and sits down next to me with a bottle of beer. "So this is my house. I'd give you a tour, but you're sitting in the highlight."

"I thought the best part was the balcony and the view," I tease and then take a drink of raspberry flavored water.

He takes the glass from me and sets it down onto

the coffee table nearby, along with his beer. Grabbing me by the hand, he pulls me from the couch like a little boy eager to show someone what he's done.

"That's right. I forgot."

We walk past the dining room table filled with mail, and I quickly look to see if any say Mrs. March, but I don't see any. Maybe he's just a man with good taste in apartments who seems too perfect. That can happen, right?

Sliding the glass doors open, he steps out onto a balcony that's much larger than I thought it would be and extends his arm like he's offering me the view for my own. "This right here is the highlight. Forget inside. This is it. What do you think? Gorgeous, huh? It makes having to live around crazy people terrified of wreaths all worth it."

I step forward and stop short, stunned by this view he has any time he walks out onto his balcony. Warm yellow and white lights around the bay cast shimmering reflections on the water, and the dark night sky with what seems like a million stars looks so close it's like you can touch it if you reach out.

"This is beautiful, Cade. You must love being able to look out whenever you want and see this."

He moves behind me and sets his chin on my shoulder. "I like how it makes you look."

My heart races at the feel of him pressed up against the back of me. "What do I look like?" I ask in a shaky voice.

Please don't let him be the kind of murderer who throws women off balconies.

"Your eyes got big, and you looked out like you couldn't get enough of what you're seeing. I like that," he says in a low voice, his warm breath drifting over the shell of my right ear.

I want to say something but my mind is blank, except for loving how he feels pressed against me. Closing my eyes, I revel in the sensation, and when he slides his arms around my waist, I don't flinch.

And for the first time in a year, I don't fear someone holding me in their arms.

CHAPTER FOURTEEN

ade

HAILEY DOESN'T MOVE WHEN I GENTLY PULL HER TO me, and for a moment, I'm not sure what to think about that. By this time, most women are crawling up my body after seeing the view and me giving them all the signs.

Then again, she's not like anyone I've ever dated before, so I guess I shouldn't be surprised she hasn't turned around and grabbed my cock yet. It's just that the view usually does a better job than it is now.

"So what do you want to do?" I whisper near her ear.

She smells like some soft, flowery perfume, and I

take a deep breath to inhale it into me. Everything about Hailey seems soft. I like that.

"This is nice. We can stay here," she says in a quiet voice.

I brush my lips against her skin just below her ear and feel her breath hitch. She ran away once before. Will she do it again now?

As I wait for her to respond, she turns in my hold to face me. Looking up into my eyes, she says, "So I've just about decided that you're not an ax murderer and probably not married, even though that's not one hundred percent. You have a great car, a great place here, and as far as I can tell, you're nearly perfect. So why do you want me?"

After the shock of her words wears off, I smile. "Nearly perfect? What do I have to fix?"

"Nothing. I just didn't want to say perfect because there's nowhere to go after that. You haven't answered my question, Cade."

Now's my chance. I can tell her I lied last night—more of an exaggeration, really—and then everything can be perfect with her. She won't care. It's not like Hailey is one of those women who gives a damn about what kind of job I have.

Or that I have one at all.

The problem is now she's standing in front of me on my balcony looking so kind and understanding that I know as soon as I tell her, she's going to lose that look she has in her eyes. That way she stares at me that says she thinks I'm pretty fucking special.

I like her thinking of me that way. It feels good for once to have someone be interested in me for me, not for my car or my condo or how much money I have. Hailey doesn't seem to care at all about any of that.

So as much as I know I should say something to clear up the tiny misconception she may have about what I do, I can't bring myself to say the words. Not if it means she won't look at me like she is now.

"I want you because you're you. It doesn't go any deeper than that," I say with a smile that hopefully hides that tiny lie hiding out inside me.

She twists her face into an expression of disbelief. "Because I'm me? I'm not anyone. I'm just some girl who bakes stuff for her parents' restaurant hoping it will bring in more customers."

"That's enough for me. I'm just some guy who saw you looking at me through a kitchen door window and liked that."

Hailey looks around the balcony and then fixes her focus back on me. "You have all of this. You drive that great car. You own a club of your own. I'm not exactly the kind of woman anyone would pair with you. You know that, right?"

I inwardly cringe when she mentions the club. "Exactly what kind of woman am I supposed to be with? Who's doing this pairing up? Because they don't have good taste if they aren't putting me with you."

"Stop joking. I'm serious, Cade."

Cradling her face, I kiss her and hope I can quell the doubts she has about us. I might not be all I claim to be, but I'm not lying when I say I like her.

"I don't care who thinks what about us. I wanted to get to know you from the minute I met you the other day. You seem to like me, right?"

Her blue eyes open wide, and she hesitates before nodding. "Yes, I do. I just—"

I cut her off before she can think of another question about us and kiss her again. "No just. I like you and you like me. Enough said. That's all that matters."

In the distance, lightning flashes and she quickly spins around. "Was that lightning? I saw it in the reflection in the glass. Maybe we should go in."

"Only if you want to," happy to be anywhere with her.

Hailey looks back at me, her eyes wide. "I forgot. I brought you something. It's in my bag."

As she hurries back inside, I follow behind, curious about what she could have gotten me. "I was wondering why you brought that big bag with you. I thought maybe you were hiding an ax or something."

She smiles at me and shakes her head. "I'm not the ax murderer here."

Reaching into her bag, she pulls out a little white box just big enough to fit a sandwich or a piece of pie. "Here. I saved you the last one."

I open the lid, and there, sitting in the center of the box surrounded by wax paper is a peach colored rose cupcake just as I imagined it would look when she told me all about them last night. "Thank you. I bet it's going to taste incredible."

"It was the last one. When Alex came to see me today, he wanted to try one of the peach cupcakes, but I had to give him a vanilla rose cupcake instead because this was my last one and I'd put it aside to give you tonight," she says sweetly, but all I hear is Alex went to Comfort Food to see her.

Why the fuck did he do that? Did he go there to try to dissuade Hailey from going out with me because of our argument?

Struggling to control my anger, I say, "Alex came to see you? What about?"

"He wanted to offer me a chance to make desserts for your family's restaurant. I had to turn him down because I don't have the time or facilities, but it was really kind of him to offer."

I push down my emotions and force a smile. "Nothing kind about it. My uncles Cassian and Kane are smart businessmen. They know a good idea when they see one."

For a moment, the two of us stand there silent in my living room as an uncomfortable tension grows between us. It's not Hailey's fault. I know that, but just hearing that Alex went there bothers me after what he said this morning.

"Will you try it? I'd love to know what you think," she says with such hope in her eyes that I can't say no.

I sit down on the chaise part of the sectional I never use and pat the cushion in front of me. "I'm sure it's going to be fantastic. Sit with me."

Opening my legs, I make a space for her. "So this is the last peach rose cupcake? Does that mean they were a hit with your customers?"

I reach in and carefully lift her creation out before setting the box on the couch to my right. The cupcake almost looks too beautiful to eat, but I can't disappoint her.

"They were," she says, beaming her happiness while I bring the cupcake to my lips. "I hope you like it too."

The first taste of the frosting on my tongue is like pure heaven. Not sickeningly sweet and not stiff like so many cake frostings generally are, it's light and delicious. "This is incredible, Hailey."

"Wait until you taste the cupcake. I put little pieces of real peach in the batter," she says, urging me to continue trying her gift.

I bite into the cupcake, and it's fluffy and just sweet enough. I taste the peach immediately, and smile. "I don't think I've ever had cake that tastes this good. I can see why these sold out today."

Hailey gives me a shy smile and reaches out to drag the pad of her thumb below my bottom lip. "You got icing on your face."

I run my tongue over the spot she touched and want more. More of this cupcake. More of her fingertips drifting over my skin. More of Hailey.

Setting the half of the cupcake left back into the box, I lean forward and press a kiss onto her lips. "Thank you for saving that last one for me."

"You don't want any more of it?" she asks with a hint of hurt tinging her words.

"I'll have more later. Right now, I want more of you," I whisper against her lips.

My cock hardens at the feel of her lips when she kisses me with all the need and want I give her in my kiss. I want to pull her down on top of me to know what it's like to have the sensation of all of her against me, but I know I have to take it slow or she may run away again. It's like teasing myself, and it's excruciating as each moment passes and all I have is her kiss.

She tentatively touches my chest, her palms pressing gently against my body. It's not enough, but I need to let her set the pace this time. Not my usual style, but I'm willing to do what I have to so Hailey doesn't bolt on me.

Each touch of her fingertips against my shirt drives me crazy. I want her to burrow her hands beneath the fabric so I can feel her skin against mine. When I can't take it anymore, I guide her hands up to my neck and love that first touch of her hands on me.

I lean back, hoping she'll inch her way closer to

me, but just then my phone vibrates in my pocket. Fuck. I know who it is without even checking.

"Your phone is making a noise," she says with a smile. "Do you want to take that?"

Shaking my head, I slide my hand around the back of her head and pull her mouth to me. "No. They can wait."

But a few seconds later, my phone vibrates again. Three more times it interrupts us, and I know it won't stop unless I call him back.

"Maybe you should take that. It sounds like someone really needs to talk to you."

I take a deep breath in and let it out slowly as a combination of anger and frustration fills me. "They don't, but they'll keep calling. Just give me a minute and I'll be right back."

By the time I get into the kitchen, I'm barely able to contain my anger. I know what I'm supposed to be doing tonight. He doesn't have to call fifty fucking times to remind me. It's not that late yet, and that place can do without me for a few more goddamned hours.

Before I can call him back, my father calls yet again and this time I answer it. "You know, calling a dozen times isn't going to make things happen any faster," I say in a low voice. "I'll be there soon."

"You were supposed to be here for eight, Cade. You're an hour and a half late right now, and something tells me you aren't anywhere close to this building."

"I'm coming."

I want to say so much more, but I keep it all in. He wants this from me, but I want something, and right now, that's far more important to me.

"Are you going to be here by ten?" he asks sharply.

"Probably not, but I'll get there. I told you I would."

Lost in my anger at this whole situation, I don't see Hailey standing in the doorway. When I look up at her, she's shaking her head and looks upset.

"I have to go. Bye."

I stuff my phone into my pocket. I hurry to try to explain away the call, but she's already walking away toward the front door.

"I knew you were too perfect to be real," she says with so much sadness in her voice that my chest hurts just hearing it. "I'm going, Cade. Goodbye."

She doesn't get to the door before I catch up with her. "No, don't go. That wasn't anything. I'm sorry they interrupted us. Let's go back and pick up where we were."

Hailey spins around to face me and shakes her head at me again. "Who was that? It sounded like a wife or a girlfriend. I'm so stupid. Why would anyone like you want someone like me? All my joking about red Jag girls. You already have one of those. Just wanted to go slumming for a little while? Was that what I was? And I was so naïve to fall for it all. You must think I'm just some moron, don't you?"

I open my mouth to tell her that call was definitely not from the wife or girlfriend I don't have, but she doesn't give me a chance to get a word in. When she finishes, she turns to leave again, but this time, I grab hold of her arm.

"Let me go! I'm leaving!"

"Don't. I swear. That wasn't a wife or girlfriend. Honest. I don't have either. And none of what you said is right. I like you. Why can't you believe that?"

She rips her arm from my hold and shakes her head, but this time her eyes are full of tears. "Why? Because I know what I look like, Cade. I know what I do for a living. You're not the first guy I've ever wanted to be with who was just playing. I just didn't think I was stupid enough to fall for this trick again."

I stare at her in confusion, knowing I should tell her just how beautiful she is and how much I like being around her. That isn't what I want to do, though, and why should I? It hasn't worked yet.

Actions speak louder than words, and I'm done talking.

Pulling her to me, I kiss her hard on the mouth and stuff my hand into her hair to keep her where she needs to be. I'm done with this pretending we just like one another and it's enough to just hang out on the couch watching TV.

That's not what I want, and by the way she's reacting to a simple call, that's not what she wants either.

CHAPTER FIFTEEN

$\mathcal{H}$ailey

CADE'S KISS TAKES ME BY SURPRISE, AND FOR A FEW seconds, I don't know how to react. I don't believe that call was to a friend or one of his cousins. I have no idea if I'm right about him having a girlfriend or a wife, but the last thing I want to do is kiss him right now.

Except the way his tongue glides over mine, teasing me with a promise of how incredible it would feel on every other part of my body, makes pulling away so hard.

He holds me against him tightly, like if I wanted to leave I couldn't. A mixture of fear and desire overwhelms me, and I don't know what to do.

When he lifts his head and smiles down at me, it's almost like he's taunting me. Like he was talking to his girlfriend or wife and now he thinks he can have me too.

Not so quick there, loverboy.

"Thanks for the kiss. I have to go. Bye, Cade," I say and hope my legs weak from that kiss let me walk out the door with some grace.

"No. I'm not letting you run away again, Hailey. You want me, and I want you. Stop trying to fight that."

"I'm not fighting anything that shouldn't be fought. I can't be with you. Goodbye."

Still, he won't let me go.

"You can and you want to be. Why are you acting like this isn't what you want? We had fun talking last night. You brought me that cupcake because you like me. Why fight this?"

"Because you have a girlfriend! Or even worse, a wife!" I scream, hating that everything he says is how I feel and still I know I have to leave.

He reaches into his pocket and pulls out his phone. "Here. Look at who the calls were from. Look at who I called."

Pushing his hand away, I shake my head. "No! I don't want to be that person who doesn't trust someone like that. Just let me go."

But he won't give up.

"Take it. Look. You accuse me of doing something I'm not, so let me show you you're wrong."

God, I don't want to do this. Not here. Not now. Not ever. I swore I'd never let myself be in another situation where I suspected someone was cheating and didn't listen to my gut. Well, at this moment standing in this hallway, my gut says this man is too perfect and now I know why.

When I refuse to take the phone out of his hand, he taps on the screen to bring up the calls. Holding the phone in front of me, he says quietly, "Not a girlfriend or wife. Just my father."

I look at the screen and see one word listed down the screen. Dad. Dad. Dad. Dad. Dad. Dad.

"All those calls were from your father? Is anything wrong?"

Not that I have any right to be asking that, but I suddenly feel so bad for the way I've acted in the past ten minutes that I have to say something.

Cade's shoulders sag, like the weight of my question is a heavy burden on him. "No. That's just the way he is," he says with a sigh.

Knowing the truth makes knowing what to say impossible now, so I mumble the only words I can think of to escape this humiliation I've brought on myself. "I'm sorry. I better go."

"Still? I didn't lie, Hailey. There's no one else, and still you want to run away?" he asks in a voice that fills me with regret.

I hang my head, unable to face him now. "I'm the problem, Cade. That's always how it is. This is all me, and I'm sorry."

As much as I hate to admit the truth, there it is. He isn't the one who caused all of this tonight. It's me. It's always me, and no matter what Dr. Thorpe or Meadow thinks, I'm obviously still not able to trust like someone like Cade deserves.

This time, he doesn't stop me when I turn toward the door, but behind me, he says, "Don't go. I don't know what happened before you met me, but you can trust me. I won't do whatever they did."

I stare at his front door and want to believe him. I'm so tired of being this way. I want to be happy. I want to have fun. I want to believe all men aren't liars and cheats. Being afraid is so exhausting.

With a heavy sigh, I turn around and see Cade's smile. Not the sexy one that makes me think of all the delicious things I would love to do with him, but the sweet one that lights up his dark brown eyes.

"Why would you want to be bothered with someone who's so fucked up?"

And there is the question I've asked myself every moment since he and I started talking.

Cade steps toward me and stops before taking my face in his hands. Tilting my head back, he looks down into my eyes as I try to push away the urge to run. "Everyone's got something they're fucked up about,

Hailey. I'm not afraid of yours, if you aren't afraid of mine."

I close my eyes and let the warmth of his skin against mine course through me. It's gentle but protective, and I want to believe in it.

"Yours? What are you fucked up about?" I whisper.

His lips brush mine, and he kisses me instead of answering. I don't believe he's like me. He doesn't fear everything and everyone, no matter how hard he tries not to like I do.

But at this moment, I don't want to think about that. All I want to think about is how incredible it feels to be kissed like this by someone like Cade.

MY HAND IN HIS, WE WALK BACK THROUGH THE apartment, neither of us saying a word. My insecurities run through me like rampaging villains, tearing up all the sweet thoughts I have about what's about to happen and replacing them with doubts that begin to eat at me even before we reach the bedroom.

I try to stay quiet, to not give voice to the ugly things they whisper in my head, but I can't stop myself, even as I know I may ruin this night for the second time. "I don't know about this, Cade."

He closes the door behind us, and in the dim light coming through the window, I see him smile at me. "I do. It's okay to let someone in. It doesn't always end bad."

As much as I want to believe that, my past says he's wrong. But now as I watch him slowly unbutton his dress shirt and shrug his shoulders to free himself from it, I want to let him in.

How could any sane woman not want that? The body only hinted at through his clothes now stands before me, muscular and tattooed and utterly beautiful.

My gaze drifts over his shoulders and chest while I try to make out the designs of each tattoo on his skin. A bright blue star on his chest. A grey and black design that looks foreign or tribal and covers from his shoulder down to his left ribs. A phoenix or some kind of bird with beautiful feathers of black and red across his stomach.

The urge to reach out and touch those images he's created on his body overcomes me, and I extend my hand to brush my fingertips over the area just between the muscles that create a pronounced V near his hips. Toned, it's divided in half with a thin line of dark hair that continues beneath his pants. His soft skin quivers beneath my touch, a movement that surprises and charms me.

A low moan escapes from his throat, like the sound an animal makes when he's sizing up his prey, and I see in his expression a darkness full of need. "See the effect you have on me?"

I shake my head, utterly unsure of anything but the effect he's having on me. Still fully dressed, I stare in awe at how beautiful he is before me.

Cade unzips his pants, and they hang open just enough to hint at what lies behind them. I wait for him to take them off, but instead, he crouches down in front of me and runs his hands over my dress.

"You have no idea how beautiful you look sitting there on my bed. I've wanted this since that first day I saw you."

Those doubts in my head grow louder now as my insecurities scream that's all he ever wanted from me. But is that so bad? Is it so bad for a gorgeous man to want me for sex? He could have wanted me for money, not that I have any. Or any other reason that would give me no pleasure.

There are far worse things than a man like Cade wanting to sleep with me. I tell myself that as he slides his hands under my dress and up my thighs. His strong hands press against my skin, exciting me with his mere touch.

"You're not talking. Is that good or bad?" he asks and stops right before he gets to where I so desperately want him to be.

"Neither," I answer with a smile as the last of my doubts return to their usual hiding places inside me.

Cade lifts himself to kiss me softly and whispers against my lips, "You don't have to be afraid, Hailey. I promise I'm not hiding any axes."

"I thought men didn't like when women laugh at times like this, but you're telling jokes."

Leveling his gaze on me, he gives me a wicked grin. "I'm not worried about you laughing. I just wanted to see you smile."

He doesn't give me a chance to say a word before he moves his hands to the inside of my thighs. Every cell in my body comes alive when his thumbs graze the front of my panties, sending a shot of electricity straight to my clit. Cade watches my reaction, smiling at his effect on me, and touches me again, making need surge inside me.

I'm wet, and he knows it. That very fact frightens me because it makes me vulnerable. What if he's just toying with me to see if he can get me excited to want him but he doesn't want me? Is that why he's still wearing his pants?

God, don't let me ruin this, please! No man, no matter how stunning he is, does anything like that. Only in my insecure head does that kind of thing even exist.

Sex is always something men want. A woman wanting it too isn't a problem for them.

All of this races through my mind as he stands up and plants his hands on the bed near my head. Leaning down, he begins to kiss me and lowers his body on top of mine, making sure not to crush me. I feel his hard cock nudge against my hip and react, letting a moan out at what's coming.

"You're so sweet. I bet you taste like heaven on my tongue," Cade whispers in my ear before sliding down my body.

He slips my panties down my legs and licks his lips. I want to say something sexy, something confident that will make him want me more, but my brain is empty. Blank. A void. It's like the mere thought of him going down on me has rendered me mindless.

His hands push my dress up over my waist, and with one last sinful grin, he looks up at me. "Let me hear the wild woman I know lives inside you come out."

A second later, the first flick of his tongue against my pussy makes my eyes roll back in my head. The beautiful mouth that made my legs go weak from his kisses playfully teases me, sucking my clit and running his tongue the length of me so all I want to do is beg him for more.

His left hand presses on my thigh, forcing me open for him, and I arch my back, whimpering with every time he drags his tongue over my clit. Lost in my own delirium, I feel his finger pass over my lips, and a second later when he sinks his teeth ever so slightly into the tender skin between my legs, I suck his fingertip into my mouth. He tastes sweet, like the peach cupcake I saved just for him.

When his other hand leaves my leg, I feel relief for the briefest of moments, but then my need and desire come crashing through me with one finger slid inside me. I suck his forefinger harder, desperate for something to ground me as my body begins to feel like I'm flying with every flick of his tongue and every stab into my wet and willing body.

Moaning against my skin, he adds a second finger and begins to fuck me as he concentrates his mouth on my clit. I arch my back, craving every part of his touch on me to relieve this need, and he pistons his fingers into me faster as he inches me closer and closer to release.

My hips ache my legs are open so wide, but the pain mixes with the pure pleasure of his mouth on me and his fingers fucking me that I don't care how much it hurts. So close, I rock my hips to get to that sweet point, wanting the release of all that's been pent up inside me.

With one last flick of his tongue, I see fireworks behind my eyes and suck hard on his finger as I come with abandon like I've never done before. I cry out in pure ecstasy, and Cade rides each wave of my orgasm, his mouth and tongue lapping against me and creating new aftershocks one after another.

Finally, I wriggle out from under his hold when I can't take it anymore. "I think you're going to kill me if you keep going."

He lifts his head and licks his lips. With one of his wicked smiles, he sighs and says, "Just as sweet as I thought. Like heaven."

"Did you get some kind of specialized training or something in that? I think you might be a master at it," I say and feel my cheeks heat up.

Cade instantly notices and points up at me. "I love that you're turning red right now. I was just between your legs eating your pussy but asking me that question makes you blush."

I cover my face, embarrassed at my body's need to do that. "Is there anything you can't do?"

He climbs up onto the bed next to me and pries my hands away so I can't avoid seeing him. "I can't make things like you do. I'm afraid I'm going to have to live with just being a sex god."

"Oh, so now you're a sex god? Such an ego, Cade March. Pretty cocky."

With a wink, he says, "It's not cocky if it's true. Then it's just facts. Just wait until next time. You'll see."

Disappointment tears through me. We're not doing anything more?

"Next time? Is this time over?"

He sighs and nods. "Yep. That phone call put a definite end time to this date, but I promise the next one will go as long as you want."

I try to imagine that and smile. "As long as I want?"

With one of those wicked smiles, he nods. "I promise. I'll go as long as you want me to."

When I first met Cade, I had a sense he was one of

those men I should be afraid of. I was wrong in one sense, but in another very real way, I should be afraid. Any man this charming and this good with his tongue to make you want more of him that his leaving early disappoints you is a very dangerous man.

And if I'm not careful, I'm going to fall madly in love with him, no matter how much I don't want to.

CHAPTER SIXTEEN

ade

WHEN I WALK INTO CLUB X THREE HOURS LATE, I'M
happy with what happened with Hailey tonight and
pissed I had to cut short our night together. Sort of a
mixed blessing, except I didn't get to come and I'm
putting the blame on my father for that.

Blue balls, courtesy of your family. That's some
shit I'm going to need a therapist for, no doubt.

The place is packed, as usual, and the crowd in
front of the main bar downstairs looks like it's about to
crush Cici and Cam. The newest bartenders, from
what I gathered from my conversation last month with
my father, they don't seem to have matured well
behind the bar in the past few weeks. She looks

practically dumbstruck trying to serve the next customer, and he appears to have a single speed.

Slow.

Like turtle slow. In a club like this one, that shit doesn't play. Not for long, anyway.

I see the legendary Stefan March come out of his office, look around, and set his eagle-eyed gaze on me, and I know he wants to talk. He always wants to talk. You'd think my interest in getting behind the bar to help his newbies would overrule his need to lecture me about being late, but I can tell by the disgruntled look on his face as he weaves through the crowd that he's in a talking mood.

Or maybe a yelling mood.

"Cade, I want to talk to you," he says when he gets about three feet away from me.

I point toward his hapless workers and say, "Can we do this after I rescue those two? They've got a line three people deep and ten people long wanting drinks. Who's setting up your shifts here these days? Whoever it is, they need to be retrained or fired."

His eyes narrow at my attack on his scheduler, who I know is him. It's always him. He likes being a hands-on kind of owner, and while that's not a bad thing, he's slipping if he thinks these two are up to the job of the main bar.

"Maya is on her break. They'll be fine once she gets back," he says defensively, and I know I've struck a nerve.

"Then I'll take over until she comes back from her break. I'll come to see you in the office then," I call back as I stride away toward the bar.

I know he hates that I just basically dismissed him, but what he hates even more is the idea that his bar isn't being manned properly. I can fix that, at least. Everything else between us tonight will go to hell pretty quickly once I step into his office, but at least I can get his main source of income here straightened out in the meantime.

As I come around the corner of the bar, I flash a blond in my way a smile and announce, "Ladies and gentlemen, what are we all drinking?"

They all call out drinks and I laugh that no one got the joke. Okay, I guess it was an inside thing. Cici and Cam look at me like they aren't sure if I'm there to help or cause a hassle, so I call them in toward me.

"Cici, take the end of the bar down there. Don't get flustered. Just do one drink at a time, and do it as fast as you can. Cam, you do the middle third, and I'll do this end down here. Don't worry about how many people there are. They all want drinks, so they'll wait a minute. Just don't make them wait two. Okay, let's go!"

They scurry away to where I've told them to go, and I turn to see the pretty blond giving me the eye. "What can I do for you tonight, beautiful?" I ask and get a sexy smile in return.

"Moscow mule. I'm Kirsten. What's your name?

Superman come to save the day?" she yells over the crowd cheering about something a few feet away.

I toss her a smile and nod as I begin to pour her drink. "Feel free to call me Superman. Give me a few seconds and I'll have you taken care of."

"Are you the man in charge?" she asks, and I shake my head.

"Not me. I'm just some off-the-street guy come to do a little bartending. The guy in charge is wearing the black suit and green tie and looks like he doesn't know what a good time is," I say, leaning over to place her drink in front of her.

She slides me a twenty and a piece of paper before flashing me another smile. "Well, Superman, keep the change and give me a call sometime. I'd love to see what kind of other superhero feats you can perform."

I could explain to her that I've got someone, even though I'm not sure that's the God's honest truth about what Hailey and I are doing, but what's the point? This is a bar, the blonde wants to flirt, and I'm a bartender whose job is to make customers happy. So I smile and give her wink.

"Time for me to go save more citizens of Metropolis."

With that, I make my way to the cash register and give the mighty Stefan March his take and pocket the ten I made with just a smile and a little sweet talk. It's too bad I hate doing this job. It's not hard and I could probably haul away half a grand tonight, if my father hadn't scheduled Maya too. Why does he insist on having me come in if he doesn't need me?

Well, he needs me, but that would mean sending poor Cici and Cam home. But my father has other plans for me, I'm sure.

Twenty minutes later, my third of the bar has more people than the rest of it because my two co-workers took my pep talk and disregarded every word. I'm halfway to what I might have made all night because of them, so I guess I can't be too disgusted with how bad they are at this job.

I'm not the one who's in charge of who works and who gets fired here, but if I was, they'd both be gone.

"Stefan Junior," a voice says behind me, and I turn to see Maya back from her break.

She knows I hate that little swipe she takes at me every time we meet up. One month of working together and she thinks I'm as bad as my father. I'd get rid of her too if this was my place, but not because she's shitty behind the bar. She isn't. In fact, she's been known to be damn good sometimes and the customers love her.

I'd get rid of her because she insists on calling me that little name.

"Maya, how great to see you again," I coo, obviously not happy to see her. "Taking half-hour breaks now? Seems pretty early in the night. Boyfriend couldn't wait?"

And that's my swipe back at her. I know her

boyfriend broke up with her last month. My father had to babysit her weepy ass for a week because she couldn't keep it together. Yours truly got to fill in for her then too and got to have the privilege of seeing how kind the great Stefan March could be to someone who isn't me.

Maya's green eyes open wide at my insult. "Fuck you, Cade! Get out of my way. This is my bar tonight."

Taking a fifty from my final customer, I head toward the register and get him his change. When he kindly leaves me a ten for a tip, I pocket that and look over at her.

"Then act like it so I don't have to come in here and clean up your fucking mess. You used to be good behind the bar. Maybe you could try to be that again."

Before she can clap back with some attempt at a witty retort, I slide around the edge of the bar and head into the crowd. Not two steps toward the stairs, I see my father wave me over toward him as he stands outside his office.

So much for getting away unscathed.

By the time I reach him, my stomach's in a knot and I'm preemptively hating the conversation we're about to have. He gives me a scowl and heads into the office with me following.

"I see you and Maya haven't made up. I thought you two would have been able to get past what happened last summer by now. It's been nearly a year," he says as he walks over to his chair behind his desk.

"Well, she's the same person she was, and I'm the same person I was, and the problem is still there, so I don't know why you would think we'd get past anything by now, Dad."

He leans back in his chair and takes a deep breath in. After he lets it out so slowly that I'm wondering if he's counting back from ten before he explodes, he points at the chair in front of his desk.

"Take a seat, Cade. No need to stand."

I prefer to stand because standing is one step closer to walking, which is what I want to do at this moment. After a great time with Hailey and a decent time working the bar, the last thing I want tonight is to sit here in this office and listen to another one of my father's lectures.

But I do as he says because it's easier than fighting him. I know how to pick my battles, and whether or not I bother to sit isn't one worth anything.

"You looked good out there. As soon as you got behind the bar, things started working a hundred times better. Those two took your guidance, and the customers love you," he says with a broad smile.

I think this is his way of complimenting me. That's not a bad thing, but I have a sense he might be going for the compliment sandwich thing tonight, so that means what's coming next won't be so wonderful.

"It's not rocket science, Dad. You smile, you flirt,

you pour drinks. People pay you, and if you've made them feel good, they give you some money to take home. As for Frick and Frack out there, they might be better at one of the other bars. Maybe the back bar that gets less traffic. Or even better, the second-floor bar away from the bathrooms. Maya has no customer skills whatsoever, but people seem to tolerate her. I still don't know why."

He sighs again, this time letting the air out in a rush. "Your mother was always an incredible bartender too, and she never wanted to do that either. I guess you take after her."

Well, this might not be horrible after all. Usually when he brings my mother into the conversation, he's feeling good about something. I definitely want to keep her as the topic, at least for the moment.

"How is Mom? I haven't talked to her in over a week. Is she busy at school?"

My father nods and his expression changes to that one he always wears when he talks about my mother's work. As much as he has no real idea what she's working on when it comes to the specifics of her research, he's proud of her and that shows all over his face.

"She is. I'll tell her to call you when she gets a chance. You know how she is when she's in the middle of her research. I'm sure you'll hear from her soon, though."

The two of us sit there with his desk separating us,

two men looking at one another and seeing very similar faces. My father and I look so alike that no one could ever wonder if we're related. Like him, I have dark hair and brown eyes, different from his brothers and their blue eyes. We take after my grandmother and her side of the family, while Cassian and Kane take after my grandfather's side.

All of this wanders through my mind as I sit and wait for him to lower the boom on why he insisted on dragging me in here to talk to me instead of just letting me work like I'm supposed to. I'm assuming I'm going to get the lecture about not being late, but with my father, you never know what he's going to be unhappy about.

"So I hear you have a girlfriend," he finally says, breaking the silence and stunning me at the same time.

Then again, in this family, nothing should surprise me, including Cassian blabbing like some old gossip to my father about what happened at CK the other night. Or was it Alex? He seems to be full of opinions on my life lately. Maybe he shared some of those with my father.

"Really? The March family gossip mill running full steam these days?"

He throws his head back and laughs at my snappy question. "You know how this family is, Cade. I saw your uncle and Alex yesterday and Cassian mentioned to me that you were at the restaurant to see some girl. From what Alex says, she's a gifted chef. Impressive."

Great. So it was both of them. Like father, like son. At least in their case.

"Is that what you called me in to talk about? Because I'm not sure I'd call her my girlfriend. She's someone I'm interested in, and yes, she is talented at her job."

Even as the words leave my mouth, I know I'm acting far too defensive about Hailey. The gossip grapevine in my family is nothing new. Hell, I take part in it from time to time myself. It's not really a shock that my uncle or even Alex would mention my interest in Hailey.

"No, it's not," my father says in a much harsher voice than just a few moments ago. "I just liked hearing that you were seeing someone who is so accomplished."

"Since I usually just see untalented sluts?"

My father frowns and lets out another sigh. "That's not what I was saying. You always think I'm attacking your choices. All I was saying about this girl is I'm glad you're seeing someone who is so successful. You deserve that."

Before I can stop myself, I say, "She isn't successful. She makes desserts at a little hole-in-the-wall restaurant to help her parents with their business."

I don't know why I tell him that. Not that every word of it isn't technically true, but it makes Hailey sound like so much less than she is.

"Well, Alex raved about her. He says she's a first-class chef."

"Well, if Alex says that, then it must be true."

This meeting has quickly gone to hell, and for possibly the first time in my life, I can't blame my father for that. I don't know why, but hearing him mention what Alex thinks of Hailey makes my blood boil. I don't give a fuck what anyone thinks of her. Let them not think of her at all. That would be even better.

A look of sadness permeates my father's expression now as he stares across the desk at me. "Does it always have to be a pitched battle between us, Cade? I just wanted you to know that I'm happy you're seeing someone so wonderful. What's the problem in that?"

I turn away, hating how disappointed he looks at this moment. "No. Sorry. Thanks. Is this what you wanted to talk about?"

Before I look back at him, I hear the emotion has hardened in his voice. "No. The club is celebrating its five-year anniversary after the flood, and I need you here at the front bar Friday night. It's going to be huge, like a packed house huge, so I can't have you being late."

Nodding, I turn to face him. "Got it. Friday night. I'll be here by six for the staff meeting."

The look of surprise I get for that I deserve. Even when I worked here full-time, I rarely bothered with attending my father's staff meetings. He loves those things. My mother told me once that he used to run them when he was just the manager of the bar, and since then, he's held one every night before opening. She thinks it's a ritual for him. I think it's his way to show everyone just who the boss is here.

"Great, great! I'll be happy to see you there."

"One favor, though, Dad. Put Maya somewhere I'm not. If that means you put me upstairs and she gets the main bar, so be it. I'm fine with that. Whatever you think works. I just don't want to have to deal with her all night while putting on my good time bartender face."

"Remind me again why she hates you?" he asks, showing hints of that gossip gene that runs so strong in my family.

I tilt my head back to look at the ceiling as I decide just how much I want to tell my father about why one of his favorite bartenders hates his son. She's probably whitewashed the whole story by now, but tonight I'm feeling the urge to spread some truth about that.

With a wince, I say, "Well, she hates me because we slept together a few times and then I broke it off. I generally don't shit where I eat, but she caught me in a moment of weakness. Actually, a few moments last summer after Emma. Once I told her I just wanted to be co-workers, that was it. Now she calls me Stefan Junior whenever she sees me. I personally think you should get rid of her since she's a bitch on wheels to the customers ninety percent of the time, but you seem to favor her."

"Hmmm...Stefan Junior. That doesn't sound complimentary," he says with a laugh before adding, "To either one of us, in fact."

"No, it doesn't. So that's why Maya hates me and why if you want your big celebration to go smoothly, you'll keep us separated."

With a nod, he says, "Fine. You'll be at the main bar, and I'll put her at the back bar. To keep her happy, I'll make sure something big happens back there so she doesn't think she's being punished."

As much as I shouldn't comment out loud on him keeping her happy, I can't stop myself. "God forbid she think that being a shit to your only son would get her punished."

My father ignores that broadside and smiles. "That's all I wanted to talk to you about. Any chance we'll get to see your girlfriend Friday night? I'll be happy to let Tannick at the door know so she and any guests she wants to bring will get V.I.P. passes."

The very thought of Hailey here at Club X makes the top of my head feel like it's going to blow off. No. Not in this life or the next one. Not even in a third fucking lifetime would I want her to be here while I have to work.

"She's got a lot going on, Dad. She's pretty shy, too. I don't think this would be her thing."

The disappointment returns to his face. "Oh, okay. I'd love to meet her, and I thought here at the club would be a nice casual way that could happen. Your cousins Alex and Cash are planning to come, and I think Kane said Liam would. I'm not sure about Wilder, though."

I stand to leave, already uncomfortable with how much my family is interested in Hailey. "No one is sure about Wilder, Dad. He's still messed up from everything. If that's all, I'm going to go back out there and see how the second floor is faring."

That gets me a huge smile from him, like I've just announced I know the way to bring in a million bucks a night. "What's that face for?"

My father shrugs, still beaming that silly smile. "I didn't even have to tell you where to go. You just knew. No matter if you want to accept it or not, you're a natural, Cade."

I don't bother replying to that. Choosing to check the upper level isn't rocket science. I already know the main bar and the back bar are doing fine. It's only logical to head upstairs.

That's not being a natural at anything here. He just wants to think that because he hopes I'll take after him some day.

Never going to happen.

CHAPTER SEVENTEEN

$\mathcal{H}$ailey

MY PHONE BUZZES ACROSS MY TABLE, AND I SEE Cade's name come up in the center of the screen. I shouldn't be so excited to hear from him, but my heart practically skips a beat and I hurry to clean off my hands before reaching for the phone to read his message.

I'm sitting in a booth wishing the world's best cupcake maker was sitting with me.

That's so sweet. Where is he?

I begin to type out my question, but I stop and run to look out the window into the dining room. There in the booth where I first met him Cade sits smiling at me. He waves for me to come out, and without even checking how I look, I hurry out to join him.

"What are you doing here? I wish you told me you were coming. I would have come out so you didn't have to sit here alone," I say as I slide into the booth on the other side of the table.

"It's okay. I don't mind sitting here for a few minutes. I was going to mention to your father that I was here to see you, but I didn't see him either. Are you busy?"

I shake my head, and at that moment, I realize I'm still wearing my apron covered in chocolate batter from today's dessert creation disaster. I look down in horror to see it's even worse than I thought.

"Oh, God. I must look like a mess. I'm sorry. I didn't think to take this off before I came out here. I'm glad I sat over here because if I had slid in next to you, you'd be covered in chocolate," I say as my cheeks heat up from embarrassment.

Cade reaches across the table and takes hold of my hand. Instantly, I feel like my anxiety calms. "It's okay. You look great. When are you off work?"

"I don't even know what time it is," I say as I look over toward the big round clock on the wall behind the counter. "It's one o'clock already? Wow, time does fly when you're making a mess."

He laughs at my mistake with the saying. "I'm not sure that's how it goes. What were you making that ended up all over you?"

"Well, I started with these cookies I wanted to try. They came out okay, but I wasn't happy with them, so I threw them away. So then I got really ambitious and tried a chocolate torte with a chocolate glaze and ribbons made of chocolate. The torte worked out, but I wasn't crazy about the glaze and the ribbons ended up as a disaster."

Pointing at my apron, I say, "Thus the chocolate everywhere."

"I bet the cookies and everything were terrific, even if you did end up wearing most of it."

"I wish. I really wanted that cake to turn out great. It would have looked so incredible in the case, and each piece would have been gorgeous," I say, still disappointed I couldn't get those ribbons to work for me.

"So what time are you off?" Cade asks for a second time.

"I can go whenever I want. I'm not really even an actual employee, to be honest," I explain, letting him know the truth for the first time.

"What do you mean? You work here, even if it's for your family. That sounds like an employee."

I force a smile, but it's always hard to explain that what I do for my parents isn't really work. At first when I came home last summer, having me in the kitchen was a way for them to make sure I was okay. Those days were rough, so leaving me alone wasn't anything either of my parents thought was a good idea.

Out of that grew what I do now. They never meant for it to be permanent or anything, really, which is why whenever anyone says I'm some fancy pastry chef or baker I balk at the very mention of those.

I'm just Hailey, someone who tinkers around with chocolate and ends up wearing it more often than not.

Shaking my head, I ease my hand away from Cade's and put it in my lap. I've dreaded knowing I'd have to admit the truth to him at some point. I guess I thought it might never happen or it would happen later than this.

But after last night, I don't want to lie to him. Not about anything, even what I do here at the restaurant or the reason why.

Unable to look up at him, I stare at the silver and gold design on the table and begin. "I never call myself anything fancy. I know Alex likes to say I'm some kind of chef, but that's not true. I have no formal training, and until last year, all I ever did here was wait on tables sometimes for extra money when I was in high school."

That's the easy part. Now comes the hard part of what I have to say.

"Last year, I was in school for psychology. I was a grad student and life was going just as I planned. Then in a matter of weeks, my life turned upside down."

"What happened?" Cade asks, probably thinking I'm going to say something like I failed a class.

If only it was that simple or that minor.

I look up at him and try to smile, but I can't fake it when I have to tell him the truth about what happened. "I fell apart when something in my life changed."

Those aren't the words I know I should say, but using the word breakdown always sounds so damn pathetic. I don't want to tell him I had a mental breakdown.

He doesn't say anything, but I see on his face he's confused. I don't blame him. I'm almost talking in code because I dread having to admit the truth in case it chases him away.

"This time last year, I was engaged to be married. My life was perfect, at least I thought it was. I was well on my way to the career I'd planned for years, and I had a fiancé who I thought wanted to get married like I did. I found out that wasn't true, though, one night when I walked into his apartment and found him in bed with her."

"Damn, Hailey. I'm sorry."

"I don't remember much after that. I drove back to my place somehow—God only knows how because I was a mess—and I crawled into bed. And then I didn't get out of bed for months. By the time my parents stepped in, I'd lost thirty pounds and I'd failed out of school so I didn't have any money to pay rent or my car payments anymore, so the bank repossessed that."

The look on Cade's face is the one I see when I tell people what happened. Not too many people have gotten the full story, but I always see a mixture of horror and sadness looking back at me. Pity sometimes too. I hate seeing that, but I understand why someone would feel that way when they hear what happened.

Thankfully, I don't see pity in Cade now. I don't think I could handle that.

He remains silent but nods his understanding. I know why he has nothing to say. I get it. I wouldn't know what to say either if someone told me this story.

But I want him to know the whole truth because if we're going to keep seeing one another, he deserves that from me.

"So since I was such a mess and my parents weren't sure what I'd do if left to my own devices, they had me come here every day to keep an eye on me so I didn't do anything to hurt myself. I wasn't suicidal, though. I just didn't care about myself or if I kept going. I didn't see any reason to."

My eyes fill with tears like they do when I think about those days. Now I can't even imagine feeling that way. I don't know that person I was then, and it hurts to remember how little happiness I had in those days.

"Making sweet things gave me reason to go on. I

found some kind of joy in that, so my parents encouraged it. I know it probably sounds strange, like how could that help someone come back from falling apart, but it did. Every day I would come in here and go back to my little spot in the kitchen where I could hide out and play with ingredients to make things. At first, they were just for me and then my parents too, but after a while, I agreed to let them put them out for their customers."

I wipe under my eyes so I don't look like some deranged and sad raccoon in front of Cade. I see him smile at me, but it's not his usual grin.

"You don't have to tell me this if you don't want to, Hailey," he says softly.

"Yes, I do. I want to be honest with you. My fiancé wasn't honest with me, and it crushed me. If he had just told me the truth, I would have been heartbroken, but I wouldn't have fallen apart like I did. Even if you walk out of this restaurant when I'm done and decide never to see me again, I think you deserve to know who you spent your time with."

"I'm not going to do that, so you don't have to worry."

"Well, whatever happens, I want you to know who Hailey Canton is. I see a therapist, and she's been terrific. I know why all that happened now and why I reacted like I did, but I also know it's my defense mechanism to push people away. I've done it with you and every person I've met since all that happened last year. I work on that, on not doing it, but I'm not very good yet. You have no idea how much I wanted to run away last night. If you hadn't kept talking to me when I was at your front door, I would have run, Cade."

A slow smile lights up his beautiful face at my mention of last night, and I assume he's going to say something about what we did. When he doesn't, I know I haven't made a mistake telling him all of this today.

"Well, you ran away on me that day in the parking lot here, so I had a feeling you're a runner. I think I knew if I didn't do something to keep you there last night, you'd never agree to see me again."

"I'm sorry about that. I have trust issues, which sounds like some lame excuse for bad behavior, but I do."

He has no idea how many times I've run away from him in my head. That first day. In the parking lot. At CK. While we walked that night. When I thought he was talking to a woman on the phone last night. When we were in his bedroom.

Every time I had to fight that familiar impulse to run away when something scared me.

But I don't want to be that scared little version of Hailey anymore.

"It's okay. I like a challenge," he says sweetly.

"I'm not trying to pressure you into anything with all of this. I'm guessing you're feeling pretty overwhelmed by this story, and I don't blame you.

Whatever you decide to do with this is okay, Cade. I just wanted to tell you because you deserve the truth."

Whether it's what happened to me or something else, I sense what I've just said bothers him. A look of sadness crosses his face for a brief moment before he makes himself smile, I suspect for me more than him.

"I'm glad you told me, but none of that changes the fact that I like you, Hailey. I also think you're downplaying how talented you are at what you do in that kitchen, but being humble is no crime. So all that said, I'm here, so let's get out of here and have fun."

"How do you know I'm off?" I ask with a giggle.

"You just told me this isn't really a job, so I figured I could steal you away from here whenever I wanted."

"I did, didn't I?" I admit sheepishly. "It's actually sort of a job in that I have to tell my father I'm leaving. Give me a couple minutes to find him and get out of this apron and then I'll be able to leave."

Cade sits back and stretches his arms along the back of the booth. "Then I'll wait."

"Okay. Let me find him and clean myself up."

As I hurry off to the kitchen, I look back to see Cade watching me. He really is a great guy, even better than I expected when I took a chance and didn't run away in CK's parking lot.

I'm glad I told him the truth about what happened with me. He told me the truth last night, so he deserved me being honest with him.

Bursting through the kitchen doors, I call out,

"Daddy, I'm leaving for the day. Tell Mom I don't know when I'll be home."

My father pokes his head out from behind a freezer door and nods. "Okay, honey. Stay safe. Are you and Meadow going somewhere?"

With a big smile, I answer his question. "I'm going to spend the day doing something fun with Cade."

I like the sound of that.

CHAPTER EIGHTEEN

ade

"SO WHAT SHOULD WE DO FIRST?" I ASK AS HAILEY and I walk toward my building. "Swim or go jet skiing?"

Her eyes grow wide. "I've never gone jet skiing. I don't think I can drive one of those things. I might kill someone."

"Then you can sit behind me, and I'll be the one at the controls. You'll love it. It's a good time."

"Are you sure it's not dangerous? I've watched people before doing it. They fly around on the water like maniacs."

Waving away her concerns, I laugh as the memory of the last time Alex and I went out and nearly drowned because of some asshole and his girlfriend playing around out there. Fucking newbies.

I can see she's still worried, so I weave my fingers through hers and bring her hand to my mouth to press a kiss onto her thumb. "I promise it'll be fine. I don't drive like a madman in the Jag, so why would you think I drive a jet ski like that?"

"You do sort of drive like a madman in your car, though, Cade. Didn't you notice me hanging on to the door a few times the other night?"

"No, but I was too busy looking at the woman sitting next to me to notice that. It wasn't that bad. Well, that one turn I took a little fast, but you didn't scream, so I figured I was fine."

She laughs at my explanation, making her look even more beautiful than usual. "That's a weird litmus test you have there for if you're driving too fast."

"I guess I could use someone jumping out of the car, but that wouldn't be fair. No one has ever jumped out while I'm driving. So screaming sounds about right."

"Because someone has screamed before?"

With a shrug, I have to admit the truth. "A couple times. People can be excitable sometimes. I chalk it up to that."

As the elevator doors open, I tug Hailey in and press the button for the fifteenth floor. Alone with her, finally, I slide my arms around her waist and pull her to me. After what she told me back at the restaurant, I feel like I need to make sure she knows I'm not like that asshole who fucked her life up last year.

"We could just forget about doing anything but hanging out in the house. It's not like we can't go out later. You know, it is pretty hot out today."

She looks up at me and raises her eyebrows. "Have you lived in Tampa a while? It's May. This isn't as hot as it gets."

"I've lived here all my life, actually. I was just looking for an excuse to keep us inside, preferably in bed."

And at that moment, I see suspicion fill her eyes. She thinks I'm a guy who just wants to fuck her and that's it. Smooth, Cade. Real smooth.

I don't give her the chance to pull away or say anything. "I didn't mean that the way it came out. I'm all about jet skiing all afternoon, if that's what you want to do."

"So you don't want to sleep with me? Is that what you mean?" she asks with such innocence that I realize I've gotten myself into a hole I need to get out of quickly.

Shaking my head, I work to change what she's thinking before she bolts as soon as the elevator doors open. "No, no. That came out wrong too. Let me start again. I'd love to spend all afternoon in bed with you, but that's not all I want to do with you. Yeah, that sounds closer to what I meant."

For a few moments, I watch to see if that made

things any better, and finally right before the elevator stops on my floor, Hailey gives me one of her sweet smiles. "I knew what you meant. I was just playing with you. You're cute when you're like that, though."

"Like what?" I ask just as the doors open.

"Sweet. Thoughtful. You don't look like you'd be that kind of guy, but you are, and I like that."

The doors begin to close as I lower my head to kiss her, but one of my neighbors stops them and marches into the elevator, interrupting us. It's that guy from across the hall who likes to wear Hawaiian shirts all the time and pulls his hair back into a man bun.

"Oh, sorry. Didn't realize it was that late in the day."

Hailey's cheeks turn bright red, and she hurries out of the elevator while I give him a nasty look on my way out. "Yeah, like there's a time when a guy can kiss someone in here. Aloha, dude."

By the time I get down the hall, she's giggling uncontrollably. "Did you just say aloha, dude to a guy wearing a Hawaiian shirt? What did he say back?"

"Nothing. He's an asshole. Like this is some puritan building that doesn't allow me to kiss you in the elevator. That guy needs to get laid and change his clothes. The seventies want their look back."

As I open my door, she whispers next to me, "Don't be mad. I don't think he meant any harm."

I turn my head so our mouths are just inches away from one another. "He ruined a sexy moment on me.

He'll pay in the future. I'll make sure of that. It will be painful and torturous. Maybe it will involve a wreath."

"If I kiss you now, will that spare that man all that pain?" she asks with a gentle smile.

"No, but that's because he's been a Hawaiian shirt wearing dick for years," I say before leaning toward her and kissing her on the lips.

"Hell hath no fury like a man denied a kiss in an elevator," she says as she walks into my place.

"Othello, right? Or maybe Hamlet? Sounds pretty tragic, so I'm guessing one of those," I joke before following her into the living room.

Wrapping my arms around her, I snuggle up to her back and press a kiss to her neck. "So did we decide if we're staying in or going out? I don't remember."

Hailey slides her hands out from beneath mine at her waist and pretends to weigh the choices. "Hmmm…go out and possibly get killed by a maniac driver on a jet ski or stay in and have sex. What's a girl to choose?"

"Just one question before we decide. Am I the maniac driver?" I ask before nuzzling her neck.

Giggling, she wriggles out of my hold and turns around to face me. "Yes, I'm sorry to say you are, so that only leaves us with sex. I hope you aren't too disappointed."

I reach out and pull her back to me, loving how her body feels on mine. "I'll get over it. I can go jet skiing with one of my cousins or my friends."

We stand there with me holding her to me for a while, neither one of us saying a word, and I can't remember the last time I was this quiet with anyone, but especially with a woman. I use talking to get what I want. Always have. It's just how I am.

But with Hailey, I want to be quiet sometimes. Like now, when we're standing in my living room and her eyes are closed and I have a feeling she wants to run.

I have to make it that she can't, though, and I have a feeling that isn't with anything I can say right now.

Finally, she whispers into the silence we've created together, "So you got quiet there. Everything okay?"

"I was just thinking the same exact thing."

She looks up at me and nods. "Yeah, everything's okay."

"Good. I liked that, though."

With a smile that lights up her beautiful blue eyes, she says, "I liked it too. It made me feel calm."

"I thought maybe you might want to run there for a few seconds."

Before she says another word, I know by the look in her eyes she did feel like running. But she didn't, and that's all that matters.

"I did, but I remembered what my therapist told me to do and made a list in my head of all the reasons I shouldn't. Want to know what was on the top of that list?"

For a moment, a flash of doubt crosses my mind

and I wonder if I actually do want to know the most important reason why she stayed. That passes, though, and I say, "Yeah."

Taking my hand, she begins to walk us toward my bedroom as I wait for her to give me that reason. When we reach the doorway, she turns around and says, "The number one reason I had for not leaving is after last time, I'd be crazy not to sleep with you. Any man who can do what you did with your mouth has to be good in bed."

I nod, smiling at how cute she is. "Well, I'm glad you liked my skills. I think you're going to like what I can do with the rest of me too."

"I'm sure I will."

"So what was reason number two?" I ask while I begin to strip her out of her pink T-shirt and jeans shorts.

Looking up, I see her smiling at me when I tug her shorts down her legs. "I'll tell you later."

I don't know why whatever this is between us feels so easy, like it's right that she's here and we're about to sleep together. When I've been with other women, it's never felt wrong, but it didn't feel like this.

Sweet. That's what this feels. Sweet, like two people who make each other smile looking to find happiness in one another.

I can't remember any time with a woman before that felt so comfortable like this.

As she steps out of her shorts and kicks them off to

the side, I move to her T-shirt, pulling it over her head. She's left standing in matching pink bra and panties, there in front of me with innocence in her blue eyes.

"Not that I wouldn't do this, but I didn't wear these thinking you and I were going to sleep together today. I wish I was that kind of woman, but I'm not that coordinated in the morning."

Glancing up and down her body, I nod my approval. "Whatever reason you did it, I like it. Then again, I'd like you in seaweed underwear and a coconut bra, so keep that in mind."

Hailey scrunches up her face like she just sucked on a lemon. "Seaweed underwear? That sounds gross. I think you might have just ripped me out of the mood."

I wrap my arms around her and pull her against me. "Then it's my job to get you back in the mood because there's no way we're wasting a fine coordinated underwear and bra day."

She looks up at me like she's studying my face for a long moment. "Are you always this cute?"

"Pro tip: men like to think they're masculine and tough. Being called cute makes us worry we're like puppies, and no guy wants to be like a puppy."

While her fingers fumble with my zipper, she says, "Well, I'm sticking with cute. Funny, cute, and sexy. Any of those work for you, He-Man?"

"I hear women love funny guys. You make a girl

laugh and boom! Her panties fall off. So I'll take funny and definitely sexy."

When she reaches inside my pants and palms my cock, I see a sly smile form on her lips. "Still thinking I'm just cute?"

Her tongue glides along her bottom lip and she reaches inside my underwear. The first touch of her hand on my skin makes me hard as a rock, and at this moment, I wouldn't care if she liked me because I have straight teeth.

"Maybe not just cute. You do have some fine attributes. I've got one in my hand right now."

She strokes it from base to tip, making my eyes roll back in my head. "I don't think anyone's every called my cock one of my fine attributes," I croak out, barely able to form the words this feels so fucking good.

I watch in amazement as she lowers herself to the floor and kneels in front of me. "I figure since you did me last time, I should return the favor. You know, since your attribute is so fine and all."

A second later, she wraps her pretty little mouth around my cock and her tongue hits the underside of the head to send me straight to heaven. Instinctively, I stuff my hands into her hair and tighten around the soft blond strands, but then I remember this is Hailey and not one of the usual women I've been known to sleep with.

When I release my hold, she looks up with confusion in her eyes. Leaning back, she eases my cock out of her mouth and asks, "Did I do something wrong?"

"No, not at all. Definitely not. I just didn't want to…"

"You don't have to treat me with kid gloves, Cade. I'm okay."

"Trust me. You're better than okay."

Hailey smiles, and then she returns to sucking my cock. I watch, amazed at how she can be both so sweet and so good at giving head both at the same time. The combination excites me more than I ever imagined possible.

As much as I love the way her mouth feels on me, I want more for our first time together. Next time, she can finish me this way.

Tilting her head back gently, I smile down at her. "Time to switch positions."

Again, she looks confused as I help her up. "Something's definitely wrong, right?"

"No, definitely right, but I have something else in mind," I say while I strip out of my clothes.

"Something else?"

A couple seconds later, I get those pretty pink panties and bra off and kiss her deep, tasting that tongue that made me feel like I'd died and gone to heaven. "Something else, as in you against this wall and me fucking you."

Those innocent blue eyes seem to get a wicked twinkle in them now, and when I lift her up, she wraps her legs around my waist. She's sexy and beautiful, and when she looks at me as I ease her down onto my cock, I'm not sure I can handle how sweet she is.

More times than I want to remember, fucking a woman was nothing but a physical act. A way for me to get off. A good time had by all, but that was it.

With Hailey, this feels different. More, like something was missing all those other times and now I just realize it.

I want something more than just getting off. I want what Hailey makes me feel right now.

Her lips brush the shell of my ear, and she moans softly when I ease out of her and fill her again. "Mmmm...that feels so good. I knew I wasn't wrong about you being just as good at this as you were with your mouth."

Kissing her neck, I say against her skin, "Hold on because you ain't seen nothing yet."

She rakes her fingernails across my shoulders, turning me on even more, and my body kicks into high gear. I thrust into her, and she meets my need with her own, rolling her hips and taking all of me. Her body feels fucking incredible, like her cunt was made to fit my cock like a glove. We rock back and forth, in and out with a perfect rhythm like we're in sync from the start.

Our bodies are damp with sweat, but I could fuck her all day. She kisses me hard on the lips and moans into my mouth, and a second later, that snug cunt of hers tightens even more around my cock and she comes with a squeal of satisfaction that sounds like music to my ears.

A few thrusts later, I come and then sag against the wall, holding her to me as we both fight to catch our breath. Our fucking was all I had hoped for and even more because of Hailey.

Gently, she runs her fingertips over the back of my neck, teasing the drenched ends of my hair. "That was incredible. I don't think my legs work, though, so you might have to carry me over to the bed."

I lean back and smile at her compliment before pressing a soft kiss onto her forehead. "That was incredible. Next round will be on the bed then so your legs can recover."

Her cheeks pinken from a blush at my mention of us going again, and when I lay her down onto the bed, she pulls me down on top of her. "Time for round two?"

"Definitely."

I ease into her again and roll over onto my back so she's on top of me this time. She looks like a fucking goddess sitting on me with my cock inside her. Setting my hands on her hips, I keep her still for a moment so I can take in how beautiful she is.

Pulling her mouth down to mine, I kiss her and whisper against her lips, "Promise me you won't run."

Her hair drapes over me, tickling my skin, and she

pushes it off her face so I see the fear in her eyes. "I'll try not to. I can promise that."

"I'll take it."

It's a start to something I can't believe I even want, but with Hailey, everything seems different. Good. I've had enough of the way my life was going.

CHAPTER NINETEEN

ade

MY FATHER BEAMS A SMILE THAT COULD LIGHT UP A small city as he explains to the crew for the night that this fifth anniversary celebration is going to be the biggest ever. Some local media is due to arrive at any minute, and people are already lined up on the sidewalk outside dying to get in here and drink until they black out.

"So I want to see you have a good time tonight because without you, Club X wouldn't be here. Smile, enjoy yourself, and make those customers see why you're the best in the business, okay?"

Everyone around me yells and claps, and I join in when I see him looking at me like I'm ruining his big night by not being as enthusiastic as the rest of these people. Why not, right? I'm happy and loving life, so why not give my father some bit of happiness too?

"Any problems, you know to see your section leaders or me, but see them first," he says, and everyone laughs.

"Okay, have a great night!"

More clapping before the crowd of my co-workers breaks up and people start their prep to get ready for opening. Even though I made it for his nightly pep talk, I don't know where he's got me scheduled, so I follow him into his office.

"Cade, what can I do for you?" he asks as he rifles through a stack of papers.

"Not sure what you want me to do tonight."

He looks up and smiles like he's thrilled about what he has to tell me. "Oh, I want you up at the main bar, for sure. I want you playing to those people here from Tampa Scene Magazine. Lots of smiling and do that thing you used to do with the bottles. People love that."

"I didn't realize people still read magazines."

My father rolls his eyes. "It's online. They just call it that, I guess. I don't really know, to be honest. I just know that the publicist I hired for this has all these people coming in to take pictures and record videos of the crowd to put all over social media. She also has them doing other things I don't really know about, so if someone sticks a phone or a mic in your face tonight, turn it on like only you can, okay?"

Thank God I had six cups of coffee today or I wouldn't be of any use to him for this anniversary shindig.

"Got it. Turn on the charm. Anything else?"

He thinks for a second and shakes his head before something comes to him. "Oh, yeah. Is that girlfriend of yours coming tonight?"

Something in the way he calls Hailey my girlfriend makes me bristle at the very sound of it, and I shake my head. "She's not coming, no."

"Fine. Then you'll be able to be the guy you were last summer?"

I nod, not really sure what he means by that. "Yeah, I guess. I might be a little taller. I think I had a growth spurt this year."

"Stop busting my chops, Cade. I've got about three million things going on right now. You know what I'm talking about."

Yeah, I know. I didn't want to think about it, but I know.

"Sure. I'll be that guy for you tonight."

"Great. Now have a good time and come find me if you run into any problems. I put Maya at the back bar and made sure we've got a bunch of promo shit going on back there, so she'll be happy. Cici and Cam are at the upstairs bar that gets the least amount of business. And you're at the main bar with the twins."

"Katelyn and Kalli?" I wonder aloud, not sure those are even their names. It's been a few months, and everyone just calls them the twins.

My father thinks for a minute, as if he isn't sure of their actual names either. "Kalli? I think it's Kylie."

"So Cade, Katelyn, and Kylie at the main bar. Going for a theme?"

He shakes his head, clearly not amused by my question. "I'm going for the two most gorgeous females behind the bar and the one and only Cade March. Your reputation precedes you. Use it to your advantage."

"My reputation precedes me? I haven't tended bar on a regular basis here for nearly a year, Dad. I doubt anyone even remembers me. You're going to have a hell of a lot more success with the twins, I think."

"Don't kid yourself. I've been in this business a long time. I know when someone is memorable."

Now it's my time to not be amused. "I think you might be biased then. Put your faith in the twins."

As I make my way toward the door, he says, "One of the people from that magazine or whatever it's called remembered you, so I think you made an impression on her, at least."

"I think she has me confused with someone else. No matter. Everyone will get the guy they're expecting, and the twins and I will have the main bar rocking."

"Good! See? You're a natural at this."

He wishes I was. I wish I was back at my place with Hailey. Neither one of us gets what we want tonight.

MY FATHER DIDN'T EXAGGERATE WHEN HE SAID IT would be a celebration. By ten o'clock, people stand shoulder to shoulder in front of the bar, and the twins and I barely have time to catch a breath between customers. I see a hand go up at the end of the bar and hurry down to find the March and Jackson family contingent fresh in the door and thirsty.

Alex drops a hundred on the bar in front of me and smiles. "Are we still being a bitch about things, or should we find one of the other bars?"

I take his money and hand it back to him, shaking my head. "Fuck you, and your money's no good here tonight. If the almighty Stefan March insists I work this hoedown, then my family and friends drink for free."

His brother Cash leans in and looks at me with that intense blue-eyed stare so like his father's. "Planning on bankrupting your father before he forces you to take over the place?" he asks and then laughs. "If I had known tonight was free, I would have better prepared. How've you been, Cade? Alex tells me your father is pulling hard on the reins lately."

I shake my head at him and roll my eyes. "Everyone in this family is like fucking hens. All you do is gossip." Turning to look at my cousin Liam, I say, "Let me guess. You know all my goddamned business too, right?"

My uncle Kane's older son, he's quiet like his father, something I appreciate since it usually means he's not interested in the family bullshit. But tonight, it seems even Liam is here to bust my balls.

With a shit-eating grin, he answers, "You know how fast word travels in this family. Don't worry, though. Looks like you got yourself a job, so your father will get off your back. Speaking of that, do you serve drinks at this job, or do you just talk to people dying of thirst?"

All three of them laugh, but I get it. As close as we've all been all our lives, it's not surprising they think they should ride me about my father's latest scheme to get me to run this place. I should have expected them to show up and act like they are.

"Fuck you guys, and if you aren't careful, I'll let the twins handle you."

My cousins turn their heads and look down the bar at the two gorgeous bartenders I get to work with tonight. Both have their blond hair up in ponytails, and both are wearing shirts that I'm pretty sure defy the laws of nature, or at least fabric, and show off as much of their tits without being naked.

"Christ, what is the tensile strength of those buttons?" Cash asks as the three of them stare at exactly what both twins hope male customers will notice and pay nicely to see as they get their drinks tonight. "They have to be super glued because there's no way that one little button is holding back all of that."

Liam smiles, and Alex taps me on the arm to get my attention. "I think you misunderstand the idea of punishment, man. There's no reason for us not to bust your ass all night long if we get them instead of you."

"Fuck off. Now you get whatever I decide to pour you three."

I leave them staring at the twins' assets and return a minute later with three whiskeys. When Alex doesn't see one for me, he stops his brother and Liam from taking a drink.

"First drink, you have to join us. It's a tradition."

"I can't get hammered tonight. There are like a million fucking people here. This job gets hard when your head is up your ass."

"One drink," Cash says, egging me on like he usually does. "You won't even feel it."

Grabbing the bottle off the shelf, I give in and pour myself a glass of whiskey. "One, but then I have to get back to work. What are we toasting to?" I ask as I lift my glass.

The four of us clink our glasses together, and Alex says with a grin, "To new beginnings."

"To new beginnings," the three of us repeat and then each of us takes a drink.

I know that's Alex's way of saying he's sorry for

giving me a hard time about Hailey. I can forgive him. I have to. He's my best friend, and even if I didn't want to let things go, this family isn't going to let that continue on for long.

"We're going to go see what's happening, but we'll check back. Don't work too hard," he says with a laugh.

Since it's better to ignore him as he's just being a bust ass, I head off to get drinks for paying customers. I'll catch up with them later, assuming my father doesn't have me giving interviews to some lame online magazine about how great working at Club X is.

That is definitely not what he wants to happen. I hope he knows that.

AN HOUR LATER, ONE OF THE TWINS LOOKS LIKE SHE needs a break from all the adoration the male customers are giving her. Her smile seems forced, so I head down to her end of the bar to check that she's okay.

Over the music, which has gotten so loud in the past few minutes that I can barely hear myself think, I say into her ear, "Everything okay? You need a couple minutes away?"

I don't use her name because I'm not sure if it's Katelyn or Kylie, but whichever one she is nods and leans in toward me. "Thanks! I just need a minute or two to get some fresh air and maybe splash some water on my face. I won't be long."

"We'll be fine."

"Okay. Thanks, Cade. Kylie still looks like she's going strong, so she'll be good if you get a huge rush, but I promise I won't be long. I'll be back in a minute."

Good to know this is Katelyn. Okay. I quickly scan her face and see she's wearing gold hoop earrings. Turning to look at her sister, I see no hoops. Good. Katelyn is hoops and Kylie isn't. That works.

Not thirty seconds after she walks out from behind the bar, all hell breaks loose. That media person my father said remembered me pushes her way to the front of the bar, and I instantly have a flashback as to why she knows me.

Easter weekend two years ago. Too much tequila. Way too much. A brunette and a redhead, sisters home from college. Or maybe they were on vacation. I didn't pay attention to their story much at the time. I actually wondered if somewhere nearby there was a blonde to round out the look we had going on.

Now the redhead stands in front of me, all smiles with some guy with a camera behind her. How did that weekend turn out? I can't remember, but I don't think anyone left with hurt feelings. Why would they? We were just three people having a good time.

"Cade March, baby, you are a sight for sore eyes. When your father told my producer that his son was going to be the star of this party tonight, I thought he meant you. Seeing you now brings all those memories back of that weekend my sister and I spent with you at the beach. Remember?"

I flash the smile I know I have to and nod like I'm happy to see her. Except I don't know her name.

"How've you been?" I ask, leaving my question hanging in mid-air in the hopes that she'll fill in her name.

She smiles, like she has my ploy all figured out, and leans over the bar to grab my shirt by the collar. Pulling me toward her, she plants a kiss full on my lips.

"Taryn. And I'm great, honey. I'm working with Tampa Scene and we're here to cover this anniversary party that's kicking. I was going to have my guy focus on those gorgeous girls that have been flanking you all night, but now I'm thinking all three of you are better. Sort of like bringing back old memories, right?"

"Great!" I yell over the music and look for anyone needing a drink. "Just let me know what you need."

A minute later, Katelyn returns, and I hear over the sound system someone announce that something's happening at the main bar. What the fuck is going on?

I look at the twins, but they shake their heads like they don't have a clue either. I see Alex coming toward me like he needs to talk to me, but before he can reach me, Taryn and her camera guy are making their way around to behind the bar.

"Okay, let's get a shot of you three gorgeous people

in your native environment," Taryn says as she directs her guy to stand a few feet back from her.

Kylie eagerly runs over to her and asks, "What is this for? Is this for something in the press?"

As Taryn explains who she is and where she works, Katelyn tugs on my shirt to get my attention. "Cade, what's going on? Your father didn't say anything about people interviewing us."

"It's fine. Just smile a lot and do your job. That's all I plan on doing. Your sister seems happy about this, though."

I see Katelyn shake her head and wonder why she looks so worried. It doesn't take long to find out.

CHAPTER TWENTY

*H*ailey

I CLING TO MEADOW'S ARM AS SHE MAKES A PATH for us through the standing-room only crowd. Everyone seems drunk and it's so incredibly loud that she can't hear a thing I try to say to her. No wonder I don't hang out in clubs much.

She turns her head and yells, "That announcement said something was happening at the front bar, so let's go there."

Nodding, I tighten my hold on her wrist and hope to God we don't get separated. I have no idea where I'd end up if this sea of people took me away.

We have to stop about ten feet away from our

destination when the crowd gets so densely packed that we can't move. Looking back at me, she yells, "Hold on. I think I see a hole over there near the wall. We might not see everything, but it will be closer."

Unsure if it's possible to be closer to any of these people as their arms and legs rub up against my body while we make our way toward the wall, I weave through those body parts as they flail this way and that with excitement. Finally, I see that hole Meadow mentioned and breathe a tiny sigh of relief. If I can just get a few inches between me and the next person, I'd be happy.

"Tonight, as we celebrate the fifth anniversary of Club X coming back from being underwater, let me hear everyone give a cheer for the hottest club in town!" a female's voice says over the sound system.

Meadow and I stop against the wall as the crowd erupts into cheers and yelling. Hundreds of drunk partiers all at once begin to chant, "Club X! Club X!" It's like nothing I've ever experienced, and after a few times, I start yelling it too.

"Look at you!" Meadow says in my ear.

I turn to look at her and smile. "I'm definitely a fish out of water here, but I figure I should try to blend in. When in Rome..."

"I'm just so glad you agreed to come. When Alex offered me the V.I.P. passes, I didn't know if you'd say yes. It's so great you did! And I love you in that dress!"

She hadn't mentioned if Cade would be here, but I secretly harbored the hope he would since Alex had called Meadow to give her the passes. She didn't know how he'd gotten them, but Meadow is always up for a good time, unlike me.

Tonight is different, though. I feel different. Spending time with Cade has made me feel like a new person, a more confident person.

Not confident enough to ask Meadow if she knew if Cade would be here, though. He told me he had work when I asked him what he was doing tonight, so I probably won't get to see him. But maybe because he's the manager of his own club, he had someone take over since his cousin has tickets to this place.

Of course, all of that stayed in my mind when I was talking to him and Meadow. It's enough that I dressed in one of her tiniest dresses and her heels that are two inches higher than any shoes I've ever worn. I'm not brave enough to let people know how much I love seeing him.

"I don't see Alex anywhere," she says in my ear.

Her disappointment comes through loud and clear. From the moment she laid eyes on him that night at CK, she's been talking about how much she hopes they'll get together. I hope so too since he's a great guy and she's my best friend.

"How can you tell in this crowd? I'd be lucky to find my own hand while we were walking through all those people."

"I know this isn't your type of place, but isn't it great?" she asks just as the woman on the sound system starts talking again. "It's so alive!"

A little too alive for me, but I'm here, so I don't want to ruin her time. Smiling, I point up toward the ceiling and say, "I think they're about to announce something."

"Ladies and gentlemen, tonight at the main bar here we have the most delicious trio you'll ever see. If you haven't met them already, here are the twins Katelyn and Kylie, and sandwiched between them like you know he loves being is the famous, well actually, infamous Cade! Give them a hand and let them know how much you love all three of them!"

The crowd erupts into cheers again, and I crane my neck to see the three beautiful bartenders just described. The twins are stunning with bodies to die for, but I can't see the other one. Just hearing that name makes me wish my Cade was here with me right now.

My Cade. I like how that sounds. But if we could be together right now instead of me being here and him being at work, I'd rather if we were at his place enjoying each other and the silence I never realized I loved until about twenty minutes ago.

Meadow grabs my hand and tugs me away from the wall. "Honey, we have to go. This place is getting too crowded. I feel like we're going to get crushed at any moment. Let's leave and call it a night, okay?"

I love that idea, so I hurry to keep up with her, happy I'll get some fresh air and elbow room once we leave this bar. All around me, people cheer and the sound system begins to play the striptease song. Curious, I look back, wondering if those women actual take their clothes off when they bartend, and what I see stops me cold.

Meadow tries to keep me walking toward the door, but I yank her back next to me as I watch one of the twins and Cade standing on the bar. My Cade. His shirt is wide open, and the woman lowers herself down until she's eyelevel with his zipper. As the crowd cheers her on, she stuffs her hands into his black pants and moves her face toward him. I can't see what she's doing, but everyone around us screams in excitement.

"Honey, why couldn't you just leave when I wanted to?" Meadow asks sadly as tears fill my eyes.

I shake my head in disbelief. Cade doesn't look unhappy that this gorgeous woman with enormous breasts is licking his stomach or whatever she's doing. I can't tell, but I can imagine what a woman does when her face is that close to his crotch.

He lied to me. He said he had to work at the club he manages. He never said he was a bartender and put on whatever the hell kind of show this is for a living. I asked him specifically what he was doing tonight since I didn't want to say yes to Meadow to come to this place if he and I could be together.

Now I know what he had to do that was better than spending time with me.

The woman stands up to her full height and takes a bow on the bar while everyone around us cheers. All I want to do is leave. That and throw up as the memory of finding Malcolm with that woman in the bed we shared fills my head.

All Cade had to do was tell me the truth. Now I can't help but wonder why he lied. Is he with this woman? It sure looks like they know each other well. Was he talking to her the other night? Was the name Dad in his phone just some decoy to hide that he's with her?

The infamous Cade. Sounds like I'm the only person in this bar who doesn't know who Cade March really is.

God, I'm so stupid. All along, I wondered why he would ever want to bother with me. I pushed that doubt and fear away because Dr. Thorpe and Meadow keep telling me it's not real.

But it is fucking real. It's real and it's standing on the bar in front of me, right now.

Meadow tugs my arm to leave, but right before I start toward the door, I make eye contact with Cade. I instantly see the guilt in his expression. He lied, and he knows he's been caught.

All he had to do was not lie. Why did he lie? Did he lie about everything?

"Come on, Hailey!" she yells, and this time I don't try to fight her.

I don't want to be here anymore. The person I thought was a fun guy who genuinely liked me isn't who he pretended to be.

He lied, and I don't know why.

I just know this hurts.

CHAPTER TWENTY-ONE

ade

I LOOK DOWN IN HORROR AT KYLIE DOING HER whatever the fuck she's doing right near my zipper and see Taryn and her camera guy getting the whole thing to spread across social media. No, this can't happen. I don't know what Kylie's going for with this faux fellatio act she's got going on, but she needs to get the fuck up off my crotch right now.

"Enough!" I yell at her, but the crowd's too loud for her to hear anything.

Behind me, her sister tries to get her attention, begging her to stop. "Kylie! What are you doing? Stop this!"

Nothing seems to faze her, so I grab her ponytail

and yank her head back roughly. She looks up at me with confusion written all over her face, like she can't understand why I'd be unhappy at this moment.

"Up. The show is over," I bark.

She doesn't fight me, and a second later, she's up on her feet taking a bow to the delight of the crowd in front of us that cheers and hollers for more. Taryn's right there when Kylie climbs down off the bar to interview her, although I can't imagine what she needs to ask her.

Maybe why, exactly, was she acting like pretend blowjobs are part of our job here? That sounds like a good question to start off with.

I glance out at the crowd and see Hailey staring up at me. What the fuck is she doing here? She's far enough away that she can't read my lips when I try to tell her this isn't what she thinks. What it is I'll need a hell of a lot more than a few mouthed words to explain, but I see in her eyes she can't believe what she's just watched.

Fuck!

Jumping down off the bar, I turn to look for Katelyn. She shakes her head like she's in shock at what her sister just pulled in front of the entire fucking crowd, but I don't have time to discuss that.

"I have to leave for a few minutes. Pry your sister away from the camera and you two handle things here," I snap, not interested in having any discussion with her.

"I'm so sorry, Cade. Kylie's been trying to get an audition—" she says, her eyes filling with tears as she attempts to give me an explanation for what her sister just did.

Pushing past her, I shake my head. "Not interested. Just take care of things and don't let it get to be a shitshow while I'm gone. I'll be back in a couple minutes."

My eyes dart left and right as I scan the crowd for any sign of Hailey. Too many people get in the way, and when I come around the corner of the bar where Taryn has been talking to Kylie, I feel someone's hand clamp down on my forearm.

"Cade, come talk to all my fans at Tampa Scene. After that show you two put on, I'm sure people want to know more about you," Taryn coos, like there's anything to fucking say about what just happened.

I tear my arm from her hold and flash Kylie a look that says I'm barely containing the rage inside me at this moment. "There's nothing to tell. It was all her."

She doesn't get a chance to say another word before I plow into the mob of people all jacked up from our little show. The music slams into me with every step I take, but I don't see Hailey anywhere. Damnit! I'm losing precious time to find her and explain everything.

Assuming she's even willing to give me a chance and listen to a goddamned word I have to say.

Right before I reach the door, someone grabs my

arm to stop me, and I turn to see it's Alex. With a smile, he asks, "Hey, what the fuck was that all about up there?"

I throw him a look like I just gave to Kylie. "What the fuck was that all about? A better fucking question is why the fuck Hailey was here, Alex. I didn't tell her about this tonight. Did you?"

Before he can answer my question, the sheepish look that comes over his face does it for him. I shove him away from me and force my way through more people to finally get to the door.

The warm night air hits me before I even step outside, and I run into the street to see if I can find her. She wouldn't have come alone, but she might drive her own car. I look for it, my gaze darting up and down the road searching for that white car of hers.

But I don't see it.

"Cade, she's gone by now," Alex says as he comes up behind me.

I spin around, livid and barely able to see straight as I stare at the person I know is responsible for this mess. "What the fuck was she doing here in the first place?"

That sheepish look from a minute ago is now full of regret as he winces like my goddamned question hurts him. When he doesn't answer me, I snap.

Pushing my hands against his shoulders, I send

him flying back away from me. "What did you do? Why was she here tonight? Tell me!"

"I gave her friend Meadow V.I.P. tickets. I was hoping she'd swing by so she and I could have a drink and get to know each other more. I didn't think she'd invite Hailey. I swear, Cade. This isn't Hailey's kind of thing. I never thought she'd come with Meadow."

Every word just enrages me more, but when he gets to the part where he seems to think he knows anything about Hailey, I practically explode. "Why the hell do you think you know what Hailey's kind of thing is? You don't know her. You talked to her a couple times for like ten minutes tops. So that makes you some kind of goddamned expert on the woman I've been spending all my free time with? Don't act like you know what Hailey likes or what she's into because you don't know her."

Cash and Liam walk out of the club and come up behind Alex, stopping just as I finish barking at him. The two of them seem confused and look at one another and then me.

"What happened?" Cash asks in his calm way that at this moment makes me want to kill him.

I point at Alex in disgust. "Ask your fucking brother. He can tell you."

He and Liam focus on Alex, but he doesn't seem to have anything to say. I don't have the time to do what I want to do with him, so I push past all three of them and head back into the bar.

"What's wrong with him?" Liam asks as I walk by. "Does this have to do with the girl on the bar? Is that the one you were talking about, Alex?"

"No, it doesn't, but he can have her," I bark back at the three of them. "Feel free, Alex. She's ripe for the picking. Maybe then you can keep your nose out of my fucking business."

By the time I get back inside, I can barely keep my anger at bay. I should have stayed outside to cool down for another minute, but even a few more seconds being anywhere near Alex and I would have pounded the fuck out of him.

I see my father coming toward me through the crowd and know for damn sure the last thing I want to do is deal with him right now. Looking around for some escape, I head toward the back bar but see Maya standing there giving me a smug smile like she knows something terrible has happened to me tonight.

"Cade, where are you going? Why aren't you up at the front bar like you're supposed to be?" my father asks, yelling over the music and the ten or so people that separate us.

Fuck, I need some peace and quiet to think. Where the hell can I find that in this place? I see his office door, and as much as I don't want to have to talk to him, at least I'll be able to hear myself think for a moment or two before he comes charging in with his hundreds of questions I have no intention of answering.

I slip in and slam the door behind me, shutting out all that noise and all those people I can't handle right now. I need to find a way to talk to Hailey and explain what happened. I'd rather do it in person, but since I don't seem to have that option open to me at the moment, I'll have to take the next best thing and call her.

Her phone rings twice and then goes to voicemail. She's avoiding me. I try again and the same thing happens. A third time the call goes directly to voicemail.

Things are getting worse, not better. I could text her, but what I have to say doesn't belong in some bullshit message she'll probably delete as soon as she sees it's from me.

The office door opens, and the pounding music outside in the bar intrudes on my silence. I turn my head to look over at the door and see my father walk through, smiling like it's the best night of his life.

Good for him. My life is falling apart, but at least he's had a nice cash haul from the hundreds of drunks in attendance tonight.

"What a night, huh?" he says as he heads toward his desk. "That was some show you and Kylie put on. She's a real go-getter, that one."

"Yeah, real go-getter. Dad, I have something I have to deal with, so is it possible we could talk some other time?"

He looks up from the papers he's been shuffling

around the top of his desk and nods. "Yeah, sure. Everything okay? Why aren't you out behind the bar?"

Always the job with him. Can't he tell I'm going through something right now? I just fucking told him I have something I have to deal with. Do I have to give him chapter and verse to find a little damn peace and quiet?

"Because I just said I have to handle something. Don't worry. I'll get back out there and pimp myself out for all the drunk women in a minute. In the meantime, the twins can manage the bar just fine. It's obvious Kylie has a grip on things tonight."

My father's expression morphs into one I rarely see from him. Concern. The usual look I get from him is a mixture of irritation and disappointment. Sometimes he mixes in disgust, for good measure.

But the way he looks now doesn't happen often with me. Ava gets that look, but that's because she's his little girl, the apple of his eye he's worried might be harmed by some jackass guy.

Someone like me. Or him.

"What's going on, Cade? You look like you're going to be sick. Are you okay?"

I look away because I can't explain that the last thing I am at this moment is okay. "I'll be fine. Just have something I need to figure out."

"Are you in trouble?" he asks quietly, like he's genuinely afraid the answer to his question is yes.

Shaking my head, even as I know I'm in trouble that I may not be able to get out of with Hailey, I give him my best bullshit smile all those people outside that door get. "Me? No. I'll be fine. Always am."

"Well, if you're not, let me know," he says with worry in his eyes.

I don't know why that makes me snap, especially since he said that with some genuine sincerity, but suddenly, I can't stop myself from laughing. "Why? What are you going to do? Ask the other twin to do her little dance behind me while Kylie does a second show for the crowd? Figure out some way I can help make this night the best one in the club's history?"

My father's eyes open wide in shock. "What is wrong with you tonight? It looked like you were having fun up there with Kylie. It's all a show anyway. Nothing is real about what you guys do out there. Nobody knows that better than you do. It's why you're such a natural at this."

I storm over to his desk and plant my palms on the top of it, leaning down so we're eye-to-eye. "I don't want to be a natural at this. Why can't you understand that? I didn't want Kylie doing her little thing, whatever the fuck that was, with me in front of the entire bar. I'm here to serve drinks and pretend I fucking like people as I do it, so I smile and do just that, but I never signed up for that shit she pulled out there."

My outburst stuns him for a few seconds. Leaning

back in his chair, he nods like he understands and says, "Okay. That's fair. But honestly, Cade, how is that any different from what you used to do when you bartended last summer?"

He doesn't understand how much I hate thinking back to those days, so of course he'd ask that question. I regret nearly everything I did then. If I could blame it on being stupid, I would, but I can't.

I knew what I was doing, and I loved it. Every fucking minute of it. And now, all I can do is cringe at those memories.

"It may not be different, but I am. I'm different," I say, hanging my head as the regret courses through me so hard it makes my body ache.

"Okay. Then don't do anything like that. We don't need any of it."

I see in my father's eyes he has no idea what I'm talking about. How could he? What's happened with Hailey came out of nowhere and turned my life upside down so fast that I haven't had a chance to truly understand what's going on. I can't blame him for not knowing.

"Cade, what's wrong with you tonight? I'm not talking about what happened with Kylie. I mean what's really going on," he asks in that softer voice he's only ever used when I was a little boy and he thought I'd been hurt on the field or lost a big game.

I look up at him and wish I could tell him about Hailey. For one moment, I'd like not to be fighting my father on everything in my life. I can't, though. Not yet. I know as soon as I say something to him, he'll tell my mother and she'll tell my aunts, which means the rest of the family will know.

I'm not ready to share Hailey with them yet. I might not even have her to share after tonight, but if I can get her to forgive me for what she saw, I want to keep what we have to ourselves for a few days more.

"I'm okay, Dad. Thanks for asking. And thanks for letting me use your office for a few minutes to get my head together."

He smiles as if we've had some breakthrough between us. "Anytime. And Cade, if this is about a girl, the truth never fails. If you haven't tried being honest yet, see what happens with that."

I don't have a choice now. The truth is all I've got. I can only hope Hailey is interested in hearing it.

CHAPTER TWENTY-TWO

ade

TEN TEXTS OVER THREE HOURS FOLLOWED BY another five when they didn't get me an answer have me crossing into full-blown stalker territory. They also leave me still unsure if Hailey will ever speak to me again.

I want to tell her what happened and that it meant nothing to me. I tried in the messages, but they didn't do much other than make me spiral out of control for a few hours as I attempted to tend bar and playact like I was having the time of my life while the whole time all I wanted to do was find Hailey and make her see how sorry I am.

"Why don't you go to her house?" Alex suggests as

the last of the crowd trails out the doors to end the night.

"I forgave you for your stupid move, dude. Suggesting I go to her house in the middle of the night tells me you want that ass kicking I threatened to give you earlier," I say, still pissed off at him.

"I didn't mean right now, for God's sake. I meant tomorrow morning before she goes to work."

As I start cleaning up behind the bar, I have to admit I have no idea where she lives. "One problem with that. I've never been to her house. I don't know where that is. So that's going to make the riding in on my white horse act difficult, don't you think?"

"Then go to the restaurant. You know she'll be there."

I nod at that idea, which seems logical, but that shows Alex doesn't really know Hailey. After what she told me about how she fell apart when she found that asshole boyfriend of hers in bed with another woman, I have no idea if she'll be at the restaurant in the morning.

My chest aches at the thought that I hurt her like that guy did. No, I didn't sleep with another woman, but I know what she went through, and I know she hurts easily.

If only I had just told her the truth.

As that little nugget of reality settles into my brain, I shake my head. It wouldn't have mattered if she knew what I really do for a living or not. Seeing me standing up on top of a bar while Kylie dropped to her knees and played around with my pants would have hurt her no matter what amount of truth she had from me.

"I'll try the restaurant then. And if she won't talk to me, I'll just have to set up camp near her car until she comes out and has to see me."

Alex chuckles at my newfound attitude. "Nice. Stalker 101. I'm a little surprised you're like this with her, though, Cade. I thought you were more about playing than anything else when it comes to women."

I finish washing a glass and set it onto the mat below the bar. He's not wrong. I've always been more about playing at relationships than actually being in them. Everything needed to stay fun and light. As long as that happened, I loved being with someone.

And when it turned into something else and I had to be honest about things, that's when everything fell apart. Every time. Without fail. I'm nothing if not reliable in my failures.

"Hailey's different. Some people you don't play around with. Some people deserve more than that."

A slow smile lights up his face, and he shakes his head. "I can't believe you finally found someone who you can say that about. Wait till Liam hears he won the bet. I'm never going to live this down considering I'm your best friend."

I stop and study his expression, trying to

understand what he's talking about. "You guys bet on my love life?"

"You know Cash. He'd bet on virtually anything, if given the chance. The four of us made a bet when you'd finally find someone who would force you to change your bullshit. I lost by about three years. Cash had you at twenty-five, I think. Liam said twenty-three, and Wilder said never. But you know how he is."

"When did this happen? Where was I when you were taking bets on my future happiness?" I ask, stunned but not really surprised since Cash will bet on anything and get everyone to join in.

"Fourth of July picnic out at Grandma's house. Remember Cash got a little buzzed and when we were talking about that girl he just broke up with, he got pretty defensive saying none of us were doing any better?"

"Dude, I'd remember us all betting on when I'd finally meet someone I cared for. I was drinking that night, but I wasn't as fucked up as you guys."

Alex shrugs, like all of this is so common in his life that he can't remember the details. "You left early after you and some girl had an argument on the phone. I think she was pissed you didn't bring her to the party. As if you ever do that."

I think back to that Fourth of July party out at the house and remember that fight. I can't even think of her name right now, but she was sure I was up to no good and didn't believe I was actually at my grandmother's house for a family get-together. I ended up leaving early, disgusted and not interested in celebrating anything after a half hour of trying to convince someone I didn't even love that I wasn't cheating on her or doing anything other than hanging out with my cousins.

"Nice. I can't trust any of you people, can I? What was the bet for?"

"Hundred bucks. No one was really willing to pony up much since I wasn't too confident it would ever happen but then went with twenty-six," Alex says with a smile.

"Well, I guess Liam gets three hundred now, assuming Hailey will ever speak to me again. Or is the whole bet just based on me caring for someone and not if she cares about me in return?"

Waving away my scolding, Alex grimaces at my potential misery. "Don't think like that. She's going to hear you out. She likes you. Trust me."

"Trust you? You got me into this mess," I say, shoving my hand against his shoulder.

"First, no I didn't. If you didn't lie to begin with, this wouldn't have been a problem."

I stop him before he can get to whatever he thinks is the second point he should make. "You can't imagine seeing one of the twins acting like she's about to go down on me would be okay with Hailey."

He thinks for a moment and nods. "Okay, granted

that would have gone over badly. But it doesn't matter because she likes you. She has from the first day we all met. Just tell her the truth and don't fuck it up so she can give you another chance. And then don't fuck that up."

"You act like I intentionally sabotage things for myself," I say with a chuckle.

Alex doesn't bother to answer, instead just leveling his judgmental gaze on me. Fuck him. That's crazy. What kind of madman would deliberately ruin a good thing that makes him happy?

MY STOMACH TWISTS INTO A TIGHT KNOT OF anxiety as I pull into the parking lot at Comfort Food. Hailey's car is parked on the side, like usual, so she's here. Now I just have to get her to listen to me so she can know the truth.

I take a look in the rearview mirror and silently give myself the pep talk I've recited since I opened my eyes this morning. "She just needs to hear the truth. That's all. Tell her the truth and it'll be fine."

None of that has truly sunk in as real yet, but I can hope.

Walking toward the front door, I'm not sure my legs are going to hold me up and my palms feel like someone's dipped them in warm water. I take a deep breath and push the door open to walk in, only to see her father glaring at me from behind the counter.

"You need to turn around and go back where you came from, son," he says in an ominously threatening tone.

Things are not starting out well.

"Is Hailey here? I was hoping to talk to her."

My voice sounds suspiciously like that time I brought my prom date home at four in the morning and lied to her parents that the car broke down. They didn't buy it then, and Hailey's father isn't taking too kindly to me right now, if his angry frown and eyebrows drawn in expression is any indication.

"Did you hear what I said? You need to go. Now."

I'm not getting anywhere with him, so I crane my neck to look back toward the kitchen. If I can see her back there, I'll try to get her attention and bypass this whole angry dad thing in front of me.

He's not having any of that, though, and comes around the counter looking like a bull charging the red blanket in front of him. And I'm the damn blanket!

"Why are you still standing here when I told you to leave?" he barks in my face.

Well, I guess I don't have to wonder if he knows what happened. I doubt anything I can say is going to make him happy right now, but I figure it won't hurt to try.

"I just want to talk to Hailey and explain everything. It was all a misunderstanding. I swear. If I can just talk to her, she'll see that too and everything will be okay."

Anger flashes in his faded blue eyes, and for a moment, I'm not sure he's not planning to physically throw me out of his restaurant. I get ready for him to grab me by the collar, but then Hailey walks out of the kitchen and touches her father's arm to get his attention.

"Daddy, let me talk to Cade for a minute, okay?"

Her father doesn't budge for so long that I wonder if he intends on standing between us during our conversation. Finally, after what seems like forever having those blue eyes staring at me in utter disapproval, he steps aside.

"You just let me know if you need me, Hailey. I'll be right over here," he grumbles before walking back behind the counter.

My first real chance to see Hailey makes my chest ache just like it did last night when I thought about her being hurt by what she saw. Her beautiful blue eyes don't look at me with that glare of hatred like her father's have in them, though.

It's worse than that. In hers, I see nothing but sadness.

"What do you want, Cade? I have to get back to my work," she says in a flat voice devoid of emotion.

"I just wanted to explain about last night," I say quietly as I realize some of the restaurant's customers are listening to us talk.

Before she can say anything, like go away or I never want to see you again, I touch her arm and motion toward the door. "Can we talk outside?"

Pulling away from me, she shakes her head. "I don't think so."

"Please? I just want to tell you some things."

I see by the hurt in her eyes that she wants to say no, but she's kind and good, so she nods and gives me a chance. Now I just have to make sure I don't blow it.

We walk out the door and go around to the side of the building before we stop. She won't look at me now but instead stares down at the ground.

"I know what you saw last night upset you, and I don't blame you, Hailey. I swear I had no part in that. The other bartender just started doing things, and before I knew it, she was kneeling in front of me. I never wanted that."

Still refusing to look at me, she shakes her head and continues to stare at that damn grease spot on the concrete near her feet. "It doesn't matter. Last night just proved what I thought all along. You and I aren't right for each other."

Fuck, I can feel her already walking away from me before she takes a single step. It's like she's closed herself off and won't let me in anymore.

I touch her arm and try again to make her understand what happened on top of that bar was nothing she should care about. "I swear, Hailey. I don't know why she did that, but I didn't want her to. Honestly."

Finally, she looks up at me, and in an instant, I see so much pain in her eyes that I wish she hadn't lifted her head. "You lied to me, Cade. That's the problem. Not that girl doing that to you up on that bar."

Her words stun me. Kylie's fake porn act isn't why she's upset with me?

"You mean about working at Club X? I'm sorry about that too."

"I have to go now."

My hand tightens around her wrist in a desperate attempt to keep her there with me for even a few seconds more. "No, don't go yet. Please let me explain. I can explain everything. I swear."

Those beautiful blue eyes of hers fill with tears. "I don't need you to explain, Cade. As I said, I figured it out a long time ago. We don't belong together. I'm not a red Jag kind of girl. I'm not an infamous Cade March kind of girl. Now just go and leave me alone, okay?"

My heart sinks at every word that comes out of her mouth, and when she pulls her arm from my hold, I stand there watching her walk away like I've lost everything I care about in the world. I don't know what to do.

I've never been at this point with a woman. Usually by now, I've checked out of the relationship and it's just a matter of time before whoever she is breaks up with me. It's a relief and I move on, like always.

Only this time I can't. I can't move on because I care about this woman.

So what am I supposed to do now?

CHAPTER TWENTY-THREE

*H*ailey

MY FATHER STOPS IN FRONT OF MY WORKSPACE AND lets out one of those sighs of his that says he has something on his mind. I know what he wants to talk about. Cade. It's just that I don't want to talk about him or anything about the last couple weeks I spent with him.

It hurts too much.

"So you know, he's sat out in my parking lot all day in that car of his. He hasn't left once, not even to go to the bathroom. He must have some soda bottle in there with him."

I look up and frown at the thought of that. "Nice,

Dad. Don't worry about him. He'll go away when I leave in a couple minutes."

"You know, I did my best angry dad act when he came in. He didn't give up, though. That usually scares people off. At least it scared your sisters' boyfriends when I did it with them. Do you think I'm losing my touch?" my father asks, his sly smile giving away what he really thinks.

But I don't want to play this game with him right now.

"I don't think you're losing it, Dad. You still look like a terrifying guy when you do your angry dad shtick," I say as I clean up my area to leave.

"Nobody said anything about losing it. That makes me sound like I'm going crazy. I was merely wondering if I had gotten soft in my old age. That's it."

"I have to go, Dad. I'll see you later. I think I'm going to go for a drive."

When I turn to leave, he stops me and kisses me on the cheek. "Okay, honey. Whatever makes you happy."

I force a smile and walk to the back door in the semi-conscious state I've been in all day. I think Hector says something as I pass him, but I'm not sure. I'm a million miles away.

Actually, I don't know where I am exactly. Or how I feel. Or what I'm doing. All I know is I hate feeling this way.

Again.

Stepping out into the late afternoon sun, I shield my eyes from the brightness after being in the kitchen for so long, but I trip over a can the cooks use for their cigarettes and go tumbling toward the pavement. Right before I hit, I feel hands on me, and then a moment later, I'm standing face-to-face with Cade.

"Glad I was here to catch you. That could have been a nasty fall."

Instinctively, I pull away from him, hating that's what I feel about him now. "Thanks."

We stand there for a moment in horrible silence. Well, it's horrible to me because I don't want to go but I don't know what to say to him.

"Hailey, please talk to me. Or if you won't talk to me, say you'll listen to what I have to say. I waited all day for you to come out in the hope that you'll hear what I have to tell you."

I look into his dark eyes and see him pleading with them too. I swore not twenty-four hours ago to never let myself be lured in by those eyes and that body, yet here I am doing just that.

"What could you possibly have to say that would be okay now, Cade? You lied to me. You told me you ran a club, but I saw that's not true. Why didn't you tell me it's your father's club and you bartend?"

"Because I don't. Not until recently, that is. Well, that's not exactly true either."

I put my hand up to stop him before he goes any further. "You seem to have trouble with the truth.

That's reason enough for me to say you should stop now. I need to go."

"That's not what I meant. I bartended at Club X last summer. I hated it. I don't know if I hated it because I had to work for my father or because I just don't like bartending, even if I seem to be good at it."

I can't stop myself from saying, "Well, from what I saw last night, you put on quite a show. You're a natural as far as I can tell."

A look of hurt settles into his face. "That's not what I usually do when I bartend. All I usually do is pour drinks for people and smile, even though behind the bar is the last place I want to be. I stopped working at Club X after the summer, but now I don't really have a choice so I went back last week."

As much as I don't want to be curious, I ask, "Why don't you have a choice? Does your father really need help because someone quit on him and he doesn't have a replacement?"

Cade shakes his head, that silent answer the only one I get for nearly a minute. When he finally begins speaking again, he sounds so different from every other time I've heard him talk—like he's defeated about something—that I can't help but feel bad for him.

"I don't have a job. I never have. I graduated from college over a year ago and haven't done anything since. That's the absolute and ugly truth, as much as I wanted to hide that from you."

In my mind, visions of his car, his condo, his jet skis flash like facts to once again dispute his version of the truth. "Then how do you have all the stuff you own? People who don't have jobs don't drive the kind of car you do, Cade. I thought you were going to tell me the truth. To be honest, this seems like a strange thing to lie about."

"I wish it was a lie. I don't have a job. I have a trust fund that gives me more money than I need. That's how I can afford the car and the condo and everything else."

None of this makes any sense, even though he looks sincere as he explains all of it. "People don't lie about being wealthy, Cade. Or is it that you knew I wasn't wealthy so you decided to hide it from me? Was that it?"

A tiny smile brightens his gloomy face. "You sound like Alex. He always asks me why I lie about not having a job. I don't know why I lie. The messed-up part of all of it is I could manage Club X. Nothing would make my father happier. I think he could die the happiest man in the world tomorrow if I told him today that I'd take over the club. He literally wants nothing else from me."

I narrow my eyes in confusion, unsure why anyone would act the way this man does. "So you lie about something you could be doing but don't instead of actually telling the truth that you're wealthy and don't have to do that thing you don't want to do? Am I getting this straight?"

"Not exactly. As of last week, I have to do something, or I'm cut off from my trust fund. The almighty Stefan March lowered the boom on me, I suspect to get me to come back to work at the club, so now I have to get a paying job or work for him. I chose to work for him, and that's what I was doing there last night."

For a few seconds, I don't know what to say. This all sounds ridiculous. Wealthy people don't lie about where they get their money, and trust fund guys certainly don't. Not that I know many of them. Or any, other than the one standing in front of me at the moment.

But it doesn't make any sense.

"Why should I believe you?" I ask, unable to be anything but that blunt right now.

Cade frowns and then lets out a heavy sigh. "Because all of it is the truth. We can drive over to the club right now and my father can vouch for every word I told you. Of course, that would mean my entire family would find out about us and I'm not sure you're up for that."

"Why? Are you ashamed of me because I don't have a trust fund like all of you?" I ask with as much defensiveness as I possess inside me.

He quickly grabs my hand, probably afraid I'm about to run away. He's not entirely wrong if he believes that. This whole conversation is making my flight instinct go haywire.

"No! That's not it at all. The problem with my family is once they find out about us, we're going to have to go to every picnic, barbeque, birthday celebration, and get-together they have, and trust me on this. My family knows nothing better than how to party."

"And you wouldn't want to do those things with me?"

He brings my hand to his mouth and lightly kisses my knuckles. "I was sort of hoping to enjoy it just being the two of us before the March and Jackson clan descends on us. I'm used to it since I've lived it my whole life, but it can be a little overwhelming."

"Oh. Have your other girlfriends told you that when you brought them around your family?" I ask, obviously fishing to find out how many there have been before me who met them all.

Cade shakes his head at my question. "I've never brought anyone around my family."

"Because they can be overwhelming?"

Again, he shakes his head, but this time he gives me a smile when he answers, "Because I never felt like that for anyone before."

"Before?"

"Before you."

"Oh."

He kisses the back of my hand again and smiles

one of those Cade smiles that could charm the birds out of the trees. "I'm sorry I lied. And I'm sorry you saw what you saw last night. And I'm sorry for how I made you feel. I didn't mean for that to happen. I would never hurt you, Hailey. I swear."

God, I promised myself I wouldn't fall for his charms and give in, but now that I'm standing here and he's apologizing for everything under the sun, how can I run away? He sounds sincere. I want to believe him.

But a nagging thought remains, and I can't take him back until I ask about it.

"If that isn't what you usually do when you bartend, why did you do it last night?"

He blows the air out of his lungs in a whoosh as a sheepish look comes over him. "Okay, here's the absolute truth. I don't know for sure why Kylie jumped up on the bar, and I definitely shouldn't have gone up there to get her down. I think it had to do with the woman from Tampa Scene magazine being there with a camera guy. Kylie might have been playing it up for Taryn."

When he stops talking, I have a sense he isn't finished. "Okay. Is that it?"

Cade winces and then says, "I slept with Taryn last Easter. Taryn and her sister. It wasn't anything big and was over as quickly as it started. One weekend. That was it."

"And Kylie? Is she an ex too?"

Shaking his head, he waves his hand in front of him like he wants to erase that idea from existence. "No, no. No Kylie or her sister. I'm sorry I told you about Taryn and her sister, but I promised to tell you the truth. I'd really rather you not know that about me."

"That you took advantage of being a good-looking man and had sex with women whenever you wanted? This isn't a shock to me, Cade. The only shock, actually, is that you would want to be with me after those women. I'm not exactly the jump up on the bar kind of girl."

Fear fills his eyes, and he holds onto my hand even tighter now. "You're exactly the kind of girl I want, though. None of that meant anything, and not just to me but to those women too. That's not who I am now, Hailey. I promise. I'm exactly the guy you thought I was before last night."

For the first time since all that happened, I give him a smile. "You don't have to worry. I'm not going to run away this time. And for the record, I didn't run away last night. Meadow and I were leaving when I saw you up on that bar."

"You didn't like the club? Too noisy and too crowded for you?"

"Actually, I think she saw you before I did and was trying to protect me. To be honest, though, right before we started to head for the door, I was thinking I would have preferred to be with you on your balcony looking at the stars instead of being plastered against all those people and not being able to hear myself think because the music was so loud."

Leaning down, he presses a kiss to my lips and leans back to smile. "I would have preferred that too."

And just when I think I couldn't be happier than at this very moment, he presses his forehead to mine and whispers, "What do you say we go to my place right now and wait for the stars to come out?"

I close my eyes and smile as I tell him I'd love to. When he takes me into his arms and holds me like I'm the most important thing in the world to him, I want to believe some quiet creature like me can be enough for the man who stood up on that bar and looked like a god to all those people and liked it. Because as much as he says he hates bartending and that's not what he usually does at his job, I saw how natural showing off was for him last night.

Will quiet nights and staring up at the stars be enough for Cade?

CHAPTER TWENTY-FOUR

Hailey

HIS APARTMENT LOOKS THE SAME AS IT DID THE LAST time I was here, but something feels different. I can't put my finger on exactly what that could be, though. My eyes scan the living room for something new. Nothing. It looks just like it did that night I was here.

Same neutral-colored walls. Same black sectional. Same end tables.

"Did you change something since I was here last?" I ask as he heads for the kitchen.

Cade looks back and shakes his head. "No. I haven't touched a thing since the designer came in and did her thing. That was over a year ago."

I follow him into the kitchen and glance around in

this room. It looks the same, but I can't shake the nagging feeling something's different in his place.

"I'm parched. What do you want to drink?" he asks from behind the refrigerator door.

"Whatever you have," I answer absentmindedly, still searching for what's changed here.

He pops his head up from behind the door and holds up a container of water and a jug of lemonade. "Either one of these work? I have some beer if you're feeling like drinking."

"Lemonade might be good. I had water all day."

We sound like two people who've been together for forty years. When did that happen? And why can't I figure out what's different about his apartment?

Then it comes to me. Nothing's changed here. Not the furniture or the décor or even Cade. They're all the same as the last time we were here together.

I'm the one that's changed. What happened last night has made me feel like I need to be on the lookout for anything different here.

I hate that. I don't want to constantly be thinking he's doing something behind my back so I need to inspect every square inch of this place every time I come here. That's not who I am or who I want to be.

Cade hands me a glass of lemonade and clinks my glass with his glass of water. "You were quiet all the way over here, so here's to us talking more. Actually, just you talking more. I've talked more today than I think I have in the entire last year."

I take a sip of the sweet drink with a hint of tartness that hits my tongue like the taste of lemonade always does and set my glass down on the counter. "I'm trying really hard not to be scared right now. I hope that doesn't sound ridiculous."

God, that makes me sound so vulnerable. I didn't mean to say it like that.

But he doesn't seem bothered by what I said at all and walks over to stand in front of me. Smiling, he brushes my hair away from my face and kisses me softly on the lips. "It doesn't sound ridiculous. I fucked up, so it's only natural you'd be a little gun-shy. But you don't have to be. There's absolutely nothing between us that isn't true. I even told you some stuff that I never wanted you to know, so there's nothing to hide here."

His brown eyes look so sincere that I hate I even let myself think like I did when I walked into this place. He did tell me some pretty real stuff back at the restaurant, but I liked hearing all of it.

"You can tell me anything, Cade. Honest. I won't hold your past against you. All I care about is how you are while we're together. That's why last night bothered me so much, but you said your piece and I believe you, so today is a fresh start."

"Good. I want you to know something else, though."

When he doesn't continue, my stomach does a flip and butterflies fill me. I wait for him to continue, but he doesn't. Instead, he simply stares down into my eyes, which only makes me sure he's about to tell me something upsetting.

"If it's bad, you don't have to. It's okay."

He slides his arms around my waist and in a low voice says, "I feel like you're trying to run away right now. Are you?"

Looking away, I nod. "When you didn't say what you said you wanted to, I got a little freaked out." I stop and take a deep breath before turning my head to face him. "But I'm not going anywhere physically, so I'm making progress. Don't you think?"

With a sweet smile, he sighs. "I do. But I must be getting better at picking up on it because it felt like you were a million miles away and I wanted to make sure you stayed, so I wrapped my arms around you. You don't have to run from me, Hailey. I promise I won't fuck up again."

I touch my palms to his chest, feeling the muscles underneath his shirt and wishing I could touch his body beneath the fabric. "So what did you want to tell me?"

He takes my right hand and places it over his heart. "I wanted you to know that I missed you. I know it was only one night, really, but I couldn't stop thinking that I'd never get to be like this with you again. Every time I thought that, it felt like someone was pressing down on my chest right where your hand is."

His skin feels warm against mine, like he's so much more alive than I am. I don't know if it's because he's fearless and not afraid of being hurt or if this is just who he is, but his ability to confess something like that leaves me in awe.

"I missed you too. I was sure I'd never be here with you again, and that made me sad."

"Well, no more sadness. No more missing either. The past is gone, and now we get to spend tonight together. Any ideas of what we should do?"

The way his eyes sparkle practically telegraphs what he's thinking. The feel of his hard cock pressing against my hip gives me an even bigger clue.

"Not that I can read minds or anything, but I think I know what you want to do," I say and giggle as I angle my hip toward the front of his pants.

Worry fills his eyes, and he shakes his head. "I don't want you to think that's all I want to do. I get that I fucked up. If that means we don't sleep together tonight, that's fine. My cock thinks other things, though, but you don't have to listen to him. He has a mind of his own, pretty much."

Cradling his face, I kiss him long and deep, sliding my tongue into his mouth to taste him like I've wanted to for so long today. When I lean back and smile, he looks relieved, like he didn't expect me to let him back in so quickly.

"I'm not the type of person to punish you for something you've said you're sorry for, Cade. I accepted your apology, so not sleeping with you tonight would be petty."

I slide my hand along the hard ridge in his pants and smile up at him. "Plus, punishing you punishes me, and I definitely don't think I deserve to be punished like that."

"You very well might be the perfect woman. Most women I've known love to punish guys that way," he says before letting out a low moan while I continue to rub him through his pants.

"Not perfect. It's just the way I am."

He nuzzles my neck, making me want so much more than just talking here in his kitchen. "Well, I like the way you are. The more I find out about you, the more I like, in fact."

My fingers slowly comb through his soft hair as he plants kisses just under my ear. I'd have to be insane to not want to sleep with Cade tonight or any night. Assuming he lives up to his promises. No woman in her right mind would deny herself what he has to offer after he's apologized.

I might be afraid of a million things in life and still working out my problems with my doctor, but I'm no fool. It's not every day a gorgeous man like Cade March walks into your life. Only a woman who doesn't enjoy feeling good would say no to sex with him tonight.

. . .

HE WRAPS HIS ARMS AROUND ME FROM BEHIND, AND as much as I want us to be in that bed together fucking because he's got me so excited, I love how safe and protected he makes me feel when he holds me like this. I lean my head back against his chest and cover his hands on my stomach with mine.

"I could stay like this all night," he whispers in my ear.

"That would make sex difficult since we're both dressed," I say with a giggle.

His hands slide up my body to cup my breasts while he nudges his cock against my lower back. "I like the way you have no problem wanting sex. That's pretty cool. No games or using it as a punishment. I like that."

Turning in his arms, I slide my hands under his black T-shirt to feel his soft, warm skin against my palms. "I'm a hundred other problems, I admit, but when it comes to sex, I'm not ashamed to say I like it. I particularly like it with you."

"Oh yeah? Why's that?"

I drag my fingernails along the space between his hipbones and feel his skin flutter from my touch. "Fishing for compliments? Okay, I like giving them when someone deserves it. The last time we were together, I thought I might pass out when I came. That's how good you are, so not being with you tonight was never not going to happen. I mean, once you came to see me and apologized. From that moment, it was game on."

His eyes grow wide as I tell him the truth, and when I finish, he shakes his head and smiles. "Damn. I didn't think you could get sexier, but that's fucking hot. Did you really almost pass out?"

I sense this isn't fishing but true disbelief, so I nod and shrug. "Yeah. It was good. Or maybe I just have low blood pressure."

Cade slides his tongue seductively along his lower lip. "I'm going with option one. It was that damn good."

"Well, you should because I've never had any blood pressure issues high or low. I think you might just be a great lay."

Again, his eyes get wide, but this time I think he's really shocked at how I describe him. No point in lying. Cade March is incredible in bed.

"I don't know if I'm taking that as a compliment or just blown away that a woman said that to me that way. Either one works."

With my fingernail, I trace the outline of his very erect cock through his pants and smile up at him. "I'm having a hard time believing no woman has ever said that to you before."

He tilts his head back and moans when I circle the tip of it a few times. "Not that I can remember, but maybe it's just the way you phrased it. God, I don't know what you're doing with your fingernail right now, but it feels fucking fantastic."

"Better than what I can do with my tongue?" I tease.

Cade looks down at me and scowls. "No way. That's a hundred times better."

"Then maybe we should do that," I say with a smile as I unzip his pants.

His gaze stays fixed on my face while I lower myself to the floor. Kneeling in front of him, I tug his cock out of his pants and bite my lip at how sexy he looks staring down at me in anticipation of the first moment my tongue will touch him.

For a few seconds, I close my eyes and inhale a deep breath to take his scent in. He's all male, muskiness mixed with the clean scent of soap that makes me want him even more.

With a gentle grip, I guide his cock to my mouth. Just as I part my lips, I open my eyes and look up at Cade to see him watching me with rapt fascination. His intense gaze tells me he's dying to feel my mouth on him, and a second later, I give him what he wants.

What we both want.

A hint of saltiness hits my taste buds when he glides over my tongue toward the back of my throat as I take as much of him into me as I can. Long and thick, he's blessed with a great cock, but I'm not blessed with the skills to deep throat, so I only get a little over half of him into my mouth before I have to back off.

"Jesus, that feels so fucking good," he groans above me, making my inability to do what I really wish I could do a little less disappointing.

His hands burrow into my hair, tugging me back down onto him faster this time. Afraid he might slam into the back of my throat so I gag, I keep my hand at the base of his cock, tightening it with every inch I go lower.

We fall into a rhythm that I like and he loves, if his moans above me are any clue. I flick my tongue along the underside of him, over the vein that runs the full length of his cock, and each time, he tightens his fists in my hair a little more so licks of pain skitter across my scalp.

"Fuck, Hailey...don't stop. That feels incredible," he whispers breathlessly, and I look up to see his eyes closed now.

I sense he's not far from coming, so I speed up just a little and begin to move my hand to stroke his cock in time with my mouth sucking him. With my left hand, I drag my fingernails across his skin between his hips, and he reacts immediately with another sultry moan that sounds like it comes from deep inside him.

He's sensual and erotic standing above me, and I can't get enough of how it feels to please him. His happiness makes me happy. His pleasure gives me pleasure.

All of a sudden, his hands leave my hair and I see him look down at me, his eyes big like he's scared of something. Before he can say anything, the first taste of cum hits my tongue and I moan against his cock, closing my eyes as I continue to take every inch of him I can.

When he finishes, I sit back on my heels and tilt my head to look up at him. He looks flushed and satisfied. If it's possible, he's even better looking than ever before.

"I took my hands away and hoped you knew that was me trying to say I was about to come. I guess we got our signals crossed?" he asks quietly.

God, he can be cute.

Shaking my head, I smile. "I had a feeling that's what you meant, but I didn't need a signal. I knew you were almost there."

"So you're not angry I came in your mouth?" he asks innocently.

"No. I guess I could have had you come on my chest, but since I'm still dressed, that would make a mess. Did you want to come somewhere else?"

I know the answer to that, but he's too cute about all of this so I can't resist teasing him a little. A look of recognition comes over him a few seconds later, and he pulls me up to kiss him.

"You are officially the sexiest woman I've ever known. Hands down."

"Because I had you come in my mouth? That

seems like a pretty low bar since you went down on me and finished."

His dark eyes dance as he looks down at me and shakes his head. "Seriously, the sexiest woman. You have no idea what it means that you aren't pissed. I was bracing for some real anger there."

"That sounds like a mood killer. What kind of women have you been with before me?"

"All the wrong ones," he says sweetly before kissing me again. "Definitely all the wrong ones."

CHAPTER TWENTY-FIVE

ade

I ROLL ONTO MY BACK, MY SKIN COVERED IN SWEAT and my body aching in places I didn't realize I had muscles. Hailey lies next to me, her head on the pillow and her hair spread out behind her so she looks like a mermaid.

An unbelievably sexy mermaid who may have just fucked me into oblivion.

"So, I'm not sure how to phrase this, so I'm going to go with what's in my head and hope you don't get upset. Were you a call girl in a prior life or something?"

She laughs and rolls her eyes, instantly putting me at ease because I suspected she might throw a punch for a question like that. "Why do men always assume you can only learn to be good in bed if you do it a lot? Haven't you guys ever heard of reading?"

"So you read how-to books on sex? Whatever they are, you clearly got what they were teaching."

Hailey inches over and kisses me. "No, but I read romance books. They were a few of the things that got me through when I didn't want to go on all those months. There are some pretty graphic ones, and I just mimicked what I read."

"Really?"

Is it possible this woman is that incredible that she learned how to be fucking fantastic in bed from reading? What are these books with such magic in them?

"Yeah," she says like it's just the normal kind of thing everyone does. "It's how I learned to bake, and it's how I learned to fuck."

I wrap my arm around her and pull her to me, loving the feel of her next to my body. "I think you might be the most amazing person I've ever met."

"I bet you'd find lots of women read romance novels and learn some skills from them. I don't think it's anything amazing," she says nonchalantly as she curls up against my side.

"Well, I love it."

And then, as if the words have a mind of their own and I can't stop them, I say the three words I've never uttered to a woman. "I love you."

They sound strange coming out of my mouth, and for a long moment they hang in the air around us, neither one of us saying a word to break the silence. My heartbeat pounds in my ears when I realize what I just said for the first time in my life.

I told someone I love them. And as odd as that is, it feels worse since she isn't saying it back to me.

Hailey lifts her head off my chest and looks at me strangely, like she isn't sure she heard correctly. "Did you just say you love me?"

Now seems like as good a time as any for some humor, so I shake my head. "Nah. I wouldn't say that. I mean, I could since I know those three words, but that would be crazy. Right?"

"Well, okay. I was going to say I love you too, but since you didn't say that, I won't say that either. Glad we got that straightened out."

She moves to set her head down on my chest again, but I roll her over onto her back and kiss her. "So if I did say it, you wouldn't run from the room in terror?"

Those beautiful blue eyes stare up at me with such sweetness in them as she shakes her head and smiles. "No. No running. I'd stay right here, and I might even say them back."

"Should we try a second take and see what happens?"

Hailey lifts her head off the pillow and kisses me. "Let's try."

As much as I always thought saying those three words would be the scariest thing I could ever utter, they come out like they're the most natural thing I could say to her at this moment. "I love you, Hailey."

She doesn't miss a beat before she says the words that sound like music to my ears. "I love you, Cade."

"I've never said that in my life."

"You did a good job. All the words came out in the right order and very clear. I understood every one of them," she says with a giggle.

"I don't know why they came out, but I'm glad they did."

"I'm glad they did too because I feel that way. I know it's probably crazy because we haven't been seeing each other for very long at all, but I have said those words before, and I know I felt a little like this when I did."

Jealousy races through me at hearing her say she's told someone before me she loved them. Not that I should be surprised since she was engaged to that jackass who cheated on her. Of course, she said it to him.

I just never thought about how much I hate that idea until this very moment.

"Oh, yeah. I guess you would have. So this time felt like that time?"

Hailey shakes her head and wraps her arms around my body to pull me close. "Sort of, but not exactly. It took six months for us to say it to one another. I guess that should have been a clue, huh?"

"So a little over two weeks and after one major fuck up seems fast, I guess."

"It seems right, Cade. And to celebrate it, I think we should have sex again. There's this thing I want to try that involves me on top and my legs out to the side. I have an idea in my head about it, but I'd like to see if it will work. You up for it?"

I roll my hips so she can feel I'm ready to go again. "You're not just trying to distract me from thinking about you and that guy saying you love each other are you? Because I'm fine if you are. I'm not going to turn down sex with you, so if that's what you're doing, I'm all in."

She wraps her legs around my waist and presses her pussy against my cock. "You don't have to worry about him. He found someone else before he even left me, so there's nothing there. I'm really a one-man kind of woman, so since I already said I loved you, I guess you're that man."

Looking down into her soft eyes, I feel my jealousy ebb away. "You must think I'm crazy to be jealous of someone I've never met."

Hailey trails her fingertips down over my chest and stomach. "I was jealous of a woman I only saw from twenty feet away and never spoke to, so I don't think it's that crazy."

I can't let her think for even a second Kylie meant

anything with that dance of hers, so I tilt Hailey's chin up and press a kiss to her lips. "I know why you were, but you had no reason to be jealous."

"Promise?"

Her eyes fill with so much hope and anticipation that I can't let her down now. But honestly, I'd promise her the moon at this moment, so promising there's no reason to be jealous of any other woman on the planet is the easiest thing in the world to do.

"I promise. It's all you, Hailey."

"Okay."

"So we should probably get to having sex again because any more talk and both of us are going to get out of the mood."

That gets me an adorable smile. "I think we both know that's not going to happen."

She's the perfect woman. That seals it.

CLUB X DURING THE DAY ALWAYS REMINDS ME OF what I see when I first wake up in the morning after having a wild party at my house the night before. Even if I cleaned up before crashing, my place looks too stark, too bright when I wake up.

Normally, that's because I'm so hungover I can't handle the sunlight trying to find its way into my room. But the club looks like that every time I come here during the daytime.

Stark and brutal.

At night, it's all fun and games. The colored lights break up the pitch black but just enough to make everyone look like a far more interesting version of themselves. The music adds to the fun, so people appear like in some kind of wild dream.

If they walked in here right now, I wouldn't recognize them. They wouldn't recognize me either. That's the beauty of night and the terrible reality of day for you.

The club stands empty, like a hollow cavern devoid of all its good times. No one's here since it's only early afternoon, but in the office, I hear a noise that sounds like someone talking on the phone.

I push the door open and see my father with his feet up on the desk and his cell phone to his ear. This is the image I have of him from my earliest memories as a child. My mother used to bring me here to see him and the three of us would eat lunch together in this office with no windows and only that one door.

Even as a three-year-old kid, I always felt trapped as soon as I walked in, but my father loved this part of the club. Everyone else thinks the fun is out there on the dance floor and at the bar, but for Stefan March, the truly good stuff happens right here where he makes his plans and runs the entire show from that desk he's had all my life.

When he sees me walk in, his eyes get wide and he waves me over, like he's eager to talk to me. He probably wants to rave about that damn anniversary party again.

"Let me talk to you later, Dan. My son just walked in, so I want to see what he's up to," he says, again waving me over to sit down.

Smiling, he nods at whatever the guy on the phone is talking about and says, "Got it! Sounds good. Okay, let's catch up with each other later in the week and see what's going on. Talk to you later, Dan."

A second later, he tosses the cell phone onto his desk and leans back in his chair as he runs his hand through his hair. "There's no way in hell I'm working with that son of a bitch again. I don't care how much he thinks he can sweet talk me."

I give him a half-hearted smile since I have no idea who this son of a bitch is or what he did in the past to make him persona non grata with my father. He probably cheated him on something. That's a surefire way to get on his bad side.

"So what brings you down here in the middle of the day? I can't remember the last time you saw this place when the sun was out."

Probably when he had me running the club and I had to deal with all those goddamned vendors and the million and a half problems that come with them. I don't say that, though, since I don't want to get into a conversation about that again.

"I need to talk to you about something, Dad. Before I get into this, I want you to know this is nonnegotiable. If you can't agree to this, then I can't work here anymore. I don't think I'm being unreasonable, but if you do, then I guess we'll be at an impasse."

When I finish speaking, he nods and gives me a big smile. "Sounds pretty serious. Only one problem."

"What's that?" I ask, already fucking defensive.

"You haven't even told me what you're here about and already you've got me unwilling to agree with you. At least give me a chance to be a hard ass, Cade."

Damn. I'd been so convinced he'd say no immediately, I never even got to what I won't be doing anymore if I keep working here.

"Oh, yeah. Well, I guess that would help," I admit, feeling pretty foolish.

My father chuckles and puts his hands back behind his head, clearly enjoying this more than I am. "You never know. I might disappoint you this time and think you're right. It has happened before, you know."

"Not often," I mumble.

"Well, how about we try to make it happen more often? You're not a boy anymore, and as your mother reminds me more often than I like, you have your own life to lead. So tell me what's on your mind and we can take it from there."

So be it. He wants to know what I'm thinking? Now he will.

"If I'm going to be bartending here anymore, I'm not going to do any more of that bullshit that Kylie pulled the other night. I nearly lost someone I care about because of that. So no more."

He shrugs and gives me a nod. "Okay. No more. We talked about this the other night, though. Didn't we?"

"The other night I was out of my mind angry. Today, I'm thinking straight. I won't do that again and risk Hailey finding out. She wouldn't understand."

My mention of her name makes him lean forward. "So your girlfriend's name is Hailey. Is this the infamous young woman who my brothers and Alex can't say enough about with the desserts? Is that the same Hailey?"

I cringe at the thought that my family has already begun to discuss my girlfriend. Nothing good can come from that.

"Yes, and I never realized all the men in the family were such gossips. Maybe you guys could talk about something else. We have sports teams in this city I know you guys are fans of. You could talk about them. Or a million other topics. You've known each other all your lives, right?"

My father smiles but remains silent for a long moment. Folding his arms across his chest, he finally says, "You're a little touchy about this subject, Cade. I'm not saying we were all sitting around talking about this woman. Your uncles and cousin were actually very impressed with her talent at making desserts. That's all. Nobody's gossiping about her."

I need to change the subject now before we go down this rabbit hole and he starts pumping me for information I don't want to give any of them just yet. Better to focus on my reason for being here.

"Whatever. The point is I'm not interested in being a show pony anymore. I'll tend bar. That's it. If that means you have to put me at the back bar or upstairs, that's fine. I'm not doing this for money anyway."

He surprises me when he nods again. "Okay, that works for me. But I'm a little confused. The other night, you didn't act like Hailey was anyone important. How was I to know what Kylie was doing would be a problem? You wouldn't even refer to Hailey as your girlfriend, if I remember correctly."

As much as I hate to admit it, he is remembering correctly. That was then, though. This is now, and now she's my girlfriend.

"That's true, but things have changed."

To me, this conversation is over, so I move to leave, happy to have gotten all I wanted out of our little talk. But as I stand up, my father asks the question I always dread about anyone I'm seeing.

"Will we get to meet this girlfriend any time soon?"

I wince at the very words when they hit my ears. Nothing would make him and my mother happier than my bringing a girlfriend to meet them, have dinner, and hang out for a few hours. And nothing makes my stomach twist into knots more.

"We'll see, Dad."

On my way to the door, he adds, "Because I know your mother would be over the moon to finally meet one of your girlfriends. She never gets a chance, but she'd be thrilled to, Cade."

The doubt in his voice tells me he doesn't think it will ever happen. Good. Maybe he won't mention it to my mother and I won't have to deal with having to put her off about this topic yet again like I have countless times.

"Well, then don't tell her about it and she won't get her hopes up. We've only been dating for two weeks, so it's a little early for all this talk anyway."

I hear him chuckle behind me and turn around to see him grinning at me. "Something funny?"

"Just that I thought this was farther along than it is. Two weeks is nothing in Cade time. I thought this was something more involved."

The smug look on his face bothers me, and even though I know I shouldn't let him bait me like he always does, I walk back toward him and ask, "What the hell is Cade time?"

My father shrugs. "Just the way we think of how long you generally are with your girlfriends. Here today, gone tomorrow. Two weeks is nothing. When it gets to be a couple months, then it will be something."

"It's something now," I snap, barely able to contain the anger rising in me.

"Sure, sure, but you're famous for going through women like a fish goes through water, Cade. You can't expect your mother to get excited about every girl you see. She'd be finding out about a new one every few days."

I shouldn't say anything to that, but I can't stop myself. "It's like you don't remember being my age, Dad. Like having a good time is a problem. But for your information, I'm not just having a good time with Hailey. Not that I plan on bringing her around any of you guys in our fine family since it's clear everyone thinks I'm nothing but a guy who goes through women like I change my underwear. I can imagine the word manwhore being thrown around."

Damnit, I hate that every time my father and I talk for more than two goddamned minutes it ends up like this. I don't know if it's because we're too alike or too different. Whatever it is that makes us like this, it's fucking exhausting.

Before he can keep this thing between us going, I turn around and head for the door. "See you later, Dad. Tell Mom I'll call her."

"Call your sister too, Cade. Ava thinks you've fallen off the face of the earth."

"Got it. Call all the women. Bye!"

CHAPTER TWENTY-SIX

$\mathcal{H}$ailey

EVERYONE FROM HECTOR TO MY MOTHER HAS BEEN giving me strange looks since I got to the restaurant this morning. I can't tell if they're worried about me or if they can't figure out why I'm happy. I catch them looking over at me while they're working and then when I meet their gazes, they quickly turn away all sheepishly.

"Honey, the apple tarts are all gone already. Did you make more?" my mother asks in her usual way, but I sense she's looking for a way to start a conversation.

About what, I don't know. Well, that's not true. I think she might want to ask about what happened with Cade because I haven't said a word about it since I walked in this morning.

I grab the tray of tarts behind me and hand them to her. "All set and ready to go!"

She doesn't walk away, so after a few seconds, I can't avoid glancing up at her. She's giving me that look of anticipation, like she's hoping this is the time when she'll find her in and be able to ask me all about what happened yesterday.

"You okay, Mom? Anything wrong with the tarts?" I ask, barely able to keep the smile from my face as she squirms trying to think of a way to ask me the question she's been dying to for hours.

Nodding, she gives me a smirk as her dark blond hair falls into her eyes. She looks around for somewhere to set the tray down so she can push it off her face, so I reach out to take it from her.

"Here, I got that for you. You seem flustered today, Mom. Everything all right?"

When she finishes fixing her hair, she reaches out for the tray again, still looking like she wants to talk but doesn't know how to start the conversation. "I'm fine. How are you?"

There's her in.

"I'm good. Really good. You sure you're okay? Because it feels like you might want to talk about something, but you don't seem to say much every time you come back to my area here."

Now I can't stop myself from smiling. Teasing her is too much fun.

"Stop playing with me, Hailey Marie Canton. You know what I want to talk about. You've known all day while you let me twist in the wind trying to find a way to ask," she says, giving me her best angry Mom grimace complete with furious pursed lips and frustrated pulled in eyebrows that nearly meet in the center of her nose.

"Why didn't you just ask then?"

Her frown deepens, if that's possible. "Your father said I should let you bring it up. That's what I get for listening to his suggestions. Do you know he wanted to make tuna fish and have it as a Tuesday special? 'Tuna for Tuesday,' he said. Just crazy."

I listen to her go off on my father for a little bit and finally she stops to take a breath. "Don't the tarts need to go out to the case?" I ask.

"No. Well, yes, but they can wait."

"Okay. So what did you want to ask me then?"

Her frustration practically boils over, and she huffs, "Well, what happened with Cade, of course? You were upset yesterday and then you left with him and we didn't see you until you showed up here for work this morning. Did you two make up?"

Now my smile reflects my genuine happiness in being able to say we did. "Yes. He explained things, and I accepted his apology."

For the first time today, she smiles, and it seems

like all the stress drains from her body right in front of me. "Oh, that's good! I know you like spending time with him, honey. As long as you're happy, I'm happy. I think your father likes him too. He seemed genuinely pleased that Cade came over and you two were talking yesterday."

A laugh escapes from my throat after how he acted yesterday. "He gave him the angry dad face. I think he thought he was helping."

"Oh, that's your father's way of being a dad. He did that with your sisters too. Danielle used to tell him not to do it all the time. I swear every boyfriend she had got that look," she says, waving away the concern she thinks I have about my father trying to act all tough for me.

"He didn't have to, Mom. Cade's a good guy. It was just a misunderstanding. Everything's fine now."

"Good. I'm glad. Well, I better get these tarts out front," she says before hurrying off.

Calling after her, I say, "Be sure to tell Dad what we talked about. I'm sure he's dying to know."

From across the kitchen, Hector says, "That's all he could talk about yesterday. We all were worried about you."

He gives me a wink like he does whenever he says something sweet, and I smile back. I'm not a fan of having my private life spread all over the restaurant, but I know my father meant no harm. I know Hector and the rest of the cooks are just curious. How could they not be when my father probably spent the entire night talking about how worried he was?

They saw me at my worst when I first came back here to work a year ago. Then my parents watched over me like a baby bird, worried that at any minute I might give up on everything. To the people in the kitchen, I think I started out as some oddity and gradually became someone they cared about. It's only natural that they're interested in my life now that something's actually happening in it.

My mother rushes into the kitchen, her arms waving in front of her like something's on fire. I jump up from my chair as she runs up to me, unsure what could be wrong.

"Mom, what's happened?"

Her eyes wide and flashing with excitement, she says, "That food blogger who was on the morning show the other day is out talking to your father about your tarts! She's raving about them, Hailey!"

"Who? What morning show? The local one or the national one? What's her name, Mom?" I ask as my heart races in anticipation of my hearing who this woman is who loves my apple tarts so much.

"Brooke Dunning!" my mother answers, saying her name like I should know her.

"I don't know who that is, Mom."

"She's huge! I saw her on the local morning show, but they said she's a food blogger who's known around the world. You should go out to talk to her. She's just as nice as can be, and she's got the cutest hair. Go out and see."

I hurry to pull my apron over my head and brush myself off since I'm covered in flour from making the tarts. Oh, God! Why did I have to make such a simple dessert today? Apple tarts are so basic. Any fool with some flour and apples can make them. Why didn't I try the macarons I wanted to? They would have been so much better.

My mother tugs my arm to get me to move. "What are you waiting for, Hailey? Get out there and talk to her. I promise you she's very nice. Not conceited or pretentious at all like some of those foodies have been."

It suddenly dawns on me that Brooke Dunning, famous food blogger, is talking to my father, a man who sees no use for what she does and has nothing but disdain for people like her. At this very moment, he's probably lecturing her on why food blogger posts shouldn't include all that information about them and should focus on the restaurant, the chef, and the food, most of all. If I don't get out there right now, he'll likely chase her away with his bad attitude about what she's chosen to do with her life.

I rush toward the kitchen doors and suddenly stop to spin around to face my mother. "Do I look okay? Is there anything on my face that shouldn't be there?"

She gives me one of those wonderful smiles that

have always made everything okay. "You look beautiful, honey. Now go out there and impress her."

One deep breath in and out and I walk through the doors to find my father giving his talk on how important the restaurant is compared to any story about the food. I cringe at how long it took me to get out here and hurry over, hoping to stop him before he says something really insulting.

"Hi! Dad, I'm sure Brooke isn't interested in all this talk about how you'd write about food."

My father takes the hint, thankfully, and excuses himself so Brooke and I are left alone. Beautiful, with short black hair and stunning green eyes that remind me of a cat's, she's tall and willowy like a model. I'm instantly impressed and intimidated, all at the same time.

"Hailey, it's so nice to meet you. You are all anyone can talk about in this town when it comes to food, so I knew I had to make my way down here to Comfort Food to meet you and try one of your delectable desserts. I am absolutely in love with this apple tart! I've never had anything so light and yet so sweet in my life."

As she talks, she touches my forearms and I notice she has very long nails and they're painted in a French manicure. I can't imagine how she makes any dish with those things at the end of her fingers.

"It's so great to meet you too," I say, not as gushing as her but still very polite. "And thank you for saying such kind things about the tarts. I wish I knew you were coming today. I would have made something far more elaborate and special."

She waves her right hand through the air between us, those long nails flying past my nose. "No need. The most special food in the world is the kind that makes people feel good. That's what I always say. And those tarts of yours made me feel out of this world. I'll have to do three extra spin classes just to work off all those calories, but it was so worth it."

My gaze instinctively drops for a moment at her mention of calories, and I glance down at her flat stomach and tiny waist highlighted by the black belt on her red dress. Three extra spin classes might make her so thin she'll slip under the door.

I quickly look up and smile. "I'm so happy you enjoyed them. They're one of my favorite desserts to make."

For a second time, she waves her hand in the air in front of me, but this time the left-hand joins in. I gently lean back just an inch or so and give her a bigger smile as I hope she doesn't notice how uneasy those nails of hers make me.

"So let me get to the point of my visit. I want you to join me on my podcast. You're on the lips of every food blogger in this area, so while I'm here, I want to make sure I get you on with me. Now you should know I never take no for an answer—it's the secret to my success—so don't even think of saying anything but yes."

All I can think of at this moment is that single word she insists I say. Of course, I'd agree to do her podcast. I'd be crazy not to jump at this chance.

"I'd love to," I say as calmly as I can, struggling to keep my voice from quivering.

Brooke's eyes get wide, and she waves her hands yet again in between us. "Oh, that's fantastic! Now usually you can do a podcast from your house or anywhere for that matter, but since I'm in town and we can be together, I'd love for you to come to my hotel next Friday. We'll talk food, you can tell my listeners all about your favorites, and everyone will love it. Feel free to bring whatever desserts you want. I'll block off time for those extra spin classes on my calendar today because I'm going to try every one of the delectable treats you bring."

"Next Friday it is, then," I say as my mind races to figure out what I can find to make in the next eight days that will bowl her over and impress whoever might be listening to her podcast.

She hands me her business card and flips it over in my hand. "My number is on there, so call me the day before and I'll tell you my hotel and room number. My publicist has me in one I'm not crazy about at the moment, so I'm thinking that's got to change. It doesn't even have a restaurant inside! Can you believe that? Who would ever think to put me in a hotel without a restaurant?"

I don't get the chance to say a word in response before she wraps her arms around my shoulders and brings me in for a big, unexpected hug. "Next Friday. I can't wait. See you then!"

"See you then."

Rushing away toward the door, she stops right before she reaches it and turns around looking almost guilty. "Any chance I can get another one of those apple tarts? I simply love them!"

"Of course! Let me grab you one," I say before hurrying over to the case and picking out two of the best-looking tarts.

When I hand her the bag, she beams a smile and leans in to whisper in my ear, "This is going to mean four more spin classes, but it will be so worth it."

And then she walks away out the door, my apple tarts with her, and jumps into a black car before leaving as I stand there in the middle of my parents' little restaurant in shock at what's just happened. I don't get long to let it sink in before my mother and father rush out from the kitchen to ask me a million questions.

"We were watching through the window. She seemed so nice, Hailey. Did she take more tarts with her when she left?" my mother asks, practically breathless with excitement.

"She did. I gave her two more, and she had already had one with Daddy before I came out."

My father nods like he approves of all he's seen today. "She seemed very interested in your desserts. I think she must eat a lot of sugar to be that enthusiastic."

That gets my father a disapproving slap on the arm from my mother. "Robert! She was enthusiastic because of our daughter's fantastic apple tarts."

I don't bother adding that I think Brooke Dunning might be naturally hyper with a healthy dose of caffeine and sugar mixed in. Four spin classes to work off two apple tarts does seem like a bit much.

"She wants me to appear on her podcast next Friday. We're going to do it in her hotel. She said I should bring some of my desserts. What should I make? Maybe I could perfect the macarons before then, but they aren't elaborate or anything. Then again, she did say that food doesn't have to be elaborate. It just has to make someone feel good, and they would do the trick there. No, she said that about special food. Maybe. I don't know. It all happened so fast."

I don't know why, but now I feel like waving my hands around like Brooke did. I don't have beautiful nails like hers, so I wouldn't be putting anyone in danger of losing an eye either.

My mother wraps her arms around me in a hug I sense is probably her way of trying to calm me down.

Ever since I fell apart last year, if she thinks I'm unraveling even the slightest bit, she likes to hold me. It does help, but I'm not freaking out right now.

I'm just happy.

"It's okay, Mom. I'm good. Just excited. So many good things are happening right now."

Leaning back, she smiles at me before kissing my cheek. "All things you absolutely deserve."

"So what are you going to do now? You can't sit in that kitchen all day after having that kind of thing happen," my father says with a chuckle. "Seems like the kind of thing a young woman would want to tell a certain guy."

I feel my cheeks heat up at his thinly veiled mention of Cade. "I will. First, though, I have to tell Meadow. She's been predicting something big would happen ever since that first food blogger came in here and wrote about my desserts."

"Okay, honey. It's only right you remember the people who were there with you when you were nobody just starting out," he says, teasing me. "You will remember us little people when you hit the big time, won't you?"

Rolling my eyes, I give his arm a gentle nudge with my elbow. "Funny, Dad."

"Congratulations, honey. I'm so proud of you."

I give him a kiss on the cheek and head back to the kitchen to call Meadow. Ten minutes and nearly a dozen shrieks of excitement later, she makes me promise to tell her everything that happens with Brooke Dunning.

"It won't be as exciting as what you told me about Cade, but I'm here for any and all good news with you, Hailey. Promise me we'll go out to celebrate after you do her podcast. We have a lot to celebrate lately."

"I promise. I just hope I don't mess it all up. I've never done a podcast. What if I freeze and can't remember what to talk about?"

With a laugh, she says, "From what you told me about that Brooke woman, you will have to fight to get a word in edgewise. Don't worry. You're going to be great."

"Thanks, Meadow. I'll let you know how it goes as soon as I get done at her hotel room." I start to say goodbye, but then I remember she hasn't said anything about Alex yet.

"Hey, did you ever get to meet up with Alex that night we went to Club X? I feel bad about the fact that you had to rush me out of there and didn't get to even see him."

She lets out a sigh of frustration. "We've tried a few times, but our schedules aren't helping any. I'm not giving up on getting together with him yet, though," she says with her usual determination. "That man is way too hot to let work get in the way. But I have to go now. I want all the details on the food lady's podcast and your adventures with her as soon as it happens, so don't forget."

"I won't. Thanks, Meadow."

"You deserve it, Hailey. The podcast and how much fun you're having with Cade. Remember that."

As I call the man himself, I think about how hard it would have been to imagine so much good coming to me just six months ago. I don't know if I deserve it, like Meadow says, but I like it.

Actually, I love it.

CHAPTER TWENTY-SEVEN

*H*ailey

AFTER NEARLY AN HOUR SITTING IN THE PASSENGER seat of Cade's car wearing a blindfold, I think I might be getting carsick. Between all the starts and stops and his tendency to drive fast, my body doesn't know what to do from one second to the next.

"Not to ruin whatever you're doing with this surprise, but if I don't look out the window and get my bearings, I think I might get sick."

Cade touches my hand resting on my leg and gives my fingers a gentle squeeze. "I promise. Only a little while more. I want you to be surprised. You asked me to help you get away for a few days before your big meeting, and that's exactly what we're doing."

I turn to face where I think he is and smile. "If I could just lift this blindfold for a second, I think I might be okay. I had no idea not being able to see where I'm going would do this to me."

"Just a couple minutes more. I promise."

The feel of his touch on my hand helps, but something about this blindfold and moving makes my stomach turn. Not exactly the way I wanted to start out this three-day vacation we're taking.

When I called Cade and told him about Brooke Dunning and her podcast, I began to unravel, just as my mother worried I would. Nothing too bad. Certainly nothing like what happened last year. But enough that I asked Cade if we could do something to take my mind off things for a couple days. I thought he'd suggest we hang out at his place, but he came up with the idea of going to a hotel and relaxing like a little mini-vacation.

How could I say no? It sounded perfect, and with him there with me, I knew it would be just what I need. So I whipped up a few batches of cherry turnovers, enough to last the time that I'll be gone, and told my parents I'd see them in a few days.

Now, however, I'm struggling not to throw up all over the inside of Cade's car because of this blindfold he insists I wear to keep where we're going a complete surprise.

"Okay, you can take it off. We're here!" he says

with so much excitement in his voice that I practically rip the thing off my head.

I focus my eyes to see a sea green and white house with three floors looming in front of me. When we get out of the car, I see the house is even bigger up close.

Turning my head to the sound of a boat behind us, I see water as I look through the side yard. "Where are we? I thought you said we were going to a hotel for a few days."

Cade cups my elbow with his hand and guides me toward the house in front of me. "I was going to do that, but then I heard of somewhere even better. Welcome to the newest house owned by Alexandria March. I think she's thinking of calling it something like Cupid's Cove. When you meet her, you'll understand why that makes sense."

We walk through the front door and begin to climb the white painted steps toward the second floor. "Alexandria March? Is Alex named after her?"

Behind me, Cade laughs. "Yep. My mother and his mother, my aunt Olivia, were pregnant at the same time. Both of them were thinking of naming us Alexander after her, but they finally decided he would get that name, even though he was born three months after me. I got the consolation prize of having Alexander as my middle name, though."

I look back at him as we near the top of the steps and ask, "Is his middle name Cade then?"

He stops when we reach the second floor and

thinks for a moment. "I don't think so, but I just realized now I don't think I know what Alex's middle name is. If his brother wasn't named after their father, I'd guess Cassian, but he is, so I don't know."

"Maybe Oliver after his mother?" I ask, half-joking.

Cade shrugs. "Maybe. So what do you think of the place?"

For the first time, I look at the home he's brought me to and nearly have trouble catching my breath. The pale blue painted room seems to go on forever, and there are windows everywhere so you can see out onto the water. It might be the prettiest room I've ever stood in.

"It's beautiful, Cade. This is your grandmother's home?"

He sets down our bags on a nearby table and shakes his head. "No. Just one she bought. She's all about real estate. She's pretty much the reason I bought my condo. When I first started getting my trust fund, she sat me down and told me all the reasons she thinks a home is the most important thing a person can own. I had no intentions of buying a condo before that, but she convinced me. I think this is her third home on the island here."

"Where are we? I don't think I've ever been to this island in my life."

Waving me over to him, he takes my hand and

begins to walk toward the windows. "Anna Maria Island. She says it's her favorite place on earth."

"And she doesn't have a problem with the two of us spending the next few days here?" I ask as the image of an old woman coming at me with a rolling pin in her hand for sleeping in the same bed as her grandson flashes through my mind.

My question makes him throw his head back and laugh. "No way. My grandmother had to deal with three sons who were nothing but trouble when they were my age. She's the one who suggested we use this place until she figures out what she wants to do with it. She basically collects houses. She also likes to spoil all of her grandchildren rotten. So you don't have to worry."

As I look out onto the blue water below, I can't believe how beautiful this view is or that I'm standing here with Cade getting to enjoy it. "This is incredible. Thank you so much for bringing me here. I just wanted to relax for a couple days before I have to go do Brooke Dunning's podcast. I know it doesn't sound like much, but it made me get a little crazy there for a minute or two, and that's why I asked you to help me get away. I never expected anything like this, Cade. I would have been happy with a couple nights at your condo or even a motel on the side of the highway."

Nuzzling my neck, he moves behind me and wraps his arms around my shoulders. I love when he holds me like this every time we look out at the water off his balcony. Here it feels even better because he made this happen just for me.

"I don't think I've ever seen the Gulf look so good, you know that?" he says in a soft voice near my ear.

"I didn't even know that was the water I was looking at. I thought maybe it was some bay. You're so lucky to have this in your life. You really are. Your family must be really incredible to let you enjoy this."

He chuckles low in my ear before kissing my neck. "Some of them are, but what I'm lucky to have in my life is you."

The way he says that makes me feel so safe and loved. I missed this feeling all those months when I hid away and swore I'd never take a chance on another relationship and another guy again.

Covering his hands with mine, he tells me about how when he was a little boy, he and his cousins would come to this island and play on the beach building sandcastles and burying one another in the sand. The way he talks about growing up like that makes me hopeful I'll get to meet more of his family other than Alex. So far, if he's any indication of what the rest of the March clan is like, I can't see why I won't adore all of them.

"You sound like you had a great childhood," I say, looking back at him.

He thinks about that for a second and nods. "Some of it was really great. I didn't have any brothers, but I had Alex who was like a twin brother since we were born three months apart and my cousins were like brothers. I think if you said that to my sister she might have a different opinion since there are no other girls, though. Well, except for my uncle Kane and aunt Abbi's daughter, but she's older than the rest of us so by the time we were old enough to play together, she was in high school and couldn't be bothered with us."

"So your cousins are all close in age with you?"

Cade rests his chin on my shoulder as he explains, "Four boys born within three years' time. My family pretty much exploded in thirty-six months. Then my uncle Kane decided he wanted to adopt Wilder after all he'd been through, so by the time we all were teenagers, there were five of us. Trust me, we were the terrors of our high school. Be glad you didn't meet me or Alex back then. You'd never speak to either of us again."

The way he says that doesn't scare me off but intrigues me, so I turn my back on the beautiful scene of the Gulf late in the afternoon and look up at him. "I bet you guys were heartbreakers. Way too cute for your own good and way too cocky for everyone else's good."

Cade gives me a sexy smile that never fails to make me think he's even more gorgeous than he was the last time I looked at him. "Times the cockiness by ten. I'm not sure you'd call us heartbreakers, though. More like bumbling fools who thought they were way too slick for high school. Trust me, you shouldn't be surprised if we're out in public one day and some woman walks right up to me and slaps me across the face. I may not even remember her, but with the way we were, I probably have it coming in spades."

"Why would anyone do that?" I wonder aloud, sure this incredible guy who did all of this for me just because I asked couldn't deserve that kind of treatment.

For a moment, he bites his bottom lip like he isn't sure he wants to tell me just how bad he and his cousins were back then. "Well, let's just say the five of us had reputations for being less than wonderful guys at times and leave it at that."

The image of Cade being a bad boy doesn't really force me to stretch my mind much, but that doesn't bother me. Who he was before he met me, even if he was that person just days before, doesn't matter. It's who he is now I care about, and today, he's the man who brought me to this beautiful home overlooking the Gulf of Mexico to relax with him for the next few days.

I press my palms against his chest and stand on my tiptoes to kiss him. "Thankfully, no one holds who we were in high school against us."

With a wink, he says with a grin, "Except that woman who slaps me across the face one day. She's going to be holding a lot against me."

More relaxed than I've been in so long I can't remember, I rest my head on his chest and let out a heavy sigh. These past two weeks have been incredible and devastating and then incredible again. Everything seems to be going my way these days.

So, of course, I'm worried that right around the corner some horrible nightmare is going to come into my life and ruin everything.

Cade's fingers slowly slide through my hair while I listen to his heartbeat lull me into a state I'd only dreamed of before meeting him. Never in my life have I felt so safe, so protected, and secure. Other women may want the bad boy he probably was before, but not me. I love the feeling of his arms around me as we stand together silently, only the sound of our breathing interrupting the quiet.

"You aren't falling asleep on me, are you?" he whispers against the top of my head.

I smile against his chest and answer, "No. I don't think I can fall asleep standing up. I'm just loving how relaxed and calm I feel at this moment. Like the world outside can't touch us, and we're safe and sound right here."

His hand cups the back of my head and tilts it back so I'm looking up at him as he stares down at me with dark eyes full of concern. "You're always safe with me, Hailey. I promise that. I won't let anyone hurt you, not even me. I swear."

"I believe you. And I didn't feel safe because we're alone. It's just that this place is so peaceful. Everyday life has no solitude, and when you wrapped your arms around me and I put my head on your chest, I felt more at peace than I can ever remember. You have no idea how much I appreciate that."

He presses a soft kiss to my forehead and lets his lips linger against my skin for a moment before whispering, "I like that I bring you peace. That makes me feel good."

When I close my eyes, I try to think of another human being who has ever made me feel the way Cade does. First he terrified me. Then he intrigued me. When we finally got together, he thrilled me.

And then that night at the club, what I saw shattered me.

But then he did what no one has ever done before with me. He made me want to believe in him again. Believe in us again.

I'm glad I didn't listen to my head when I saw him standing there in the restaurant the other day. All my brain could say was he couldn't be trusted, that he's like all other men.

My heart had a different story to tell. That one said to give him another chance.

This time, my heart was right.

CHAPTER TWENTY-EIGHT

ade

HAILEY SITS BACK ON THE CHAISE LOUNGE NEAR THE pool, and I watch her for a moment as the last yellows and pinks and purples of the sunset fade away. When she told me how relaxed this place made her feel, all I could think about was how I could make her life like that all the time.

I've never felt this way about another soul in the world before her. It's why I can't help but just watch her in the hope that I'll somehow figure out how in such a short time I went from who I was without her to who I am with her.

No wonder my family was betting I'd never find anyone. I barely recognize that Cade from a couple weeks ago. That guy would never have thought to bring a woman here just to spend time together.

Why bother doing that when I have a perfectly good condo with a perfectly good bed?

Yet the moment Hailey asked if we could hang out for a few days so she could stay calm and not freak out about this meeting with that big food blogger, the first thing that popped into my head was taking her away to somewhere quiet and out of town so the two of us could be alone. It was like that was the most natural reaction in the world.

She felt like she was starting to spiral out of control, so I wanted to do whatever I could to stop it. I didn't even think twice.

"Are you watching this gorgeous sunset?" she asks before turning her head to look over at me. "I swear everything in this place is perfect."

"It's like someone painted it for us," I say as I make my way around the pool deck to where she sits.

"Do you want to go swimming?" She giggles and then says, "We could go skinny dipping."

I love how open she is when she says things like that. Looking down at her lying there in her blue tank top and jean shorts, I wonder if any of the neighbors are home.

"Hailey is a skinny-dipping girl. Well, now I've heard everything."

She rolls her eyes at my teasing and sits up to kiss me. "I don't look like someone who'd skinny dip?"

I let my gaze roll over her and shake my head. "No, not really. You bake cookies and look too sweet for that."

Hailey's mouth drops open in shock. "And after all the great sex we've had, you pull that cookie baking good girl thing on me?"

"That's true. Okay, I take it back. You do look like a skinny-dipping chick."

She stands up from the chaise lounge and unzips her shorts in front of me. As they fall to the ground, she says, "Well, I'm not because I've never skinny dipped before, but tonight I am. You joining me?"

Before I can get my answer out, she rips her shirt over her head and tosses it on top of her shorts. As I watch in complete surprise, she sheds her bra and panties and then she's standing in front of me and the entire Gulf naked.

"You're way behind, Cade. Catch up. Skinny dipping isn't a solitary sport, you know," Hailey says with a giggle before jumping into the pool.

I don't need to be told twice to get naked for a beautiful woman, so I quickly strip out of my clothes and jump into the water. It's cooler than I expected, but it doesn't take long to get accustomed to it.

"So now we're both skinny dipping people. I think that's one step away from swingers, you know," she says with a playful grin as I make my way over to her.

I kiss her wet lips and smile against them. "I'm not

sure I'm ready to be a swinger. That's a whole lifestyle. I think it requires special furniture."

"And special clothes. Easy on and easy off so you don't get caught unprepared when someone wants to get busy," she says so adorably.

Her body presses up against mine, the water lapping around us as we tread water. "You seem to have put some thought into this whole swinger thing. I'm not sure how I feel about sharing you with other guys."

Hailey wraps her arms around my neck and kisses me long and deep. "Mmmm...actually, there's a guy at the restaurant who says he's a swinger, but his hair is all greasy and he combs it over to hide his bald spot, so he might just be saying that."

I can't stop myself from making a face full of disgust just thinking about that greasy guy banging bunches of women. Gross. He's probably in his sixties and hoping to just get some by bragging to someone like Hailey.

Pressing her breasts against me, she nudges her pussy against my cock. "And as for sharing me with other guys," she says and then runs her tongue along the seam of my mouth, "my vote is no on that and that goes twice as much the other way with you and other women. I don't share well with others."

I slide my hands down her back to cup her ass and pull her into me even more. My cock is as hard as steel and getting harder with every time she rolls her hips.

"Good, because I wasn't happy with the idea of you and anyone but me. Glad we got that settled."

She reaches down between us to grip my cock and strokes from base to head once and then twice before kissing me again. "No way I'm sharing this with another woman. No way, no how."

I've had enough foreplay, so I lift her out of the water and position her at the perfect height so I can slide my cock inside that perfect cunt of hers. She looks down at me like some goddess straight from the sea, and when I lower her down onto me, she narrows her eyes to give me that sexy look I love to see when I'm inside her.

"Is your grandmother going to be mad that we're having sex in her pool?" she asks with such innocence to her voice that it feels wrong to be fucking her.

Moving toward the side of the pool, I shake my head. "I don't plan on telling her, to be honest."

I feel the cool tile wall against the base of my spine, so I lean back to brace myself. Hailey rolls her hips again, taking every inch of me, and wraps her legs around my waist.

"Why do I have the feeling you've done this whole pool sex thing before?" I ask and then thrust my hips forward to fill her.

She shakes her head and smiles. "Mmmm...no. Remember? This is my first time skinny dipping. I did read about it, though. You?"

At the moment, I can't think about anything but

how good she feels riding my cock with all this water sloshing around between us, so I give her a noncommittal shrug and focus on fucking her. I don't want to remember whoever I had sex with in some guy's pool in high school. None of that means anything to me now.

I pull her mouth to mine and kiss her as every cell in my body screams how fucking good this feels. Her breasts bounce up and down in the water and rub against my skin to send a wave of sensation through me.

Stuffing my hands in her wet hair, I tug hard and she makes a moaning sound into my mouth that I swear goes straight to my cock. "Mmmm...baby, you are the perfect skinny dipper."

Suddenly, Hailey stops moving, and I open my eyes to see her staring up at the deck, her eyes wide and full of something that looks like she's seen a ghost. "Cade—"

She doesn't get another word out before a voice behind me says, "I guess we stopped in at a bad time."

A second later, I spin my head around to see Wilder and two of his friends standing there staring down at us like some kind of asshole Peeping Toms. Hailey practically crawls beneath me to hide, so I push her against the wall of the pool and cover her with my body as I stand up to my full height.

"What are you doing here, Wilder?" I ask, barely able to hide my disgust at seeing him standing there.

"Just came over to hang out for a little while. My father said the place was empty, so he didn't see why it would be a problem," he answers in his usual snide tone.

"Well, your father was wrong, obviously. Why don't you and your friends go back the way you came in? We're here for the next few days."

I look down and see Hailey cringing at every moment she has to stand there naked. "Cade, who are these people?"

"My cousin and his friends," I say to her and then look back up at Wilder. "And they're leaving. Now."

One of his friends who looks a little older than me cranes his neck to look down into the pool and grins. "I'm always up for a gang bang. What about you guys?"

Barely able to contain my rage on most occasions with my cousin, now I want to tear his head off and both his buddies' heads. "Get them the fuck out of here, Wilder. And try finding a better class of friends than a scumbag like that one."

The asshole with the smart mouth starts to cock off, but Wilder understands now's not the time to be playing with me. I don't care if I have to climb out of this fucking water buck naked and kick their asses before I dry off. No punk ass friend of my least favorite cousin is going to talk about my girlfriend like that.

I glare up at Wilder, and it doesn't take long before

he gets the idea. "Let's go. We can hang out somewhere else."

Both of his friends take one last look at Hailey and me and shrug before walking away. When they're all inside, I look down at her and let out a heavy sigh. "And that's Wilder, the world's worst cock block, ladies and gentleman. I'm sorry about that. He's bad enough, but his friends are always pure assholes. Are you okay?"

"I'm fine. I just didn't know what to do when I saw them standing there watching us," she says. "So that's another one of your family members? I hope you don't mind me saying I like Alex better than this one."

Nodding, I can't disagree with that. "Everyone does. Alex is a good time. Wilder's nothing but sulky bullshit and trouble."

With a smile, she says, "Not that I got a really good look before you hid me away, thank you very much for that, by the way, but he doesn't look like you and Alex. I think I just assumed you guys would all look alike."

I hear the downstairs door finally slam shut and breathe a sigh of relief. I didn't have beating the hell out of Wilder and his jackass friends with my dick hanging out on my schedule today.

"That's because he's adopted, although, he sort of looks a little like my uncle Kane, strangely enough. Most of us look like Alex and me. Brown hair, brown eyes, you know—like us. But Liam and Cash look like that side of the family with dark hair and blue eyes. It's just a coincidence that Wilder looks like them, I guess. Enough talking about him. Let's get back to what we were doing."

As I move to nuzzle Hailey's neck, she pushes me away, shaking her head. "I can't, Cade. That was definitely a mood killer."

Fucking Wilder. Add this to the million other reasons I can't stand him.

Trying not to sulk, I nod and force a smile. "I get it. Well, since they're gone, we can get out and dry off before we get something to eat. How's that sound?"

She cradles my face and kisses me sweetly, which only makes me want what she doesn't even more. "Thank you for understanding. That just freaked me out a little. Maybe it's because it's my first time skinny dipping?"

I can't help but laugh at how cute she is. Lifting her out of the pool, I let myself enjoy the view of her body with the water droplets rolling off her tan skin. Fucking Wilder and his friends.

"You were doing fine at your first time until my cousin loped in here. Blame it on him."

Hailey hands me a towel from the bin on the other side of the desk, and her eyes wander down my body before she looks up at me with a smile. "I was having a very good time. I hope you know that."

"I do."

"And I loved how you protected me and made

them go away. I was worried you might have to get out of the pool and fight them," she says with worry hanging off every word. "It would have been three-on-one."

"And me with my dick hanging out," I joke as I knot the towel at my hip. "But Wilder wouldn't have let it get that far. There's no love lost between the two of us, but he's part of the family, so he would have stopped his friends. Or I would have put on a show for you and hope you liked men who do their best ancient Greco-Roman wrestling imitation."

Hailey's eyes narrow, and she shakes her head. "Your what?"

"Nothing. Just something I saw on TV the other day. Back in ancient times, the men wrestled naked."

A look of surprise settles into her expression. "Really. Now I'm going to have that image in my head all night."

I pull her to me and kiss her, wishing we were still in the pool. "I think I'll try to give you something else to think about."

"Even better," she says, giving me one of those Hailey smiles that lights up her face and makes her so beautiful.

CHAPTER TWENTY-NINE

ade

BACKING OUT OF THE GARAGE FROM THE ISLAND house, I wish Hailey and I never had to leave this place. Other than my cousin and his asshole friends crashing our party that first night, we spent the next two days lying around adoring one another and having sex. That was it, except for a few times we got out of bed to put some food into our stomachs.

Hailey leans over and kisses me softly on the cheek. "Thank you for these last few days, Cade. They were just what I needed. Today, I'm going to go into the restaurant and I'm going to start making the best desserts I've ever made."

As we drive away, I thread my fingers through

hers and step on the gas. "And I'm going to bartend this weekend and wish I was sitting at the restaurant trying out all the desserts you're making."

"Do you have to work all weekend?"

I hear the disappointment in her voice come through loud and clear. I know how she feels. I'm disappointed I have to work too. I'd much rather spend my time eating cookies and cakes and then falling asleep with her next to me in bed.

Forcing a smile, I nod as I make a turn onto the main road. "All weekend. Sunday the club isn't open, but I know he's going to be having me do inventory or some damn thing." I look over at her as I bring her hand up to my mouth to kiss it. "But come Monday, I'll be at Comfort Food ready to see all those incredible desserts you came up with this weekend. I promise."

Like always, her face lights up when she talks about what she creates. "I really want to wow her on Friday. I hope I can come up with something amazing."

"You will, and then maybe you'll get people to start paying you what you deserve for your creations."

"Oh, I don't know about that. I just want more people to hear about my parents' restaurant and come in to help their business. That's why I do this. They've been so incredible all my life but especially this past year, Cade. I just want to help them out, and since this is the best way I know to do it, I want to show Brooke

Dunning how great the desserts are so she'll tell her fans to come to the restaurant."

I kiss her hand and smile over at her. "I know you will. Don't worry. You got this."

Worry comes off her in waves, though, so the whole way back home, I tell her stories about the March and Jackson clan and the trouble we all used to get into. Nothing makes people laugh more than the idiocy of teenage boys and the messes they cause, and at least for a little while, she doesn't think about all the importance she's put on this podcast with the food lady.

When I pull the car into the Comfort Food parking lot, I'm sorry we had to return to the city so soon. I could spend a month out at the island house, away from everything and everyone but her.

"Thanks for bringing me to the restaurant. I want to get started working on things immediately. Call me when you have time. I know you have to work, and you probably usually sleep late the day after, but when you have a chance…"

Gently pulling her to me, I kiss her lips to stop her from talking. "You don't have to worry. I'll wake up early to call. I got up early the other day to come over here to convince you to take me back, so I can do it again."

Hailey gives me a tiny smile and nods. "Okay. Should I tell you to have fun at work? Is it fun?" she asks with trepidation in her voice.

She's thinking about what she saw that night with Kylie. I need to do whatever I can to make her understand that is not what my job is supposed to be, and after that little talk with my father the other day, that won't be what my job is ever again.

I somberly shake my head. "It's anything but fun. I'd rather be with you on my balcony or anywhere else in the world with you instead of screaming over the music asking drunks what they want."

A tiny smile brightens her face. "Okay, then. Don't have fun. Save the fun for the next time I see you after the weekend," she says. "We'll do something fun on Monday night."

Her cheeks turn pink, and she adds, "Maybe I'll read a few chapters of one of my favorite books and see what I can come up with."

I love how sexy she is, even when she's talking about reading. Definitely the first time I've ever associated that with anything hot.

"Okay. You have fun this weekend. Love you."

Pressing her forehead to mine, she smiles. "I love you too. See you Monday!"

When she jumps out of the car and runs toward the front door of the restaurant, I watch her and can't help wish I didn't have to be stuck in the club tonight doing the thing I hate most in life. Just before she walks inside, she turns around and waves and then blows me a kiss.

I don't think any woman other than my mother has

ever blown me a kiss in my life. I instantly love it because it's from Hailey.

GRABBING MY PHONE, I CALL ALEX AS I'M LEAVING the parking lot. "Hey, where are you? Are you at work already or at your place?"

"I'm the early shift today, so I'm at work already. Why? I thought you and Hailey were hanging out at the Anna Maria Island house until later today," he says over the noise of the kitchen around him.

"We were, but we left early. She wants to get to work on what she's going to make for that blogger when she does her podcast next Friday, but I think fucking Wilder crashing in on us the first night freaked her out too."

Alex laughs like he always does when something frustrates me. I think he finds amusement in my unhappiness somehow.

"Wilder did what? Why did he go out there?" he asks over some whirring sound that reminds me of a broken drill.

"Dude, I can barely hear you. What the hell do you people do in that kitchen? I thought you cooked food. Why does it sound like you're standing in an auto body shop?" I ask as I head toward CK.

"Shit doesn't happen like magic, Cade," he snaps.

He gets like that when I comment on his job or how he performs it. So fucking touchy.

"Prep is noisy, man. What can I say?"

"Well, say you have a couple minutes to talk since I'm driving to the restaurant right now."

He doesn't say anything, but the ruckus in the background gets loud enough with some mixer now on that he finally yells into my ear, "Yeah, I can talk for a few. Come to the back door. Kane or my father will let you in since we aren't open yet."

Fifteen minutes later, I'm banging on that metal door for the third time and wondering if the noisy prep means no one will ever hear me out here. I pound my fist against the door one more time, and then it flies open to reveal Alex standing there looking irritated.

"What?" I ask as I walk by him. "I didn't think anyone heard me so I kept knocking."

Behind me, he mumbles, "It sounded like you were using a battering ram."

I look back at him and see his expression is miserable. His eyebrows are all drawn in toward his nose, and his frown looks like it's found a permanent place on his face. Alex isn't usually like this, even when he's peeved about me commenting on his job.

"What's up? You look like someone just ran over your best friend, which can't be the case since I'm standing here just fine."

He waves away my question, shaking his head as he pushes past me. "Nothing. So what happened with Wilder out at the house?"

I follow him to the kitchen, not sure how we're

going to talk now if we couldn't do it on the phone because of all the noise, but surprisingly, it doesn't sound like an auto body shop now. Alex points at a spot in the corner nearby and walks a few feet away to a metal table where what looks like a bushel of carrots waits for him.

"That's a lot of carrots," I say with a chuckle. "You guys getting a family of rabbits for lunch today?"

He simply rolls his eyes and picks up a knife to begin chopping the orange vegetables. "Fuck you. Now what happened with Wilder?"

Remembering his father could be anywhere nearby, I ask, "Where's Kane?"

Alex waves away yet another of my questions and gets back to chopping. "He left about ten minutes ago. You're fine."

"You know how he is about Wilder. I didn't want to get into that. As for our fantastic cousin, he brought two of his friends to the house and the fuckers walked right in and caught Hailey and me skinny dipping in the pool."

With a smile, Alex says, "I didn't have her pegged for a skinny dipping chick. I like that. So what happened when they saw you guys buck naked in the water?"

"The fuckers just stood there. One of them even fucking mentioned a gang bang. Asshole. I thought I was going to have to get out of the pool and fight them. Seriously, where does he find his friends? My car was parked out front. It's not like he doesn't know what I drive. He knew I was there and still came in with those two shitheads."

Looking over at me, Alex winces. "How did Hailey take all of this?"

"She was freaked out and rightfully so. Nothing like us having a good time and her looking up to see him and two guys staring down into the pool like we were giving the world a fucking peep show. I had to threaten them before he thought it was a good idea to leave."

After tossing the chopped up vegetables into a bowl, he pulls another pile of carrots in front of him and starts cutting them. "Sounds like him. I bet he didn't even ask Grandma before he just busted into the place. What were the three stooges planning to do there? Take a swim?"

I shake my head at that idea. "No way. Those two he was with looked like they were straight out of some dive. They were probably looking for some place to party. Two-million-dollar house and he brings that garbage to hang out there."

Behind me, a voice says, "You two finished talking shit, or do you want to continue?"

No sooner do the words filter through my brain, I'm spinning around to face Wilder himself. "Have a nice time the other night? Maybe I can invite you over to my place so you can watch my girlfriend and me fuck? Bring your friends and we can make it a party," I say with disgust just having to look at him.

"You mean like a gang bang? You didn't seem to be a fan the other night. Either did your girlfriend."

A second later, I lunge at him, slamming him into some metal rack that makes a horrible clanging noise when it crashes into the wall behind it. I've wanted to beat the hell out of this asshole for years, and that little crack is going to get him what he deserves.

What I've been holding back for far too long.

He's a little bigger than I am after his time in prison, but he isn't carrying the rage for me that I have for him. That I've had for so long I can barely see straight sometimes when I have to listen to everyone talk about how great it is that he's getting his life back together and how wonderful it is that he's making the most of his second chance.

Wilder is an asshole who gets away with all kinds of shit in our family and has all his life. Today, that ends, at least with me.

I get a few good punches in before he hits me hard in the side, taking most of the wind out of my lungs. Stunned, I stagger back, but my anger helps me regroup in only a second or two, not enough time for him to take advantage.

He moves to take my legs out from under me, but I grab him around his chest and push him back into the wall. The metal rack and the few utensils left hanging on it make that loud, clanging noise again, and I hear him grunt when he runs up against it.

I don't know when Cassian and Kane show up to pull us apart, but I feel someone's arms wrap around my shoulders and yank me off Wilder, and a second later, I look up to see Kane doing the same with his son.

"Cut it out!" Cassian barks in my ear. "Cut this shit out now, you two! What the hell are you doing brawling in my kitchen?" he asks.

Neither Wilder nor I answer his question. Instead, the two of us struggle to shake off the men holding us so we can get back to fighting.

"Enough!" Kane bellows. "That's enough!"

Behind me, Cassian angrily says in my ear, "You come with me. I want to talk to you."

Reaching out to grab Wilder as my uncle pushes me out of the kitchen, I snap, "I'm not done with him yet. Get off me! Let me go!"

Cassian tightens his hold on me and forces me out into the hallway and down to the office he shares with Kane. He kicks the door open and thrusts me into the room before pointing at the chair next to his desk.

"Don't say one fucking word until I sit down. My head is pounding, and it isn't even noon yet."

CHAPTER THIRTY

ade

WHEN HE FLOPS DOWN ONTO HIS CHAIR, CASSIAN takes a deep breath in and lets it out slowly, like he needs to calm himself down before we have this talk he so desperately wants to have with me. After a few seconds, I begin to speak, but he holds up his hand and shakes his head, a clear sign he isn't ready yet.

"Not one fucking word."

"You're already sitting down. I figured I could start talking now."

His blue eyes flash an anger rarely seen in my uncle recently. "Don't be a smart ass. You know what I meant."

"Actually, I don't know why I'm here getting this

treatment while that asshole is probably out in the dining room having a little snack to soothe his feelings."

Cassian takes another breath in and lets it out before asking, "What is with you two? You nearly came to blows on Labor Day last year, and at Christmas your grandmother thought the two of you were going to tear up her living room. This is the third time one of us has had to step in and separate you two. So what's going on?"

My heartbeat begins to slow down and return to normal now that the adrenaline isn't pumping through my body. Sagging in my chair, I look away, not wanting to have this conversation with this uncle or anyone else.

"Maybe you shouldn't separate us, and we can see how that goes."

"What is going on, Cade? All of you boys used to hang out in school. You never fought then. What's happened in the past year to make you two always want to be at each other's throats?" Cassian asks, genuinely not knowing why I've had a problem with Wilder for a long time.

Long before he showed up and he and his friends acted like dicks to Hailey.

I turn to look at my uncle and see real concern in his expression. Always the brother who wanted a big, happy family, he's bothered when any of us don't get along. By the look in his eyes now, I have a feeling he's really freaked out by what he just saw.

He has no idea how long it was in coming.

"As for why he has a problem with me, I have no idea. I haven't had a conversation with him since like eleventh grade. So you're going to have to ask him about that. As for me, my problem with Wilder is what it's been since we were kids. This past year just brought it into sharper focus."

Cassian nods, but I doubt he knows what's going on. He probably thinks it has to do with Wilder getting sent away for a year. I don't care about that. People do stupid things like stealing stuff. Wilder has always done things like that. He just happened to get caught this time.

And just as I guessed, my uncle quietly asks, "Is this about him going to jail? Everybody makes mistakes, Cade. He's family. We're supposed to support him now that he's out."

Just hearing that same tired excuse for that shithead's bad behavior makes me want to throw up. "To be honest, Cassian, I don't care about that. It was pretty inevitable that Wilder was going to end up in jail at some point or another. I mean, come on. He was trouble from the minute he showed up in our family. Was anyone really surprised that he got caught stealing money from someone? Really? But I don't care about that. What pisses me off is he always gets a fucking pass. He fails a grade? Oh, he'll do better next year, and we all have to support him. He gets in trouble with the cops the first time? Oh, well he's had a troubled life. He gets in trouble with the cops the next five times? Same excuse. Every goddamned time it's 'he's had a rough life.' Fuck that. He's had a charmed life with Kane and Abbi, and I don't know why anyone wants to pretend otherwise."

The shocked look on my uncle's face tells me he had no idea I harbored these feelings for my cousin. Oh, well. Now the truth is out. I'm sure he'll try to give me some lecture on how Wilder's life has been so tough, but I'm not buying it.

"What is all of this really about, Cade? You don't care for your cousin, but not because of him getting in trouble or even that we all are probably a little too easy on him. But that's not what this is about, is it?"

Part of me wants to stand up, toss this chair I'm sitting on across the room, and storm out of this place since he just admitted what I've known forever, and it doesn't seem to bother him. But another part of me is finally ready to say what's been on my mind about Wilder and his bullshit.

Congratulations, Cassian March. You're the lucky guy who gets to hear what I have to say today. Buckle up. It's going to get pretty fucking wild from this point on.

I lean forward toward his desk and take a deep breath, but not to calm myself down like he did a few minutes ago. I need that air in my lungs so I can get all these fucking words out I've been holding in for what feels like forever.

"You know what this is all about? I've been busting my balls being everything I was supposed to be, and when I want to take some time to figure out just what the fuck I want to do with my life, I get nothing but grief about it. Wilder, on the other hand, gets to screw up time after time after time, and nobody gives him a hassle about a single goddamned thing."

My uncle opens his mouth to say something, but I'm not done yet, so I hold up my hand to stop him. "I got great grades in high school and never failed a damn class. He failed a whole entire grade. But did anyone give him a moment's grief about it? Nope. When I graduated, I was expected to go to college, but he gets a pass because everyone is just happy he got out. I go to a top rate school and do well for four years. And what did he do in that time? He got caught stealing and got sent to prison. So then last year the two of us were fresh off college and doing time. Has he spent the last year being asked what he's going to do with his life? Is he expected to hold down even a part-time job? No on both counts."

And now comes the part that pisses me off the most.

"I never fucked up the way he did. Never. Yet I get the 'Cade, you need to have a job or you'll lose everything' speech from my father, while that son of a bitch gets to do exactly what he wants to do or doesn't

329

want to do, and nobody says a damn word to him. That's why he can bust up into the island house the other night with his two lowlife friends he probably met in jail while I'm there with my girlfriend and he has to be fucking told to leave. So yeah, it's not really about one thing. It's about a lifetime of things that he's gotten away with while I don't get a damn pass on anything."

When the last word comes out of my mouth, it feels like a ten ton weight has been lifted off me. I lean back against the chair and take another deep breath, blowing it out in a rush a second later.

That felt good. All of it. Saying what's on my mind. Not holding back. Everything.

Cassian looks like he's been slapped across the face when I finish, leaning back in his own chair like he needs to increase the space between us just in case I start talking again. He doesn't have to worry. I've got nothing more to say about the subject of my cousin and how goddamned easy he's had it all his life.

"Cade, I had no idea you were dealing with so much," he says quietly, like he's in shock after what I just told him. "I know your father means well, but I don't think he realizes the pressure he's put on you all this time."

I shake my head, not willing to let my father take the blame for everything this time. "It's not that, though. I never cared about his expectations. Well, not until recently now that he's shanghaied me back into service at the club. But it never bothered me that I was expected to do well in school and go to college and do well there too. All of us dealt with that. Alex wasn't given a pass on anything by you and Olivia. Neither was Cash. Liam either, which is strange since he's got the same parents as Wilder. It wasn't just me who was expected to do something, but then you look at how he's gotten away with so much and doesn't have to deal with a single thing, other than when the state decided he needed to do some time for taking that money. This isn't about my father and me. It's about two men with a single year yet only one of them has to get his life entirely planned out while the other has all the freedom in the world."

"He did have a rough start, Cade. His mother overdosed when he was five, and if it hadn't been for Kane and Abbi, he would have been on a path to surely repeat his mother's mistake."

I point across the desk at him when he proves exactly what I've been talking about. "That. That right there. He was five when that happened. Since then, he's been with our family and gotten to enjoy all the good stuff the rest of us have. When exactly does something that happened to him twenty years ago stop being an excuse for the rest of his life?"

Cassian hangs his head, unable to answer that question just like everyone else in our family. "I'm sorry you're unhappy working for your father, Cade. For what it's worth, I don't think he intends it as a punishment. I don't think he'd want your life to be unhappy like this."

"You don't get it. I'm not unhappy. I have a girlfriend I'm crazy about. I love my condo and my car. My best friend, who is probably still stunned I tried to go all MMA in his kitchen, and most of my family are great. So I'm happy. I just have a hard time swallowing the insistence that I figure out what I want to do with the rest of my life when Wilder, who is two years older than me and has already done time, gets to live life how he wants and bust up a night with my girlfriend at the island house with his two scumbag friends because he has no responsibilities."

"I'm not going to ask what happened there. Just tell me your grandmother's house doesn't look like the wreck you made of the kitchen a few minutes ago," Cassian says in a voice full of worry to match the panicked expression he's giving me.

The way he makes it seem like Wilder and I are the same kind of man pisses me off. I fold my arms across my chest and shake my head as I push down the urge to tell my favorite uncle to fuck off.

"I wouldn't do that to Grandma's house, Cassian. Can you say the same for him?"

He doesn't answer, which tells me all I need to know. He isn't blind to what Wilder is. Good. Now maybe he can act like it from now on.

Standing to leave, I look toward the door for the first time, remembering that Kane is nearby and might have heard everything I said. Too bad. I'm tired of pretending just for family unity and peace.

Cassian looks up at me and tries to give me a sympathetic smile. "Do you want me to talk to your father? He probably doesn't realize any of this is happening with you, so it might help if I spoke to him."

"Not necessary. My father knows perfectly well how I feel about being back at Club X. And just so everyone in this family doesn't get it wrong about me, I'm not there because I'm lazy or I can't get another job. I don't know what I want to do, but since my father demanded I work at something or lose everything that's mine, I chose to go back there. I hate it, but I don't have another choice right now."

My uncle doesn't say anything for a long moment, but then a smile lifts the corners of his mouth until he gives me a big Cassian March grin that could charm the birds out of the trees. "I sometimes forget how much you're like Stefan. I can't tell you how many times he said something very similar about your uncle back when he was close to your age. You might even find he agrees with you when it comes to Wilder. He just can't see it because he's too busy being your father."

"Well, feel free to clue him into that. I don't need you to talk to him about me or what I'm doing with my life, though. He knows already. He sees me five nights a week behind the main bar."

"Do you mind me giving you some advice I gave your father all those years ago?"

The last thing I want is advice about anything concerning how I feel about Wilder at this moment, but since I doubt it would matter if I said no, I merely give him a noncommittal shrug. I know how this family works. If he doesn't say it to me, I'm likely to get a call from someone else looking to share their wisdom about this topic with me. Better to hear it from Cassian since I like him the most out of nearly everyone, except his sons.

"Don't let resentment about this eat you up. It will steal your happiness, and you don't deserve to have that happen."

I look down at him, unconvinced he ever said that to his younger brother. "You told my father that? In those words?"

He laughs and leans back in his chair. "Well, I probably sprinkled in a few expletives and called him a name or two, but it was basically the same sentiment."

"And what was his response?" I ask, now curious about how that little talk went compared to how I'm feeling right now.

"I don't recall specifically what he said, but I imagine it involved telling me to fuck off or to mind my own business. You know your father when he gets hot about something."

"That I do," I say as I move to leave.

"Come back again," he says as I head toward the door. "But next time, don't bust up my kitchen, okay?"

I give him a nod and force a smile for my favorite uncle. "I'll see what I can do."

If Wilder's there, I can't promise anything. Just because I admitted how pissed off he gets me doesn't mean I won't want to take a swing at him the next time he shows up in front of my face.

CHAPTER THIRTY-ONE

$\mathcal{H}$ailey

ALL WEEKEND, I TRIED OUT NEW RECIPES IN MY quest to find the very best desserts to show off to Brooke Dunning. The Boston Cream Whoopee Pies with chocolate glaze turned out incredible, so they definitely made the cut. The coconut and pistachio meringue cookies didn't end up as good, though, but I might try again this week before I meet her on Friday. My tried-and-true key lime pie came through like always, but I'm not sure I want to take something so commonplace to a meeting with a nationally known food blogger.

All of this fills my head on Monday afternoon when my phone rings with a call from Cade. Thrilled to speak to him for the first time since Saturday afternoon, I quickly answer and start talking without even saying hi.

"Wait until you see what I came up with! I'm still working on a couple more, but I saved you a whoopee pie you're going to love."

"I hope it can keep until tomorrow afternoon. I have to fill in for Katelyn tonight," he says, sounding disappointed.

And I have to make it worse when I tell him I can't see him then either. "I have to work on these every day, Cade. I'm sorry. How about Tuesday night?"

"She can't work until Thursday, so that's the first night I'll be off. Any chance that pie is going to be good three days from now?"

"Probably not," I sulk. "But I have to make more for Friday, so I can save you one of those. I'm going to miss you this week."

"Me too, Hailey. I miss you already, and it's only been a couple days since I've seen you."

He sounds so down that I want to do something to cheer him up. "Well, think about what you want to do on Thursday night, and we'll go all out. Whatever you want. I'm going to need something to take the stress away because I'm probably going to be pretty strung out by then. I just hope I find some more desserts that work."

I hear a smile in his voice when he says, "You will. Don't worry. As for Thursday, we're probably not going to leave the bedroom. I miss you so much already."

My cheeks heat up as I blush at the thought of how much I wish we could be together right now. "I'm fine with that. We just have to make sure we bring in some drinks. Hydration is key in marathons," I say with a giggle.

"I'll stock up on some because I'm going to be in marathon mode by the time Thursday rolls around."

"Good. That'll make two of us."

I sense unhappiness creep into our conversation again when he falls silent, but before I can try to cheer him up with a funny story about how one of my chocolate creations blew up in my face, covering me from my neck up in melted chocolate, he clears his throat and says, "I have to go. Katelyn shows up earlier than I do because she handles the upkeep of the main bar usually, so now that's on me. I'll call you tomorrow, okay. Or maybe I'll text you tonight if it's not too busy."

The way he sounds makes me wonder if he's just miserable about going to work at the club or something else. I don't know how to ask about what that something else may be, though.

"Okay. I'm always up for texts."

"Then maybe I'll send some if I can."

Everything about him sounds so noncommittal now. Has something changed between us, I wonder?

"Is there anything you want to talk about, Cade?"

"No. I'm the same old me. Just not looking forward to work tonight. I wanted to see you instead of a bunch of drunks. Everything's okay, and I promise by Thursday night, I'll be out of this funk."

"Okay. I'll miss you."

"Me too, Hailey. Talk to you later."

When the call ends, I can't help question if there's something else that's wrong. He was so happy all those days we spent together. Now he sounds like a different person.

I shake my head to push those needless worries out of my head. He doesn't like his job. That's it. It's nothing more.

"KNOCK KNOCK! CAN YOU HAVE VISITORS?"

Lifting my head from a lump of dough that refuses to do what I want, I smile at the sight of Meadow and Alex standing in front of me. "Hi! You're the last two people I expected to see tonight."

I quickly wipe my hands on my stained apron I've been wearing all day and hope I don't have flour or anything else on my face. "What are you guys doing here?"

"When Meadow said you were hunkered down here coming up with new desserts, I told her I wanted to come over and check them out. You don't mind us intruding, do you?" Alex says, seeming genuinely concerned about interrupting me.

"You're always welcome in this kitchen. Both of you. It's almost closing time, so it's just me back here anyway. I'm hoping to stumble upon something incredible, but so far, no luck. I should have stopped playing with this dough half an hour ago. Now it's just a mess."

Meadow gives me a wide-eyed stare and glances over at Alex to let me know she's thrilled to be hanging out with him tonight. I wish I could ask her how it all came about, but since the restaurant is basically closed, I have no reason to be dragging her off to the dining room without him knowing we're gossiping about him.

"Any chance you have anything hanging around I can do a taste test on?" he asks with a sly smile.

"I have a Boston Cream Whoopee Pie I think might change your life," I joke and then point over toward the rack behind him.

He and Meadow turn around and let out audible gasps. "Hailey, it's huge!" Meadow says. "No one person can eat that and live."

"Then it's perfect for sharing."

The two of them grab forks and knives and dig in to taste what has of yet been my best creation for my meeting with Brooke Dunning. "You two enjoy. I'll be right back. I want to grab some strawberries for an idea that just came to me."

By the time I return from the refrigerator, the whoopee pie is gone. Coming around the corner, I spy

Meadow wiping chocolate from Alex's chin and I can't help but smile. They really are cute together.

"So how did that taste?" I ask as I sit down and place the case of strawberries on the table in front of me.

"Incredible. I would eat your desserts every day if you'd agree to come work at CK," Alex says, licking his lips of the last hint of chocolate on them.

"Honey, you are going to be single-handedly keeping dentists in business in this town with treats like that," Meadow says with a laugh.

I smile at her, remembering what Brooke said after she ate the apple tarts the other day. "And gyms too. The woman I'm meeting with said she needed to take three extra spin classes after indulging in the dessert she had here that day, and those were only apple tarts. What do you think what you guys just had would require? A week or two of those classes?" I ask with a chuckle.

"At least," she says. "Who is this woman? Does she look like she takes that many spin classes? I guess I always pictured food bloggers to be a softer lot since they spend all their time with food."

My attention turns to Alex, who at the moment looks confused by Meadow's idea on people who work in our industry. "I admit I might be a little soft, but I don't think he could be called soft by any stretch of the imagination."

Before he can say anything, Meadow quickly tries

to clean up her statement. Shaking her head, she says, "Oh, no. That's not what I meant. I don't think either of you are soft. No, no. I just meant I guess I thought food bloggers were."

Alex and I look at her, neither one of us smiling, and she says, "Maybe I'll just stop. How about those Rays? They played yesterday and looked pretty good. Don't you think?"

I try not to smile, but Alex simply shakes his head and rolls his eyes. "Smooth. So Hailey, what are you doing with the strawberries?"

Happy the subject has changed, Meadow asks, "Yeah, those strawberries look huge. What are you doing with them?"

Lifting one out of the case, I hold it up in front of me. "Well, most people go for dipping strawberries in chocolate. I'm not against that idea since I'm a huge chocolate fan, as you can tell by the whoopee pie you guys just enjoyed, but I wanted to come up with something different. I've tried strawberries dipped in honey and peppercorns, but I was thinking that I'd play around and maybe try chili powder or something equally as spicy. You get the heat but you get the sweet too."

"Or cayenne pepper," Alex suggests excitedly. "That's sounds good."

"I might throw in some lemon juice to see how that picks up the flavors," I explain as the two of them nod.

"You think of the most interesting stuff. I would

never even consider mixing those ingredients, but now that you're talking about it, I think I'd want to try it," Meadow says.

"I just want to impress this woman. If she likes what I make, then maybe people will start to finally come in to try my desserts. Then my parents can benefit, like I always intended in the first place."

Meadow's phone rings, and when she takes a look at who's calling, she apologizes for having to take it. "I'll just be a minute. I wouldn't answer this call, but it's a client who's been giving me a hard time and being new at the firm means I can't lose anyone. I'll be right back."

She hurries out to the dark dining room, leaving Alex and me alone. I want to ask him about Cade after that phone call with him left me wondering if anything's wrong, but I don't know how to broach the subject. He might not even know either.

Still, I have his best friend standing in front of me, so I can't let go of the chance to find out.

"Have you spoken to Cade at all in the last couple days?" I ask in a quiet voice as I focus on the strawberries and hope I don't sound too pathetic.

"Not since the other day," he says, not sounding like he wants to continue this conversation.

I look up at him to see his expression and notice he doesn't appear uncomfortable. Maybe he really has nothing to say about Cade.

"The last time I saw him he was attempting to beat

the hell out of our cousin Wilder in the middle of my kitchen."

Alex's voice holds little emotion, but what he's saying sounds like it should. I know I'd be furious if people came into my kitchen and stared a brawl near where I was working.

"Why would he do that? Is he okay? He didn't seem right when I talked to him a little while ago. Maybe that's why."

Alex shrugs, as if all of this is perfectly normal and he's seen it a hundred times before with his best friend. "He and Wilder don't get along. I'm not sure they ever have. Not that I blame Cade. I'm not a big fan of Wilder either. But don't worry. Cade got the best of him before my father and uncle broke them up."

I think back to that night at the house on the island and remember Wilder was the name of the person who interrupted us in the pool. "I think I met this Wilder person. He and two of his friends came by your grandmother's house out on Anna Maria Island when we were there. Cade was pretty frosty with him, but I thought it was just because he walked in on us."

"Just the most recent straw that broke the camel's back, I'm guessing," Alex says. "They aren't close like he and I are. In fact, Wilder's not close to any of us, even his own brother. So it's not only Cade who has a problem with him."

The way Alex defends his best friend makes me smile. "Well, I was worried they were going to get into a fight that night out at the house. I guess I shouldn't be surprised that it happened, but in your kitchen? You must have been livid."

"I'm passionate about a lot of things, including my job and my kitchen. I understand other people don't see why, but they're passionate about their own stuff. It was bound to happen at some point. The situation between them just boiled over that day. It's not like they planned to bust up my workplace."

"Was it because Wilder and his friends came to the house when we were there?" I ask, still trying to figure out what's changed with Cade to make him sound so different on the phone when we talked earlier.

Alex nods, giving me a tiny smile I sense is to make what he has to say about his best friend easier for me to hear. "That and a bunch of other things. Cade's under a lot of pressure from our family to decide what he wants to do with his life. I think it's unfair, to be honest. He isn't like me. I've known what I want to do since I was a kid. He isn't that way. Then he sees our cousin two years older than him and not knowing what he's going to do with his life, and nobody says a word about it. I think it finally just got to him."

"I like how he is. He's smart and funny, and I'm sure when he finds what he wants to do, he'll be all in on it. Having your whole life planned out isn't as good as everyone thinks either. I thought I knew what I wanted to do and that didn't turn out. Now I'm making desserts in my parents' restaurant when three years ago I could barely microwave soup."

Forcing a smile to hide my true feelings about the memories of what brought me to this point in life, I point down at the strawberries, suddenly uncomfortable with talking about this subject. "And tonight, I get to do fabulous things with strawberries. I definitely didn't need to get a degree in psychology to do that."

"I agree with you. Cade's a free spirit, and everyone trying to pin him down on something only makes him want to rebel. When he finds something he loves, he'll go headfirst into it. That's how he is. He can go from zero to hundred percent once he decides he wants something. You're proof of that. Just a few weeks ago, you two didn't even know each other. Now, you're all he thinks of. When he finds what he wants to do in life, he'll be the same way. He does nothing halfway."

His mention of how Cade is with me makes me blush, and I look away to avoid his gaze. I don't know how much his friend has told him about us, but I hope he's left out some of the sexier details. I'm not sure I could face Alex if he knew everything.

Like skinny dipping with Cade at his grandmother's house, for example. Or the specifics of our sex life.

Thankfully, Meadow returns before the silence between us grows truly awkward, and I'm thankful she doesn't pick up on it. "So that client is going to make me age overnight, you know that? I have to get to the office. I'm sorry to bail on you, Alex."

"Perfectly fine," he says with a smile. "I understand being on for the job. Hailey and I were just talking about that. I'll take you back home so you can get to work right now."

Turning to face me, Meadow asks, "Are you going to be okay here alone? Your father and everyone else are gone already. I feel terrible us leaving you here like this."

I wave away her concern, truly not worried about being the only person in the restaurant after hours. It's not the first time, and I doubt it will be the last time.

"Nonsense. Go take over the design world. I need to figure out what I want to do with these strawberries, so it's no problem. I'll see you guys later."

After they leave, I think about what Alex said about Cade and smile. I like how he's someone who can dive into something he's interested in and become engrossed by that thing. Or that person. Other women might not like how he can go from zero to one hundred percent in no time, but for someone like me who wasn't sure she'd ever be able to trust another man, that's exactly what I need.

I just hope he isn't changing his mind.

CHAPTER THIRTY-TWO

ade

DURING A LULL ON AN UNUSUALLY BUSY MONDAY night, I see Alex poke his head out of the crowd at the front bar and wave me down to him. It's not like him to be out at a club on a weeknight. He's like a kid who's always good in school—weeknights are for doing good stuff, not trolling the bar at Club X.

"What the hell are you doing here?" I ask with a smile. "Isn't it after your bedtime on a school night?"

An eye roll and a fuck you are what I get in return. "I just came from hanging out with your girlfriend. She's working hard at coming up with some great things for her meeting this week. I got to try a whoopee pie that might have sent me into sugar shock, but damn, it was worth it."

That should have been my whoopee pie. If I hadn't been called in to sub for Katelyn, I'd be with Hailey right now enjoying all sorts of things, including one of her delicious desserts.

"Yeah? Must be nice. So did you come over to rub it in my face?" I ask as I scan the bar for any customers who need a drink.

"No. Just making conversation. You planning on trying to kick my ass too? Is it some kind of thing you're doing, getting into fights with every male member of your family? Cash and Liam aren't here, so you can't get a three-for-one thing going on."

Alex is unusually snappy tonight, and I turn to see his gaze leveled on me pretty aggressively. That's not like him. What the hell is going on?

"What's up with you?" I ask, leaning forward to see him close up.

He lightens up instantly, shrugging away my question. "Nothing. Just frustrated. Give me a Jack and Coke, and go light on the soda."

I mix his drink and set it down in front of him before waiting on some guy who looks like he's going to burst if he doesn't get some alcohol in his system in the next sixty seconds. When I get back to Alex a few minutes later, half his drink is gone. That's definitely not like him. Something must be really frustrating him tonight.

"So do you want to tell me what's making you into an alcoholic, or do I have to do my best bartender routine and let you gradually confess what's wrong? I'm here all night, so feel free to take your time, but it might be easier to just tell me."

Alex downs the rest of his drink and pushes his glass forward toward me. "Get me another just like that and I'll tell you."

I mix him another Jack and Coke and set it down in front of him, ready to hear what's wrong with my best friend tonight. "There you go. Not too much soda. So what's the problem?"

After he takes a gulp, he lets out a heavy sigh. "It's Hailey's friend Meadow. I think we could have a good time, if I could ever get her to stick around for more than a half hour. She had to rush off back to work tonight. That's the third time in a row. Well, second if you aren't counting her not even sticking around here that night we were supposed to meet."

His moping and why he's so upset make me laugh. "So you have a hard time with a fellow workaholic. I'm guessing you don't appreciate the irony in all of this. Too bad because it's rich."

Alex twists his expression, shaking his head. "I'm not a workaholic. I have no idea why you think that. I don't work because there's a ton of shit to get done. I enjoy my work. I love my work. That's not the same as a workaholic," he protests before taking another drink.

"Probably wouldn't have worked out anyway. She gorgeous and all, but I doubt she's a freak like you."

I know that will get him going. He's not exactly a freak. What he likes isn't necessarily any different than most guys. What makes Alex different is the intensity of how he likes the run-of-the-mill things.

He's a pure hedonist, through and through.

"So enjoying life is being a freak? Maybe I should be a surly bastard who goes around being miserable and picking fights with people?"

I smile at his swipe at my own recent behavior. "Sounds like you're doing just that right now."

As he tilts his glass up to his mouth, he grins at me. "You know, you're lucky to be with someone like Hailey. She was working on doing something with strawberries that sounded incredible. Maybe I should change my policy of dating women in my business."

"Go find your own beautiful baker. Hailey's taken."

He looks down the bar and then up at me. "So what are you doing here on a Monday when you could be with her?"

"Filling in for Katelyn," I answer, practically grunting my disgust. "First her sister nearly makes me lose my girlfriend when she pulls that shit at the anniversary party, and now she's out until Thursday. I thought Wilder was a huge cock block. He's got nothing on the twins."

After he finishes his drink, Alex sets his glass down

on the bar and frowns. "You should have heard him after you left the other day. To hear him talk, it was all your fault."

"What? Him busting in when I'm trying to be alone with Hailey out at the house or the fight? In my opinion, both were his fault."

"No, the problem between you two. He was acting like he has no idea why you're not his biggest fan."

I roll my eyes at the thought of any excuse Wilder could come up with. "Well, I'm not even sure he has a problem with me. I mean, other than the general problem he seems to have with everyone in the world. That whole miserable fuck who hates all of humanity thing is such bullshit, but I don't know if he has a problem with me. I know I have a problem with him, and his showing up with those two shitheads the other night didn't make it any better."

"Is that why you were acting weird with Hailey when you talked to her? She asked me about it, but I sidestepped giving her an answer since I had no idea. I think she's worried, though."

Hearing Hailey told Alex something was wrong between us irritates me. "Why would she say that?"

He gives me a look like I just asked the dumbest question in the world. "Because she's worried."

"Well, she has no reason to be. I was just pissed that I had to work so many nights this week. That's all."

"Don't tell me. Tell her."

"What else could she think was wrong?" I ask, once more getting pissed off that I have to be here tonight.

Alex shrugs, but I see in his expression he thinks there could be something else. "I don't know. Maybe she's gets worried when someone acts like they're a hundred percent about her and then gets all moody. That running hot and cold thing you do isn't easy if you aren't used to it like I am, and that's only because I've known you all my life. She hasn't, Cade. It's not surprising she might get uneasy."

I nod, but I know it's more than just that. True, I do tend to run hot and cold like he said, but for Hailey, I know she's got to be wondering if the same thing that happened with that asshole who cheated on her is happening again.

Damn Katelyn and whatever crisis she's dealing with this week. She and her sister should get together with my goddamned cousin. They could be the cockblock triplets. Somebody should make up T-shirts they can wear so people know to steer clear of all three of them.

"So, are you planning on giving up on Hailey's friend? I don't think two people who love to work are a good fit," I say, teasing Alex once again.

"We'll see. She might be just like me. You never know."

The wicked look in his eyes tells me he hopes

Meadow is just like him. She seemed pretty normal to me, though. No weird wearing of cartoon costumes as an everyday way to dress. No bizarre habits like most of Alex's girlfriends. Not exactly the usual type of woman he likes to pursue.

"If all she does is work, you might never know either."

"Fuck you. I don't know why I even talk to you," he snaps before pushing his glass toward me.

"Because I'm your best friend. Are you that drunk that you forgot?" I ask with a laugh.

"Fuck you. I'm going home. You around tomorrow? I'm working early, so I'll be off by nighttime."

I shake my head as I spread my arms. "All of this is what I get until Thursday. Then I'll get to see Hailey."

"That sucks. Too bad you don't have a trust fund or something that would allow you to just relax and enjoy life," Alex says, throwing his head back and laughing. When he finishes, he smiles. "That's for busting my balls about Meadow. Now we're even."

"No, now it's my turn to say fuck you. Stop over Wednesday afternoon, if you aren't busy chopping every carrot in the known world. We can go out on the water for a few hours before I have to put the ball and chain on and come back here."

Alex slaps me on the shoulder. "Will do. Have a good one."

And with that, the most interesting part of my workday walks out, leaving me with a handful of customers in need of more booze. Too bad I don't have one of those handy, dandy trust funds.

CHAPTER THIRTY-THREE

$\mathcal{H}$ailey

EVEN THOUGH CADE AND I TALKED EVERY DAY AND he made sure to explain that nothing was wrong on Tuesday when he called, Thursday night couldn't come fast enough for me. After all my experimenting, I have five desserts I love and hope will wow Brooke Dunning on Friday.

Except for the fact that I haven't heard from her yet, and it's already four o'clock on the day before.

Did she change her mind? Or maybe she decided the apple tarts she had last week really weren't that good. They could have been better. I went a little too heavy with the cinnamon. Or maybe she doesn't want to do extra spin classes. I couldn't blame her for that. Just the thought of them makes me grimace in pain.

All of this races through my head as I wait for Cade to return from the kitchen with a drink. By the time he walks into the living room, my panicked thoughts have made my stomach twist into knots and my mouth feels like someone has sucked all the moisture out, leaving nothing but a dried-up husk for my tongue.

Definitely not the way I wanted our first night together all week to go.

"You look like something's wrong. What happened in the time between me going to get you a drink and now?" he asks as he sits down next to me on the couch and sets my glass on the coffee table in front of us.

"Nothing. Just my normal worrying. I still haven't heard from Brooke Dunning. Do you think she changed her mind?" I ask and then lean forward to grab my drink.

The cool water feels so good when it hits my tongue, and I hope it does wonders for my upset stomach. What would help is if I wouldn't get stressed out over this.

"No, I don't think she changed her mind," Cade says with a sweet smile. "I bet she's just been busy."

I don't know if I believe that, but it doesn't matter. The more I keep thinking about tomorrow, the more freaked out I get. Either she's forgotten or changed her mind, which would make me feel terrible, or everything's fine and I'll hear from her tonight about what time to go to her hotel tomorrow, which will make me feel even more nervous.

"Tonight might not have been a good idea. I don't think I'm going to be very good company."

Talk about an understatement.

"No way. I have something good planned, and you watch. You're going to love it and be so relaxed that you'll stop worrying about tomorrow. Just sit back and unwind. Tonight is all about you."

Cade's trying to be helpful, but I'm worried if all the focus is on me tonight, then I'll have nothing to occupy my mind and I'll keep stressing out about this thing with Brooke. What I need is to focus my mind on something else entirely.

"I think it might be better if it was all about you, to be honest. Then I'd be able to get my mind off what's troubling me," I confess, hoping I'm not ruining his plans.

His mouth turns up in a wicked smile that makes him look so incredibly sexy. "Well, that could work too with what I have planned."

Cade slides his hand up my thigh and leans in to kiss me. "We can take turns, or the first part of the night can be all about you and then the next part can be all about me. Whatever you like. It's your call."

As his fingers slowly creep up my leg, I feel the familiar ache I've carried with me all week since I was with him last. "Did you plan to just have sex all night?"

He stops his hand and looks up at me, all worried. "Sort of. We could do something else too, though. Whatever you want."

The way he says that sounds so sincere and almost innocent that I giggle. I don't have a problem with him wanting to spend all night in bed. The last thing I want to do is go out tonight and be around people when I've missed him so much all week.

"I'm not really hungry right now. Not for food, anyway. And I don't really want to go out."

His smile returns, lighting up his dark eyes. "Good. So do we focus on you first or me?"

"Your choice."

Gently, he pushes me back on the couch and settles in between my legs. Looking up, he watches me as he pushes my sundress up over my hips and then inches my panties down.

"This was all I could think about last night. Just lay back and let me give you something good to take your mind off everything."

He tosses my underwear behind him and pushes my legs open, his palms pressing my thighs out so I'm completely exposed to him. That ache in my belly I've had all week grows stronger now, and I can barely wait to feel his mouth on me.

Cade stops just before his mouth touches my pussy, and his warm breath teases what's about to happen. Desperate for his tongue to flick against my excited skin, I lift my hips, but he pushes me back down onto the couch.

"Somebody can't wait. I love it," he whispers so close to my pussy that each word thrills me.

"Please…" I murmur, unable to get more than just that word out as every bit of my brain focuses on the moment when he'll finally touch me.

Instead of pressing that beautiful mouth of his to me, he runs his fingertip up my wet slit until he reaches my clit. "Patience. I'm supposed to be taking your mind off your worries."

I look down at him and smile. "Trust me. You are. Now all I can think about is how much I want you to use that perfect tongue to get me off."

"Since it's your turn first, your wish is my command, my lady," he says as he stares up at me with those dark brown eyes so sensual and mischievous.

And then I finally feel what I've waited for, and it's like heaven.

His tongue drags over my delicate skin, exciting every inch it touches on its way to the bundle of nerves needy for attention, and when he flicks the tip of his tongue against it, my eyes roll back in my head it feels so damn good. Cade gently sucks my clit into his mouth and presses his fingertips into my thighs, marking the flesh so I'll probably have faint bruises for days to remind me of how much I enjoyed this.

He lets out a tiny, satisfied hum against me that

races straight to the center of my being. Arching my back, I press my pussy to his mouth, dying for all he can give me. He devours it, like a famished man with his favorite food after too long denied it. I stuff my hands into his dark hair and hold him to me as I rock my hips back and forth.

Cade rides each movement of my body, his hands holding me tightly enough that he controls every part of this for me, even if he lets me move to feel as much as I can. I whimper with each lap of his tongue up my slit and cry out softly when he sucks my clit between his lips. He sets a tempo each time—slow up and then suck. Over and over, and I wait for each part to follow the other.

Just when I think I can't take another moment of the sweet agony, he changes things up. Sliding a finger inside me, he begins to fuck me, hooking his fingertip just right so it touches that spot that makes hints of colors shatter behind my eyes. When he slides a second finger in and sucks my clit into his mouth, that's all it takes. What look like fireworks explode in my closed eyes, and I moan loudly enough that his neighbors have to be able to hear.

"Oh, God! Yes...yes...right there. God, don't stop..." I beg, and Cade's happy to keep giving me every last lick I need.

When the last tremor of my release finally subsides, he lifts his head and licks his lips. His mouth shines with my juices, and he gives me a satisfied grin like he's the one who just got off.

"That's a nice start to the night, don't you think?" he asks as he sits back on his heels looking like a conqueror who's taken some prized territory for his own.

"Definitely," I say in a dreamy voice.

I can't seem to put together a full sentence to tell him how utterly incredible he just made me feel. Stretching my legs, I feel a phantom quake from my orgasm, and I press my thighs together to make it last.

"I fucking love how you are when I do that," Cade says.

Hovering over me, he leans down and gently kisses my lips. I taste myself on them and run my tongue along my bottom lip. "I love how you do that, so it works out well."

He sits down on the couch at my feet and unzips his pants to take his cock out. Already rock hard, it stands up straight, and he gives it a few tugs before turning to look over at me with pure need in his eyes.

"Change of plans. I want that beautiful mouth on me. Now."

Cade pushes the coffee table back with his foot, making way for me to sit in front of him. I think about straddling his hips and moving things along to the next phase of the night for a moment, but I lower to my knees instead. He wants me to suck his cock, and after the release he just gave me, I'd say yes to anything the man asked at this moment.

I wrap my fingers around the base while he opens his pants to give me all the room I need. He didn't wear any underwear tonight, a sign he had planned for us to spend all night in bed. No matter. They'd just get in the way now.

My gaze locked on his, I give the underside of his cock a long lick from balls to head. His eyes go cloudy and even darker, if that's possible, like just the simple act of my tongue on his flesh changes him.

His silky soft skin tastes faintly salty, and when I take the head into my mouth, that flavor increases. He's large and forces my jaw to open more so I feel a twinge of pain, but I push it away. I want to make him feel like he just did for me.

Cade lets out a throaty moan and stuffs his hand into my hair, tightening his fingers in the strands so tiny licks of pain dance across my scalp. It's something that excites me instead of hurting me, and I respond by slowly lowering my head to take more of him into my mouth.

He's patient for a minute or so as I gradually ease his cock inside me, but that tolerance gives out about halfway down and his hand pushes me the rest of the way. He bumps up against the back of my throat, and I can't stop myself from gagging and moving away from him.

Above me, he says in a faraway voice, "Take all of it, baby. Let me see you take all of it."

God, he's so sensual that I want to do just that, so I relax and ease every last inch of his cock inside my mouth until the head touches the back of my throat again. This time, I don't gag, and he lets out a passionate moan that sounds like it comes from the depths of his soul.

"Fuck, Hailey. That feels so good. Don't stop."

I slide my mouth up his shaft and then dip down again, this time faster and harder so I slam down on him. Looking up at him, I see him watching me with rapt attention, like my sucking his cock is all he's ever wanted to see in his life.

Scratching my fingernails over the skin between his hips, I bob my head up and down, finding a rhythm that excites me. If he touched between my legs, Cade would find me drenched. I want to make him come like he did for me, and just the thought that I can thrills me so I run wet.

His hold on my hair tightens a minute later, and I sense he's getting close. He pushes my head down on him, groaning softly when I swipe my tongue over his balls when I reach the base of his cock. When I think he might be just seconds away from coming, I suck harder, my heart slamming in my chest, and a moment later, he floods my mouth with everything he has.

After he finishes, I sit back and smile up at him. He looks down at me through half-lidded eyes, so utterly sexy and satisfied that I have to stop myself from going down on him again.

"Fuck. I'm not sure I can move now," he says with a smile.

I slide my hands up his thighs and take a deep breath, ready to climb on top of him and feel him fill me up. "No need for you to move."

Straddling his hips, I kiss him on the mouth and whisper against his lips, "You have no idea how excited that got me."

Cade cups my ass and squeezes, dragging my pussy the full length of his cock. "I think I do," he says with a chuckle.

CHAPTER THIRTY-FOUR

ade

DAMN, SHE'S SO FUCKING WET AGAINST ME THAT MY strength suddenly comes roaring back. A minute ago, I wasn't sure my legs would even work, but knowing how much sucking my cock excited her has given me a second wind I thought I'd have to wait at least a few minutes for.

But I don't want to just sit here and watch Hailey ride me tonight. No, this night is about taking her mind off everything but us, so it calls for something more.

I lift the bottom of her dress and say, "Time for this to come off."

Hailey gives me a confused look but raises her

arms to help me slip the dress over her head. Underneath, she's naked, which is perfect for what I want to do next.

After I give her nipples a suck and pull her mouth down to mine to kiss her long and deep, I give her a little tap on the ass. "Up and onto the couch."

That gets me yet another confused look, but she doesn't ask what I have planned and stands up off me. I watch her sit down where I'd just been and shake my head.

"Turn around and on your knees. Hold onto the back of the couch," I say with a wink.

"Oh. Okay."

She does as I order, and I give my cock a few hard tugs looking at how beautiful she looks bent over and waiting for me to fuck her from behind. Leaning down, I press a tiny kiss to the middle of her back and make my way down to the base of her spine. Hailey arches her back with each kiss, a sign she's as eager as I am to get down to business.

I grip the base of my cock and aim it for her cunt while my other hand grabs her hair and pulls her head back. With one hard thrust, I bury myself in her and say low in her ear, "Ready?"

She whimpers her answer, and I pull out of her so just the head is still inside. Then I push my hips forward and fill her completely again as I tighten my hold in her hair.

Her cunt is wet and perfect around my cock. "That's it. This feels so fucking good."

Hailey says something, but I can't understand because her mouth is pressed against a cushion. I begin fucking her in earnest, watching how beautiful her body looks when my cock disappears into her perfect cunt. Her hands grip the back of the couch until her knuckles turn white, but she doesn't want me to stop any more than I want to.

I sink my fingers into her hips and fuck her hard, loving how she reacts. Hailey moans, and I swear my cock swells inside her so her body grips me tightly. It's like she was made for me and only me, and I can't get enough of her.

"Cade, I'm slipping.." she says, and I look down to see her knees coming off the couch.

"Don't worry. I got you."

Hooking my arm under her stomach, I lift her and move her forward so she's back on the cushion. She turns to look back and me, and I see her teeth sink into her bottom lip. Fuck, she looks sexier than I think I can handle.

A few strokes more into her and I feel her cunt tighten around me. Her hands curl into tight fists, and she lowers her head so the angle changes for us. This position feels even better, and a second later, she screams my name as she comes hard on my cock.

It only takes a few more thrusts and I'm right there with her as her body milks me to release. I rear back and sink into her one last time before it feels like the top of my head is going to blow off. I see her press her palms against the back of the couch to push back against me, and then I'm lost.

I collapse on top of her and we both fall to the couch, exhausted and satisfied out of our minds. Breathless, she and I search for air, panting after the best sex I've ever had.

"You okay under there? I'm not crushing you, am I?" I whisper in her ear and then kiss her neck softly.

She turns her head and through a curtain of hair, I see her smile. "This time, I definitely can't walk. I think I'm boneless."

I don't know why, but all I can think of when she says that is chicken. Chuckling, I kiss her again. "That was incredible."

As I sit up, she rolls over and looks at me oddly. "Then why are you laughing?"

She's so beautiful lying there that I hesitate to ruin the mood with something stupid, but I tell her the truth. "Because when you said you were boneless, I thought of chicken."

Hailey's expression twists into one of disbelief, but then she sits up and laughs. "Super hot sex makes you think of chicken? Thank God you have a big dick, or I'd have to think twice about sleeping with you again."

"Well, thank God for small favors."

Leaning over, she kisses me. "Big favors, honey. Big favors."

As we sit there after incredible sex, in each other's arms while we try to catch our breath, I think about how many women I could never have that conversation with. They'd take it personally or think it was dumb. They might even get their feelings hurt by my laughing and not accept anything I say after that.

Hailey's different, though. Different from every other woman I've ever known. I like being able to laugh with her while we're lying naked next to one another.

"Why so quiet? Thinking about getting something to eat? Boneless wings, maybe?" she asks with a cute little giggle.

I pull her to me and smile at how comfortable it feels to be with her. "Actually, I was just thinking that I like that we can be this way together."

"Silly?" she asks as she nuzzles the space between my jaw and my shoulder.

"Real. I don't have to lie to you, even when my brain thinks of something stupid, probably because of a lack of oxygen after a round of great sex. I like that about us."

Looking up at me, she nods. "I like that too."

We sit there in silence recovering and after a little while, Hailey taps her finger against my arm. "Did you fall asleep?"

I squeeze her to me, loving how this feels more natural than anything else in my life. "No. Just recharging after that round."

Before she can say anything else, her phone buzzes in her purse on the floor. Grabbing it, she holds it up in front of us. "I need to get this in case it's Brooke telling me what time tomorrow. Sorry."

On the screen, I read that Brooke Dunning wants her to come to the Regent Hotel at one o'clock tomorrow. Room 544.

Hailey points at her phone and smiles like an excited little kid. "I thought maybe she had changed her mind. This is so great!"

"It is. You're going to be great tomorrow."

She tosses her phone back into her purse and sits up next to me. Her smile is gone, replaced by a far too serious look for someone who's just gotten such good news.

"What's wrong?" I ask, unsure what could be making her so unhappy.

Looking down at her hands, she says, "Would you come with me? I know it's an imposition, but it would be so great to have you there for moral support in case it turns out I'm terrible at podcasts."

I lift her chin and give her my answer. "It's not an imposition. If you want me there, I'm there. And I don't think you're going to be terrible at podcasts. Don't you just have to talk?"

"What if my mind goes blank or I stammer a lot when she asks me questions?"

The fear in her eyes is real, so I pull her to me and press a kiss to the top of her head. "You're going to be fantastic. You're a great chef and great at sex and the best girlfriend in the world, so of course you're going to be terrific at this too."

Tilting her head back, she looks up at me. "You're going to give me a big head."

"Good. Some people should have big heads. I believe in you, Hailey."

She takes a deep breath and lets it out slowly. "Thank you. And thank you for agreeing to come with me tomorrow. Just knowing you're nearby will keep me calm."

The idea that I could do that for anyone shocks me more than it would anyone else, I imagine. The guy who runs hot and cold and can't get his life together keeps this incredible woman calm.

I'd be crazy to ever let her go just for that reason alone. But there are a million others too, and I silently promise never to forget any single one of them.

CHAPTER THIRTY-FIVE

$\mathcal{H}$ailey

MY ARMS FULL OF THE DESSERTS TO TAKE TO Brooke Dunning's hotel room, I look into the backseat of Cade's car and then back at him. "Maybe we should take my car. I don't want to ruin yours if anything spills."

He takes the top tray out of my hands and moves toward the rear of the car. "If anything spills, I'll get it detailed. You'll owe me one night of mind-blowing sex. We can put it all in the trunk and everything will be fine."

I blush at his mention of sex knowing my parents are just inside the restaurant and follow him to the back of the car. He helps me load the trays and pans and then stops to kiss me.

"I might just swerve a few times so I get that night of sex."

"Please don't. I'll deliver on the sex no matter what. I promise."

Cade laughs at me, and I sense I took him too seriously there. "I wouldn't do that. I know you need these to look as good as they taste. Presentation is everything, right?"

"Yes, and I'm sorry I'm so literal right now. I'm just a little nervous."

"No worries," he says before kissing me again. "Now let's get going. I promise to drive the speed limit for the first time in my life too."

"Okay. Let me run in and tell my parents goodbye. I'll be right back."

Busier than usual, the kitchen feels crowded now as I run in to see my mom and dad. They pretend to be busy, but I know by the way they're just standing near my station that they've been talking instead of working.

"We're going to leave now. Wish me luck!"

My mother, always the more emotional parent, opens her arms and pulls me in for a big hug. "Oh, honey. This is so exciting! Have a good time, okay?"

When she leans away from me, still holding my shoulders, though, I see hope in her eyes. While she doesn't talk about it every day, she can't escape the truth of how the restaurant is faring lately.

If only Brooke Dunning could get more people to come in because they heard about my desserts on this podcast, business would pick up. I know it would.

"I will, Mom," I say with a smile.

My father stands stoically off to the side, as if none of this podcast nonsense interests him in the least. His arms folded across his chest, he looks like he's doing his best statue impression. I know the truth, though. He may not be as hopeful as my mother that today will turn things around for Comfort Food, but he's wished something would.

I so want today to be that something.

"Will we be able to listen to this podcast thing at some point?" he asks in a serious tone.

"Yes, Dad. I don't know when, but I'll find out."

"Don't talk too fast. I swear to God every time I turn on the radio or TV, people are talking too fast. They sound like squawking chickens running around with their heads cut off."

I stare at him for a moment, not sure how a chicken without a head could make any noise. "Okay. No squawking Hailey. Got it. I have to go. I don't want to be late."

For the first time in this conversation, he finally cracks a smile as he opens his arms to hug me. "Enjoy yourself, honey. You deserve this."

"Thanks, Dad. I will."

With a kiss for both of them, I hurry back through the kitchen past well-wishes from the cooks and servers out to the car where Cade waits for me. When I jump in and we take off much slower than he usually drives, I look over at him and smile.

"Thanks for toning down the speed today."

"No problem. What did your parents have to say?"

All I can think of is my father's chicken comment. "To have a good time and don't sound like a chicken with her head cut off."

Cade switches lanes and then turns to look at me with confusion written all over his face. "Is this an inside joke in your family? How would a chicken sound without a head? Do they mean make sure not to lose your voice? I don't get it."

With a shrug, I laugh. I don't explain it to him since it's silly anyway.

THE REGENT HOTEL SITS DOWN ON THE waterfront, prime real estate in the city, and from the moment we drive into the parking garage, I sense this is very different from what I'm used to. By the time we get off the elevator on the fifth floor, I start to doubt this is something I should be doing.

"This place is nice," Cade says casually as we walk toward Room 544. "A little on the stuffy side for my tastes, but nice."

I turn to look at him in shock that he's describing this hotel as merely nice. "Did you see the fountain in the lobby? That thing goes two floors high. And all the decorations looked like gold. Not painted gold but real gold."

"Yeah, but they could have put some TVs in the lobby where all that water was. It's nice, though, I guess."

I suspect Cade is more nonchalant about the fancy style of the Regent Hotel than I am because he comes from money. To me, this place is stunning. It's the kind of hotel you see in movies when royalty have to sleep away from their castles.

He stops and points at one of the white hotel room doors. "544. Looks like we're here. Ready?"

Shaking my head, I admit the absolute truth of what I feel at this moment. "No. I'm shaking like a leaf, and my stomach feels like it's about to push out everything I've eaten this morning."

As always, he smiles and leans in to kiss me softly on the lips, his dark eyes filled with kindness he probably thinks I need so I don't unravel like a cheap suit right here in the hallway on the fifth floor of the ultra-fancy Regent Hotel. "You're going to be great. I can't wait to see you wow her with these desserts. I want you to know that after we're done I plan to eat one of those whoopee pies, so she better not block out a week of extra spin class to gobble the last one down."

"I love you. You know that?" I say, trying to find some calm inside my terrified brain.

"I do, and I love you too. So let's go in there and do some podcasting. There's a whoopee pie with my name on it, and I can practically hear it calling to me right now. If we don't get in there, I'm going to have to rescue it, so we better get this show started before I do."

His sexy smile and silly joke bring me some relief from the stress building inside me, and I knock on the door to get this day underway. Everything will be okay. What's the worst that can happen? All the desserts are terrible, she announces that to the entire world, and I go back to my parents to apologize and swear I'll learn how to waitress better than anyone ever has before to help them save on at least one salary.

As I watch for the door to open, I silently pray to God none of that happens as memories of my one and only stint as a server run through my head. I was so terrible. I tried it one summer in high school. I had a tendency to drop trays full of food, sometimes in customers' laps.

Please don't make me have to go back to that again. Nobody wants that. Really.

The door finally opens, and a tall brunette with the longest neck I've ever seen on a person is standing there. That one feature steals all my attention from her beautiful face, and I have to force myself to look up at her lovely hazel eyes and only them.

"Hello! You must be Hailey. Please come in. Brooke is waiting for you," she says in a chipper voice before stepping back to let Cade and me into the room.

As I imagined while we walked through the hotel, the room is gorgeous. Rooms is technically the correct description. We walk into what looks like a living room that's bigger than the apartment I had in college. Two white couches with tiny pink flowers face one another, one on each wall, and in between sits an enormous coffee table. The room is so big that none of these pieces of furniture make walking through the room toward a large dining table in front of a bank of windows on the far wall difficult at all.

Definitely bigger than my entire apartment.

Brooke sits at the table near the windows and practically jumps up out of her chair when we walk in. Dressed in white pants and a red shirt, she looks stunning.

"I am so glad to see you again, Hailey. You can just put everything in your hands on the coffee table. We'll be talking over at that table over there. I see you brought a guest."

I nod and hurry to introduce everyone. "Brooke, this is Cade. My boyfriend. He came to help with all the trays since I'd never be able to get these all up here. Cade, this is Brooke Dunning, a food blogger who has a national podcast."

Brooke quickly adds, "And Hailey and Cade, please meet my assistant Tabitha. She'll be helping today."

We all shake hands and smile before Cade and I set the desserts on the coffee table and I begin to arrange them. Nervous, I nearly knock over the container of pink and green macarons to send them spilling all over the floor. Thankfully, Cade catches it and sets it down on the table.

Taking my hands in his, he whispers in my ear, "It's okay. This is going to be great, right?"

I nod and take a deep breath in. This is going to be great. I've made the best desserts I can, and Brooke's going to love them.

"Your boyfriend is so nice, Hailey. My ex-husband would have just let those cookies fly everywhere and then he wouldn't have helped to clean them up either," Brooke says and then laughs.

"I'm just a little nervous. Thank God, Cade never gets nervous. He's always calm, cool, and collected."

She and Tabitha look over at him and smile. "See, that's what I like to see in a man. Cool. It's a very sexy trait but so many men just can't pull it off," Brooke says, still staring at him as her assistant turns her focus to the desserts now arranged on the coffee table.

"Brooke, look at how gorgeous all of these are!" Tabitha coos, pointing down at the white chocolate torte topped with chocolate morsels and plump raspberries. "Is that white chocolate? Did Brooke tell you that's one of our favorites?"

I smile and quietly let out a sigh of relief at my choice of that dessert for today. "It is, and I think you're going to love it. It's one of my favorites too."

"I'm going to need a month of spin classes after this, but it will all be worth it," Brooke gushes as she heads toward the desserts. "I think we should taste some now before we get started. Tell me about every one and why you made it."

Turning to face Cade, I give him a panicked look. I had planned on talking about all of that during the podcast. If I explain things now, what will I say then? He simply nods and smiles, like he knows I'm unraveling but he's here and everything's going to be okay.

"Well, I thought I'd tell that in the podcast. I don't want to bore you with telling it twice."

Brooke waves off my worry and grabs a macaroon. "Oh, don't worry about that. You can tell me then, if you like that better. Just make sure you give my listeners a full story. They're used to that after reading my recipes on my website."

My father's criticism of that very trait of food bloggers flashes through my mind, and I can't help but smile. He'd have a lot to say right now about that and so many other things. Hopefully, I can channel him when it comes time for the podcast.

"This chocolate creation is divine!" Tabitha squeals before taking her second bite of Boston Cream Whoopee Pie. "Brooke, this is to die for. I'm serious. Try this!"

I glance over at Cade and see him giving me a fake scowl, like he's not happy these two women are so focused on the dessert he wants to eat in a little while. I give him a smile and silently promise to make him his own special whoopee pie if it turns out there are none left when we leave today.

After they try each dessert, leaving a single whoopee pie for me to take home for Cade, Brooke pats her nonexistent belly like it's some huge thing and motions for me to follow her. "Time to get this thing going. I have to tell you, I think I'm in love with every single dessert, but that Boston Cream pie creation is just heavenly. Do you mind leaving that last one for me when you go? It's just so good."

Out of the corner of my eye, I see Cade smile. "Oh, that would be no problem. I'm going to make a special batch of them for Cade when I get home because he loves them too."

Brooke's eyes light up, and she looks past me toward where he's sitting on one of the couches. "He obviously has good taste. And not just in desserts. You two make such a darling couple. I love it!"

I thank her for being so sweet, and as we begin to actually talk about the desserts and me, I find I have a lot to say about many topics. Whatever fear I had before I sat down in front of her at that table evaporates, leaving me to have fun talking about why I love to bake and my parents' restaurant.

And my father won't be disappointed since I didn't talk too fast and I didn't bury all the good information about Comfort Food beneath a ton of words and some long-winded story about my childhood like food bloggers generally do.

By the time we finish, an hour has passed and I'm so excited I could talk for another sixty minutes. Brooke finishes what she calls goodies for the production crew, which seems to mean repeating something about what we talked about and who we are, and turns to me with a big smile that I hope means this was a success.

"Hailey, that was so much fun. I only have one question to ask you. Where do I find a yummy man like the one you have? He doesn't happen to have any brothers, does he?"

For a second, I wonder if she's just being nice, but the intensity in her eyes while she waits for me to answer her question tells me she's serious. "He just happened to walk into the restaurant one day. We sort of stumbled onto one another. To be honest, considering that he works at a nightclub and I rarely go out, especially to clubs, I doubt we'd ever meet. He doesn't have any brothers, but he's got a family full of cousins. One of them, Alex, looks a lot like him and is a chef at CK."

Her mouth drops open like this is the best news she's heard all day. "Really? I might have to go there before I leave town. So Cade works at a nightclub? Which one? What does he do?"

"Club X. He's a bartender there," I proudly tell her.

"A bartender and a baker. It's a perfect pairing. Thank you so much for coming here and talking to me and my listeners today. I hope your family's restaurant gets a ton of traffic because of it. It's a charming place I know so many people would love."

I have to stop myself from crying I'm so relieved at this moment. Brooke Dunning, a major food blogger with millions of fans, loves my work and had fun talking to me, a nobody when it comes to cooking.

"Thank you so much, Brooke. You've been so wonderful. I can't tell you how much I appreciate this."

When Cade and I get out into the hallway, I throw my arms around his neck and jump up and down I'm so happy. "She loved it all! I had so much fun. Did it sound okay? I think it sounded okay. I made sure to mention Comfort Food a bunch of times, and I didn't sound like a total idiot when I told the stories about why I love blueberry and lemon desserts and how chocolate should be a major food group. That didn't sound stupid, did it?"

Always the calm one, he smiles and presses a kiss to my forehead. "You were as great as I thought you would be. That's going to be her most interesting episode, I bet. I'm so proud of you, Hailey."

There isn't a happier person in the world than me right now.

CHAPTER THIRTY-SIX

ade

AFTER CELEBRATING HAILEY'S SUCCESSFUL DEBUT as a podcast star with her parents at Comfort Food, I have to drag myself away to get to work. Standing behind the main bar at Club X is the last place I want to be tonight. I don't have a choice, though. That's the worst part of it. No choice.

I intentionally miss my father's overly enthusiastic team meeting to start off the night, unable to stomach that much gung-ho tonight. Slipping in as he busies himself with some drama on the upper floor, I take my position at the front bar and get to work making sure all the liquor we may need is available and the glasses necessary for the night are ready.

When I finish, I look around wondering where the rest of the staff is for the front bar tonight. He surely didn't schedule only me to run the main bar on a Friday. My father is a better businessman than that.

As I look around for anyone to find out who's supposed to be up here with me, the man himself walks down the stairs and sees me. "I wish you'd get here for the staff meetings. I had important things to tell everyone, and you missed it all."

"Sorry. My cheerleading uniform is at the dry cleaners. I'm here, so you can tell me what I missed right now."

That snide crack gets me one of Stefan March's patented grimaces, sure to make any delicate person wither. Since I'm not sensitive and I've been on the receiving end of that look at least a million times in my life, I just shrug.

"You know I hate repeating myself. I swear you push my buttons intentionally, even though you know what the end result will be, Cade."

This is how our usual dance goes, but tonight, I'm not in the mood to fight with him. Today was great with Hailey, especially seeing her do so well with the podcast. I don't want to ruin that feeling by having yet another argument with my father.

So I do something I rarely try with him.

"I'm sorry, Dad. Today was a big day for my girlfriend, and I got caught up in that and ended up running late. What did I miss at the staff meeting?"

He takes a step back and stares at me like I've grown a second head out of my shoulder. At first, he doesn't seem to know what to say and looks around as if he needs someone to tell him that really just happened. I actually apologized.

Flustered, he takes a few moments to get his thoughts together since I'm sure he had this entire fight planned out in his head. Old habits die hard with us.

"Well, I decided I wanted to try something different tonight. The second-floor ladies' room needs some repairs, but the plumber can't come until Monday. That means I need people to spend their time down here instead of upstairs. So I've rearranged some of the usual assignments. You'll be here with three people, not two. I put the twins at the back bar and brought Maya back up here. I know that isn't what you want, but I need you to give it your best, okay?"

Still expecting an argument from me, when he finishes talking, he takes a deep breath and lets it out on a heavy sigh. "It's only for one or two nights, but if you'd rather me put you somewhere else, I can do that."

"It's okay, Dad. Maya and I will do fine. Who's our third and fourth since you moved the twins to the back?"

"Antonio and Chelsea. They're getting fruit right now, so they'll be out soon."

"Okay. We'll be a little crowded, but we'll get the job done. Don't worry. I promise I won't douse Maya with the soda sprayer tonight," I say with a chuckle, remembering the time I shot her straight in the face with water after she dumped a beer over my head.

My agreeing with him throws my father off a little, and for a few seconds, he stands in front of the bar like he doesn't know what to do now. Not fighting with me appears to have sent his world off its axis.

"So, something happened with your girlfriend that was good? What was her big day about?" he asks in a low voice as he steps forward toward the bar.

Happy to tell this story for the second time today after I gave Alex all the details on my way over here, I explain, "She's a baker. She makes desserts for her family's restaurant, a little place called Comfort Food across town. A big food blogger heard about her after other bloggers began writing about the desserts, and today she had Hailey on her podcast to talk about what she makes. She did fantastic. I'm so proud of her. She's a little self-conscious about things because she didn't go to school for cooking like Alex. She actually went to school for psychology and was going for her master's, but things happened and that couldn't continue. So she started baking for her parents' restaurant and now this happened."

I suddenly cut my story short when I realize I've ventured into parts of Hailey's life I know she wouldn't want me talking about with anyone. My father smiles as I finish, giving me a nod like he approves.

"That sounds great. From what your uncles and Alex tell me, she must have a natural talent for baking if she didn't go to school because they rave about her desserts. I'm going to have to get myself over to that restaurant and try some so I'm not the only member of our family who hasn't sampled these delicious treats."

"She makes a Boston Cream Whoopee thing I hear is pretty incredible. I haven't gotten to try it yet, but the food lady raved about it."

"Sounds good. So you guys are doing okay?" he asks, hesitating as the words come out of his mouth.

I think about that and try to come up with the right way to describe how great things are between Hailey and me. We're more than okay. She makes me smile and happier than I've ever been in my life. That's a hell of a lot better than just okay.

But I still don't want to share her with my entire family yet, so I give him a noncommittal shrug and a vague answer. "We're good. It's still early, though. I guess I could fuck it up any time now."

He nods, like he agrees and turns to walk away. "Don't be so hard on yourself, Cade. You're a good man. I'm sure your girlfriend knows that."

Stunned those words came out of my father's mouth, I watch him walk away, surprised at how all that went with him. For one of the few times in my life, I didn't jump into a fight with him, and that ended up pretty good.

To hear him say he thinks I'm a good man makes this day for me. After seeing Hailey succeed with that food lady, this puts a cherry on top of a hell of a great afternoon.

FOR THE NEXT FOUR HOURS, I FEEL LIKE I'M walking on air. The club is packed with people, the music is pumping, and my fellow bartenders and I are making a killing on tips. Even Maya, the person who hates me most at Club X, seems in a good mood, so working with her turns out to be okay tonight.

Standing down at the far end of the bar closest to the door, I've got a few newly legal drinkers and their friends partying and paying more than usual customers do, so I give them some extra attention. I may not like this job, but I know how to do it damn well. Every tip I get I think about what gift I can buy Hailey to congratulate her on what she accomplished today.

Maybe a necklace or a bracelet? She doesn't seem to wear jewelry much, but that doesn't mean she wouldn't like some. Maybe a nice dinner out? That could be fun. Maybe we could go for a few nights down the coast to a secluded hotel that won't involve my cousin busting in with his idiot friends.

Someone tapping on my shoulder rips me out of

my daydreams about Hailey's gift, and I turn my head to see Antonio in my face. Dark haired and literally the guy women come to see here at Club X, especially since he has a habit of sleeping with customers, sometimes two or three in a night, he points over his shoulder and smiles.

"Pretty lady down at the other end of the bar wants to talk to you," he says with a smile. "She asked for you by name."

Feeling like busting his ass, I say, "Not you? You must be losing your touch, man."

He screws his expression into one of disgust at my joking. "Don't you worry about my touch. It's all it's ever been."

I look down the bar to see a familiar face staring back at me—the food blogger woman. Brooke. Brooke what, though?

She waves me down to where she's standing, and as I slowly walk toward her, I try to remember her last name. Damnit. This is what I get for calling her the food lady so many times. Maybe it won't matter. It's not like we have to be formal and use last names in a bar.

"Cade March, boyfriend of the girl who makes those incredible desserts!" she squeals above the music.

Fuck. She remembers my last name. Great.

"You're a sight for sore eyes. Tabitha and I are spending our last night in Tampa and figured we should go out for a few drinks. I had no idea when I heard about Club X that it would be this crowded. We barely got in before security stopped the line," she says, thankfully moving on from names.

Glancing over her shoulder, I see her friend with the giraffe neck and smile. She's too far away to hear anything I might say, so I turn my focus back to Brooke standing at the bar.

"It's good to see you again. That was interesting today. The whole podcast thing, I mean. I know Hailey had a great time. She talked about how much fun talking to you was all the way home."

Brooke excitedly waves her hand in between us, showing off some serious purple painted claws before she drops them to my forearm. I look down, unsure we're already at the touching one another stage, but I don't want to say anything and ruin things for Hailey. If this woman can help the woman I love, then I can handle her putting her hand on me. It's not like hundreds of other Club X customers won't do the same in the next few hours.

"It was so much fun! I hope it helps her. I'd love to help her in other ways too."

Seeing my chance to do something to make that happen, I lean forward and try to encourage her. "That would be great. I know if more people got to taste what she can make, they'd be lined up outside her parents' restaurant. You tried them, so you know what I mean."

She points at her ear and shakes her head before leaning toward me. "This music is really loud. Is there any place quieter we can talk? Do you get a break?"

I quickly scan the crowd in front of the bar and wave Antonio down to me. "It's not too busy, so I'm going to take ten. I'll be right in the office if things get hairy and you need me back ASAP."

My fellow bartender seems unfazed by my leaving and simply nods, so I come around the bar and point toward my father's office. "Come with me. It's quieter in there."

She smiles and latches onto my arm as I weave through the crowd of people drinking and dancing. When we reach the office door, I open it and see my father isn't anywhere around.

Good. I don't want to talk to Brooke in front of him.

I guide her inside and shut the door, immediately drowning out all the noise from outside. Brooke takes a deep breath and looks around. It's not as impressive as her hotel room, but it will have to do.

"That's better," she says with a smile. "It really is loud out there. I don't know how you work in that night after night."

"Tonight's not even really bad," I say as I move her toward the couch over against the wall. "Sometimes it's loud enough that you wish you could wear earplugs, but then I'd never hear what anyone wants to drink. That would kill my tips, I think."

She laughs at my lame attempt at a joke, probably just being polite. I don't mind her thinking I'm stupid for that remark. I just want her to help Hailey.

"Whose office is this? Yours?"

"No. It's my father's. He owns the club. I merely work the bar."

The smile I get for that seems forced. "That's nice. You and your girlfriend work for your families' businesses."

Time to get her focused on how she can help Hailey.

"It's not really the same. I just bartend. Hailey actually creates things that her customers love. The first time I had her chocolate lace cookies, I knew they were special. Nothing I've ever mixed up tasted that good. I'd love it if more people could try them. They look like those little lace things grandmothers have around their houses and you think they're going to be light as air, but they're really creamy and very chocolatey."

"Tabitha loved the macarons. She said they were... what did she call them?"

When she can't seem to come up with the right word, I say, "Sweet?"

"Yes! That's it. I thought she said something else, but that was for that Boston Cream dessert. Tabitha said she thought it was sumptuous. Isn't that a wonderful word?" Brooke asks as she turns to face me on the couch.

"Sure. Sumptuous is a great word. I'd definitely say many of the desserts Hailey makes are sumptuous. The lighter ones might be better called tasty, but they're great too."

"I'm going to have to do a month's worth of spin classes after today. I couldn't help it, though. Those desserts seduced me into being bad."

My senses go on high alert as I listen to her talk and watch her hands move closer and closer to my thigh. Is she doing what I think she's doing?

"Is that how she got you, Cade? Did she seduce you with those tempting desserts?" Brooke asks as she nudges her leg against mine.

I know what's going on, and I need to make it very clear I'm with Hailey before this woman gets any ideas. I still hope I can get her to help Hailey more, but most important is she understands I'm all about my girlfriend. Period.

"She definitely did seduce me with them. I'm only human. One taste of her lace cookie and I was lost. What man could say no? That's why I think there's a great chance for anyone who wanted to help her get her treats out to the world."

As the last word leaves my lips, Brooke swings her leg over my lap, and a second later, she's straddling my hips. Before I can stop her, her lips cover mine in a heavy kiss and she jams her tongue halfway down my throat, moaning into my mouth.

Stunned, I push her away and shake my head.

"Brooke, whoa. I'm with Hailey. She's my girlfriend. I just wanted to get you to help her. You need to get off me. Now."

I lift her by her waist and set her on her feet, hurrying to stand up before she jumps on my lap again but wondering if I can salvage anything to help Hailey. "It's okay. I mean, I'm flattered, but I'm with Hailey. Sorry."

She smooths the front of her pants and smiles like nothing just happened. "Can't blame a girl for trying. I still want to help her get the word out because I agree that people will like her desserts. No hard feelings?"

"No, no hard feelings," I say, relieved she didn't take my rejection and twist it to hurt Hailey.

"Well, time for me to go. Tabitha and I have an early flight tomorrow morning. Have a good night, Cade."

I watch her walk out as my father comes in and hope I didn't ruin everything Hailey worked so hard at with her this afternoon. The problem is I don't think Brooke came here to talk about helping her with anything. What she wanted to do was help herself to me.

Fucking food lady.

My father walks by me on his way to his desk looking confused. "Who was that?"

"That food blogger from the podcast today."

He sits down and leans back in his chair, folding

his arms behind his head. "Oh yeah? What did she want with you?"

"Nothing. I better get back behind the bar. Thanks for letting me use the office."

When I turn to leave, he laughs and says, "I don't recall you asking, but whatever. Hope it helped."

I just hope it didn't hurt.

CHAPTER THIRTY-SEVEN

$\mathcal{H}$ailey

My phone vibrates across the dining room table, and I grab it to see who could be trying to talk to me at seven-thirty in the morning. I know it's not Cade since he didn't get home from the club until after three. His text telling me he loves me came in a three-eighteen, so it can't be him.

I vaguely recognize the number, but I answer it to hear Brooke already talking when I say hello. "We don't fly out until noon, so if you can get over here within the next half hour, I have some ideas for how to get the word out about those delicious treats of yours."

The next half hour? Thirty minutes? I'm still in the T-shirt and shorts I wore to bed last night, and I look like something the cat dragged in since I didn't remove my makeup before falling asleep!

But I can't miss an opportunity like this. Brooke might be able to help me get my desserts into the hands of someone who could write a great article about them and get even more people into the restaurant.

Jumping up from the table, I begin to dash around the house like a chicken with my head cut off. God, I really am my father's daughter!

"Okay, I'm getting ready right now. I'll be there in just a few minutes. Thank you so much, Brooke!" I say as I tear up the stairs to my bedroom.

"See you then!"

There's just enough time to wash my face and brush my teeth before I throw on a pair of capris and my favorite baby blue T-shirt with the word BELIEVE on it. Me without makeup isn't exactly the best, but when opportunity knocks, you have to answer the door no matter what you look like.

I drive like a maniac the whole way to the Regent Hotel, blowing through a red light a block away. With the sun shining in the bright blue sky, I didn't see it turn, but I doubt a cop would buy that story. I just hope no one saw me do that.

This time, I run through the hotel's lobby and barely notice anything as the furniture and decorations go by me in a blur on my way to the elevator. When the doors close and I press the button for five, I can finally catch my breath.

"This is going to be great. Just keep calm and try not to worry about not wearing makeup," I whisper into the elevator around me.

When I get to her room, I repeat that same idea and add, "You can do this. Remember you can do this."

"Hailey, it's so great you were able to come over so early today. Let's sit down and talk."

I immediately notice both Brooke and Tabitha have makeup on their faces. And they look incredible. Are those fake eyelashes they're wearing? God, my eyes must look like two pencil holes in a bedsheet compared to theirs.

Opening them as wide as I can get them, I nod and hope they don't pay too much attention to my face during this conversation. "I was so happy to hear from you today. Any help you can give me would be so appreciated."

Brooke waves her now purple tipped hands in front of her face, clearly excited about what she has to tell me this morning. "Well, I spoke to one of my fellow food bloggers, Jessie Tyson, and she wants to do a whole week of posts about you. She's local and has a really great audience, so I think it would give you a leg up you could use. She said to have you give her a call, so here's her number and all her info.

Definitely check out her site. She gets tons of visitors every day."

She reaches across the space between us over the coffee table and hands me a sheet of note paper with all the details. "She said she hopes you'll call today, so I think she's excited too."

I clutch the paper like it has the secret to eternal life scrawled on it, thrilled for this assistance from a woman I just met last week. "Thank you so much, Brooke. This is so great of you."

She smiles, but it feels forced. Then she turns to look at Tabitha, who's never sat down, and I sense something's wrong. Did they have a fight? I had wondered if they were together and not just boss and assistant. Maybe I interrupted something when I got here so quickly.

"I have something I need to tell you, but I don't know how to say it."

My heart sinks. This is something about me. Something she doesn't know how to tell me. She doesn't think my desserts are good. She didn't like them. She was only pretending. But why did she call me over here this morning if she hated my stuff? Why would she recommend me to this Jessie woman too?

"Oh?"

That's all I can get out. Oh. Not even an oh my or an oh God. Just oh. Pretty much how my hopes being dashed to pieces sounds.

"This is so hard. I really like you, Hailey, and I

think you're super sweet. I feel like in the short time we've known each other we've gotten to be like friends, and I would never let a friend be done wrong."

Now my stomach drops. "Done wrong?"

What does that mean?

She gives Tabitha another somber look and then falls silent. The seconds feel like hours as they tick by, and all I want to do is scream, "Who or what is doing me wrong and how do you know about this?"

Finally, she blurts out, "Your boyfriend. Cade? I don't think you can trust him."

Every word after his name hits me like a slap to the face, but somehow I get out, "What? Why can't I trust him? He's great."

For the first time, Tabitha speaks up as she walks over to take a seat on the couch next to Brooke. "You have no idea how much we don't want to tell you this. He seemed like such a great guy yesterday."

"He is a great guy," I say, my words trembling as they leave my mouth.

"No, he isn't," Brooke says quietly. "We saw him last night at that club he works at, and when I tried to talk to him, he was all over me. I couldn't believe it since he was so sweet with you when he was here."

"Cade wouldn't do that. He wouldn't do that to me."

"Tabitha was there. She witnessed it all."

All I can do is shake my head. They must be mistaken. Cade wouldn't do that. He just wouldn't.

"You must have him confused with someone else. Cade isn't like that."

The two women exchange looks, and then Brooke grabs her phone off the table. Holding it up, she turns it toward me, and I expect her to show me a picture of Cade doing something. Instead, I hear voices coming from it, but I can't understand what they're saying.

"Who is that?" I ask, hoping against hope that it's not Cade's voice on that phone.

"I'm only human. What man could say no? I want you to get off."

Oh, God. He sounds so wrong. The guilt is coming through loud and clear. It's his voice. His words. Him hitting on Brooke.

It feels like someone has sucked all the air out of the room and I can't fill my lungs with a single breath to sustain me. Why would he do this? Was everything we've been to each other these past few weeks a lie?

My mind races as I struggle to fight back tears. Did he want to do that thing he did with that bartender the night I was at Club X? Was that all a lie he told me too?

"Hailey, I'm sorry I had to play that for you. You don't deserve that. You're so sweet and you're so talented. I just couldn't walk around with that on my conscience and not let you know the truth about him."

I shake my head but can't say a word, terrified if I

utter a single syllable that I'll begin crying. I believed every word he said. Even when I had proof with my own eyes, I believed him.

Why would he do this to us? If he wanted someone else, why did he chase me like he did?

Through watery eyes, I look across at Brooke and know the truth. She's the type of woman he wants. She's gorgeous and successful and she probably comes from money.

Exactly the opposite of me.

"I better go, Brooke. Thanks for all your help."

"Okay. I hope I did the right thing, Hailey. I did, didn't I?" Brooke asks.

"Sure. Thanks. I have to go."

She says something as I hurry toward the door, but I can't hear her over the sound of my heartbeat pounding in my ears. Nothing she could say now matters anyway.

By the time I get to my car, I can't stop the tears from coming anymore. I sit there in the parking lot of the expensive and luxurious Regent Hotel and sob like a baby, knowing I don't belong there just like I never belonged with Cade.

How could I have been so stupid?

CHAPTER THIRTY-EIGHT

ade

ONE OF THE REASONS I HATE WORKING AT CLUB X so much is the hours. Getting home after three and not getting to sleep until four in the morning means I don't wake up until nearly noon and half the day is gone already. When it was just me, it didn't matter so much, but now that Hailey is in my life, having only a couple hours to see her before I have to go back to the club feels like a tradeoff I'm not willing to make.

I roll over and run my hand over the pillow she used the last time she slept in my bed. Pulling it to my face, I inhale deeply and smell the scent of that shampoo she uses. Vanilla? Or maybe coconut? I'm not sure. All I know is it reminds me of her.

Glancing at my phone through still-sleepy eyes, I see it's twelve-fifteen. Damn. I wanted to hang out with Hailey for a few hours before I need to be back at the club for seven.

My mind still groggy, I scrub the last of the night's sleep from my face and focus on the screen. Eleven messages. Who the fuck needed to talk to me that badly for the last eight hours that they left that many messages?

Even before I look, I'm guessing it's my father. He likes to send me an entire conversation in texts, each one two or three lines. I wake up thinking the world is on fire when it's just that he had an idea on some theme he thinks would work at the club and wants to know my opinion on it.

He's probably going to pitch that Y2K idea to me again. Dude, it wasn't good the first time you had it, so what would make you think a year later it's gotten any better? It's not a concept that's improving with age.

I set my phone back on the nightstand, not interested in dealing with that nonsense right after I wake up. That's really more of an in-person conversation anyway. Then I can shake my head when he says something really bizarre and hold my hand up to stop him before he gets too far into the crazy.

Staring up at the ceiling of my bedroom, I slowly come to life and wonder if I should read them. He's only going to continue messaging me if I don't. Then I'll have twenty or thirty to get through.

I reach my hand over and grab my phone, surrendering to the inevitability that I'll have to read them at some point. Better to get it over with now.

It only takes a split second to realize this isn't another one-sided conversation from my father. They're all from Hailey. The first message hits me like a fist to the face, stunning me.

I never want to see you again. I know what you did, and there's no way you'll talk yourself out of this one. You must think I'm so stupid, but since I believed you with the girl on the bar, I bet you thought you'd fool me with this one too.

What does she mean? My eyes roam down the screen to the next one filled with even more hurt.

How could you do this to us? Why? And why Brooke? Was it to make sure it was as painful as possible for me?

My chest tightens with each word I read. Why does she think something happened with the food lady? Did she tell her? But nothing happened. Nothing at all.

I swing my legs off the side of the bed and walk out into the kitchen as I read the next message from Hailey.

Don't call me or come looking for me at the restaurant. I don't want to ever see you again.

Instead of reading any more, which will only show me how much she's hurting, I do exactly what she said not to and call her. I need to hear her voice. I need her to hear me tell her what really happened so she can know I never did anything with Brooke.

That I wouldn't blow up all we have together. Not with some lying food lady. Not with anyone.

That I love her and would never hurt her like that.

But her phone simply rings and rings with no answer. I try again, but the same happens. And again and again for another four more times until the next time I try it goes directly to voicemail. I listen to her voice so sweet and bright when it says to leave her a message. I want to explain everything, but not in a voicemail message, for Christ's sake.

So instead I tell her the one thing that's truer now than it's ever been.

"Hailey, I love you. I'm coming over to see you, and I'm not leaving the restaurant until I talk to you. This is all a mistake, and I'm going to show you that. I love you."

I want to keep repeating that I love her so she can't think of anything else. Not whatever bullshit lie Brooke told her. Not whatever doubts she has because of what happened in her past. None of it. I just want her to know the one thing that's true is I love her.

She has to believe that.

HAILEY'S FATHER SEES ME AS I WALK IN THE FRONT door of Comfort Food, and I brace for what's likely to be the ugly scene that waits for me. I really don't want to have to fight through him to get to her, but I will today.

"Cade, good to see you!" he says as he walks over to greet me at the register. "Hailey's in the back. I'll go get her."

I quickly study his expression. It doesn't seem like he's being ironic or disingenuous in any way. Maybe he doesn't know?

"O—o—okay," I stammer out, unsure what's going on.

I read through all the messages before I got in my car and raced over here. Hailey never said she was mistaken or something had made her change her mind.

The double kitchen doors open, and she walks out looking as sweet and cheerful as usual. She doesn't smile so much as not frown, but when she stops in front of me, she points toward the door.

"I don't want to talk here. Let's go outside."

She doesn't sound furious or even sad. I don't understand.

By the time we get to the side of the restaurant out of sight, I'm totally confused. Her messages made it clear she's upset, but she's not acting like it.

Hailey stops near the corner of the building and spins around to face me. Now I see what she was hiding inside. The hurt. The anger. It's written all over her face.

"It was all a lie, wasn't it? Everything between us

just one big, fat lie to you," she says, her voice soft but shaking as she tries to hold back the tears.

"No! None of it was a lie. I love you, Hailey. I'm crazy about you. I would never do anything to hurt you, especially cheat on you with another woman and really especially with that food lady Brooke."

Her eyes well up with tears, but she shakes her head like she's willing herself to stay strong and not show me how devastated she is. She doesn't have to worry about that. I know what she's feeling. Her emotions came through loud and clear in her texts. That's why I rushed over here. I knew she was telling herself I'm just like that asshole she caught cheating on her.

But I'm not.

Hailey falls silent for so long I want to fill up the empty space with more words about how much I would never do what she thinks I did. I hate standing here with her so close but feeling like she's slipping away from me with every second that passes. I reach out to touch her, but she shakes her head and backs away.

Finally, she can't stop her tears from falling and lowers her head to hide her face from me. "I heard the recording, Cade. I heard you talking. It was your voice. I heard you kissing her. I heard it all."

"What recording? I don't know what you're talking about," I say, but it's like I'm watching her drift away as the memory of those few minutes with Brooke pass through my mind.

"I heard your voice! It was you, and you sounded so guilty. You knew what you were doing was wrong. Twice I've known the truth about you with my own senses. I saw with my very own eyes you and that girl up on that bar, but you made me disbelieve what I knew I saw. Now I heard with my very own ears your voice and hers while you and Brooke were together. Are you saying I shouldn't believe that either? Do I have to have all my senses prove what you are? Maybe I should taste another woman on you or smell her on you for proof? Do I need to feel another woman touch you to finally have enough proof that you'll admit the truth?"

Hailey begins to sob, and I know I have to tell her the whole truth. It's now or never. But nothing really happened. She has to understand that. I didn't want to offend Brooke and ruin Hailey's chances that she could really get her to help her.

"Okay, okay. There was a kiss, but I didn't kiss her. She kissed me. I should have pushed her away quicker, but I was worried that if I did anything to piss her off that she'd take it out on you. She came looking for me at the club. I didn't want to see her. She said she wanted to talk about helping you, so I took her into the office. That was all I wanted to do, but when we got in there she obviously had other plans."

I stop myself from saying anything more and try to

get Hailey to look at me. She lets me lift her chin, and when she looks up at me, her beautiful blue eyes are all watery. Looking at them breaks my heart, so I have to continue talking so she knows what happened. That I didn't do anything with that woman.

"You have to believe me, Hailey. Nothing happened. I don't know what kind of recording she has, but it's not real if you heard me saying I wanted her or even gave a damn about her. She's the food lady to me. That's it. The person who said she wanted to help you get the word out about all the great things you make."

As tears stream down her face, she stares up at me, tearing my heart out of my chest at seeing her like this. Then she says the words that make me feel like someone's carved into the center of me and left an empty space I won't be able to fill without her in my life.

"I never want to see you again, Cade. Don't text me. Don't come here and stand out in the parking lot waiting for me. Just stay away from me. Whatever I was to you I'm not anymore, so go find some other girl to play with."

Her words stun me, and I reach out to stop her from going back into the restaurant, but she pushes me away. And then she's gone, and I'm left standing there in the midday sun feeling like all the goodness in my life has been taken from me.

TIPPING THE BOTTLE UP TO MY MOUTH, I DRAIN THE last few drops of whiskey and toss it onto the couch next to me. For five hours, I've sat here trying to drown my ability to feel. It hasn't worked. If anything, I feel more, not less about losing Hailey than I did all those hours ago.

I hear the front door open and look toward the hallway to see Alex walking toward me. Not exactly the person I hoped would stop over tonight.

"Hey, what the hell are you doing sitting here? You're supposed to be at work," he says as he sits down in the chair in front of me.

"What are you? A fucking timeclock? Unless you're here to deliver more whiskey, go away."

Alex leans forward and narrows his eyes to look at me. "Are you drunk?"

"Yeah. And I plan on getting even more drunk just as soon as I can find another bottle," I announce before attempting to stand up.

Gravity or drunkenness, whichever is the more powerful force on me at the moment, sends me falling back onto the couch, and I give Alex a shrug. Guess I'm not looking for more to drink right now.

"What's going on, Cade? I've never seen you like this. You're supposed to be at work. Your father called me and asked me to come over here to see if you're home because he couldn't get in touch with you."

I grab my phone and hold it up for him to see. "I got his calls. I got his texts too. Today's been my day for texts I didn't fucking want."

"Why are you sitting here hammered when you're supposed to be at work?"

"Because I fucking hate that place, okay? Hate it!" I yell.

Alex nods like he understands. Of course, he would. He's known me for my entire life, so naturally he thinks he understands my utter loathing for that place.

"I know. You always have. But this isn't like you not to go to work. What's going on here, Cade?"

Focusing on him, I push myself up so I'm sitting. "I've always hated that club. You know that? My father spent every spare moment of his life when I was a kid there. My mother used to take me there so I could see him and we could have a normal family dinner together because he always fucking had to be at the club by six. He couldn't go in at seven. No, it had to be six. As if any of those fucking drunks that go there every night would know the difference if he waited until we had dinner at home together. He didn't even change when Ava came along."

Alex's face twists into an expression of sadness. "I know. I know you hate working there now too."

"But now I have an even better reason to hate it. First, fucking Katelyn...no, I mean Kylie...fuck, I don't know which one it was but whichever twin it was that decided she needed to put on that fucking show the night Hailey came nearly made me lose her. Then that fucking food lady decided to trap me and fucking tape us together. What kind of manipulative fucking bitch does that? And for what? We didn't do anything, but she told Hailey we did. Now she says all her senses tell her the truth about me."

His sadness gives way to confusion, which is written all over his face even before he starts talking again. "Wait. What? What happened with Hailey?"

I hang my head, too drunk and too sad to look at him when I explain. "She broke up with me. Brooke, the food lady who said she wanted to help her, came to the club and when we went into the office to talk about her helping Hailey, she made a move on me. I don't know how, but she recorded the whole thing and then played it for Hailey. And I really don't know how she made it sound like she and I were together. But she did, and Hailey's gone."

"Did you talk to her? Tell her it didn't happen?"

"Of course, I did. She doesn't believe me. Why would she? She saw what happened with the twins, and now she's heard what supposedly happened with that Brooke bitch. I even went over to her hotel to convince her to tell Hailey the truth, but she left already."

"Why would this Brooke woman do that to her? I thought she wanted to help Hailey because she loved her stuff."

"Isn't that the question of the day? I've sat here for hours trying to figure out why food bitch would do that to someone she just met. Nothing makes sense, but then again, I've been blasted for most of that time, so that could be why I can't work out what the fuck made her do that."

"Maybe she's jealous," Alex says, nodding like he approves of that explanation. "She probably doesn't have the talent Hailey has in her little finger in her entire body."

Leaning back, I let my head rest against the couch cushion. I'm tired of trying to figure out what food lady's motive was.

"It doesn't matter why she did it. All that matters is Hailey's gone."

Alex jumps up from the chair and begins moving around the room. That's how he acts when he's excited about something. What he could be excited about in all of this, I have no clue.

"Okay, here's what you have to do. Find out where you can locate this Brooke woman and talk to her. She clearly isn't any friend of Hailey's, and I doubt she has any interest in helping her after what she did to you. Just make her tell the truth and this will all be cleared up. You and Hailey will be back together."

Fuck, he makes it all sound so simple. Or maybe that's just because my drunken mind only understood about half of what he just said.

"It doesn't matter, Alex. It's over. Hailey was right

in the beginning. She's not a red Jag girl, and I'm not a guy who deserves someone like her. Karma got me, man. Every woman I've ever been with said this would happen, and lo and behold, it has."

He starts to say something, but I'm too drunk and too tired to listen to anymore. I just want to fall asleep thinking about Hailey and how she'd look at me like she loved me.

Like I could be someone she could love.

CHAPTER THIRTY-NINE

$\mathcal{H}$ailey

IN MY BEST EFFORT TO KEEP BUSY AND NOT LET myself think of Cade, I hide out in the kitchen with chocolate and attempt to create something new. The problem is I can't stop thinking of him, and after about an hour, I've eaten more of the chocolate than doing anything else with it.

The air around me smells like pancakes and sausage, the most popular item on the menu every Sunday morning. While the restaurant struggles during the week, Sunday mornings are always a busy time, thankfully. If it wasn't for the breakfast rush each weekend, my parents might have to close the place down.

I peek out the windows in the kitchen doors and see the crowds have thinned a bit since the last time I looked. Good. That will give my mom and dad a break, to say nothing of the servers and cooks.

As I'm staring out into the dining room, I see a man walk through the front door who catches my attention. Tall with dark hair and a hint of gray at the temples, he's attractive, but I think my mind must be playing games on me because he looks like an older version of the person I'm trying so very hard not to think about this morning.

Or ever again.

Curious, I step out to take a better look. Who is this man? Is it just a coincidence that he looks like the spitting image of Cade?

"Hailey, someone to see you!" Hannah calls back to me.

I walk toward where she stands with him, cautious that I might be going crazy. Too much Cade on my brain.

"Yes?" I say with a smile I hope doesn't show how odd I feel at this moment.

Hannah walks away, leaving me standing in front of this older lookalike of the man I so desperately want to not have on my mind anymore. Is this the universe playing some kind of cruel trick on me? Isn't it bad enough I trusted Cade and he made me look like a fool? Do I really need to see his face in every guy that shows up here?

"Hailey? It's nice to meet you," the man says as he extends his hand to shake mine. "I'm Stefan March, Cade's father."

A nervous giggle escapes from my throat. "I guess what they say is true. You can't plant peas and get corn. You look just like him."

Stefan gives me a big smile and leans in toward me. "I think I get to say he looks just like me since I came first."

"I guess. Yes, that would be right."

"Do you have a few minutes? I'd like to speak to you," he says in a kind voice that sounds so much like his son's it's unnerving.

But I can't talk to him or anyone else about Cade today. It's too soon. My emotions are too raw, too close to the surface, and there's no way I'll get through a conversation with him about his son and not cry.

"I'm not sure that would be a good idea right now."

"Well, then will you let me show you something? No talking. Just showing. I promise it won't take much of your time."

Still unsure if I should even do this, I point toward an open booth on the far side of the restaurant. "Okay. We can sit over there."

Good to his word, he doesn't try to make conversation at all as we walk to the booth. When we sit, he remains silent but sets a laptop on the table.

Spinning it around, he lifts the top and presses a

button to light up the screen. "All I ask is that you watch."

I look over the laptop and give him a smile, noticing how similar his deep brown eyes are to his son's. Deep brown eyes that I've looked into so many times and found the calm I needed.

"Okay."

When I look back at the screen, I see a black and white picture. It's a recording of some sort, but I don't know from where or of what.

As if he's reading my mind, Stefan says, "This is the security camera footage of my office from Friday night. The sound will come up in a few seconds."

For a moment, I panic. I don't want to watch this. I can't see Cade with someone else. Why would his father come here to show me that? Is it that he doesn't want the two of us together? Because if that's the case, he didn't have to bother coming all the way over here to show me the video proof his son cheated on me. I already heard the audio.

But then I see on the screen Cade and Brooke standing there in the middle of his office talking, and it's not like she said it happened at all. He's talking about how he hopes she'll help me. He doesn't look like he's interested in her. Everything he's saying is for my benefit.

Then I see her climb on top of him and kiss him, just like he claimed she did. It's only for a second or two, though, and then I hear him say the words any girlfriend would want to hear in this situation.

"Brooke, whoa. I'm with Hailey. She's my girlfriend. I just wanted to get you to help her. You need to get off me. Now."

I stare at the screen as she makes some excuse about why she hit on him, but I'm not listening anymore. All I can see is Cade doing exactly what he told me he did.

Stefan closes the laptop and lets out a heavy sigh after Brooke leaves the office. "Nobody is harder on Cade than I am, but he's a good man. He wouldn't do anything to hurt someone he truly loved, and he loves you. That's obvious. I just thought you should see this since I've been told you heard some version of it that isn't true."

"What did he tell you?"

He shakes his head and smiles. "My son wouldn't tell me anything. We aren't like that. That's my fault, but that's the way it is. His cousin Alex told me after he found him drunk last night when he didn't come into work."

"She told me they were together. She played me a recording with his voice on it saying those words he said on the security tape, but not all of them. She twisted everything to make it seem like they were together."

Stefan nods. "Doctored. Probably just a splice job. It isn't hard to do. If she has someone around her who knows anything about production, it could have been a very convincing version of what happened."

Someone like the production guy she has who helps with her podcast. I've been such a fool! I barely knew her, but I believed her lies over what the man I love was trying to tell me.

I cover my face with my hands, not wanting Cade's father to see me fall apart. "God, I said such horrible things to him. He must be so hurt. I was so angry, though."

"Something tells me it's not too late."

Wiping my eyes, I can't help but feel like it might be. "I wanted so much for Brooke to help me get the word out about my desserts to help my parents keep this place open that I couldn't see anything but that. I feel so foolish, and I've hurt Cade because I wanted to believe her."

"For what it's worth, you did hear his voice on the tape. I don't think anyone could blame you for believing what she told you."

I look down at the table to avoid meeting Stefan's gaze as the real truth becomes clear. "I believed it because it was something I always feared. I always worried I wasn't the type of person he should be with. I'm not really a red Jag kind of girl, as you can tell."

"Well, my son doesn't let his mother or me meet most of the women he dates, but we hear things since he and Alex are so close. Cade's never felt for any of them what he feels for you. That I do know. He even told me about you the other night. He said you went to school for psychology but something made you change your career path to begin baking here for your parents' customers. And from what I hear from my brothers and Alex, they'd love to have your desserts to serve their customers at CK."

He stops and lets out a heavy sigh. "Cade is a lot like me when I was his age. I think that's why we lock horns so often. That and I want him to take over the club so I can walk away knowing it's in the best hands possible and he hates the place. In that way, we're very different. I loved living the life of a single guy until I met his mother. Then, it was like someone suddenly turned on a light and I saw I didn't want to live like that because I wanted her in my life more. I think that's what Cade's found out with you. I'd hate to see him lose that because of someone's malicious attempt to break you two up."

Maybe it isn't too late.

"I need to talk to him. Right now. I'm sorry, Stefan, but I have to go."

I shimmy across the seat to leave, but he stops me. "Wait. I'm tired of being the only one who hasn't tasted one of your creations. Do you have any today?"

"Hang on. I'll be right back."

When I return to the table, I set an apple tart in front of him. "All I could do today was mope over a bowl of chocolate. This was from what I took that awful woman, but I promise it's still good."

"I'm sure it is," he says with a smile so similar to his son's. "Thank you for listening, Hailey. It was very nice to meet you. I think I'm going to enjoy this."

"Thank you very much for coming here to help me see the truth, Stefan. I hope this isn't the last time we meet."

With a shake of his head, he says, "I don't think it will be."

AFTER RACING THROUGH TRAFFIC, I GET TO CADE'S condo in record time after treating stop lights as optional on at least two occasions and the stop sign near his building as more of a glide sign. I run past the people walking in and get into the elevator to take me to the fifteenth floor. A few people getting on two floors up means I have to wait an extra thirty seconds to get to him, and by the time I reach his floor, I'm more nervous than I was the first time I came here.

I knock on his door, but I get no answer. I was in such a hurry to get to him that I forgot to check to see if his car was in the parking lot. He might not even be here.

Disappointed, I knock one more time and wait as each second that goes by I lose hope that I'm going to get to talk to him. I give the door knob a jiggle in a last-ditch attempt to get inside, and I'm thrilled when it actually opens.

Rushing in, I look around but don't see him. I

hurry into his bedroom, but the bed looks like it hasn't even been slept in. Did he go out and stay somewhere else last night?

The very idea of him licking his wounds over our breakup with someone else makes me feel sick. Disheartened, I walk out to the living room and there on the couch all curled up is Cade sleeping.

I crouch down beside him and press a kiss to his lips. Slowly, he wakes and looks at me like he isn't sure what he's seeing.

"Hailey? What are you doing here?"

"I came to tell you I was wrong. I'm sorry, Cade. I'm sorry I believed her. I'm sorry I said all those awful things to you."

Wide awake after hearing that, he sits up in front of me. "It doesn't matter. You were right. Who I am is the problem," he says sadly.

"No! It wasn't you. I know that now."

Cade sighs and shakes his head. "It's karma. Every single woman I've ever been with said this would happen. Now it has. It's cosmic payback for how I was with them, for who I was before I met you."

I grab his shoulders and shake him, desperate to make him understand. "Stop this! I know what happened with Brooke. Or better yet, I know what didn't happen. I'm sorry I didn't believe you when you told me nothing happened between you two."

"You don't believe her anymore?" he asks,

sounding so hopeful that I just want to take him into my arms and hold him forever.

Looking into his eyes, I see hope there too. "No. I saw the whole thing on the security tape from your father's office that night. I know you didn't do anything wrong. I heard what you said to her. You were trying to help me, like you always are."

"How did you see the security tape?"

"Your father. He came to see me at the restaurant this morning to show me. I'm so sorry, Cade. I should have believed you, but that recording sounded so real. It was just my insecurities blinding me to the truth. I should have known it never happened the way she said it did."

Cade sighs, his shoulders sagging in relief. "My father came to see you?"

"Yes. He played the tape from when you and Brooke were talking in his office, and I saw it all. It happened just like you said it did."

"How about that? Just when I think he and I might never get along, he goes and does something like this."

"I thought when I first saw him that he was some kind of memory sent to haunt me," I say, giggling. "You two look so much alike. If that's what your future is, I'm all in. You have good genes."

"Good old Stefan March. Just when you think you know the guy, he surprises you."

I lean forward and press a kiss to Cade's lips as he smiles. "So you forgive me?"

"Of course. I love you, Hailey."

Hearing that, I climb onto the couch to sit next to him, nuzzling my face in his neck. He feels just like he always has next to me.

Right. Perfect. Just where I want to be.

"You know, I drank like a bottle of whiskey last night. I'm sure I smell like the floor of a bar right now."

I take a deep breath in and definitely smell alcohol. "It's okay. I probably smell like chocolate after eating half a bowl of it today. If you're fine with that, I'm fine with you just as you are."

Cade hugs me tightly to him and kisses the top of my head. "I have a better idea. Let's jump in the shower. We can think of it as a fresh start."

"Good idea. We'll wash everything from the past couple days away and start over," I say as I stand up from the couch.

He gets up and wraps his arm around me. "And we'll have great shower sex because what is making up without that?"

No wonder I love this man.

CHAPTER FORTY

$\mathcal{H}$ailey

My stomach feels queasy like it always does when I'm moving but can't see where I'm going. I know Cade loves surprises, but I just wish he didn't require me to wear a blindfold for them.

"I think I might be sick. I'm just not good with not seeing the road when I'm in a car. I can't even sit in the backseat because I get carsick on trips."

He takes my hand and gives it a gentle squeeze. "Just one block more. If you're really not feeling good, take off the blindfold but keep your eyes closed, okay?"

"That doesn't really solve the problem, but thanks."

I feel the car slow down, and then a few seconds later, we come to a stop. Thank God. I really don't want to throw up all over whatever the surprise is.

"Okay, just let me come around and open your door. No peeking."

I hear the driver's side door open and feel a blast of hot air enter the car before it disappears when the door slams shut. Then when he opens my door, heat from the outside on this late July day rushes into where I sit. I feel his hand take hold of mine, and I turn to get out of the car.

"Watch your head," he cautions as I slowly stand up and step onto the curb.

"Ready? You can take off the blindfold now," Cade happily announces.

I push it up over the top of my head and see a store's windows in front of me. There's no name on them and no sign above on the building, though.

Turning to look at him, I see Cade beaming a smile. I love that he's so happy, but what's going on here?

"Do you know what this is?" he excitedly asks, clearly not understanding how in the dark I still am, even after taking the blindfold off.

"No. What is it?"

He brings my hand to his lips to kiss it. "This is your new bakery shop. You can still make anything you want for your parents' restaurant, and you'll be able to make all those desserts for CK too. Cassian and Kane told me their customers have been raving about them since you started making them last month, so this will help you do that and anything else you want to do."

I shake my head in disbelief. "You bought me a bakery?"

"Wait until you see it, Hailey. I asked Alex to tell me exactly what you might need for any kind of cake or pie or cookie or pastry or whatever you want to make. Whatever you can create, you have the kitchen to do it. He had one of his friends who's a pastry chef at one of the finest restaurants in New Orleans make a list, a dream list of everything he would love to have in his ideal kitchen, and that along with Alex's ideas is what you have in there. If you can think it, you can make it now."

Happiness fills me, and I start to cry. "You did this for me? How? This must have cost a fortune."

"That trust fund of mine needed to do something other than buy me more stuff I don't need. Seems even though I've been pretty much a loafer this past year, the bank thinks I'm a good risk. Don't worry about how much it cost. Just make whatever your heart desires here and it will all be worth it."

Tears stream down my face as I try to understand someone giving me such a gift. "I don't know what to say."

Cade kisses me and smiles. "Say you love me and you're going to make those incredible desserts and whatever else makes you happy, Hailey."

"I love you, Cade, and when I get over the shock of the man I love buying me a bakery shop, I'm sure I'm going to think up a thousand things I want to try. I've never had anyone do anything this wonderful for me before."

"Well, I had to do something for our three-month anniversary, especially after how great things went with that Jessie woman once she and all her blogger friends found out what Brooke tried to do to you."

"She really was so kind, wasn't she? I still don't understand how anyone found out since you swear you didn't tell anyone."

A sly smile turns up the corners of Cade's mouth. "You do know! Tell me. If it wasn't you, then who?"

"Alex. He's got lots of friends in the food biz, and all it took was telling the right person and the story had legs from there. My best friend is not only a committed hedonist but also someone who likes seeing people get their just desserts."

So it was someone in Cade's family all along. I had a feeling it was, but I couldn't be sure.

"I'd say Brooke Dunning got her just desserts. Jessie says she's practically a pariah in the food blogger world now. Nobody wants to do her podcast these days."

"Good. That's what being a jealous bitch gets her. But enough about food lady."

"You're right. No more talk about her."

"Now that you're making desserts for CK in addition to your parents' restaurant and their business is doing so well because of everything you make, I figured you needed the right kind of kitchen. Plus, when I tell you about the second surprise I have for you today, you're going to understand that this is the least I can do. Trust me on that."

I wipe the tears of joy from my eyes and laugh at how silly he can be. "So what's the second surprise?" I ask, curious how what he has next for me would make me think he needed to buy me an actual top of the line bakery.

"No blindfold needed for that one, although you might tell me later you wish you had to wear one."

"What is it? Nothing can be that bad."

He shakes his head and sighs. "Today, you get to meet the entire March and Jackson family, and by entire, I mean everyone from my cousins to my grandmother and everyone in between."

"And that's a bad thing? I've already met your parents and Alex and Kane, and I guess I technically met Wilder that night out at the island house. How bad could it be?"

He rolls his eyes. "Brace yourself for stories from my childhood and a million questions about us."

I wrap my arms around him and hold him to me.

He sounds like he's dreading this get-together today far more than I ever would.

"Well, I for one, can't wait to hear all about you as a little boy. Your mother told me a few things that were adorable. As for the questions, what is there to say about us? You bought me a bakery. I'm madly in love with you. That's the whole story, right?"

"Trust me. My family is going to want to know if we're getting married, where we plan to live, how many kids we plan to have, what their names will be, and a dozen other questions, and that's five minutes after we walk in the door."

This is the first time he's ever mentioned us getting married and doing all those other things. Cade and I have been happier than I thought two people could be after that mess with Brooke Dunning, but neither one of us has ever brought up the word marriage.

Until now.

"Well, what do you want me to say if they ask me those questions?"

He presses a kiss to the top of my head as I look at the front of the bakery he bought me just to make me happy. "Tell them you don't know. It drives the group of them crazy. That's my standard answer for anything, and they hate it."

Looking up at him, I search his face for the answer to the question that's now on my mind. "Okay, but do we know?"

He doesn't answer immediately, and I wonder if he

regrets mentioning marriage, even in the way he did. I wait for him to say something, but I feel like I ruined everything by pushing this issue.

"Do you love me?" he asks in a serious tone that makes me nervous.

"Yes."

"And do you believe I love you more than anything in this world?"

"Yes."

A smile lights up his face, making his dark eyes sparkle as he looks down at me like I'm the most important thing in his life. "Then we know. When it's time for them to know, we'll tell them."

He's right. We do know, and what I know more than anything else is I love this man and he loves me.

Everything else is icing on the cake.

Cade takes my hand and brings it up to his mouth in a kiss. "Who knows? Maybe Cash won some big pot in a poker game everyone will want to talk about, or Liam finally decided to take that job he's been thinking about for weeks and no one will be interested in paying attention to us today."

I roll my eyes at how cute he can be. "Like the infamous Cade March finally bringing a girlfriend to one of the March family parties isn't going to be the major topic of discussion? I doubt it, but I'm ready."

"Well, let me show you your brand-new kitchen before we tackle all of that," he says as he tugs me toward the building's front door.

My brand-new kitchen. My brand-new bakery.

"Okay, but before I get all tongue-tied and awestruck, I want to tell you something."

"What's that?" he asks, holding up the keys to my new business.

"I love you, and not because you bought me an entire building with a super new kitchen so I can make anything I want. I love you because you're you, Cade."

He smiles, and it's like he lights up from the inside at hearing me say that. "I love you too. Now let's go check out that kitchen of yours. I've been dying to show you this for days, so don't make me wait anymore."

Impatient, he hurriedly opens the door and rushes into the building. "Alex made me promise I'd show you something first, but now that I'm here, I can't remember what it is," he says with a laugh.

I watch him make a beeline for the back of the building and can't help but smile at how happy giving me this gift makes him. Not that I'm surprised. I don't know what other guys with trust funds are like, but Cade doesn't have a selfish or stingy bone in his body.

He turns around and looks at me with excitement flashing in his eyes. "You coming?"

"I'm right behind you!" I yell back as I make my way toward my new kitchen.

How did I ever think for a second I wouldn't fall madly in love with this man?

CHAPTER FORTY-ONE

ade

I FEEL THE PRESSURE FILL MY CHEST AS I DRIVE UP to my grandmother's house. All the cars tell me everyone in my family is here already.

This will be fine. I'm my grandmother's favorite grandchild. Or at least one of them. I think she might favor Alex a little more since they share a name and I think Alexandria March was a hedonist in her day.

No, this will be okay. It's just me bringing a girlfriend to meet my family. All eight hundred and sixty-two of them. At the same time.

"Cade, are you okay? You haven't put the car in park, and you're squeezing my hand so hard I think the circulation is getting cut off to my fingertips."

I turn to look at Hailey and realize I totally zoned out from panic for a few seconds there. Opening my hand, I force a smile.

"I'm sorry. I didn't mean to crush your fingers. Are you okay?"

She smiles sweetly, shaking her head. "I'm fine, honey. My hands have gone one-on-one with a mixer and barely won more times than I want to count. I was just worried because you seemed to go blank for a little bit. Are you really that worried about me meeting your grandmother and everyone else?"

Hurt simmers beneath that question, so I quickly move to help her understand why this family get-together is freaking me out. After I put the Jag into park and turn off the engine, I turn to face her and hope I can find the right words.

"It's not you, Hailey. My family can be a lot sometimes, and I'm related to all of these people. I've seen them converge like a pack of hyenas on other girlfriends a few of my cousins have brought to family parties."

Hailey smiles, and I know she thinks I'm exaggerating. I wish I was.

"Hyenas? Cade, they're probably just like your mother and father, and the first time I met them was great. Remember, you were nervous that night too? You were sure your father would make you sound like the world's biggest manwhore and your mother would tell me terribly embarrassing stories about when you were a little boy. Neither of those things happened, and we had a great time. Then Ava and I had a great time together when the three of us went to lunch. This is going to be just like that, I bet."

That dinner with my parents did go pretty well, after all. My father didn't feel the need to play my greatest hits and bring up the name of every woman I've ever dated, and my mother kept her story time to a minimum, sharing only about when I was five and thought people were like dinosaurs and laid eggs instead of giving birth.

But that wasn't my extended family.

"Well, that night didn't include my uncles and aunts, notorious for their questions and gossip more than anyone in the family, except my grandmother. Once Olivia and Abbi get a hold of you, God only knows what kind of information the two of them will wriggle out of you about us. One minute you'll be smiling and explaining how nice you think my grandmother's house is, and the next you'll be inexplicably talking about my favorite place to have sex and how often we sleep together. My aunts are like the CIA, Hailey. And don't even get me started on my uncles."

None of what I'm saying seems to be scaring her, unfortunately. With a giggle, she takes my hand and brings it to her lips in a kiss. "I've never met men who were that gossipy, Cade. I'm sure they're just like your father, and Stefan has been wonderful every time we've spent time together."

I shake my head, wishing I could explain how wrong she is about that. "My uncles are nothing like my father. I love them, but no. They look like they're cool, and Kane has a badass vibe to him that makes it seem like he's quiet and all that, but once their wives are around, forget it. Cassian will be the one to ask when we're going to get married, if his wife or Abbi hasn't first. You'd think it would be my grandmother, but it'll be him. He's got this whole family thing about him, and the thought of adding more people to the tribe practically makes him giddy."

"Well, we already decided my answer is that I don't know, right? I doubt he's going to ask for more than that."

The image of Cassian stepping back all gentlemanly and his wife and Abbi coming in for the second attempt flashes through my mind. I'll probably be talking to Alex about something, and they'll swoop in like vultures with their questions.

Maybe this was a bad idea. We can do this some other time. Maybe in a year or so. Or never. Never works too.

As I reach down to start the car, Hailey leans over and kisses my lips, stopping me. "It will be okay, Cade. I'm sure they're all great people. I love you, and Alex is one of my favorite people in the world after only a couple months now that he and I work together on the desserts for your uncles' restaurant. It's going to be okay. Have some faith."

I close my eyes and let out a heavy sigh. "I just worry that you're meeting people who've known me for my entire life."

"Look at me, Cade."

After I take in another deep breath and let it out, I do as she wants and open my eyes to see her looking at me like I'm the best thing she's ever seen. "They know all the good, the bad, and the ugly, and even if they don't mean to, I'm worried they're going to make you think you made a mistake."

"A mistake? How?"

"By staying with me after all that happened at the beginning when we first started dating."

She cradles my face and looks into my eyes with that gentle stare that never fails to make me think I'm the luckiest man in the world. "Baby, it was no mistake believing in you. I told you. I don't hold your past against you. Do you know why?"

I shake my head as I realize I don't know the answer to that. I guess I just always assumed it was because she's a good person.

"Because I don't want people to hold my past against me. What if you found out a little over a year ago I was a mess and that made you think you shouldn't take a chance on being with me?"

"It wouldn't."

"Well, for some people it might. People change,

Cade. Being around you has brought out a lot of things in me that were hidden for a long time when I was with Malcolm and then after what happened with him. I like that change in me. I think you're a different person too, and even if your family brings up that you've been with a lot of women before me, which I doubt they will, that's okay. Your past is your past. What we have now is our present."

She never fails to make me happy. "And we have our future."

"Exactly. And our future. So don't worry about what they ask when you're not there or that they tell stories about when you were little. All of it just makes me love you even more, okay?"

"All right, but don't say I didn't warn you."

As I move to get out of the car, she says, "You worry a lot for a guy who's so carefree. How bad could these stories be?"

I glance back at her as half a dozen tales of my escapades throughout my life march through my memory. "Remember me mentioning about that woman who's going to at some point walk up to me and slap me across the face?"

"Yes."

"Well, there's at least one other person, probably an old man by now, who would still call the cops on me without even saying hello first. In my defense, though, it wasn't just me. Alex, Cash, and Liam were usually right alongside me causing the trouble."

When I turn away, I hear a tiny giggle escape from her. "I bet you four were just the cutest little hellions this town had ever seen."

"That's not exactly the way we've been described."

MY GRANDMOTHER STANDS IN THE FRONT DOORWAY to her house in white pants and a pale blue top, thankfully alone and not flanked by every member of my family peeking their heads out from behind her. Her ear to ear smile reminds me of how she looked when I first learned how to ride a bike without training wheels.

"Cade! I'm so happy you're here! Come give me a hug and introduce me to this beautiful young woman."

Hailey squeezes my hand for a moment and then loosens her hold. Turning to look over at her, I quietly say, "This is the easy part. My grandmother is going to be the easiest part of this day. Trust me."

We climb the steps to the porch and I open my arms to give my grandmother a hug. "Hi, Grandma. You look great. Did you take up long distance running? Whatever you're doing, don't stop."

She leans back from our embrace and gives me that look of hers that says she knows I'm simply flattering her. "You're just like your father, even if you don't want to think you are. He always knew just how to charm people too when he was your age."

"I'll take that comparison, Grandma."

Looking around me, she smiles. "And who is this beautiful girl in the yellow dress looking like the personification of summer?"

As if she doesn't know all the vital statistics like the back of her hand already.

I reach out and take Hailey's hand to pull her to my side. "Grandma, this is Hailey, my girlfriend. And Hailey, this is my grandmother, the one and only, Alexandria March."

For a moment, she stares at us, and I wonder if I underestimated how she'd react to my not being single anymore. Terror races through me at the idea that right here at the front door we're going to have to deal with the first of many comments about how no one ever thought I'd settle down.

Then she smiles and my stress melts away for the moment. "You are just the cutest couple I've ever seen. You have beautiful blue eyes, Hailey, and I've always been partial to blue eyes since two of my sons have them from my late husband. It's so wonderful to have you here with my grandson. He's probably told you he's my favorite hasn't he?"

Leaning in toward us, she whispers, "He is, but don't tell anyone. Their feelings would be hurt, but how could he not be my favorite? Just look at him."

Not surprising since my father always has been her favorite son. She probably just favors us because we take after her in the looks department.

"So everyone is here already and out back on the

porch. They can't wait to meet you, Hailey, but let me give you a little piece of advice. If you just say 'I don't know' to any question they throw at you, they give up relatively soon."

My grandmother turns to look at me and winks. "Isn't that right, Cade?"

"I told her always go with I don't know. It drives them crazy and you don't have to tell them anything."

She nods and gives us a wicked smile. "He learned that from me, you know. A big family means lots of people wanting to know every tiny tidbit of your life. I don't tell them everything, though. You need to keep them in the dark about some things, don't you think?"

Hailey chuckles and looks over at me. "I think your grandson here takes after you. He prefers the idea of remaining a mystery too."

"It's the only way to be," I say with a shrug. "Once you start giving them details, forget it. Then people start having opinions about your life, and the next thing you know, there's someone explaining how you can't do what you want while you're trying to eat a hot dog and enjoy a cold beer."

My grandmother laughs at that little bit of truth. "Always remain a mystery. It's the secret to how I get away with all I do in this world. Now let's go in, and remember, no matter what we all seem, we love each other in this family."

She turns on her heel and walks into the house before I look over at Hailey and ask, "Ready?"

"I am, and your grandmother is as wonderful as you said she was. I don't know how old she is, but she's sassy, and I love that. I can see her putting someone in their place and smiling the whole time."

We walk inside and I say, "She can tell someone to go to hell and make them thankful she bothered to take the time to mention it."

The sound of my family having a good time outside filters through the house, but all I feel is dread. We can be a lot to handle. I hope it wasn't a mistake bringing Hailey here today.

She gives my hand a squeeze, and I turn to see her smiling. "This is going to be fun. Try to look like you want to be here, Cade."

CHAPTER FORTY-TWO

$\mathcal{H}$ailey

CADE'S GRIP ON MY HAND TIGHTENS AS WE WALK through his grandmother's house, and by the time we reach the back door to the porch, I worry he might spin the two of us around and bolt before I even get the chance to see another member of his family. I'm starting to worry there really might be a reason I wouldn't want to meet the entire March and Jackson clan.

I lean over and kiss his cheek as he looks out toward the group of people assembled outside. "There's nothing anyone can tell me that would make me love you any less, okay?"

He turns to look at me, and I see genuine concern

in his dark eyes. "I hope you mean that because it's about to get tested this afternoon."

"Don't worry. I love you, and I have a feeling after today, I'm going to love you even more. By the way, I think I saw Wilder out there. Can we make a deal that you won't fight him today? I think your grandmother might hate that."

That breaks the tension, and Cade rolls his eyes. "Okay. I promise. Time to meet the family."

"Who's first?" I ask as I glance out and see a blond woman standing next to a redhead with expressions that say they're dying to meet me.

Cade looks out the door and smiles. "My aunts Abbi and Olivia. The blonde is Abbi, and she's married to Kane. Olivia is Alex's mother. I want to say they're both cool, but by the looks of it, they're about to burst from about a million questions. Last chance to leave. You say the word and we're out of here. My grandmother won't care. She'll think it's mysterious."

"It's going to be great. I know the drill. Lots of I don't knows and smiles."

"Brace yourself for so many stories about when I was little from Olivia. I spent a lot of time at their house with Alex."

The dread in his voice is clear, so I kiss him again and whisper in his ear, "It's okay. I don't think she could tell me anything more embarrassing than the story you told me about when you and Alex peed in your sleeping bags because his brother stuck your hands in warm water."

A nervous laugh explodes out of him, and he shakes his head. "You have no idea. Pissing in sleeping bags might be the least disgusting thing Alex and I did as boys. Just remember you love me, okay?"

Before I can tell him I would never forget, I hear a man's voice call out, "Cade, you can't hide in there forever. Come on out and let us meet your girlfriend."

He pushes the door open as he explains, "That's Cassian. He's married to the redhead. He used to be my favorite uncle until about five seconds ago."

We step out onto the porch and Alex greets us with a beer for Cade. "I didn't know what to get you, Hailey, but considering that you two are all my mother and Abbi have talked about all day, I figured a drink would be in order."

"I think I better stay sober today," I joke as Cade tilts the bottle up to his mouth and takes a gulp of beer. "I tend to get a little dopey when I drink."

Alex smiles and reaches over toward the porch railing for a bottle of lemonade. "Understood. Hey, what did you think of the kitchen over at the bakery? Cade said he was going to show you before you came over."

I open my mouth to tell him how much I love all the cool things he insisted should be included in the kitchen, but before I can say a word, Cade's aunts hurry over to say hello. Both beautiful women, I instantly can tell that Olivia is the chatty one and Abbi is a little more reserved.

And like Cade warned, they immediately begin to ask questions about how we met, how long we've been dating, and a dozen other topics, but I've got a plan ready. Standing next to me, Cade tries to interject answers to save me, and he succeeds for a few seconds.

"Abbi and Olivia, Hailey's going to be around for a long time, so trust me, you'll get to know her," he says when they begin to ask about our plans for the future.

Time to change the subject.

While I search my purse for my phone, I ask them, "Did you know Cade bought me a bakery? Want to see pictures?"

And just like that, his two aunts fall silent, their mouths open in shock.

I hold up my phone in front of them and smile at Cade. "Alex helped him decide on what machines he should buy and how it should be set up. Now when I'm making my desserts, I have a brand-new kitchen to make them in."

Out of the corner of my eye, I see Stefan walk up the stairs and take a peek at the picture of the bakery. Leaning in, he kisses me on the cheek and whispers in my ear, "That's how you do it in this family. Congratulations on the new business."

As Abbi and Olivia watch Cade scroll through the dozens of pictures I took earlier, I give his father a smile. "I'll make sure one of the first things I do is whip up a batch of those lace cookies you love."

His eyes roll back in his head, and he sighs. "Oh, I do love those. Just tell me when and I'll be there."

"Is Shay here?" I ask before scanning the faces below in the yard.

"She will be later, I hope. Her research has her tied up the last couple days."

Disappointed she isn't here to chat with, I nod. "I wanted to show her the new bakery pics."

Even more, I hoped she would help me with her sisters-in-law.

"It looks like you'll be tied up for a while with these two," he says with a smile, pointing at Olivia and Abbi.

"Ladies, ladies, let Hailey have some breathing room," Cade's grandmother announces a few moments later, probably after her son said something to her on his way inside the house. "She's going to be here with us all day, so let her enjoy her lemonade and relax for a few minutes."

Cade takes the opportunity to whisk me down to the beach as his aunts and uncles talk amongst themselves about the new bakery. Alex follows behind, and we join two men who look very much like the uncles we just walked away from on the porch.

"Hailey, I'd like you to meet my cousin Cash and my cousin Liam. Cash is the redhead's son, and Liam is the blonde's."

The two of them look so much like their fathers that there'd be no way I couldn't figure out they were related. "You guys really do only have two looks going on in this family, don't you?"

Laughing, Cade nods. "You either look like my father or their fathers. Nothing in between."

"Not true," Cash says. "Ava looks like your mother more than Stefan."

They all agree, and I can't help but wonder why Olivia and Abbi's traits don't appear to have moved to the next generation. "So not a single redhead or blonde in the bunch here?"

Liam shakes his head. "Strange, isn't it? I guess red and blond hair are recessive genes, and they were no match for the brown hair with brown eyes on one side and the black hair and blue eyes on the other."

"Maybe it skips a generation," Cade suggests as we all sit down on beach chairs arranged in a circle in the sand.

Alex elbows him, and with a sly smile whispers far too loudly, "I guess we're going to see with you soon, huh?"

And here I thought the aunts would be the ones asking the uncomfortable questions.

Cade looks at me and rolls his eyes before elbowing Alex in return. "First of all, dude, where did you learn to whisper? That kitchen of yours? And second, any redheads will be coming from you and Cash here, not me, and Liam will have the chance at a blond kid. I come from two people with dark hair, remember?"

"I definitely didn't expect to have a conversation about genetics today," I say with a chuckle, leaning back to close my eyes and enjoy the feeling of the sun on my face.

"Just wait," Alex says. "A few more beers and we'll be having all kinds of conversations."

"And Cash will have us betting on who's going to have the redheaded kid," Cade jokes. "I forgot to mention to you that these family get-togethers always end up with him offering some kind of bet."

I open my eyes to see Cash smiling. I can definitely see him being able to charm women with that grin.

"It's all in fun. Right, guys?"

Alex and Cade nod, but when I look to my left at Liam, I see he's checking his phone. His expression grows serious before he looks up at us and smiles.

"My luck is changing for the better, it seems. I got that job as a bodyguard I was waiting to hear about for the past couple weeks. Looks like today's my last day of real freedom, so we better make it good," Liam says.

Like his father Kane, he's not as outgoing as his cousins, but I sense he's got a kind heart under that gruff exterior. Cade mentioned he's been hoping to get this job, so I'm not surprised when the other three men toast their congratulations.

"Hey, everyone, Liam's got good news!" Cade yells

up to the rest of the family on the porch. "Tomorrow he becomes a bodyguard to the stars!"

"Don't be an asshole," Liam mumbles. "Now I'm going to have to deal with the million questions from my mother and Olivia."

I can barely stifle a smile when Cade laughs and says, "Exactly! Thank God for you and that girl you'll be guarding because now Hailey and I don't have to be under the microscope today."

As the three of them laugh, Liam turns to me and scowls. "He's a son of a bitch, but I'll let him go on it today since you benefit from my good news."

"Thank you, and congratulations. It sounds like a great job."

He nods and gives me a shy smile. I get the feeling he's got a gentle giant thing going on. Only an inch or two bigger than the rest of his cousins, Liam seems bigger and the perfect bodyguard for whoever he's going to be protecting.

"Is the person you'll be working for famous?"

"Not the way Cade said, but to some people she is. She's a pianist. Her name is Mia."

"Classical pianist? That's impressive."

"Even more impressive is she's young. Not even twenty yet, and she's about to set out on a tour that might end up taking her around the world," he explains.

"Then we need to get this party started," Alex

announces as he stands up from his chair. "Refills for everyone, and Hailey, still sticking with lemonade?"

"Maybe I'll have one beer now that the pressure's off."

Alex slaps Cade on the back as he starts to walk away. "She fits in perfectly with us. By day's end, we'll have her playing a game of poker with us."

He turns to look at his brother and smiles. "You brought the chips, right?"

Cash looks surprised at that question. "Do I ever not come ready to play a game of poker?"

Leaning over toward me, Cade kisses my cheek. "Sorry I was so stressed out before. I should have known you'd be great."

"So I fit in, huh?" I ask with a smile.

"Of course. That trick you pulled with the bakery pictures was perfect, by the way. Bold move. I was going to save that news for later, but you shocked everyone right out of the gate."

"Your father gave me that idea. He said he's always found deflection to work best. After the classic I don't know, of course."

Cade's smile lights up his face. "So now that you've won over the entire March and Jackson clan, what's next?"

I glance at Liam and Cash sitting around us before I kiss him. "Well, I hear there's going to be a poker game sometime today, so I need to keep my wits about me for that. There's always the friend of mine who's crazy about your best friend, so I'd like to see if I can help her case with him today. And I'm more than a little curious to know about this young pianist your cousin is going to be doing bodyguard duty for."

"Well, we like to keep things interesting in this family, for sure."

Taking his hand in mine, I bring it to my lips and press a kiss to his fingers. "Then, there's my favorite March, of course, the infamous Cade March, who deserves something incredible after today's surprise. Got any ideas for what that should be for later?"

He thinks for a few moments and then gets a wicked look in his eyes. "Read any great books lately? Maybe we could try something from one of them."

EXTRAS

Some scenes don't make it into the final book but still deserve to be read. Happy reading!

K.M.

STEFAN

My eyes feel heavy, so I lean back against the headboard and relax, ready to sleep after a long night at the club. Beside me, Shay shuffles through papers, stacking piles at her feet, on her legs, and between the two of us.

"They really should give you an award for work

above and beyond the call of duty," I sleepily say before opening one eye a crack.

She rolls her eyes at my suggestion and stacks more papers next to my right leg. "I need to get these done. My students need to know where they stand, and since this class is accelerated because it's a special course, there's no time to dilly-dally."

I sit up and stare at her until she looks over at me. "Dilly-dally? You've never once in your life dilly-dallied. Seriously."

Leaning over, she kisses me sweetly on the lips. "Exactly, and this is no time to start."

As much as I'd love to discuss how that's not really an answer that makes sense, I'm too tired to bother now. After work and dealing with Cade, I have little more to say than my question about Shay dilly-dallying.

Right on cue, as if she can read my mind, she nudges my side. "So how did things go with Cade tonight? You said you and he talked, but then you clammed up. What's going on?"

"Clammed up? Dilly-dally? I feel like I've been transported back to the fifties," I say with a chuckle.

Shay gives me a sideways glance and shakes her head. "What would you know about the fifties?"

"I watched Happy Days in reruns when I was a kid. I know a lot about the fifties."

She tosses papers onto the pile at her feet and looks over at me with an odd expression that includes an arched eyebrow of disbelief. "Not that I'm an expert on midcentury America, but I have a feeling watching reruns of Happy Days doesn't really give a person the full treatment on the fifties, Stefan."

"What can I say? It schooled me," I say with a shrug.

"What you can say is what happened between you and our son tonight. How is he handling being back at the club?" she asks, likely knowing all too well how Cade's dealing with that.

I take a deep breath in as I try to come up with a nice way of saying he fucking hates it. I really don't want to get into an argument with my wife tonight.

"He'll adjust. He always does, Shay. He's like you were there. It was never where you belonged, but you owned every inch of it every minute you were in the building."

She squeezes my forearm and leans over to kiss me on the cheek. "I know it was hard what you had to do. It's totally not in your makeup to take away his trust fund, but he needs to understand there has to be some direction to his life. I know you hated doing that, but it's the right thing. That's why I suggested it. We should have done it before this, in my opinion."

"I guess. I just felt like my father when I had to do that to him. Cassian March the second would have done something like that and relished every minute of it."

"That's the difference between you and your father,

Stefan. Don't beat yourself up about this. You did this because we agreed he needed a fire lit under him after a year of wandering around like some wealthy playboy."

"I guess. It's pretty much what he expected of me, so it's not like it's completely out of character for me. I'm not exactly his favorite person."

Shay doesn't respond to that. Stacking up all three piles into one, she sets them down on the floor beside the bed and turns to face me.

"You know why that is, don't you?" she asks in that tone that says she thinks I'm being a lunkhead because I can't see something that's as obvious as the nose on my face.

I'm not in the mood for question and answer period tonight, so I simply shrug. Why my son and I are like oil and water has always vexed me. He looks just like me, but it's like we're night and day. No two people have ever been more different, and for the life of me, I don't know why.

"Really, Stefan? You don't know why you two are always at one another's throats over the least little thing?"

She says that like I'm one of her dimwitted freshman students she can't fathom ever making it to graduation. "Really, Shay. I mean, we're like twins, yet I fight with him more than I fight with Kane, and that's saying something. If you know what I don't, enlighten me, please."

Shay taps my arm and smiles. "It's because you're like twins that you two don't get along. He looks like you. He acts just like you. I swear sometimes when I'm talking to him, it's like I'm talking to the Stefan from twenty years ago at Club X."

"That guy was a great guy," I joke, not believing my problem with my son is because we're too alike.

She tilts her head and looks at me. "That guy is Cade. Fun-loving. Good time. Everything is light and easy. How can you not see that?"

"Because I'm still that guy and he's nothing like me. Other than the way he looks, I mean."

"Stefan, our son is so you that I can't believe it sometimes. He has that funny way of being cute one minute and infuriating the next. That's quintessential Stefan March."

Hanging my head, I try to remember when Cade was cute with me. It's been a long time. Not since he was a little boy.

"I don't get that Cade, I guess. Maybe he saves that for you and Ava."

As she turns out the light on her nightstand, she laughs, which only makes me sulk more. "You get the same Cade we do. You just find him frustrating because it's like dealing with another you."

In the darkness, I try to make heads or tails of what she's saying. None of it makes sense. If he was just like me, then we'd get along famously. Two peas in a pod. A father and son team to rival those throughout the ages.

Instead, we spend ninety percent of our time going toe to toe on everything and the other ten percent of the time avoiding one another. Pretty much like my father was with me, when he bothered to pay attention to me, that is.

I never wanted to be like my father. I wanted my son to always know I loved him and would always be his biggest champion. How did we get to a place where the only words we seem to have for one another are filled with anger?

"For the record, I think dealing with an exact replica of me would be a dream. We'd enjoy the same kinds of things, laugh at the same jokes, and get along fantastically."

Snuggling up against my side, Shay whispers in my ear, "You can trust me that he's just like you, honey. You two don't get along because you refuse to understand each other."

"So it's not just me?"

"No. Cade knocks heads with you because he wants to be his own person, but every time he looks in the mirror, he sees you. Can you understand why that would make him want to be rebellious?"

When she puts it that way, I guess I can sort of understand, even though seeing me in the mirror is a hell of a lot better than seeing many other people staring back at him. He could look like my great-grandfather with his turn of the century dour expression and complete lack of style. Every time I saw pictures of that guy when I was a child, all I could think was life must have been miserable back then.

Into the silence of our bedroom, I ask the question that I've never figured out the answer to, even as I try to understand our son. "Is that why he doesn't want to take over the club, even though I'm more than happy to simply hand it over to him? No muss. No fuss. Just here are the keys and enjoy yourself and all the money you'll make. Because he's a natural at running the place. He's just like you, Shay. He's not there five minutes and he picks out all the issues and sets to solving them."

"He wants to be his own man, Stefan. You can understand that, can't you? That's all you wanted when you were his age. You just didn't have a lookalike father telling you what to do."

True. By the time I was Cade's age, my father was dead and there were no more chances for us to have any relationship at all.

"Well, maybe I'll give up on him taking over Club X and start to look for buyers. I just didn't want him to miss out on me being able to give him that to get him started in life. That's all."

"Give him some time. You might find that in a couple years, he'll be more interested in that gift. But if he isn't, it isn't a slight against you, Stefan. It's just not who he is."

She kisses me and lays her head on the pillow next to me. "You know, you do have another child. Maybe Ava will want to be the owner of Club X."

A million thoughts, each more horrible than the last, race through my mind about my little girl being in charge of the club. Oh, no. No, no, no.

"You better be joking, Shay, because I swear I'm going to have nightmares now of Ava around the people who frequent the club. I might not get any sleep at all tonight after that."

My wife giggles, amused by the horror she's injected into my brain right before bed. "You know, you weren't such a caveman when it came to females before Ava. Do you forget that? I think you would have had me run the club if it came down to it."

I turn my back to her and punch my pillow to fluff it up. Whoever I was then or now or whenever has nothing to do with my daughter running Club X. Oh, no. Just the thought of the men there slithering up to her and trying out their lines on her makes my stomach twist into a knot.

"Goodnight, Shay."

She wraps her arms around my waist and gives me a gentle squeeze. "Goodnight, honey. Don't worry about the kids or the club. It will all work out. I know it will."

Like always, Shay's asleep in less than a minute, leaving me to stare at the wall in the darkness and try to forget what she said. Better to focus on Cade and that business about us being too alike.

Maybe we are.

KEEP READING FOR THE RECIPES HAILEY USED TO MAKE ALL THOSE DELICIOUS DESSERTS!

MACARONS

Ingredients for 30 macarons

Macarons

- 1 ¾ cups powdered sugar
- 1 cup almond flour, finely ground
- 1 teaspoon salt, divided
- 3 egg whites, at room temperature
- ¼ cup granulated sugar
- ½ teaspoon vanilla extract
- 2 drops pink gel food coloring

Vanilla Buttercream

- 1 cup unsalted butter, 2 sticks, at room temperature
- 3 cups powdered sugar
- 1 teaspoon vanilla extract
- 3 tablespoons heavy cream

Preparation

1. Make the macarons: In the bowl of a food processor, combine the powdered sugar, almond flour, and ½ teaspoon of salt, and process on low speed, until extra fine. Sift the almond flour mixture through a fine-mesh sieve into a large bowl.
2. In a separate large bowl, beat the egg whites and the remaining ½ teaspoon of salt with an electric hand mixer until soft peaks form. Gradually add the granulated sugar until fully incorporated. Continue to beat until stiff peaks form (you should be able to turn the bowl upside down without anything falling out).
3. Add the vanilla and beat until incorporated. Add the food coloring and beat until just combined.
4. Add about ⅓ of the sifted almond flour mixture at a time to the beaten egg whites and use a spatula to gently fold until combined. After the last addition of almond flour, continue to fold slowly until the batter falls into ribbons and you can make a figure 8 while holding the spatula up.
5. Transfer the macaron batter into a piping bag fitted with a round tip.

6. Place 4 dots of the batter in each corner of a rimmed baking sheet, and place a piece of parchment paper over it, using the batter to help adhere the parchment to the baking sheet.

7. Pipe the macarons onto the parchment paper in 1½-inch (3-cm) circles, spacing at least 1-inch (2-cm) apart.

8. Tap the baking sheet on a flat surface 5 times to release any air bubbles.

9. Let the macarons sit at room temperature for 30 minutes to 1 hour, until dry to the touch.

10. Preheat the oven to 300°F (150°C).

11. Bake the macarons for 17 minutes, until the feet are well-risen and the macarons don't stick to the parchment paper.

12. Transfer the macarons to a wire rack to cool completely before filling.

13. Make the buttercream: In a large bowl, add the butter and beat with a mixer for 1 minute until light and fluffy. Sift in the powdered sugar and beat until fully incorporated. Add the vanilla and beat to combine. Add the cream, 1 tablespoon at a time, and beat to combine, until desired consistency is reached.

14. Transfer the buttercream to a piping bag fitted with a round tip.

15. Add a dollop of buttercream to one macaron shell. Top it with another macaron shell to create a sandwich. Repeat with remaining macaron shells and buttercream.
16. Place in an airtight container for 24 hours to "bloom"

Credit: https://tasty.co/recipe/macarons

CHOCOLATE GLAZED BOSTON CREAM WHOOPIE PIES

Ingredients
Vanilla Pastry Cream
1 1/4 cups whole milk

1/4 cup sugar

2 large egg yolks

2 tablespoons cornstarch

1/8 teaspoon kosher salt

1 tablespoon unsalted butter, cut into pieces

1 teaspoon pure vanilla extract

Cake Cookies
1 1/4 cups Silvana's Kitchen Gluten-Free All-Purpose Flour

1/2 teaspoon baking soda

1/2 teaspoon kosher salt

1 stick unsalted butter, at room temperature

3/4 cup sugar

1 large egg, at room temperature

2 teaspoons pure vanilla extract

1/2 cup buttermilk

Chocolate Glaze

4 ounces semisweet chocolate, chopped

3 tablespoons unsalted butter

1 tablespoon corn syrup or brown rice syrup

Directions

Make the pastry cream

Step 1

In a medium saucepan, whisk the milk with the sugar, egg yolks, cornstarch and salt; bring to a boil over medium heat, whisking frequently. Simmer until thickened, about 1 minute. Remove from the heat and whisk in the butter and vanilla extract until smooth. Transfer the pastry cream to a medium bowl. Press plastic wrap onto the surface of the pastry cream and refrigerate until chilled, about 2 hours.

Meanwhile, make the cookies

Step 2

Preheat the oven to 350° and line 2 baking sheets with parchment paper. In a medium bowl, sift the flour with the baking soda and salt.

Step 3

In another medium bowl, beat the butter and sugar with a handheld electric mixer until fluffy, 3 minutes. Beat in the egg and vanilla. Beat in half the flour mixture, then all the buttermilk, followed by the remaining flour mixture, beating until smooth.

Step 4

Arrange twelve 1/4-cup scoops of batter 2 inches apart on the prepared baking sheets; using an offset spatula, spread the batter into 3/4-inch-thick rounds. Refrigerate for 15 minutes.

Step 5

Bake the cookies for 12 to 15 minutes, rotating the baking sheets halfway through, until a toothpick inserted in the center comes out dry. Let the cookies cool on the baking sheets for 5 minutes, then transfer them to a rack to cool completely.

Make the chocolate glaze

Step 6

In a small bowl set over a saucepan of barely simmering water, whisk the chocolate with the butter and corn syrup until smooth. Let cool slightly.

Step 7

To assemble, arrange 6 cookies flat side up on a work surface. Beat the cold pastry cream with a wooden spoon and spread 3 tablespoons of cream onto each cookie. Top the cream with another cookie. Using an offset spatula, spread the chocolate glaze on top of each whoopie pie, letting it drip down the sides. Before serving, let the pies stand until the glaze is firm, about 1 hour.

Credit: https://www.foodandwine.com/recipes/chocolate-glazed-boston-cream-whoopie-pies

HONEY-PEPPERED STRAWBERRIES

Ingredients

Fresh strawberries

Honey

Cracked black peppercorns

(In the story, Alex suggests cayenne pepper, which is a variation on this recipe)

Step 1

Dip strawberries in honey and roll in cracked black peppercorns.

Credit: https://www.bhg.com/recipe/appetizers-snacks/honey-peppered-strawberries/

WHITE CHOCOLATE TORTE WITH CHOCOLATE Morsels and Raspberries

Ingredients

For the Crust

- 1/3 cup (75g) unsalted butter, melted
- 2 and 1/2 cups (250g) gingernut biscuits/gingersnaps crumbs

For the Mousse

- 3 and 1/2 cups (600g) white chocolate, coarsely chopped
- 1 cup (240g) Greek style yogurt
- 4 gelatin leaves

- 2 and 1/2 cups (600ml) heavy cream, whipped to soft peaks
- Raspberries and chocolate chips, to garnish

INSTRUCTIONS

For the Crust

1. Grease the base and sides of a 9-inch spring form pan. Set aside.
2. Mix together the biscuit crumbs and melted butter. Press the crumbs into the prepared pan, and chill whilst preparing the filling.

For the Mousse

1. Add the white chocolate to a large microwave-safe bowl, and heat in 20 second intervals, stirring after each one, until melted and smooth. Allow to cool slightly.
2. Place the gelatin into a heatproof bowl. Add 4 tablespoons of cold water and soak for 10 minutes until soft, then place in the microwave and heat until dissolved.
3. Stir together the melted chocolate and yogurt. Stir in the gelatin, then fold in the whipped cream.

4. Pour the mixture over the biscuit crumb base, and spread out evenly. Chill for at least 4 hours or overnight.

Credit: https://marshasbakingaddiction.com/white-chocolate-torte/

Be sure to look for the next book, The Ambitious Bad Boy, Cash March's story! And don't miss the Club X series, the original series of the March and Jackson family!

ABOUT THE AUTHOR

K.M. Scott writes contemporary romance stories of sexy, intense, and unforgettable love. A New York Times and USA Today bestselling author, she's been in love with romance since reading her first romance novel in junior high (she was a very curious girl!). Under her Gabrielle Bisset name, she writes paranormal and historical romance. She lives in Pennsylvania with a herd of animals and when she's not writing can be found reading or feeding her TV addiction.

Be sure to visit K.M.'s Facebook page at **https://www.facebook.com/kmscottauthor** for all the latest on her books, along with giveaways and other goodies! And to hear all the news on K.M. Scott books first, sign up for her newsletter today and be sure to visit her website at **http://www.kmscottbooks.com**

BOOKS BY K.M. SCOTT

HEART OF STONE SERIES

Crash Into Me (Heart of Stone #1)

Fall Into Me (Heart of Stone #2)

Give In To Me (Heart of Stone #3)

Heart of Stone Volume One

Ever After (Heart of Stone #4)

A Heart of Stone Christmas (Heart of Stone #5)

Return To Me (Heart of Stone #6)

Forever With Me (Heart of Stone #7)

Heart of Stone Volume Two

Hard As Stone (Heart of Stone #8)

Set In Stone (Heart of Stone #9)

Silent As A Stone (Heart of Stone #10)

Heart of Stone Volume Three

All of Me (Heart of Stone #11)

CLUB X SERIES

Temptation (Club X #1)

Surrender (Club X #2)

Possession (Club X #3)

Satisfaction (Club X #4)

PROJECT ARTEMIS SERIES

In The Darkness (Project Artemis #1)

After The Storm (Project Artemis #2)

Behind The Scenes (Project Artemis #3)

Project Artemis Box Set

FINDING THE ONE SERIES

Hard Work (Finding The One #1)

Big Love (Finding The One #2)

DIRTY BOSS SERIES

Sweet Things (Dirty Boss #1)

Private Secretary (Dirty Boss #2)

Play Date (Dirty Boss #3)

Dirty Boss Volume One

K.M.'S BOOKS ARE IN AUDIOBOOK TOO!

Masquerade

The Victorian Erotic Romance Trilogy